ELIZABETH WOODCRAFT

BABYFACE

HarperCollins*Publishers*

This novel is entirely a work of fiction. The names, characters
and incidents portrayed in it are the work of the author's imagination.
Any resemblance to actual persons, living or dead, events or
localities is entirely coincidental.

HarperCollins*Publishers*
77–85 Fulham Palace Road, London W6 8JB

www.**fire**and**water**.com

This paperback edition 2003

First published in Great Britain
in 2002 by HarperCollins*Publishers*

1 3 5 7 9 10 8 6 4 2

A catalogue record for this book
is available from the British Library

ISBN 0 00 651480 4

Set in PostScript Linotype Meridien

Typeset by Rowland Phototypesetting Ltd,
Bury St Edmunds, Suffolk

Printed and bound in Great Britain by
Clays Ltd, St Ives plc

For my mother, Peggy Perry

My thanks go to the criminal practitioners in chambers, in particular Joel Bennathan. His assistance was invaluable and his advice exemplary, any errors are my responsibility. I would like to thank the members of the family law team all of whom have given support. The clerking team have also been very understanding (and I should point out that Gavin's band is not based on any clerk's band that I know). My thanks also go to Chief Superintendent Anthony Wills of the Metropolitan Police for his comments and assistance. And thanks to my agent Annette Green; to Julia Wisdom, Anne O'Brien, Catherine Dey and the team at HarperCollins, and to Caroline for making it all possible.

ONE

Tuesday Afternoon

I was just getting into the rhythm of packing when the phone rang. I was slinging socks and a toothbrush into my bag and wondering if I could get away with one suit for the rest of the week.

It was Gavin, my clerk. 'You're still at home then?' he said.

The obviousness of the question left me silent.

'Your solicitor's just rung to say the inquiry has been put back till two thirty.'

'So I don't have to go up at all tonight. I can go in the morning. That's great.' I began to unbutton my black shirt. I was wearing my work outfit so there'd be less to carry. Already I was planning my evening. I could have a great night out in Stoke Newington with a few close friends, go to Fox's wine bar, share a couple of bottles of wine, cruise a little.

'Well.' There was a pause which meant Gavin was trying to choose his next words carefully.

'Oh God, Gavin,' I said. 'You're going to say something to make me regret answering the phone, aren't you?'

'It's just a short matter in the morning. You're going up there anyway. You'll be away by ten thirty. Loads of time to get to the inquiry in the afternoon.'

I said nothing.

'It's a PDH at the Crown Court.'

'Gavin, how many times do I have to tell you, I don't do crime. A pleas and directions hearing will turn into a guilty plea. I will have to do the mitigation, the judge will adjourn it till after lunch. I will have to go back after lunch thereby missing the beginning of the inquiry, and then my clients, or even the panel itself, will sack me. Great.'

'There is no way this will turn into a plea,' he said. 'It's Simon's corpseless murder.'

'Then Simon can do it. Simon should do it. Isn't that the rule? The person who does the trial does the directions hearing?'

'Unless there's a very good reason. And there is. He's ill.'

'What's wrong with him?'

'He's twisted his ankle.'

I spurted with laughter and was about to say, 'Pull the other one.'

'No, honestly,' Gavin said. 'He was jogging.'

Once again my theory was proved correct. There is an inherent contradiction between personal fitness and personal safety.

'Have a heart, Frankie,' Gavin said. 'I know you don't want to do it but Simon's very careful who he returns his cases to, and he did say you were his first choice.'

'The first choice out of all the people from chambers who will be in Birmingham tomorrow?'

'Is that sarcasm, Frankie? Unattractive trait. But seriously, Simon was delighted when I suggested you.'

'Huh,' I said, pleased. 'But if he's ill, is he going to be fit to do the trial?'

'He'll be fine by Monday.'

'Gavin, I really don't need this. I'm still getting papers for tomorrow, my fax is about to expire with all the statements my solicitor is sending me. Plus the comments on the statements. And the comments on the comments.'

'Frankie, there isn't anyone else and if the brief goes out of chambers we risk losing it altogether. Don't do it for me, do it for Simon.'

Simon was a senior member of my chambers. Like most barristers he worried about his practice and I knew that with this case he was hoping to consolidate his reputation as a heavyweight criminal practitioner which would lead to his shortly applying to become Queen's Counsel, to wear the robes of silk. Slowly I buttoned up my shirt.

'How am I going to get the papers? There's no time to get the papers to me.'

'When are you leaving? I'll fax them through to you.'

'My plan had been to leave in about half an hour, to miss the rush hour, but that was before you said that the inquiry had been put back till tomorrow afternoon. At which point, for a split second I began planning a social life for myself in London.'

'Yes, but wouldn't you rather be doing something for chambers?'

'Quite frankly, no. But, before you start again Gavin, OK,' I said, 'I will do it, but you owe me one.' A thought struck me. 'Oh no, the client must be in custody, so I'll have to go and see him in the cells, won't I? Then he'll either say, "I don't want a woman", which will be embarrassing, or he'll demand I stay on as Simon's junior, which isn't going to happen.'

'They're not bringing him,' Gavin said, with hardly a pause for breath. 'You're first on at ten o'clock, His Honour Judge Norman, Court 7.'

'Is this in chambers or do I have to robe?'

'I'm not sure about Birmingham, you'd better take your wig and gown just in case. Now, have I got your cousin's number?'

He'd won, and meekly I gave him Julie's details.

'Email?' he asked.

'Oh, for goodness' sake,' I said.

The fax machine rang and slowly pages from the brief in Simon's case appeared.

I shouldn't have agreed to do the PDH. I really needed a clear head for the start of the inquiry. This was a big one for me, my first really big case. I still wasn't sure how it came about that I had been instructed. I was representing twelve adults, five men and seven women, who had been physically and sexually abused in their residential home by five carers. Some wanted vengeance, some simply wanted to know how it had been allowed to happen, they all wanted to stop it happening to anyone else.

It had been in my diary for over six months, the date being put back every couple of months because the chair of the inquiry had other commitments, or someone's solicitor was ill, or a team manager was on holiday.

I'd had one conference with my clients, which had been raucous to say the least. Not only were they fed up with the delays, but three different solicitors within the firm had dealt with the case since I'd been instructed. I hadn't even met the most recent one. The clients were seething. But I was determined to keep the brief. A case like this could make your career. Or break it.

My fax machine had stopped. Ten pages had come through from Gavin. Ten of ten. That didn't seem a lot for a tricky murder, but if Simon felt that was enough then it must be enough. I glanced at the back sheet and realised that Gavin had failed to mention that the instructing solicitor in Simon's case was Kay Davidson. I wondered if he had done it deliberately. I thought of ringing him to ask, but I knew that the answer would probably irritate me. Kay was one of Gavin's favourite solicitors. The fact that she was an ex of mine was only a minor complication. Anyway, apart from a brief phonecall after the hearing tomorrow morning to let her know the outcome, I wouldn't need to have any contact with her, which was probably best for all of us.

I shovelled the new papers and the huge brief for the inquiry into a second bag, threw in an alarm clock, and my packing was finished. I glanced round the living room and reluctantly I carried two empty wine glasses and a used coffee mug into the kitchen. Then I picked up three old copies of the *Guardian* from the sofa, straightened the rug in front of the fireplace, and, having switched on the timer that worked the two lamps, I left.

TWO

Birmingham

Of course I didn't miss the rush hour at all. Well, I missed it for a bit, but my car, an L-reg Renault, was taking it steady, so that by the time I got to the turn off for Luton Airport and was wishing I'd brought my passport, as I always do on that stretch of road, the rush hour caught up with me and stayed by my side, jostling and pushing, till we got past Watford Gap.

I arrived at Julie's redbrick terraced house in Selly Oak at eight o'clock. Marnie, her fifteen-year-old daughter, answered the door. Ever since she was eleven I have been surprised each time I see her by the growing maturity of her appearance. She kissed me effusively then went back across the room to watch the TV. I made my way through the living room to the back of the house.

Julie was in the kitchen, looking at a pizza in the oven. You could tell Julie and I were blood relatives, neither of us liked cooking.

She hugged me and suggested I take my things up to my room before supper. 'Marnie!' she called, 'show Frankie where everything is.'

Marnie stomped ahead of me up the narrow, dark staircase to the first floor, and then up another flight to the loft, the room that was to be my home away from home for as long as the inquiry lasted.

'It's great,' I said. I hadn't seen it since Julie had converted it into an extra room. Pale wooden floorboards, white walls and a television standing on a chest of drawers. I didn't need anything else. I knew I would be happy here. At one end of the room was the bed, with a duvet in a royal-blue cotton cover. 'That goes into a sofa,' Marnie said, following my gaze. 'And there's this lamp.' She switched on a small white lamp with a bendy neck. 'That was mine,' she said, with a trace of bitterness.

'Well, I was intending to bring up some stuff of my own next week,' I said, quickly. 'Including a couple of lamps.'

She thought for a moment. 'What if I like yours more than mine?' she said.

'We can swap,' I said. 'Thanks for a great guided tour, I think I can hear the TV calling you.'

In a second she had slipped out of the room.

As well as the futon there was a good-sized table and a sensible office chair, beside which stood an empty bookcase. I imagined the shelves filled with a few of my favourite books, looking colourful and interesting. My cassette player would fit just nicely on the bottom shelf. I turned to the clock radio by the bed and fiddled with the dial. Having found the easy rhythm of 'The Way You Do the Things You Do' I fell back onto the bed. With my hands behind my head and the Temptations harmonising gently round the room I felt content, and I had a sense that my problems were sorting themselves out.

My practice and my bank balance might actually

improve as a result of doing this inquiry, which in turn could lead to a new car and some new clothes. And then, looking sleek and successful and driving a shiny new vehicle, I would inexorably start a rich and satisfying relationship, filled with passion, good music and true love. A relationship of my own, not sharing with anyone, not thinking mixed and angry thoughts about Kay, or just falling for the wrong kind of gal – although who could resist a woman singing soft and sexy love songs, in a red sequin dress with curves and high-heel shoes . . . ?

I was beginning to get maudlin, I could feel it, and the Four Tops were reminding me that they were 'Standing in the Shadows of Love'. I jumped off the bed to unpack.

I laid my two briefs in neat piles on the bed. The brief in Simon's case was small and narrow. I had wrapped it in a piece of the pink ribbon which grows at the bottom of all my work bags. It wouldn't take long to read. I'd do it after supper.

My inquiry brief was enormous, but I'd read most of it. I skimmed through the latest thoughts of my inquiry clients. They had met as a group on their own several times, they had written letters, they had even organised demonstrations. Now they wanted some legal action, and they wanted to get started.

I made a few notes on matters I should raise with them tomorrow afternoon – whether they were still anxious to put our case first, double check exactly who wanted to give evidence, whether we should ask for a view of Haslam Hall, and remind them what the procedure at the inquiry was likely to be.

Then I closed my notebook and followed the smell of

burning pizza down to the small dining room. Julie, Marnie and I sat round the square utility table covered in maroon oilskin, by the window that looked out over the side passage at the back of the house where Julie had hung pots of geraniums. Marnie ate her Hawaiian with extra caramelised pineapple in silence, sighing loudly from time to time, as Julie and I exchanged family gossip, mainly about our mothers, who were sisters.

When Julie said to me, 'Your hair looks nice,' Marnie looked at me and then back at Julie.

'It's just like yours,' she said to her mother.

Julie's hair was short at the back and had a floppy fringe that skimmed her eyebrows.

'Your hair is really nice,' I said to Julie.

Marnie tutted in disgust and stroked her own hair, which was pulled back from her face in a thick golden-brown ponytail.

As soon as she had finished her pizza she excused herself and slid back into the living room. Julie made tea and as we sat at the table, talking about GCSEs and the last time Julie had been out on her own and what films were on in town, I felt the comfort and security of staying somewhere with other people to talk to and discuss articles in the *Guardian* with. The words to 'We are Family' drifted through my head. I shook myself and made a mental note to be alert for further signs of the family vortex thing. So easy to slip into, so hard to climb out of.

It was a quarter to eleven when I sat cross-legged on the bed and began to read through the papers in Simon's case. If I had done it earlier I might have rung Gavin back and shouted 'Be serious!' and laughed maniacally down the phone. Of course Gavin knows how I work, so he deliberately faxed me the papers just as I was leaving. He calculated how long it would take me to get to Birmingham, unpack, have something to eat, an hour or so of chat with my cousin, and bingo, it's eleven o'clock and far too late to return the brief. I felt like ringing him up and laughing maniacally down the phone anyway.

For a start it quickly became clear that I had nowhere near enough papers. The ten sheets of paper that had come through my machine included the fax letter, and also the back sheet to the brief, which in terms of legal importance is the equivalent of an envelope. To attend court to sort out the final directions for a trial, which I read was listed to last for three weeks, I had eight pages of information. Kay is a very good solicitor and her instructions, dense and informative, ran to six pages. But she had obviously prepared the brief for tomorrow morning's hearing thinking Simon was doing it; Simon who had had days to read everything.

From what she had written it was clear that some-where – probably on the floor in Simon's room in chambers – there were about six lever arch files containing statements, reports, interviews, even, I read, a couple of videos, in other words a detailed description of everything Danny Richards was meant to have done and how the prosecution were going to prove it. And I had eight pages of it. I just hoped the judge wouldn't ask me any trick questions. Or any questions at all.

The last paragraph of my instructions read:

'As counsel will remember, Mr Richards is a difficult client who has had much experience of dealing with the legal profession. Counsel is reminded that he has sacked one firm of solicitors and two counsel already. As well as doing his best at this hearing, counsel is required to ensure that Mr Richards is satisfied with the service he receives.'

And how would the difficult Mr Richards react if he knew that instead of the big, firm assertive Simon Allison, the smaller, slimmer family practitioner Miss F. Richmond was appearing on his behalf? Good job he wouldn't be there to see it.

The last two pages of the fax were 'the missing pages of his CRO as requested' – information from the Criminal Records Office of Mr Richards' previous convictions. If these were the missing pages I dreaded to think what the other pages contained and how many there were. These pages were crammed with entries. The first page covered the early seventies and the second the late eighties.

For a defence barrister this man was very bad news. Just looking at the pages I had I could see he had visited most of the juvenile courts in the South of England, on at least fifteen occasions. Not a local boy then. The pages revealed no violence against women, which was something. The first page ran from 1969 to 1974. Two of his convictions were for 'common assault against another youth' for which he had been bound over, which meant it was probably a bit of weekend strutting about, but his weakness had obviously been cars, stealing them, driving them away, without a licence, without insurance, without due care and attention. By the time he was fourteen, in 1974, he'd been banned from driving for twenty years.

Of course, looking at that sheet through the eyes of a self-styled liberal, it seemed as if he'd never had a chance. He was dealt with harshly from the start, sentenced to Intermediate Treatment, Detention Centre, Borstal. The second sheet jumped ahead eleven years, and was now based round Crown Courts in the Midlands. The inevitable had happened. It looked as if he had fallen in with a bad crowd in his late twenties, there was an affray in 1985 and in 1988, a serious GBH. He'd been sentenced to five years for that. In 1993 there was an attempted murder – a man had lost a leg – and Danny Richards had said goodbye to the outside world for nine years, but on appeal it was reduced to seven.

I wondered who the man with one leg was. I wondered what he thought about the reduction in Danny Richards' sentence.

And now he was on a charge of murder. With an unlikely victim, certainly as far as pages three and four of the instructions were concerned. An underworld villain, Terry Fleming, had disappeared. He was a small-time crook and heavy man, who hired out his services to local businessmen, in between selling cars and playing a mean hand of blackjack. Some nine months previously, three days after Danny Richards had been released from HM Prison, Parkhurst, having completed five years of the seven-year sentence, Fleming had gone out for a birthday celebration, dressed in his finest and newest four-button, mohair grey suit, and never come home. His body had never been found. He had last been seen at one of Birmingham's brightest and hottest nightspots, the Lambada Casino.

Perhaps there would be the chance of a night at the casino, I thought, to feel the atmosphere Fleming had been in, to see what he had seen. I could wear a cool black jacket, some black patent shoes, try a twist of the poker cards, slide some chips across the green baize, *faire mes jeux*.

But what was I thinking? I had no intention of having anything more to do with Danny Richards' case after tomorrow. On the stroke of half past ten I would announce to the judge that my time was up, and I would rise and tie the pink ribbon firmly round the papers, write Simon's name on the back sheet in large letters and walk out of the court building without a backward glance.

As you can imagine.

Of course the trouble with a good juicy criminal brief is that you get sucked in, you get involved and excited by the possibilities. I made a list of things I would do if this case were mine:

Check the Malaga coast line. No corpse can so often mean no murder.

Check police missing-persons files for reports of disappeared young, nubile women to see if Fleming had run off with someone (or nubile men – what better reason for a man to leave the country than if he thinks he'll lose his reputation as a hard man if his sexuality is revealed?)

Investigate other reasons for wanting to disappear. Had he fallen out with someone? Was he trying to go straight? Was he threatening to tell all?

Consider the possibility of suicide – did he have any reason to commit suicide (see above)? Are there any forms of suicide that allow the body to self-destruct so that no traces remain – e.g. throwing oneself into a vat of acid?

Who might want to kill him? What would Danny Richards' motive be?

According to Kay's instructions, the prosecution case against Danny Richards was pretty weak, based on circumstantial evidence. The statements of the witnesses offered little information other than the fact that Danny and Fleming had never got on. There was a hint of a long-standing quarrel, a suggestion of an argument the night before he disappeared. No more than that. The case could well be thrown out at half-time, at the end of the prosecution case, after a stirring submission of no case to answer. From the way Kay was describing it, Simon could probably make that submission on the papers alone, before a word of oral evidence had been given.

This was good. This meant I could be extremely condescending to the prosecution, and swagger round the courtroom in controlled indignation.

But reading between the lines of her upbeat instructions, I could tell that Danny Richards was going to have an uphill struggle. He'd apparently said some fairly stupid things to the police, which could amount to admissions of guilt. It would be difficult to keep them from going in front of the jury without calling the police liars. That counted out the possibility of an early submission. It also meant the risk of the jury hearing about his previous convictions. The jury wouldn't like him at all. And then, almost as a throwaway comment at the end of the instructions, there was a mention of the laughable 'forensic evidence' Simon was being asked to consider. From the instructions I couldn't tell what it was. A finger print? A spot of blood? Fibres? Kay had written that it was harmless enough on its own but in the context of the trial, could be fairly damning. The possibility of an acquittal seemed remote.

But tomorrow my main task was to hang on to him. It was a good thing he wasn't going to be there, to ask me hard questions like, 'Am I going to get off?'

It was midnight. I could still ring up Simon and demand his limping attendance. Or Gavin, to demand his, to explain to the judge why Simon wasn't there. But I couldn't do that. It was beneath me. I had to take it like a woman.

The best thing to do was to get a good night's sleep to be fresh and clear-eyed for the judge.

THREE

Wednesday Morning – Crown Court

But it wasn't just the judge, it was Danny too. Because of course, they brought him.

I went to the cells, just in case, and asked nonchalantly whether they had him.

'Oh yes, madam.' The jailer had a cup of tea and a copy of the *Sun* open on the desk in front of him. I gave him my name. 'Just you is it?' he asked in the false anxious tone they use to wind-up women barristers. 'You want to go in on your own?'

Gavin had assured me that, whatever impression the papers might give, the client was a pussycat. I wasn't sure what that meant. Personally I won't have a cat in the house.

'If you would make your way to room number three, madam,' the jailer said, reluctantly rising to press the intercom to ask for Danny Richards to be brought through. I walked down the corridor, under fluorescent lights, to the small concrete room with a table and three tubular chairs.

I laid my wig and a packet of Benson & Hedges on the table.

The interview began badly. 'Where's my brief?' he said shortly as he barged into the room. He was big,

16

stocky, with a face that would have been pleasant if it wasn't for the very short hairstyle. He was wearing a tight, short-sleeved, camouflage green T-shirt, over bulging biceps and baggy combat trousers. He was on remand, he was still considered innocent, so he could wear what he liked. Simon would doubtless advise him to get a different outfit for the trial.

He slumped into the other chair in the room. 'Where's my brief?' His hands curled into fists on the table.

'If you mean Simon Allison,' I said, 'he's in hospital having a pin put in his ankle.' I made a mental note to tell Simon that. 'On the other hand, this morning and this morning only,' I inclined my head towards my wig, 'I'm your brief. My name is Frankie Richmond.' I held out my hand. He looked at it reluctantly. Then decided not to shake it.

I smoothed open my blue counsel's notebook.

'Mr Richards, the purpose of this morning's hearing is to make the final preparations for the trial.'

He looked at me with a bored expression, picking up the pack of cigarettes and removing the cellophane.

'It's pleas and directions. You pleaded not guilty on . . .' I rifled through my ten pages, knowing the date on which Danny had entered his plea was one of the many things they did not contain.

'I'm thinking of changing that. My plea. I'm thinking of going guilty.'

'Oh no you're not.'

'I can do what I like, I'm paying your fees.'

'No,' I said, 'I think someone else is paying my fees. But perhaps your name isn't Richards at all, perhaps it's Aid, or can I call you Legal?'

'That's Mr Aid to you.'

'Of course,' I said.

'Don't get smart,' he said. 'I've got a right to representation, same as that bloke Saunders did. And the Maxwell brothers.'

'Of course you have, probably more,' I said. 'But we're getting off the point. You are not going to change your plea. Your lawyers having been working very hard for . . .' I rustled my papers, 'a long time, and they are . . .' I coughed, 'confident of victory.'

He nodded. 'But I'm going to be convicted.' He took out a cigarette and I handed him a box of matches. As he struck the match he said, 'Where is my barrister really?'

'Simon's at hospital. There's something wrong with his ankle. He'll be fine for the trial, but he particularly wanted me to do this hearing for you this morning.'

'Why?'

'That's a question I have been asking myself since the moment my clerk told me about today, Mr Richards,' I said. 'I think in another life I must have done something really terrible to him.'

His face cracked into a smile. 'I like you,' he said.

Oh God.

I looked at my watch.

'We've got twenty minutes before Norman has us in,' he said, knowledgeably. 'Look, they've stitched me up and they've done a good job. You've read the papers. You can see, can't you?'

I shook my head vaguely.

'It's funny really. I've known him for years. Never liked him – a self-important twat. I expect your old dad always told you never to trust a secondhand car dealer. Well, Terry Fleming is the reason why. But there's loads more people I would rather have taken a pop at. But he disappears and they come and arrest me. And what have they got?'

'A "no-comment" interview.' I knew that much.

'Yeah, but they've got the other stuff. What I said in the car. I admit I did say one or two things behind my hand, being ironic. And that is how they think they've got me admitting to this murder. And what with the forensics.' He stopped. 'Let's just say, I want to change my plea. I've been in front of Norman before, he doesn't like me, I know how this is going to go.'

'But the conversation in the car . . .' I hesitated. I was on difficult ground here, I wasn't entirely clear what he'd said, what he'd said he'd said or what they said he'd said. 'Simon can argue that's inadmissable.'

'He could, but it'll go in. Then somehow my previous convictions will go in, probably thanks to my co-defendant, Mr Catcher, who as you know is charged with conspiracy, but who I would no more conspire with than get in a spat with.'

I made a surreptitious note. A co-defendant was good. If he was first on the indictment, the charge sheet, I might not have to say a word during the hearing this morning.

'So my previous goes in and the jury hears about my climb up the ladder of physical violence – common assault, ABH, GBH, and attempted murder. The pross says something like, "And now the charge is murder. In criminal terms, members of the jury, he has come of age."' He inhaled deeply and hunched forward in his chair. It was a good imitation of a pompous prosecution barrister. 'Then what chance have I got? Down I go and Freddy Hanging's-too-good-for-them Norman recommends thirty years for a "heartless gangland execution". I might as well go guilty now and he knocks some time off in consideration.'

Part of me knew he had a point. But another part of me knew I was not prepared for a plea in mitigation. A shard of desperation told me there was a chance he would win if he fought the case. And a sense of justice told me he should fight it, if he hadn't done it.

'But you might win,' I said.

He snorted and sat back in his chair with a grin on his face, leaving me with a small internal war going on. I didn't know what else to say. I certainly couldn't say 'Actually, I'm not really meant to be here, in fact I'm not even a criminal barrister any more, and I am starting a case with some uppity clients at two thirty, a case which is going to open the path to heaven and possibly a fleet of fancy cars for me, and if I do your plea they'll sack me.' He was lighting a cigarette from the embers of his first one. The room was cold and full of misty smoke, like being on Dartmoor. I could almost hear small ponies neighing and pawing the ground.

I said, 'We're not ready for a plea today. I'd want to spend a long time with you to prepare your mitigation, and we don't have time for that now. Also,' here we go, 'I'll be straight with you. I have to be somewhere else this afternoon.'

'What did they send you for if you can't do it?'

'Because "it" is listed as a thirty minute PDH.'

'Which stands for pleas and directions. And that's what I want. I want to put in a plea, a guilty plea and get a direction that the whole thing is over and done with today. You just want me to stay not guilty because you want to get away. Where are you going?'

20

'I have a case. I'm representing . . .' I paused. Mentally I was checking my professional position. This was not breaching confidentiality. 'I'm representing some people at an inquiry.'

'Oh yeah?' He was interested. 'Who you representing?'

'The victims. Look, I do want to get away, but it's not going to make any difference to your sentence if you plead guilty today or next week,' I said. 'But for God's sake, you've got so little to lose by fighting it. Plead guilty, you get life. Plead not guilty and lose, you get life. And I think there are investigations to be made – I don't know if they've been done – that could help your case.'

'Like what?'

'Like, I don't know, checking local newspaper reports for the month Fleming disappeared, retracing his last known steps, talking to his mum.'

'All right, you can stop worrying.' He rolled his cigarette between his fingers. 'Write this down. "This morning, I will not ask to change my plea."' I scribbled on my faxed back sheet. He held out his hand for the pen and signed his initials. 'You're a good little barrister, aren't you? I'd like to see you cross-examining someone.'

'Yes, I'm a real Rottweiler,' I said.

'No, I'd say you were more of a – what are they called?'

'A Borzoi?' I said, imagining something elegant and sophisticated.

'No, no, I was thinking more like a Jack Russell.'

FOUR

Wednesday – Court 7

The prosecutor didn't like me. He was a young man with a five o'clock shadow, his accent obviously having shattered his shaving mirror. His first words were, 'Counsel from London?' He pronounced it kine-sel.

'That's right,' I said cheerfully. They hate it when you come from out of town, stealing their work, stealing their hooks in the Robing Room, stealing their women.

'Which chambers?'

When I told him he said, 'And why does a case like this need counsel from 17 Kings Bench Walk?'

That was a good question, to which I didn't have an answer. I thought of getting personal and saying 'Because at 17 KBW we got rid of five o'clock shadows at the end of the last century.' Which wasn't even true. But he had strutted off to speak to a police officer. I wondered if I should try to create a friendship for Simon's sake. Perhaps I should run after him and say something appeasing, something barristerial, like 'What's the best pudding they do in the Bar Mess?' But it stuck in my throat.

A woman with dark hair and red lipstick came over to me. She was wearing a spotless wing collar and snowy-white tabs, a true professional. 'So you've met the Birmingham Bar's roving ambassador? That's Ewan Phillips,' she said. I liked her at once. 'I'm Roseanna Newson, I'm for Ronald Catcher.' Her thick black hair, cut in harsh, geometric lines, highlighted the delicacy of her neat heart-shaped face.

'I'm Frankie Richmond, for Danny Richards,' I said, stroking my neck to hide my creased, cream collarette.

'It'll be good co-defending with a woman,' she said.

'Unfortunately, I'm not doing the trial,' I said. 'I'm standing in for Simon Allison for the day. He's done something to his ankle.'

Roseanna's neat little rosebud mouth formed an O of concern. 'Oh, dear. Norman's not going to like that. He said on the last occasion that trial counsel must attend this hearing. And if Ewan is Birmingham's ambassador, Judge Norman is our honorary consul. He's a bit of a fool, but he's a stickler for procedure.'

I knew it, I knew it. This is exactly why I don't do crime, why I don't do returns from other people, why I don't like to leave London. I hadn't even got a medical note to back up Simon's story. Norman would make me do the trial.

We were called on at ten o'clock precisely.

And of course, Danny Richards' name was first on the indictment which meant that after the prosecution had opened the case I would be required to stand and say my piece. But even before Ewan Phillips had introduced all three counsel, the judge barked, 'Miss Richmond, we haven't seen you in this matter before?'

'No, Mr Richards has recently changed his represen-tation.'

'And we will have the pleasure of your company throughout this trial.' It wasn't a question.

'I don't want her representing me!' Danny shouted from the back of the court. I turned to the dock in horror. Danny was on his feet, grasping the rail. The security guard had risen beside him. Danny's co-defendant, a thin, hunched man, in a grey T-shirt and jeans, didn't even look up. He'd probably seen it all before, if Danny really did make a habit of sacking his representatives. Then Danny winked at me. He was doing this to help me. He was trying to make it look as if I was meant to be doing the trial but now he'd decided he didn't want me.

'Mr Richards, I hear what you say. Now be quiet.'

'I'm not having her. I want a real barrister.' But he was going further than I considered absolutely necessary. 'I want someone who knows what they're doing.' Much further.

'That's enough, Mr Richards. It may be that your objections are well-founded, but I have told you before, this court is not to be used as a soapbox. One more word and you will go below.' He turned his gaze to me. 'Are you prepared to represent Mr Richards?'

'I'm certainly prepared to represent him.' This was true in so far as I was prepared to represent him this morning, although I was not prepared to represent him in the widest sense and certainly not beyond today.

The judge rifled through some loose papers on his desk, found what he was looking for and peered at the page. My heart sank. He was going to ask me a question. 'I have a letter here from your instructing solicitors. A *Miss* Davidson.' He held up the page between the tips of his fingers. 'This is your latest team of representatives is it, Mr Richards? *Miss* Davidson and *Miss* Richmond? A *London* team? Very well. And why is the witness referred to at page 213 of the bundle a fully bound witness?'

I didn't have a clue as to why that witness was required to give oral evidence at the trial instead of having his or her evidence read. I didn't have page 213. I didn't even have a bundle. I rose to my feet, flicking through the ten faxed pages I did have, hoping the answer would come to me through ESP. Roseanna slid her bundle across to me, open at page 213. Quickly I scanned the page. Not quickly enough.

'Miss Richmond, you just told me that you were ready to represent this defendant. That is patently not so. What are you doing in my court without being prepared for the case?'

'I am in your court because my colleague Simon Allison is in hospital at this moment having surgery on his ankle.' Oh God, let that be true, I prayed. 'And as for not being prepared, I am prepared for what usually happens in a Pleas and Directions Hearing. As for the attendance of Dr . . .' I glanced at the page '. . . Rowland Quirk. Quite clearly . . .' I skimmed through the paragraphs '. . . his evidence is of a forensic nature.'

'Rowland Quirk. Rowland Quirk? Was he ever in Saudi Arabia?'

'I – eh – don't think . . .'

'Had a terrible problem with his business interests? What, about seventeen years ago?'

'Eh . . .'

'Do you know, I think I represented him.'

A small rattle left my throat.

'He was in terrible trouble. Owed millions. Well, if I have represented him, and he is to be called to give oral evidence as a result of the way the defence wish to run

25

their case, then I must step down at this very, very late stage, because I cannot hear this case. The case will have to come out of the list. So be it, if the defence wish to call Roger Quirk, they must pay the price.'

'Rowland Quirk.'

'Oh Rowland Quirk. Oh, no, not the same man. I don't think I know him. So? Why do you need him?' he barked.

Roseanna rose and I sank to my seat. 'Your Honour may remember that this witness is one of a series of expert witnesses which both defendants seek to cross-examine at trial. Your Honour indicated on the last occasion that an investigation of this area of the case was the only appropriate way to take the matter forward.'

The judge opened his mouth but nothing came out. Ewan Phillips rose to his feet. 'I wonder if I could be of some assistance as to the availability of prosecution witnesses.' Judge Norman turned a beaming smile on him. 'Dr Quirk is available to give his evidence during the second and third weeks of the trial.'

'Ewan and the judge come from the same set of chambers,' Roseanna whispered to me. 'Ewan's very intelligent, he'll go far, Norman isn't and hasn't.'

'I will say again, Miss Richmond,' the judge's voice boomed around the room. 'Has there been a meeting of all the professional witnesses to see if there is any way that this matter can be shortened?'

I knew the answer to that one. 'Yes there has.'

'And still you wish to call them?'

'Yes,' I said wildly. 'I think that's quite usual for a trial, isn't it?'

Ewan Phillips rose slowly, insolently, to his feet. 'Of course, your Honour,' he said, 'as your Honour has pointed out, my learned friend for Mr Richards is from London.' He said it as if I had just flown in from the twin towns of Sodom and Gomorrah. 'In Birmingham, and in particular in your Honour's court, close attention is always paid to the detail and it is pertinent at every stage of the proceedings to consider whether there is a way to save time or prevent a drain on the public purse. Perhaps my learned friend's instructing solicitors, a London firm –' he shuddered ' – are unaware that there is a right way and a wrong way to do things.'

'Precisely, Mr Phillips,' the judge said. 'Well, Miss Richmond?'

'My learned friend for the prosecution may not know that, in London, matters such as this are usually dealt with outside court in order to save the court the trouble of enquiring into every small detail. In London,' I emphasised the 'L', 'in London, we ensure that the Judge is able to deal with the big picture.' Roseanna was tugging the sleeve of my gown, hissing, 'Shut up, sit down! Shut up, sit down!' 'In London,' I ploughed on, 'counsel have the skill and ability to ensure that a case goes forward smoothly and properly, without incurring unnecessary costs. In London, members of the Bar are regarded as professional and competent. Which they are.'

'Have you finished Miss Richmond?'

I thought for a second and then nodded.

'Which chambers are you from?' His Honour Judge Norman leaned forward, licking his lips.

He was going to write to my head of chambers. Or he was going to report me to the Bar Council. I told him my chambers address and he made a great show of writing it all down, including the postcode.

So there. I'd lost my career at the Bar for a client who wasn't even mine. And I'd probably lost the client. If I hadn't lost him when I first stood up without the papers, I'd lost him now, after he'd seen me shouting my mouth off at the judge. I sagged in my seat, taking a desultory note, while Ewan Phillips completed the last technicalities. Then we all rose, bowed and His Honour Judge Norman left the courtroom.

And then Danny Richards hissed at me. He was being led away, between two men in short-sleeved shirts and with self-important chains on their belts. No words, just a hiss. I looked at my watch. It was ten thirty. I had so much to do, so much to read. So much money to earn before I was deprived of my livelihood. I was bruised and battered, I needed to lick my wounds, not go three more rounds with Danny Richards.

I looked over at him. He grinned and winked. Oh no.

He inclined his head towards the back of the dock, wanting me to go down to the cells. I walked over to the dock. 'Have you got a minute?' he said.

'Not really. Can't it wait? Can't you tell Simon?' I emphasised the word Simon, to remind him where his future lay. I was not getting any further involved in this case.

'No, it can't, this is important stuff,' he murmured so I had to strain towards him to hear. 'I enjoyed that, though.' He rubbed his hands together. 'I was right, you are.'

I frowned.

'Just like a Jack Russell.'

Roseanna and I stood outside the door leading to the cells. Each of us held our wig in one hand and a pile of papers in the other. As we waited for a jailer to let us in Roseanna said, 'I'm sorry I tugged your arm.'

'I'm glad you did. I don't know what more I might have made up if you hadn't. What do you think he'll do?'

'I don't know. Probably nothing, he's too lazy. Have you got time for coffee after this?' she asked.

'I can't.' I pressed the bell again. 'I'm starting an inquiry this afternoon and I've got to meet my solicitor who says a load more papers arrived last night.' Chambers had rung me at Julie's this morning.

'Oh, you're in the abuse inquiry,' she said.

'There's more than one inquiry?'

'There's the environmental one, that's been going a couple of weeks, and the abuse one.'

'Well, then yes, I suppose I'm in the abuse one.'

'Everybody from here to Leicester has been after at least one inquiry brief. All that lovely money. I thought in the end that it was mostly solicitors doing the representation in the Haslam Hall case.'

'I'm representing the victims,' I said.

'Oh, you have the poisoned chalice,' she said. 'Good luck.'

'I don't know what you mean,' I said.

'No, no, I'm being unfair,' she said. 'I'm sure you'll get on well with everyone. Are you staying up or are you commuting?'

'I'm staying at my cousin's in Selly Oak,' I said.

'Well, keep in touch,' she said. 'I'm at Bournville Chambers.' She pulled a card out of her bag. 'If you fancy a drink or dinner one night, just give me a call. I don't want you to think that all the legal profession up here are unfriendly oafs.'

'Don't worry, despite what I said in court, unfriendly oafs are, unfortunately, everywhere,' I said. 'But thanks, that's great. I'll take you up on that offer.'

The door was opened and we were directed into separate rooms to await our clients.

Danny Richards came in humming. He grinned at me. 'I think you got under old Norman's skin there for a bit.'

I looked at him.

He danced over to his chair. He was light on his feet. 'Look,' he said, 'I just wanted to say, and you can pass this on, I may or may not change my plea. If Catcher's fighting it, I might as well go the distance. It'll put the wind up him for me to go not guilty. But I don't want anyone taking any trouble, all that cross-examination of prosecution witnesses. I don't want any of that.' He held my gaze. He sighed. 'Some things just have to follow their natural course.'

'Maybe so, but you've got some natural points to make. The fact that the argument you had with Terry Fleming was so long ago. They can't rely on that.'

'Fortunately for you, you don't know what you're talking about. And nor do most people round here. People do things, other things happen. It's the way of the world. All right? What will be, will be.'

'Is that meant to be religion?'

'I thought it was Doris Day. Whatever. Call it what you like, it's realism, anyway.'

I was too bedraggled from my voyage under HHJ Norman's skin to argue. Danny Richards leaned back in his chair and, from his trouser pocket, drew out the packet of cigarettes I had given him. He kept humming as he took out a cigarette and lit it.

Unusually the jailer appeared at the door. He didn't even look at me. 'You've got a visitor,' he said to Danny.

I could have ignored the interruption, but I feared that if I stayed, Danny might really start to like me. I stood up and said goodbye.

'Don't say goodbye,' he said, 'say "so long."'

'Mr Richards,' I said, 'this is no longer my case.' I remember saying it very clearly. And then I left the cells.

As I took the lift back up to the Robing Room, I found myself humming Danny's tune. I knew it, I knew I knew it. It was a seventies song, I was sure. Dum, dum, dum. A bit of a heart-catching voice. Dum de dum de dum, 'Bad Company'! At least he had a sense of humour.

But now I could forget Danny Richards and start to think about my inquiry, get myself into a different mode, relax. First of all divest myself of my robes. I slid my wig back into its tin and rolled up my gown. I looked at myself in the mirror. I would have worn a different shirt if I hadn't had to robe. Something sharper, with a collar, more likely to impress my colleagues at the inquiry, although if what Roseanna had said was right, perhaps I should have just worn a suit of armour.

As I walked out of the building into the hot, dry sunshine of the street, it was already half past eleven. A figure stepped in front of me and I took a step sideways to avoid her. She stepped with me and for a few seconds we swayed in a repetitive dance on the pavement. Finally I said, 'Do you come here often?'

'You're Danny's brief, aren't you?'

I thought back over my life as a barrister. Had there ever been a client called Danny?

'Danny, Danny,' I said, hoping that saying the name would bring an image to my mind.

31

'Danny Richards,' she said disdainfully. 'He was your client this morning.'

'OK,' I said neutrally, hoping she thought my vagueness was actually a result of my duty of confidentiality.

'I'm Yolande.'

The name didn't ring a bell, I wondered which part of his life she was involved in, in which volume of the brief I might have read about her, if I'd had all the papers.

'Mmm,' I said, cautiously.

She was thin, blond and tanned. She had to be Danny Richards' girlfriend. She looked tired, her face was lined, as if she'd spent too much time in the sun, and I was conscious that she was wearing a lot of gold jewellery. She looked like my idea of a gangster's moll.

'Have you got time for a coffee?'

'I can't talk to you about his case,' I said. 'I'm only here for the morning. You should get in touch with his solicitor.'

'Oh her,' she said, dismissively. 'I don't even know her. She's only been on the case a week.'

'Has she?' I was surprised. The brief I didn't have was obviously prepared in her usual meticulous style.

'Two weeks,' she amended.

'Look, Mr Richards hasn't said I can talk to you,' I said, thinking he probably would have, if we'd got round to it. 'It's his case, I can't.'

Her face twisted in anguish. 'I'm not going to be able to see him before this trial. Someone's got to do something.'

'OK,' I sighed. 'If you like, you can tell me what you want to tell me and I'll pass it on.'

She smiled, a big wide smile.

* * *

I thought we would go to a rather nice café with large windows and the smell of coffee beans; I envisaged a little espresso with some hot milk on the side; I saw myself considering a slightly warm apricot danish pastry. But we were sitting on two rickety chairs in the back room of a shop, drinking Tesco's own brand and eating non-chocolate Hob Nobs. I felt quite at home, it reminded me of my life in Colchester, days spent in my dad's garage. And compared to that, this was high class, because in those days it was Rich Tea or nothing.

We had walked for about five minutes, in silence, away from the city centre, down Dalton Street and round behind the hospital. She walked like a model, moving confidently, head straight, a small smile on her lips. Men looked at her, and kept watching as we passed, twisting their necks, shaking their heads. Till we arrived at the shop. 'This is Danny's shop,' she said. My heart sank. I shouldn't be here. Kay was going to kill me.

I would make it short. It would be very short. She had unlocked the front door ('There's just me, during the week, when Danny's away,' she explained. 'Sometimes I have extra help on a Saturday.') and we had walked through a forest of armchairs and sofas, covered in mottled blue and grey velvet, and beige and orange corduroy, with matching footstools, guarded by nests of tables. The kind of things I always say I would never have in my home, but that are always fantastically comfortable and comforting to sit on, unlike my own furniture.

I had watched Yolande as she had fiddled with the kettle, carrying it to a room I assumed was the toilet to fill it, as she had removed two mugs from a cupboard on the wall and as she spooned powder from the jar.

All with her left hand. I gazed at the long pale-pink painted fingernails incongruously but expertly, left-handedly, completing the coffee-making process. I once fell in love with a person on the basis of left-handedness alone. The relationship didn't last long, but while it did, whenever anything manual came up I was in heaven, watching her write, watching her make a point, watching her look at the time on the other wrist.

But today I was here for professional reasons.

Yolande eased carefully back in her chair and stretched out her long legs. Not that I was watching.

She wore two thick gold rings on the third finger of her left hand, one splattered with stones that looked like diamonds. She wore a thick gold chain round her left wrist. Her blonde hair was caught up in a sleek chignon and she wore expensive cream clothes. She looked like she had stepped out of the eighties, the seventies. She was obviously older than me, and older than Danny Richards, but as she relaxed, nibbling at a Hob Nob, sipping her coffee, she seemed to grow younger. Maybe that's what classic clothes and hair do for you. Or perhaps good biscuits. Or possibly good company. I smiled.

She crushed it. 'You know who I'm married to?' she said. I couldn't work out if it was a statement or a question.

'No.'

'He's a bastard.'

'OK.'

'He hates the fact that I'm having an affair with Danny.'

'Well he would.'

'No, he wouldn't. Not for the reasons you're thinking.

He doesn't care about me.' Uh-oh, we were into the barrister-as-priest situation. I fixed a bland but caring expression on my face. 'But I actually care about him.'

'Mmm hmm.' Whatever gets you through the night, I thought.

'He's fifteen years older than me. To him I'm a kind of trophy. That's what he wanted when he asked me to marry him. And that's what he got. Look at me. Long legs, blonde hair, good face.'

'He's a lucky man,' I said, meaning it, uncertain where the conversation was going.

'We've been married fifteen years.'

'That's good. Did you care about him when you married him?'

'Good question,' she said. I felt a small glow of pleasure. 'I don't know. I suppose I married him because he asked me. And it made my sister's eyes pop. And he was very rich,' she added. 'So I suppose in one way I married him for his money. And he's got his money's worth.' She ran a hand down her leg. 'He's been good to me. It's just . . . he can't help Danny with this . . . thing.' She stared at the pieces of carpet on the floor.

'That's understandable.'

'And I wondered if you could.'

My head snapped up from the turquoise swirls on the floor. I was more than happy for her to ask me to go for coffee because of my personal charm. I was also happy to be a listening ear, even to offer a little bit of moral support. But I wasn't sure what concepts we were now dealing with. What might a husband do? Put up shelves? Have a toolbox with screwdrivers in? Plan a jailbreak? We could be heading towards a conflict of interests. 'I'm Danny's barrister,' I said. I was already in too deep, I was calling the client by his first name. 'Does he know you're talking to me?'

'Oh yes, I just went to see him. He said he thought you were OK.'

'That's nice, but I can't represent anybody else.'

'But I thought that after today, you weren't going to be his barrister. You could give me some advice.'

'No, no, no. There are professional considerations here. I really shouldn't be talking to you at all.'

'Professional considerations! Where have I heard that before?'

'I don't know, but I'm no good to anybody if I'm not professional. You have got to go through Kay Davidson, the solicitor.'

'I don't know her, I don't know if I can trust her.'

'She's straight,' I said, adding to myself, professionally speaking. 'I know her, you have absolutely nothing to worry about from her. But, if you don't trust her, what's she doing being Danny's . . . Mr Richards' solicitor? Not to mention the fact she's in London.' It's not unheard of to have a solicitor from out of town, even on Legal Aid, but it is unusual.

'Because he – he needed a new solicitor. For this, he needed a new solicitor.'

'I thought all his recent offences were serious assaults? Why change now?'

'He'd . . . had the old one for years. He needed someone new. And we heard she was good. She was in London, away from Birmingham. But I've never met her. You can get a feel of people when you meet them. You know who to trust.' Her expression changed. 'Danny's got to get off this.'

'You can trust Kay Davidson,' I said. 'Ask her.' I was

so anxious not to know about Danny Richards and his problems. I could feel myself slipping down into a large vat of golden syrup. Nice, especially if you had a slice of bread and butter with you, but really difficult to get out of.

'But she's only been to see him a couple of times. She won't even speak to me on the phone.'

I lifted my hand. 'It's probably because she hasn't been given the say-so from Danny to speak to you.' Oh God, Kay was going to kill me for talking to Yolande. 'It really is tricky in a case like this, who you talk to, who you don't. Why don't you go and see Danny? He's on remand, you can go any time, can't you? Tell him to talk to Kay.'

'I can't take any more time off,' she said, gesturing round the room with a biscuit.

'Really?' I asked. 'Don't you have an early closing day? Or a late opening?'

'I've lost too much time already.' She saw my expression. 'I can't go, all right?' A small flush rose up her neck.

'Then tell Simon, the barrister, when he comes up.'

'For the start of the trial? No, that's too late. Danny will have pleaded guilty by then. And I don't want that on my conscience.' She took a mouthful of coffee. 'If he goes down for this, he'll be inside for years. He won't get time off because he never does, he won't show remorse. He can't go down for this.' She shuddered.

'But why did he bother getting a new solicitor if all he wants to do is plead guilty?'

'I made that happen. I wanted someone to fight for him.'

'But it's his choice, surely.'

'No, it's not!' she said sharply. 'There are other people involved.' She took a mouthful of coffee and paused. 'He just needs time.'

It wasn't only Danny who needed time. I leaned over to pick up another biscuit, casually easing up the sleeve of my jacket. It was getting late.

'Look, you obviously stopped him pleading guilty this morning,' she went on. 'You had a go at the judge. You've got to help me.'

'Ehhh . . .'

She leaned down and picked up her handbag from the floor. She took out a small gold-covered diary and a slim, gold ballpoint pen. She turned to the back of the diary and looked up at me. 'What's your number?'

She wanted my number. She shouldn't have my number. She wanted my number so that she could write it down. With her left hand. She could find my chambers' number in any directory.

'020 7249 . . .' I was giving her my home number. I hesitated. I shouldn't. There wasn't anything I could do for her. I was a barrister, not a private detective. Her hand moved gracefully across the paper, covering each digit as she wrote it, elegant, liquid, smoother in every way than writing with the right hand. I was putty. I gave her the rest of my number.

'Mmm, a London number. I come to London sometimes.' She smiled at me, her eyes a stunning dark blue.

'So call me.' It just slipped out.

'OK.' She pushed back her chair and stood up.

We walked through the shop together. I threw a last regretful glance at the comfy sofas. I might have to come back to do some furniture research.

FIVE

Wednesday Afternoon – The Inquiry

It was quarter to two. How had that happened? My solicitor's office was on Broad Street, near the Convention Centre. There was little point in trekking all the way over there if the inquiry was starting at two thirty. I rang him from the street on my mobile. I realised it was the first time we had spoken to each other. He was new to the firm and most of our communication had been by email. Now, he sounded weary. 'Don't worry about the fresh paper. It's nothing urgent,' he said.

'Is it stuff I ought to know before this afternoon?'

'Oh no. Some statements from two social workers from London saying they visited the children on a regular basis. And there's a couple of reports from other inquiries. I'll bring them down to the Grange. I thought you were coming in this morning to pick them up,' he said vaguely.

'Unfortunately I had to do a directions hearing for a colleague and it went on rather longer than I expected.'

'Who was your judge?' he asked.

'Norman?'

'You were lucky to get out alive.'

'Given how things turned out, death might have been a blissful release.'

He laughed.

Encouraged, I went on, 'One of the barristers there said . . . Do you know any reason why our case, well, this brief would be regarded as the poisoned chalice?' I asked him.

'No, not at all,' he said. But then he'd only been on the case about three weeks. 'Look, I'd better go now. Do you know how to get to the Grange?'

I told him I did and then he said he'd got to find a fresh shirt before we started this afternoon. I wasn't sure whether I should be reassured that personal presentation was important to him or worry that he had to change shirts in the middle of the day. Perhaps it was the Birmingham way. I looked down at my own, black, shirt, it was creased and sticking to parts of my body. Perhaps I had things to learn from the Midlands.

The inquiry was being held at the Grange on Dalton Street. The name, the Grange, might make you think it was a large old country building covered in ivy, with fields of cows somehow miraculously nearby. But no. It was a square 1950s concrete municipal office block, grey and flat with wide steps leading up to a vast glass door. The upside was that inside the building were long wide corridors which led into large airy rooms. I was directed to the first floor, down one of the long corridors, through a wide vestibule to the room where the inquiry was to be held. In fact it was two rooms whose shared middle wall was folded back to create an enormous space with one huge glass wall, looking out over a scratchy piece of lawn. Inside the room were historically daring light fitments, municipal chairs and long trestle tables.

Lawyers are not used to appearing in rooms with natural light and I wondered if it was the glare of the sun that made the room seem empty. A woman in a short purple jacket and black slacks was straightening green baize on the top table. She looked up at me with a polite smile. 'Can I help?'

'I'm Frances Richmond, counsel for the . . . victims,' I said breathlessly. I had to find another name for my clients. Calling them victims made them sound weak and pathetic when they were actually angry and frustrated and hungry for action. I looked wildly round the room. Whatever they were called, they weren't here.

'Oh,' she said, and gave me a puzzled look. 'I'm Mrs Gisborough, eh, Ellen Gisborough. I'm part of the administrative team. We're providing secretarial and administrative support for the inquiry. We're not starting till tomorrow. Have you not been told?' That was the reason for the look.

With a rush of paranoia I wondered if it was just me who didn't know, or if it was our team who hadn't been given the information. Was this what Roseanna had meant?

'So you won't know it's the press conference this afternoon.'

'Ah,' I said. We both looked round the room. 'Not for the clients then?'

'Not really. I think your solicitor said something about them not wanting photos.'

'Of course.'

'Yes, this afternoon is just – what would you call it? – a bit of PR for the inquiry.' She stopped as if she had said too much. Which she probably had. Busily, she began to pull the other tables in the room into a straight line facing the head table. There was nothing to do but help her.

At twenty-five past two, lawyers began to appear. You could tell they were lawyers because they carried large pigskin briefcases. Three of them were men who I would, at some stage, be able to distinguish from each other. At the moment they all had plump cheeks, varying shades of grey hair and wore subdued navy suits. As a gesture to the press conference, I assumed, they were all wearing snazzy ties. A woman introduced herself as Catherine Delahaye, the advocate to the inquiry. She and the only other woman wore careful, understated peach-coloured lipsticks and small, black polished shoes. I felt worn and dusty, the word 'hack' seemed to hang over my head like the ghost of things to come.

At two thirty the panel of three came into the room and we all stood. The panel sat and then so did we. I had placed myself next to a large man who looked in his late fifties, wearing a double-breasted suit and a navy blue tie with large red spots. I put a low pile of my papers in front of me, then, leaning across my neighbour, took a glass from the tray Mrs Gisborough had anxiously provided, and poured myself some water. 'Water?' I asked him, but he obviously didn't hear.

Mrs Gisborough ushered in the press and I began writing, as if I were preparing incisive, justice-provoking, questions. I wrote 'Bad Company' – I ought to dig it out and play it. Then I wrote 'Pay bills'. Then 'New Suit?' Finally I added, 'Solve the mystery of Danny's murder charge (personal interest only). Possibly need more info from Yolande. Tell Kay? No.'

There was a camera crew with several metres of trailing wire and a BBC logo on their camera, and two journalists who looked more dishevelled than I did. They were almost professionally crumpled, as if how to wear baggy corduroy was something they had learned on their media studies courses. The journalists eagerly wrote down every word as the Chair of the panel introduced the panel members, a senior social worker from Sussex, a childcare expert from a Scottish university, and himself, Henry Curston QC. I vaguely recognised him. He was something auspicious at the Bar Council and his face had been in *Counsel* magazine on one or two occasions.

The BBC crew moved away from the panel and directed their attention to the legal representatives. As the TV camera panned round towards me, I put down my pen and bent confidentially towards my neighbour and began talking earnestly about the weather.

He looked at me with disdain, then turned firmly away from me and spoke to the person on his left.

The camera panned away. The Chair bent across the table, looking questioningly from side to side, murmuring to his colleagues. The journalists craned forward excitedly, their pens poised, waiting for some details, some hint of the dreadful stories to come, to thrill their readers, to please their editors, to make their mark, then sank back despondently as the panel nodded to each other and rose and left the room. The press conference was over and the press disappeared like grease spots when you squirt Fairy Liquid into the washing-up bowl. The lawyers pushed back their chairs, picked up their pigskin bags and, laughing and joking with each other as if they'd all been friends for years, filed out of the door. I was left packing my notebooks into my non-pigskin bag. I didn't want them to like me, I didn't want them to be my friends, but I felt loneliness lapping at my ankles.

'The chair has asked me to say we're starting at ten thirty tomorrow morning.' Catherine Delahaye had stepped back into the room. I looked round to see who she was talking to. It was me. I just stopped myself throwing my arms round her neck. She took out a sheet of paper from a plastic folder. 'I thought it would be useful if I circulated a list of all the legal representatives' phone numbers, so I can be in touch if anything crops up. Especially people from out of town.'

'Do you mean here, or in London?' I took the sheet of paper which was divided with two meticulously ruled lines.

'Both.'

I tugged a pen out of my jacket pocket and, with what I hoped was a friendly grin, enthusiastically scribbled Julie's number in Birmingham and my number in London. I didn't give her the number for my mobile as I never switched it on, and I had recently become aware that the ringing tone didn't always work.

She slid the list back into the plastic folder. She was obviously from the Miss Neatly Organised school of advocacy and I reminded myself sharply that, like a pupil on her first day at a new school, I must beware of making friends with the first person who wants to play with me. I went back to rearranging my notebooks, when I heard Catherine Delahaye's resigned, 'Oh, hello.'

A young man who looked about sixteen with short brown hair and small rimless glasses, his tie at a forty-five degree angle to his collar, approached me, with his hand out, saying breathlessly, 'Hello, I'm Adam Owen. You're . . . ?'

'Frankie Richmond, yes, hi.' My heart sank. This child was my solicitor. What would he know? How could he

44

help me? Had I imagined it or had he done a double take when he saw me? Perhaps it was just a guilty start. He was late after all.

He looked round the room. 'Oh God,' he said. 'I've missed it haven't I? The senior partner even let me drive one of the cars to get here. I'm meant to be getting as much publicity for the firm as I can. I'm really, really sorry.'

I shook my head.

'One of our clients had a crisis, social services were threatening to take her son into care, I've just spent an hour at her house, trying to reason with them. And they've got dogs,' he said, looking down at his trousers. As he got closer I could see white dog hairs from knee to ankle. He followed my glance. 'I wouldn't mind but they were only about six inches high, they just bounced a lot.' He looked round the room. 'Did anything happen?'

It was four o'clock. 'Let's go and have a drink and I'll tell you what you missed,' I said. 'While you pick dog hairs off your trousers.'

He grinned. 'And that way I don't have to go back to the office. Perfect. And if you're good, I'll let you pick off the dog hairs.'

'Now then,' I said.

We walked out of the room as a couple appeared at the top of the stairs into the lobby. I thought hard, this was . . . yes, Mr and Mrs Springer. They had been at the one conference I'd had with my clients. Mr Springer was my actual client, but it was his wife whose face was working with indignation. Today, as on the day of the conference, she was wearing a thick sheepskin coat, which she held

45

tightly round herself with thin, red hands. I noticed that her wedding ring was too big for her finger, slipping back and forth to her knuckle.

'I told them not to come,' Adam muttered to me, as we advanced with apology on our faces.

Gregory Springer sank into himself, shaking his head and telling us not to worry, so sorry to be troublesome. Mrs Springer looked around angrily, as if expecting to catch a glimpse of the other clients, hiding behind pillars or in the stairwell. 'Why shouldn't we come?' she asked.

'When I rang them, most people decided they didn't want to be photographed,' Adam said.

'Our story has a right to be heard,' she said. 'There's been too much whitewashing already.'

'The press may well be here tomorrow,' I said. 'They do want to hear what people have to say. But Mr Springer, I thought you had decided not to give oral evidence.'

'Yes, well, he's still considering his position.' Mrs Springer spoke before her husband could answer. 'Come on Gregory,' she said. 'I took the afternoon off work for this.'

'I'm so sorry,' I said, 'but we'll see you tomorrow morning.'

'Yes,' said Mr Springer, as his wife said, 'Maybe.'

Adam knew a tapas bar behind the inquiry building. We dashed the last ten yards as it started to rain and immediately ordered some tortilla and patatas bravas (egg and chips) to make up for the lunch I hadn't had, and a bottle of red, oaky wine to make up for everything.

'Nice shirt,' I said, looking at the crisp pink creases as he shook off his jacket and hung it over a chair.

He laughed, embarrassed. 'I cycle to work, and we're usually quite casual in the office, but I didn't think . . . you . . . would go for lycra.'

He said he had rung chambers again this morning as soon as he had learned of the press conference, and left a message. So it wasn't that the victims were being victimised before the inquiry started, or that my solicitor was hopeless, it was just chambers being useless and failing to ring me, probably Gavin not wanting another earful about Simon's case. I made a mental note to speak to Gavin.

In any event it made me feel happier about Adam, so I could relax, and because we had the time, discuss the other lawyers. Adam ran through the list of representatives. Because the abuse had happened twenty years before, not everyone who had worked at Haslam Hall was going to be represented. The perpetrators, the five men whose names had been given to the police, were in prison. Some of the other staff could not be found, one or two had died, and a few simply wanted to forget it had happened.

But David Wyatt, the man who had been principal of the home at the time of the abuse, was being represented. He had not been charged with any offence and was now, it said in his statements, anxious to help the inquiry. His solicitor was Mr Frodsham, who from Adam's description was the man I had attempted to swap meteorological niceties with earlier. Frodsham worked for Stiversons, Adam told me – the Carter Ruck of Birmingham – an old firm situated in a narrow alley off Corporation Street. Six social workers were participating in the inquiry, they were from four local authorities and were represented by two solicitors' firms in

Leicester. The two care workers who had never been implicated in the abuse had chosen a firm in Sutton Coldfield.

Adam was an assistant solicitor in the firm of Painter, Pavish and Rutland. PPR, as he called them, was regarded with suspicion by the other solicitors in the inquiry. Although the partners were old school, recent recruitment had brought in lots of bright young things with too many degrees for their own good, earning enormous amounts of money. 'Not me, though,' Adam explained, 'being the most junior solicitor in the firm.' PPR had new, modern offices near the Convention Centre, and an intense work ethic.

I devoured the potatoes and tortilla, and he picked at a piece of bread, and we watched the rain falling steadily outside. 'I still don't know how come I was instructed,' I said.

Adam's face began to colour. 'Well . . .' he began. 'I had nothing to do with it, because it was before my time. But I was quite surprised to see you. You weren't . . . quite what I expected.' He opened a crisp yellow file and began flicking through a deep pile of correspondence and attendance notes, held together by a metal pin. 'You were instructed before my time. Yes, here.' He held back a bunch of papers and read from a note dated the autumn of the year before. It had been sent to someone who had been a new trainee, who had since left the firm without finishing his training. 'David, ring 19 Kings Bench Walk to instruct Francis Richmond to represent the victims, whom they have requested.'

'17,' I corrected. 'My chambers are at 17 Kings Bench Walk.'

'19,' he repeated, staring at the scrawl on the note. 'Francis with an "I".'

'That's not me.'

'Apparently not.' There was a beat of silence. 'But the clients haven't said anything, which is obviously why it wasn't picked up. And they're obviously happy.'

Francis Richmond had been a well-known and apparently well-liked Birmingham solicitor who had decided to become a barrister. He divided his time between London and Birmingham, where his wife remained. When she had fallen ill with a wasting illness, he was forced to stay in London where he could find better, more lucrative work. A prolonged period in Birmingham on this inquiry would have been a godsend for him. The money, the proximity to his wife, the quiet rhythm you get into in an inquiry.

Instead the trainee had made a mistake looking up the number in the Bar directory. He had rung my chambers and got me. 'I should have noticed there are several different numbers for your chambers,' he said.

I shook my head. Not only was I not the right person, but I was positively the wrong person. And they all knew it.

I made a note to ask Gavin if he had known. I had a horrible feeling that he had. When your world is falling all around you, shoot the clerk. I added it to my mental list of things to do.

'It may have been 19 KBW that I rang this morning about the press conference,' he said.

I was still going to shoot Gavin.

When I got back to Julie's, my shoulder sagging with the weight of my soaking wet bags, which I had dragged through the rain, from a parking place halfway down the street, Marnie was curled, dry and comfy, on the sofa in front of the TV. 'I just saw you on the news!' she crowed as she let me in. 'Can I come down and watch you one day? Ooh, you're wet.' I dropped a dripping bag. 'But who was that horrible man?'

'Which one?'

'The one who slapped his thigh and turned his back on you. He was so rude. I wanted to punch him.'

'Perhaps you should come to the inquiry as my minder,' I said carelessly.

'Yeah!'

'No.'

'But I want to meet all your lawyer friends.'

'That would not be possible,' I said bitterly. 'I have no lawyer friends.' I dragged the two bags ostentatiously across the room. 'I'll just take these heavy wet bags upstairs then.'

'OK,' she said cheerfully. 'Oh, Mum said to tell you she's working late, so we should take something out of the freezer.'

'Oh great,' I murmured as I climbed the stairs. Julie's freezer was like mine. Everything was three years old, nothing had labels, and it was all mince.

As I threw the bags onto the floor of my room, I noticed the stitching in my work bag had perished in several places and a corner of my brief was poking through. It was wet. Everything was wet. What a lousy start to the inquiry. Water is not my medium. My star sign is not a water sign. And clearly my bag was not waterproof. Not now anyway. I was going to have to buy a new work bag. And, on top of everything, I was about to have melted mince for my supper. I needed warmth, I needed human kindness, so, foolishly, I fished my mobile out of my bag, sat on the edge of the bed and rang chambers for my messages. There were none.

'Forget the freezer food,' I said to Marnie, stomping back down the stairs. 'We're going to have a takeaway, and we're going to have it delivered.'

'Oh cool,' Marnie crowed. 'Can I order it?'

An hour later I was back in my room.

I pulled out my files. I made a list for myself of all the witnesses to be called. It gives you an idea of the shape of the case, how it might go. But really it's just to make you feel you're doing something.

Time Table
Opening submissions – half a day
My clients – three days?
Social workers – a day?
Teachers – two days
Mr Wyatt – principal – a day
The medical experts –
called by my clients
   Psychologists × 2) – 1 to be called to give oral
   evidence – half a day
) – 1 written evidence to be read
   Paediatrician   ) – half a day
   GPs   ) – written evidence
   Counsellors × 1) – written evidence
   Therapists × 2) – written evidence
called by advocate to the inquiry
   Two psychologists re theory of sexual abuse – 1 day
called by the principal

Child-development expert – ? an hour
Other experts –
called by the advocate to the inquiry
Architect – half a day
Safety officer – ? an hour
Training officer – ? half a day
Management consultant – ? an hour
University lecturer in social work – half a day
called by the social workers
Field worker in child abuse – half a day
Others –
Police – ? one day
View of Haslam Hall?? – half a day?

I gazed at the list. I could be up here for weeks.

SIX

Thursday – Inquiry

The rain drummed on the plate-glass window in relent-
less waves. Through the fluorescent lights the air was
grey while Shelly Dean gave her evidence. She was
wearing a neat black jacket and a loose white Tricel
blouse. Her round face was flushed with concentration.

We had decided at the conference that Shelly would
be the first witness. She was confident, spoke clearly
and made good points. Like many of the other clients,
she had had a difficult life – it was her complaints to
the police about abuse by her father which had led to
her reception into care, only for her to be abused at the
children's home. Shelly was determined that the system
would give answers for what had happened to her in
her childhood. She had high hopes for the inquiry.

The lawyers had finished their opening submissions
in the morning. Each advocate had stressed how his or
her clients wanted to assist the panel in every way, to
ensure such things never happened again. I had said it
myself. Before Shelly went into the witness box, as my
clients milled around in the lobby at the end of the lunch
break, tense and garrulous, she had approached me,
holding a cigarette in a trembling hand and asked me
again what would happen. 'We're all fighting on the

perhaps as an example of the damage done by the abuse my client suffered. I assume Mr Frodsham asked that question on instructions from his client, Mr Wyatt. I simply say again, it's not relevant.'

Henry Curston shuffled his papers. 'If you hadn't been so quick off the mark, Miss Richmond, I was about to say the same thing myself.'

It was the afternoon tea break and Adam and I left the inquiry room. Catherine Delahaye approached us with a sheaf of paper. She gave me a sheet and Adam a sheet. It was a timetable for the inquiry. It looked rather similar to mine, except she had set out the days the witnesses would be attending and her time estimate was longer. At this rate I would be here till Christmas.

'By the way,' she said, looking across the lobby, 'Mr Frodsham would like to know which of your clients will be giving evidence.'

'I bet he would.'

She hesitated, but when I said no more she moved on to speak to the other advocates.

The clients had gathered in a loose group protecting Shelly. She was smoking. I moved towards her purpose-fully, trying to convey a sense of achievement I did not feel. Shelly hadn't asked, or even expected, to be treated so badly. I had to reassure her, and the others who were due to give evidence, that going through a horrible time in the witness box had served some purpose. 'You were good,' I said to her. 'You were clearly telling it exactly like it happened.' I noticed Wyatt hovering on the edge of the group, with a caring smile fixed to his lips. 'Get rid of him,' I said to Adam, from the corner of my mouth.

Adam ushered Wyatt away. I went on, 'For some

reason you put the wind up Frodsham. I think we're making some good points.'

'Yeah, that last one were a killer.'

'That was irrelevant. You were the first witness, Frodsham was just trying impress his little personality on the proceedings, to worry you. It reflected worse on him.'

'I probably had him too,' she said. She took a long drag on her cigarette. 'He probably wants his fifteen quid back.'

Frodsham's plan, if that's what it was, had worked. Leanne Scott and Janine Telford who were to give their evidence after the break, looked grey and anxious. I asked Adam to make sure everyone had a biscuit so we would all have the necessary blood sugar levels for the next session and I left the room, saying I had to make a phonecall.

Earlier in the morning, wandering round the building, I had found a set of telephone kiosks in the basement that no one seemed to use. I stood in the phone booth now, staring at the wall. It was important not to get things out of perspective, I told myself. Being an advocate was my job, getting shouted at was my job. But protecting the clients was also my job and I hadn't done that very well just now. I simply hadn't seen it coming. But it wasn't my fault, I told myself sensibly, Frodsham wasn't playing by the rules. What were the rules? Perhaps I'd made up my own rules and everyone else was working to a completely different set. No, Frodsham was out of order. I was sure of it.

After the break Leanne and Janine told their stories. They too had been regularly 'punished' for minor misdemeanours at the home. The advocate to the inquiry asked them clinical questions about the systematic nature of the abuse, the days of the week, the time of day. The women held their heads high, occasionally looking over at me, and I tried to offer support without moving a muscle of my face. Wyatt's name was not mentioned and Frodsham's cross-examination was desultory.

We were adjourned until ten thirty on Monday, because Henry Curston had a case in the Court of Appeal. I could see my youth disappearing while I staggered through this inquiry in Birmingham.

Leanne and Janine mingled with the others in the foyer, pleased not to have been attacked in the witness chair, but a little disappointed they hadn't had the chance to shout at Frodsham. Perhaps I was wrong about Frodsham. The three women who had given evidence walked towards the stairs, sharing their feelings. After they had gone a few steps, I could hear them laughing.

I went to my phone booths in the basement and rang chambers. 'So you've started then?' Gavin said.

'Yes, but we're not sitting tomorrow. In fact, I think we're unlikely to go straight through. From the time-table, it looks as if we're going to be jumping about with days here and there, to fit in with everybody's other commitments.'

'You'd better fax the timetable to me,' Gavin said, 'or bring it into chambers.'

'Only if you promise not to book anything else in for me.'

'OK,' he said. 'If you're sure.'

'Have I got any messages?' I asked.

'I'll hand you to Jenna.'

'Hello.' Jenna's pleasant voice was happy and enthusiastic. She had just been promoted to junior junior clerk.

'You've got one message. Oh, it's from Iotha.' She was surprised that it was from another member of chambers. 'Can you ring her? I don't know what that's about.'

'Is there anything in my pigeon-hole?' I asked. 'Like a cheque?'

She went away to look and I passed a few hopeful seconds dreaming of what I would do if she found a massive cheque there. Or even a small cheque. I could buy a new suit for work. I could pay my mortgage.

'No cheques, I'm afraid, but you have got a memo, well, it's an invitation really, well it's a memo.'

'What is it?' I said, 'I'm on a payphone.' I put money into the box.

'This is from Iotha, too.' Iotha was a young practitioner who did crime and family, and who had taken over three cases of mine which were coming to court during my time out of town. 'This is probably what her telephone message was about. She's having a garden party,' Jenna said.

'Oh, that's nice,' I said. 'But I thought her garden was in a terrible state.'

'That's the point. It says, "Gardening at three o'clock, dinner provided at seven. RSVP."'

'Oh God,' I said. 'When is it?'

'Sunday.'

'Oh dear.'

'Can't you make it?'

'I'm afraid I can,' I said. 'Tell her I'll be there.' I hate almost all types of gardening, I have nothing in common with most of my colleagues in chambers, and the time I had to spend at my lovely flat over the next few weeks was going to be severely limited. But it's important to support young members of chambers, and chambers activities are necessary anyway, to raise morale. And we needed morale boosting in chambers, every one was feeling anxious about how little work there was around, about Legal Aid rates, and about the three civil practitioners who had left chambers in the past few months. I'd have to go.

It was nearly nine o'clock when I got back to Stoke Newington. I drove through Dalston and up Kingsland High Road, past the Turkish shops with their lights coming on in the dusk, lighting up bright oranges and exotic vegetables. The florists opposite Amhurst Road welcomed me home with an enormous display of red and white flowers in pots outside the shop.

I picked up my post, left by one of my upstairs neighbours in a neat pile outside my front door. It didn't look even remotely interesting. There was a catalogue, a red bill and a couple of local newspapers. And a postcard which made me catch my breath. It was a picture of Edinburgh castle at night. I knew who it was from before I turned it over.

I unlocked my front door and walked into the living room before I read it. The message was brief and heartbreaking, written in the scrawl of all her postcards.

The gig last night was fantastic. Standing room only. Three encores. I still can't believe it. Love Margo x

Heartbreaking for me.

Margo was the woman I had had a short, passionate affair with the year before, when I'd had my run-in with the police. Margo had definite priorities and I was very low down on the list, after her children and her career.

But I had been pleased when she was booked to do some backing vocals at Ronnie Scott's through a friend of a friend of mine, and then some supporting work at the Jazz Café, and when I had heard there was talk of a tour with Jools Holland I was delighted. And now I was getting postcards from her exciting new life.

I threw myself onto the sofa and gazed at the ceiling. She had sung 'Call me,' and I had, but it was a party line and someone else was talking.

I shook my head, this wouldn't do, it was too late, it was over. My eye was caught by the flashing red light of my answerphone. I pressed the button. There were two messages. The first was Gavin saying he assumed I would finish all my outstanding paperwork before I started the inquiry, since that was what he had assured my solicitor only minutes after I had been speaking to him. 'Of course,' I told the machine, trying to remember what he was talking about. The other message was from my best friend Lena asking me to ring her, because she had great news.

'Guess what, I've joined a gym,' she announced as soon as I'd said hello.

'Whatever for?'

'Fitness, toned limbs, eternal youth. Plus they've got a Bar that sells liquid grass, not the herbal kind, and I don't think I could bear to drink it in public.'

'I don't think I could bear to drink it anywhere,' I said. 'It's unnatural.'

'So, the thing is,' she said, ignoring me, 'I can take a guest in free and I wondered if you wanted to come on Saturday morning.'

'The short answer to that of course is no.'

'That's what Nicky said. And Sophie.'

'So I'm not even your first choice.'

'You were number one on my non-lovers list,' she said.

'It was very nice of you to ask. I tell you what, how about you go to your class, and then we meet for breakfast after?'

'All right,' she said reluctantly.

'What are you doing tonight?'

'Going to see *A Bout de Souffle*. It's on in Shaftesbury Avenue.'

'And would that be with Sophie or Nicky?'

We talked about Lena's complicated love life for a while and then she had to go.

So no pleasant evening with Lena, cruising in Stoke Newington Church Street, then. There was some Ryvita in the fridge and there was a scraping of Marmite left in the jar. I prepared a feast of culinary delights and opened a half-bottle of Pouilly Fumé.

Ten minutes later, remembering my list of things to do, I knelt down to my line of albums and pulled out *Bad Company*. Side two, track one. The mournful piano notes filled the room, followed by the wailing voice of the lead singer. My dad used to play it in his workshop. I think he liked the image, always on the run. For Danny, of course, it wasn't just an image. And anyway he kept getting caught.

Then I flipped the disc and played 'Can't Get Enough of Your Love', clicking my fingers round the living room. I was having a good time playing seventies rock. Oh dear, perhaps I was coming down with something.

SEVEN

Friday – Chambers

I had to go into chambers. I had rung Gavin about the paperwork immediately after breakfast, about ten thirty. As soon as he mentioned the name of the solicitor I remembered with sickening clarity what the cases were. Both had started out with different solicitors and counsel. One case involved a mother who had conceded residence of her children a year before when she really shouldn't have, and now the father was refusing to allow her contact. She wanted to know if she could go back to vary the order. The other was a father who wanted to appeal against his children being taken into care by raising Human Rights Act arguments, saying that he hadn't had a fair trial. I'd had them on my desk for two weeks and I knew I needed to look things up. I also needed to find the book on social work practice I had bought to prepare my cross-examination of the social workers at the inquiry. And I needed to catch up on chambers news.

It was a hot day and I put on black linen trousers and a loose, black silk shirt for the barristerial but casual look.

There was no one in the clerks' room but clerks and they were all busy and didn't want to chat. I was forced to go to my room, which was small and filled with an

Ikea desk and chair and pine shelves holding briefs and old notebooks. It looked out over a patch of grass and if I stood up I could see the river. From my bag I pulled out Danny Richards' brief which I still had not endorsed. I was looking at the faxed, smudged back sheet wrapped around the nine pages, which had been the source of all my problems with Judge Norman, and wondering how much of what had gone on I should actually put in writing, when the phone warbled.

Jenna said, 'I've got – em – Orlando on the phone to speak to you.'

'Orlando who?'

'I don't know.'

Jenna sounded stressed, so I said, 'OK, put him through, but if it's someone selling insurance you might find yourself with a thirty-year premium round your neck.'

'No thank you,' she said primly, 'I'm already fully covered.'

'Get you,' I said. 'OK, put him through.' The phone clicked. 'Frances Richmond speaking,' I murmured cautiously.

'Mmm,' said a husky voice, 'what a nice telephone manner you have.'

'Thank you,' I said. 'Who am I speaking to?'

'Didn't she tell you? It's Yolande.'

My heart fluttered. I did not want to speak to this woman, it meant grief all the way down the line, I knew it. 'So, Yolande, how are you?'

'I'm fine. How's the inquiry going?'

'As well as can be expected.'

'I saw you on TV. You looked very nice.'

I snorted. But perhaps I had looked nice.

'Compared to the others,' she continued, with a short laugh. 'Come and have lunch with me.'

'Where are you?' I said.

'I'm on Fleet Street,' she said. 'It's a lovely day, we could get a cab across the river. We could sit and look at the water.'

It sounded rather nice, with or without Yolande. But I couldn't. She was blonde and left-handed and she was the girlfriend of a very dangerous man, if his record was to be believed. Which it was. Plus there were professional issues. They were in the grey area of murky to say the least. On the one hand neither Danny nor Yolande was my client, but on the other, in a way I still was Danny's counsel, since I hadn't endorsed my brief or told Simon what had happened. Or even rung Kay, my instructing solicitor, I realised with a lurch of guilt. And Yolande was bound to want to talk about him, and Yolande was his girlfriend.

'I'm really busy,' I said, half-heartedly. 'I've only just got into chambers.'

'Why don't I come to you then?' she said. 'I'll bring some sandwiches.' Even over the phone I could tell she was left-handed. And there was that item on my list of things to do. Solve the mystery of Danny's case. I hate leaving things undone. 'Everybody has to eat lunch,' she whispered. That was just so true. I was starving I realised. It was at least an hour and a half since I'd had toast. What else could I do? And somehow if she came to chambers I was . . . containing things. But what if Simon saw her? That might mean trouble. I remembered that Simon wasn't in today. He was at the hospital, having his foot seen to, which is why it was all his fault anyway.

'OK,' I said.

'I'll be there in ten minutes,' she cooed. 'We'll need a few plates and two glasses.'

I shivered with anticipation.

She was sitting on a sofa in the waiting room, reading a copy of the *Financial Times*, one of the papers Jenna spread out daily on a small coffee table. She was wearing more of those clothes that only blonde, lightly tanned women can get away with. Today it was a gold-beige, probably cashmere, sweater; a gold-beige straight skirt that revealed her long legs, but only discreetly from the knees down; slim beige high-heeled shoes. And a thin gold chain around her neck. They were very expensive clothes and I wondered who had paid for them, Danny or her unhappy husband. Or maybe she had bought them herself, I could hear Lena sternly asserting, from her wages from the shop. Remembering her relaxed approach to opening hours and the absence of any customers during the two hours that I was there, I doubted that the shop could fund that level of sumptuousness.

Yolande stood up, swayed towards me and I leaned to kiss her on the cheek.

I had found some dusty, non-matching plates at the back of the cupboard in the small kitchen area at the far end of the clerks' room and, optimistically, had taken two matching glasses from the chambers box of champagne glasses. Now the plates were spread across my desk, piled with sandwiches made of interesting bread. 'I like picnics,' she said. 'And this is almost a picnic.' She gestured at the food with her left hand, the diamonds glinting heavily. 'There's a BLT, something with houmous and peppers, and a chicken thing. Oh and water.' She pulled a blue bottle out of her plastic bag, twisted the lid and poured out two glasses of fizzing mineral water.

'Sometimes you don't need alcohol to get a buzz,' I would have said, but couldn't summon enough enthusiasm.

As I ate seriously through every flavour, she nibbled at a triangle of chicken salad. She made conversation about Somerset House and the Courtauld Gallery, which she had just visited, she talked about fountains and cobble stones and ice rinks. I talked about Somerset House when it was part of the Family Division, and the hours I had spent sitting in narrow corridors, proposing compromises to angry people who thought they were preserving their dignity when their sadness was blinding them to an easier way forward.

'Coffee?' I asked, screwing up my serviette and putting it on the empty plate in front of me.

'How nice,' she smiled. 'I'll amuse myself looking out of your window.'

I flew along the corridor to the kitchen.

As I returned with two unchipped mugs of coffee, I could hear voices in my room. My heart shrank. Simon must have limped bravely back from the hospital and Jenna must have told him Yolande (or someone like that) was here. He would be furious that I was entertaining a defence witness in chambers. I wondered if I could leave the coffee outside the door, just give a tap to let her know it was there – Simon could have mine, I thought generously – and then I could leave the country and start a new life with a new identity.

'Courage,' I said to myself, and then I said it again, with a French accent. A new life in France was an option. I would think about it later. I could say she had come to see how Simon's foot was, to wish him luck for the trial. She was just sitting in my room to wait.

But it wasn't Simon, it was Marcus. I would much rather it had been Simon. Marcus was another member of chambers and he and I didn't get on. And it wasn't just because, unaccountably, he earned a lot of money and had a very nice new car. It was deeper than that. He was a slimeball. You only had to look at his hair.

And there was the smell of cigarette smoke in the room. Bastard. I hate smoking, I won't have it in my room. Yolande stood by the window, her arm half hanging out. She was the smoker. Oh. OK. But, I noticed, Marcus was chewing. He was eating our picnic.

'Hello Frankie,' he said, as if we were the greatest friends in the world. 'I just came in for a word, but I see you're . . . in conference?' His eyes flicked mockingly over the half-empty plates.

'Yes,' I said, 'absolutely.'

'Catch you later then,' he said with an easy smile. 'Great sandwiches.' He picked up half a BLT which I had been looking forward to taking home. He bit deeply into it. Even Marcus wouldn't eat the sandwiches if he thought he was interrupting a conference. 'Very nice meeting you . . . ?'

I wasn't going to tell him Yolande's name and nor was she, so Marcus backed out of the room, grinning and chewing.

Yolande flicked her cigarette out of the window. I worried briefly about the dry greensward outside while she moved plates to make room for the coffee. 'Friend of yours?' she asked.

'Not really,' I said.

'He seemed very interested in Danny's case.' She indicated the thin brief now lying on top of a pile of back copies of *Family Law*. I thought I'd thrown it onto the shelf with my notebooks when I had brought the plates in.

'Did he?' I said cautiously. Marcus must be annoyed that Simon had got the case. Corpseless murders were considered rather exotic in the world of the criminal barrister.

'He seemed a bit disappointed when he saw it was so thin.'

Silently, I moved the brief to a higher shelf and sat down.

I still wasn't sure why she was here. It didn't feel as if she was here for me, there was something else. Silence stretched between us. I yearned for a small personal activity to fill in the space. Smoking for example: I could lean across the table, take a cigarette from her packet, look round the room tapping the cigarette on the box, strike a match, inhale, look at the cigarette, look attractive. But I don't smoke and she did.

'You weren't smoking at the shop, were you?' I said.

'We're not supposed to smoke in the shop. It burns holes in the stock.' She took another cigarette out of the packet. 'Do you mind?'

'No.'

She sat smoking, relaxed, at ease, her arm draped along the window sill. As if she was just there for a pleasant lunch, a 'picnic couvert'. While I jittered, fiddling with a piece of cellophane.

I shook my head. Sod it, why not? 'Did you know Terry Fleming?' I wasn't sure if this was helping her or me.

'Vaguely.'

71

'Do you think he's dead?'

'Are you interested or are you just making conversation?'

'I thought you were interested.'

'I'm not particularly interested in Terry Fleming.'

'I thought he was the cause of all your problems.'

'My problem is to stop Danny pleading guilty to this charge.'

'Well if Simon knew more about Terry Fleming, he wouldn't have to.'

'Tell Danny that.'

'I just wondered if Terry Fleming had taken off.'

'Good point,' she said, and I had that ridiculous glow of pleasure again. 'He has disappeared before.'

'When?'

'When things got hot. When he fell out with people or had trouble with business deals, that kind of stuff. They all do. They all have their little places. Danny does.'

'Like prison you mean?'

She raised her eyebrows at me. 'They go and wait for things to calm down, for a new deal to be done.'

'I didn't get the sense that Terry Fleming was a businessman.'

'He had his car business,' she said. She looked round. I had no ashtrays. I had a small dish containing paper clips, which I now emptied into a drawer, and gave to her. 'But I meant more generally, Effo's business.'

'Who's Effo?' The question was out before I could stop it.

She looked at me with her eyebrows very slightly raised. This was obviously information that was in the papers I hadn't had. But I didn't try to explain that. And apparently she wanted to tell me.

Edward Farnigan was known as Effo to his friends, of whom there were, apparently, many and in high places. He was a well-known local businessman, a property developer, an entrepreneur, with a hand in a lot of pies. He had a number of people who worked for him, including Terry Fleming and Ronald Catcher. He owned the Lambada Casino and Hombre, the menswear shop, where Terry Fleming had bought that last fabulous suit. And Effo was successful in his work, he had a number of big cars ('A Roller,' Yolande said, 'and a really nice Jag') and a large mock-Georgian house with a swimming pool in Solihull to prove it. I wanted to say obviously not that successful, because who would choose to live in Solihull, but it was her story, so I said nothing.

'So, Terry might be lying low while some deal of Effo's gets sorted out. Where does he go? Can't we get hold of him?'

She shrugged, jutting her lower lip to exhale, relaxed, casual.

'Who knows about this? Effo? Should someone be talking to him?'

She shook her head. I felt as if I was missing the point. Perhaps all of this was clearly set out in Simon's brief.

'I don't think anyone wants Effo to be involved, if at all possible. Certainly not Sandra.'

I waited. If I showed I didn't know what she was talking about it might look as if Kay hadn't briefed me properly, and that Kay wasn't up to the job. If Kay wasn't up to the job, she might think Simon wasn't up to it either.

'Sandra, Effo?' she said, mildly irritated. 'Yolande, Danny?'

'I'm sorry, there are so many names.'

'Sandra is the one who eventually drew the short straw and got Effo.' She tapped her cigarette into the paper clip dish. 'Sandra's a natural blonde, you know. Unlike me. Effo likes the natural look. And he pays for it. All Sandra wants these days is a quiet life. I think the excitement of being with Mr Big has worn off. She's spending a lot of time in the London flat at the moment, till the heat dies down. She's always been a bit independent.'

I wasn't sure where this conversation was going, although an independent woman and a flat in London made it more interesting. 'Had Sandra and Terry Fleming been getting close?'

'If they had, then she'd be the dead one, wouldn't she?'

The easy way she said it stunned me. 'For goodness' sake, who would have killed her?'

She smiled at me and I felt like Miss Prim the Sunday school teacher. Perhaps I would be better off in the library, looking up the meaning of the term 'equality of arms'.

'So, in the past, when Terry Fleming has laid low for a bit, how long has it taken for things to calm down?'

'Depends. Depends what they've done. Effo has various people to sort things. Sometimes that's Terry, occasionally it's Danny. Depends who's in his good books. People get a call, they do a job. Could take a couple of weeks, a couple of months.'

'Well, Fleming's been missing for a lot longer than that. But what's your point?' I was thinking aloud. 'Is Effo a respectable businessman, or a member of the Birmingham . . . underworld? What's he doing using the services of someone like Danny?'

74

Smoke curled round her nostrils.

'I'm just playing Devil's Advocate,' I said.

'In Birmingham,' she said slowly, tapping her cigarette unnecessarily over the paper clip dish, 'people do things for Effo. And if they don't, people – other people – disappear.' She looked at the tip of her cigarette for a second. 'It's not just London where people end up in concrete pillars.' She laughed. 'That's a joke.'

I didn't smile. 'So who's in a concrete pillar? Fleming?'

'Maybe. Do you want another sandwich?' she said.

I shook my head. 'I want you to tell me why you're here. All this is very interesting, but I don't represent Danny and I can't really have anything to do with this.'

She tilted her head and smiled at me. 'You started this conversation.'

'You rang me, you brought the sandwiches.' Was this our first argument?

'You seem friendly. It's nice to have someone to talk to.' She gestured at the plates spread over the table. 'Someone to have lunch with.' She gazed at me.

I looked away first. 'This may sound crass but why don't you talk to Effo, or Sandra? You seem to know them quite well.'

She shook her head and inhaled deeply on her cigarette. 'I think it goes a bit further than that. Something happened twenty years ago.' She gestured her head towards the thin brief on the shelf.

I didn't know what happened, I didn't have all the papers, I wanted to say, but I was still protecting everyone's professional probity.

My face must have said it anyway. 'Don't worry,' she said. 'I doubt Danny's told this new solicitor about spats.'

'Fights?'

'In a funny kind of way.'

I waited but she said nothing more, concentrating on crushing her cigarette into the paper clip dish. Then she looked up at me and gave me that smile.

I walked out of chambers with her. The air was hot and dry as we crunched in the gravel towards the main road. It was almost two o'clock. People were hurrying back to work along Fleet Street. Men in stiff white collars and grey, pinstriped trousers and women in black suits and sensible shoes, all with briefs tucked under their arms, walked briskly towards the High Court.

'Spats?' I repeated, rolling the word round on my tongue.

'I have to go,' she said, and turned and waved her arm in the air. A taxi with its orange light glowing careered wildly towards us. She wrenched open the door, climbed in and fell into the seat, then leaned forward, as if to say something, but pulling the door shut she simply called, 'Bye!' and she and the taxi drove away.

I wondered if my frustration showed on my face as I slunk back up the stairs to chambers. All that effort, all those sandwiches. For what? For nothing. I really knew nothing new about Danny, just some confusing information about this man Effo. Her and her gold jewellery and her left-handedness. Well, that was it. That was it. I would just ring Kay and tell her I had done the hearing, with the merest hint of professional difficulty, leave a note for Simon, mentioning the page 213 point, and that would be the end of my involvement in the case of Danny Richards.

Firmly, I turned the handle of the front door.

Marcus was standing in front of the shelves of *Halsbury's Statutes* which lined the walls of the corridor leading to the clerks' room. 'I suppose you've heard,' he murmured, pulling out a grey and red volume, his desire to impart gossip obviously transcending his personal antipathy to me.

'What?' My desire to know transcending everything.

'He's going to sit.'

'Who? Tony? That's great.' Anthony Garforth QC was our head of chambers. And he was becoming a judge. It was always useful to have a judge in chambers. So this was very good news, for Tony and for the rest of us. And it meant that Tony's hard work had paid off, all the talking to judges, becoming a Bencher at his Inn, attending Criminal Bar Association dinners. 'Tony must be thrilled, where's he sitting?'

'Our head of chambers is to sit as a Mental Health Appeal Tribunal Chair.' Marcus' mouth puckered in distaste, which is what stopped me from saying, 'But Tony doesn't know anything about mental health.'

Marcus wanted to be a judge himself, and he couldn't work out why he wasn't a QC. Plus he despised Tony. He watched my face, but I didn't want to give him the pleasure of thinking I agreed with him about the strangeness of Tony's appointment. That irritated him but there was more to tell and he didn't want to lose the chance of informing the uninformed, even if it was only me. He leaned back against volumes twenty-five–twenty-seven of *Halsbury*. 'It has been decided to have a chambers party.' He was examining his fingernails. 'To congratulate Tony, and also, of course, to remind solicitors of our existence. Not that my solicitors need that kind of reminder.'

'There are solicitors who actually instruct you?' I asked. 'I thought your briefs appeared through parthenogenesis.'

He wasn't sure whether that was an insult. But he gave me the benefit of the doubt. 'Who was the attractive number in your room just now?' he asked.

I blinked at him. I couldn't be bothered to question his terminology. 'A friend,' I said, 'a concept which may be foreign to you.'

'A friend,' he mused. 'You should choose your friends more carefully. She was flicking through your briefs as I came into your room.'

'I expect she was looking for a needle in a haystack,' I said, 'searching for the story of a good man.' My heart was racing. She said he'd been the one looking, hadn't she? Oh God, which one of them was telling the truth?

'The party is in three weeks,' Marcus droned on, not certain whether his barb had hit the target. 'There's a three line whip on all members of chambers attending. Including you.' His voice lifted in surprise. 'Crime's a bit slow at the moment and apparently you still know some of the old criminal solicitors.'

Kay was the only criminal solicitor I really knew but she got a lot of very good cases. High profile political activists – the cases that got noticed, the ones where the barristers were filmed walking into court because there were no other action shots available.

'I'll have to see if I can clear my diary and fit it in,' I said. I put my shoulder against the door of the clerks' room and pushed.

'We're sending out the invitations on Monday,' Gavin said, as I stood by the printer waiting for an updated version of my diary to appear. 'Kay never comes to these things normally, and Tony's trying to do his paternal bit for the members he leaves behind, making sure the work is still coming in. I think he thought she might come if you said you'd be there.'

'All lesbians together, you mean, the lesbian Mafia? The trouble with Tony is he thinks we go round in packs, walking in step, wearing slinky clothes. If only that were true.' Something he'd said struck me. 'Tony's not leaving chambers is he? I thought you were a member for life till you went to another set.'

'Oh, his name will still be on the door, but he won't be around so much and he's stepping down as head of chambers.'

So that was the reason Marcus was trying to be friendly. He wanted to be the new head of chambers and he was on the campaign trail. Sharing gossip was his equivalent of kissing babies.

'So will you ask her?' Gavin was saying.

'I'm not sure that it's a good idea for me to be schmoozing round Kay at the moment.'

Gavin gave me a quizzical look. 'Do I need to know what that means?' He was a great clerk, but I could see him hoping he wasn't going to have to deal with my personal problems, which might take a lot of time.

'No, not at all,' I said. 'In fact there's no reason why I shouldn't invite her myself. When I ring her up to tell her about Wednesday, I'll ask her. I have nothing to be ashamed of, nothing at all.'

'Now you've really got me worried,' he said.

EIGHT

Friday Evening

It was gone five o'clock when I got home, and I was planning a pleasant evening in with *Friends* and people from Seattle, all sharing a takeaway. The phone was ringing. I threw my bag down beside the sofa and retrieved the phone from the arm of the armchair, under yesterday's *Guardian*. 'Hello?'

Kay said, 'Were you ever going to ring me to let me know what happened in Birmingham?'

'I'd thought about it.' We didn't stand on ceremony in our relationship, we just got straight back in and took up where we'd left off, eight years before. 'But then I thought phone calls didn't figure in our professional association, since you failed to ring me about the case before I started it.'

'I didn't actually know you were doing it. One might almost say I was misled by your clerk. But I would have had no objection.' She sighed. 'So?'

I sat on the chair and stretched my legs, examining my shoes. How do you get marks out of suede? 'It all went well. He is still your client. The judge wanted to know why Dr Quirk was a fully bound witness.'

'For goodness' sake! It's the whole point of the trial.'

'Exactly. And he got furious with me for not being

Simon Allison, plus we had a small argument about the different professional approaches of the London and Birmingham Bar and he took the name of my head of chambers.'

'Not to invite him to a drinks party?'

'I don't think so.'

'How long did this hearing last?'

'About twenty minutes.'

'Dear God, Frankie, you're not safe to be let out.'

'Some people like living with danger. And I only had ten pages of brief to go on.'

'I didn't know Simon couldn't do it.'

'And . . . eh . . . Danny said he wants to change his plea. He wants to plead guilty.'

'Oh, not again. What did you say to him?' I knew she was thinking of all the work she had done, which might be wasted.

'It had nothing to do with me. It was hard enough to persuade him not to do it there and then. You should be thanking me.' I felt unappreciated.

'Did he tell you he was guilty?' If a client tells you he's guilty you cannot put forward a not-guilty defence on his behalf. 'Did he say that he did it?'

'Oh no.' I thought back to our conversation. 'Although he didn't actually say he didn't.' Perhaps he felt he didn't need to. 'He's just fairly realistic about his chances of an acquittal and he wants to get some consideration for a guilty plea. Who knows, maybe he did do it.'

'The police case is very weak. At the very least we should put them to proof.' Even if the client is guilty, you can test the prosecution case to see if it stands up. 'But there's more to it than that. I don't know Danny at all, but there's something not right about this.'

'I did have a few ideas you know.' I dragged my note-book out of my bag and read the list I'd made sitting on the futon in Julie's house.

'I've already got that,' she said.

'This is my list, I just made this up,' I protested.

'Well, it's identical to the advice Simon wrote.'

'Great minds,' I said.

'I don't know about that, but perhaps you should do crime. You have a criminal mind.'

'Don't send me back there again,' I begged. Memories of being hated by everyone, the judge, prosecuting counsel, the police, even the ushers, just for represent-ing defendants, were still clear in my memory. 'I met Yolande,' I said to change the subject.

'Oh, what's she like? She's been ringing me about three times a day for the last ten days.'

'Why don't you speak to her?'

'Danny's such a tricky guy. He's given me specific instructions not to and I can't afford to mess him about. For all I know there are things she knows which I abso-lutely shouldn't know.'

'She seems to know things that might help his case. She could be an important person.'

'Oh, yeah?'

'Yes, she was very insistent, she asked me to . . . go for coffee to talk about it. Although I didn't,' I assured her, emphasising the 'I'.

'Really?' Kay said, drily. 'Just tell me this, does Yolande have blonde hair? No, let me guess – she's left-handed, isn't she?'

I retained a haughty silence. Kay could be so shallow. I certainly wasn't going to tell her about the picnic in chambers now.

'Let me tell you something,' Kay said. 'And I will say this just once. Danny is a wheeler and dealer. Which means his girlfriend is probably one too. She might well be asking you to help Danny with his case, but it could equally be that she's on some complete frolic of her own. Do you know, for example, how long they have been together?'

I was silent. Of course I didn't know. But I knew what Kay meant. If Danny's relationship with Yolande was a relatively recent thing, this could be a set-up by Yolande or someone she was working with. But they had the shop, I told myself. Or did they? It was only what Yolande had said.

Kay was still talking. 'The word is that Danny's a hit man who's killed at least two people and he's a very lucky boy because he's never done time for it.'

'Who?'

'His last counsel.'

'He killed his last counsel?'

'No, that's who informed me.'

'Well, who was it? Who did he kill?'

'And the reason you are asking?'

'I suppose I'm just interested in the kind of man he is, since I didn't get to read the whole brief. Ten pages doesn't provide a lot of information.'

'Frankie! I've already said, I didn't know you would be doing the case. But if it helps, I'm sorry. You should have had more papers.'

'Apology accepted. I was even thinking,' I ventured, now that I had her at a disadvantage, 'that I might flick through Simon's brief just to get a sense of who Danny is, try to locate where he comes in the scheme of –'

'Serial killers? Don't. Don't be interested. You're not

being paid to, you're not insured to, and I am not instructing you to. In fact I'm instructing you not to. Danny or any of his little entourage. And you know what I mean.'

'If I didn't know you better, I might think you were a teensy bit jealous.'

'Oh God, Frankie,' Kay drawled. 'Just keep it clear in your head. After today you and Danny Richards have nothing more to do with each other.'

Kay obviously didin't want me to find out who Effo was, find out what Terry Fleming or Danny had done for him, or discover what happened twenty years ago. As I put the phone down I did a silent deal with Kay. I wouldn't speak to Yolande again, except to say that I wouldn't speak to her again.

NINE

Saturday

Lena toyed with her scrambled egg. We were having breakfast in the café round the corner from the gym, just near Stoke Newington Green. The café was hot and full of the perfume of fried bread. A number of single men sat eating plates of sausage, egg and beans. Everybody had a large white mug of tea in front of them. It was nine o'clock. I couldn't imagine the time Lena had had to get up in order to go to the gym first. She looked flushed and healthy. I just looked flushed. With her thick long hair pulled back and wearing a loose pink T-shirt you couldn't tell Lena was ten years older than me. It didn't help that I was feeling ten years older than I was. I was telling her in the vaguest terms about my few depressing days at the inquiry in Birmingham.

'Just remember, you're only up there for a while,' she said. 'It will be over in a flash. What do you think that is?' She speared something on her fork. 'You don't think it's bacon, do you?'

'It's probably a bit of mushroom. Does it matter? You haven't gone vegetarian have you Lena?'

'I'm trying a new diet,' she said. 'Three days vegetables to one day meat.'

'The point being . . . ?'

'To see if I can, I think. I mean, we've got to stop eating meat. It's not good for us or the rest of the world.'

'But it's so delicious.'

'So's foie gras but we don't eat that, do we? Do we?'

'Not often,' I mumbled. 'Well, never, actually, but I might do if, say, I was going out with a racy, possibly French, torchsong singer who was also a wizard in the kitchen.'

'Remember what happened with your last torchsong singer,' Lena said sagely, spearing a dripping piece of fried tomato.

'It wasn't her fault I got arrested for murder.'

'No, but she would have been happy to see you take the rap.' Lena, trying to be kind, blamed the whole thing on Margo, but it wasn't like that. Not really.

'We never ate anything at her place. I don't know if she could even cook.' I thought back to Margo's small desolate flat, denuded of its contents by her ex-husband at the end of her marriage, all the borrowed furniture, brown and depressing.

'Exactly, she would probably have opened a tin of the stuff, all porky pink and covered in jelly.'

'You seem to know a lot about this,' I said. 'Or else you're confusing it with Spam.'

'Just stay away from nightclub singers,' she warned. 'It's the wages of foie gras.' She looked at me piercingly. 'You need help. You need to spend some money.'

We strolled along Stoke Newington High Street. 'Let's go in here,' I said.

'A furniture shop?' Lena sounded as if I'd suggested we go into an abattoir.

Overstuffed sofas were squashed one behind the other in two rows, with an aisle between them, like a chartered aircraft that was aiming for comfort as well as maximum passenger numbers.

'I just wanted to smell the smell,' I said. The smell of new fabrics and polished wood. 'I was thinking I might get a new sofa.'

'You don't need a new sofa,' Lena said, looking round the shop in despair. 'Certainly not a cream and maroon one.'

'This is the kind of place Yolande works in.'

Lena frowned, then raised an eyebrow. 'Yolande?'

'She's the girlfriend of someone in Birmingham.'

'Oh.' She was disappointed, but her eyebrow stayed where it was. 'Well, if you seriously want to buy something like this, buy it from her and get a discount.'

'What about leather?' I said.

'Don't you have to kill an awful lot of cows to cover a sofa? How could you sit comfortably with that on your conscience? And stop looking at me like that.' Lena looked down at her leather coat. 'Leather jackets are the offcuts of shoes. Or they should be. Anyway, I am aware of the contradictions that society forces us to live with. But it's very pushy, isn't it, leather furniture? Dominating. In a room. A huge leather sofa. Surely as feminists we didn't give up being dominated by men to be dominated by our furniture?'

'I was thinking of a small armchair, I thought it would feel sort of deep and intellectual.'

'Buy a pair of horn-rimmed glasses, they'd be cheaper.' She looked round the showroom again. 'Can we go now? All these smoked glass coffee tables are depressing me.'

The air was clean and fresh, even for Stoke Newington, and the sun was high in the sky as I walked back to the flat. It was going to be a really hot day. The grass in front of my house looked almost verdant. I unlocked the main front door. There was no post on the mat and no neat pile outside my front door, but on a day like this I was not going to feel miserable about Margo. I wandered into the kitchen. I leaned against the sink and gazed out of the window.

In the garden the sky was blue and the lawn ached in the light, calling to me. I shared the garden with the people in the flat upstairs, which worked rather well because I like a garden and they liked gardening. Technically my half was the half nearest the house, but they did it all, mowing, pruning, planting, weeding. That is the kind of gardening I like. I pulled open the cutlery drawer and fished out the key to the French windows.

I pushed open both doors and stepped onto the patio. Two of the rose bushes were in flower and I could smell the sweet, old-fashioned perfume. Margo's perfume had been rose, I thought woefully. But I hadn't met her till the autumn, I told myself firmly, so there was nothing here to remind me of her. In fact she'd never been to my flat, so there was no trace of her anywhere. No trace, just feelings. I could feel a bad seventies song coming on so I went back into the kitchen. While the kettle was boiling, I walked down the three steps in my hall to a small landing where the cupboard I call a shed houses all my unused gardening equipment and my deckchairs. I hauled one back up to the garden, made some coffee and sat in the sun in the green and white deckchair, gazing at the newly watered pots of geraniums and the recently cut grass.

I was drifting in and out of a doze. The phone was

ringing. I lurched into the living room, stumbling against the sofa, wondering whether I should have gone to the gym. It was Yolande.

'What are you doing this evening?'

Lena and I had made a loose arrangement to see each other in Fox's wine bar in Church Street if all else failed. 'Nothing,' I said.

'Do you want to come out for dinner? Nothing fancy, quite quiet. It might be . . . useful.'

'Ah, now then . . .' I began.

'Can you pick me up at about seven?' She said the name of a hotel in Russell Square.

'Well . . .'

'Seven it is, then. We should be at Sandra's by about seven thirty,' she said and there was a click as she broke the connection.

I held the receiver limply in my hand. Sandra? The Sandra who was Effo's girlfriend? We were going to dinner with Sandra? I tried to remember what Yolande had said about Effo and Sandra. Effo got people to do his dirty work, Danny worked for Effo, Danny was a hit man, Terry Fleming was dead, well, missing believed dead. Did people like this even eat dinner? Or did they just eat other people? A small tingle ran down my spine.

I rang Lena to consider this development. Although Danny was no longer my client I retained as much client confidentiality as I could, but she had to know something so that she could take a properly informed view. At first she was most concerned that I was going out to dinner with a person who could sell sofas like the ones in the shop this morning.

'Perhaps you should go for a walk round Heals this afternoon, as a form of inoculation.'

'We're not going to get that close,' I said doubtfully, and explained about Danny.

'So that's two reasons not to go out for dinner with her.'

'It's not like that,' I said. 'She's straight.'

'That,' she said darkly, 'is what they all say.'

'And she's married.'

'Three reasons then. Sofas, boyfriend and husband.' She paused. 'Well, if she's really straight, why are you going?'

'It's just dinner. Nothing fancy. There'll be other people there. Sandra . . . another girlfriend.'

'Another girlfriend of Danny's? Maybe that's not so dangerous then.'

'No, the girlfriend of another man.' I explained the position – Lena knows she has to be discreet – about Danny and his history of serious offences, Yolande's determination to prove him innocent, my interest in justice being done.

She sighed. 'Was it wise to take a criminal case, after your last experience?' she asked. Everything that had gone wrong the year before, from my arrest for murder through to my unsatisfactory relationship with Margo, could be traced back to a small drunk and disorderly case I had done at Highbury Corner magistrates' court.

'It's all going to be fine.'

'Darling, I think there's a chance that Danny might not like you going out with his girlfriend. And might there not be the teensiest possibility that Yolande is up to something with this Sandra? They both have relationships with rather unpleasant men. Where do you come in? Look, sweetie, I'm not one to panic, as you know, but in this particular situation, isn't there a risk that something fairly nasty might happen this evening and it might happen to you?'

'But I've said I'll go now. I'm picking her up.'

'OK. Here's a plan. You don't go. You ring her back and say we have a date. Which of course we do.'

'It'll be fine,' I assured her, starting to worry. Lena had called me 'darling' and 'sweetie' in the same breath, it made me feel vulnerable and in serious need of hot chocolate and someone to tuck me up in bed.

On the other hand, there was Yolande, with her blonde hair and ironic eyes. She knew what she wanted. I didn't, but she did. I like that in a woman. Clarity of purpose, determination. 'She's cool,' I said. 'I know she has her own agenda, which is helping Danny. But that means she wouldn't take me anywhere risky. I'm useful to her.'

'Oh Frankie,' Lena said, mournfully. 'Well, take your mobile, make sure the battery is charged and keep it switched on. And, I can't believe I'm saying this, tell that ex-girlfriend of yours, the Ice Queen.' Lena had strong negative views about Kay. 'If she's his solicitor, she ought to know.'

'Of course,' I said. But, as I replaced the receiver, I told myself that Kay didn't need to know just yet. What was there to tell? It was just dinner.

Guilt – or was it anxiety? – forced me to pull out one of my outstanding pieces of paperwork. Mr Burke had assaulted his partner and his two children and now they were in care and he was afraid the other foster children in the placement were a bad influence. He was raising Human Rights points, that he was being denied a family life and the family life the children were getting was a bad one. The eternal dilemma. Was it better for the children to be with a parent, even a not very good one, or in a rather bad placement in care? The mother wasn't appealing. She was twenty, the children were four and two. I wondered if she would rather someone else looked after them for a while just to get him off her back. Maybe she wanted to live a little. I drafted a short advice saying I needed more information. I felt flat and chilly. I didn't know if it was the sadness of some people's lives or because I was really rather concerned about the evening to come.

Suddenly it was six o'clock. It was time to think about leaving.

I put on 'Going to a Go Go' and jumped into the shower in time to the drum beat. I thought about what to wear. Nothing fancy, she'd said. I'd stick to black, just to be on the safe side.

Before I left the flat I set the video to record a TV show about barristers, which I needed to be able to discuss in sneering detail in chambers ('Oh that would never happen, as if a clerk would ever say that!' 'You'd never do that without a solicitor!'), but then I couldn't find a tape to use. I decided I could probably discuss it without seeing it (not that I approve of that). A thought flickered through my mind that I might not be around to discuss it anyway, but I didn't have time to dwell on it – I was already worried that I'd put on too much Ô de Lancôme. I switched on the radio to protect my home from intruders.

They say you're in more danger in the home than out of it, so I was being positively sensible by going out to dinner.

TEN

Saturday Evening – The Dinner Party

We planned the evening as we drove towards Hyde Park Corner. While I engaged Sandra and her other guests in deep, interesting conversation, Yolande would go and rifle through Sandra's cupboards for something which, she assured me, was an important part of Danny's case. Just normal dinner party activity.

'I haven't told them you're coming,' Yolande had said, buckling herself into the passenger seat, 'or Sandra might have smelt a rat.'

'Oh great,' I said. 'If you and Sandra are such friends, why don't you just ask her for this thing?'

'Well, we get on, but sometimes Sandra has divided loyalties.'

'How come we're even going to Sandra's?' It wasn't too late for us to find a restaurant to have dinner. Although on a Saturday night, that's not always easy. Maybe she'd like to slum it and we could go for a kebab somewhere.

'I told you, she has something I need. . . .Danny needs.'

'What am I doing here?'

'When I've got it,' she smiled, 'you'll tell me what to do with it.'

'Why don't I just wait outside and I'll tell you when you've finished dinner. Or, even better, let me tell you now. Give it to Kay Davidson.'

'I don't want to go on my own. There's nothing to worry about. Sandra doesn't concern herself with Effo's business really. It'll be a laugh. She's a good cook. Sometimes. Their relationship works quite well. He pays her bills and she hosts his dinner parties.'

I stopped the car abruptly in front of the Shaftesbury Theatre. A taxi behind hooted and swerved angrily by us. 'So, he'll be there tonight?'

Yolande ran her hand up the back of her neck, over the combs in her French pleat. The scent of vanilla perfume wafted across my face. 'No, no. Sandra's on her own in London. I think so anyway.'

'So this could be one of his dinner parties?'

'She didn't say. But whoever's there, it's probably best not to mention Danny this evening. For some reason Danny is not popular with Effo and his friends. Shall we go across Trafalgar Square and down Pall Mall?' I was so entranced to be with a woman who could give good directions that I didn't ask exactly why Danny was not a friend to Effo, whether it was his contract killing or the fact that he was so bad at staying out of prison, let alone how a relationship with Danny fitted in with having a husband, and where this friendship with me came into it.

It was a dull square block with a lift, very close to Park Lane. I didn't expect the lift to go straight into the flat. But it did, because this was a very expensive flat.

I wonder about rich people, seriously rich people. I always expect them to have fantastic taste. With all that money, they could have gone to art galleries and bought pictures, or at the very least, purchased every glossy magazine going, to get some ideas. But then some people think tan is tasteful. Sandra obviously did. She was wearing tan slacks and tan shoes and the carpet, as we stepped out of the lift, was tan. If you squinted at her, and I did, as she moved towards us in greeting, it looked like she was floating with no legs, just a head wearing a navy and gold shiny Jaeger shirt. But she was indeed little and blonde and angelic-looking with her small, baby-pink mouth and her large, baby-blue eyes. Interestingly, she was about as old as Yolande. I hadn't expected that. Yolande was introducing me.

'Frankie,' Sandra said, with a tight smile, 'that's an unusual name.' She turned to Yolande, 'I wasn't expecting . . . Frankie.' I wondered who she was expecting, or whether I was a complete surprise. Perhaps she'd envisaged a quiet evening with Yolande, a good chat over a couple of TV dinners, and a chance to catch up on all the news, to discuss Danny's life of crime and Effo's life of instigating crime. And now I'd put paid to that intimacy. Or perhaps she just didn't have enough salad.

She led us into a large L-shaped room dominated by a window which took the place of one whole wall and looked out over Hyde Park. In the distance I could see the lights beginning to twinkle in the dusk – was it the lamps slung along the trees in the park, I thought romantically, or just the tourist coaches waiting on Park Lane? And sitting in low, square armchairs upholstered in shades of ginger and gold bouclé, were Roger, Barbara and Charles. So I hadn't broken up a cosy evening *à deux*.

Roger, Barbara and Charles were also wearing clothes

in various tones of tan, a chocolate-coloured dress, more tan slacks, a raw silk skirt in pale coffee. Even their soft leather shoes were in muted shades of caramel and chestnut. I wondered if that was why they were here. They all shared an interest in brown. Even Yolande, I realised, with her loose beige linen top and trousers was part of the gang. My black jeans felt crude and wrong. I felt that Yolande had not properly prepared me for this evening.

Yolande and I sat on a matching sofa and Sandra gave us each a small glass of sherry. It probably cost £60 a bottle but it tasted like Harvey's Bristol Cream. Licking my lips and reflecting on this, it took me a little while to realise that no one was speaking to me. They were talking about the European community, the top rates of income tax, and something that sounded like petro-chemicals, and they weren't talking to me. When Yolande described some shares she had recently pur-chased, they glanced quickly at me with bemusement, to see if I was possibly her broker, or a management consultant. Which I obviously wasn't.

But who were they? Were they friends of Effo's? They all spoke with upper-class accents, except for Yolande and Sandra who both had the merest lilt of Birmingham. But Yolande seemed to fit right in. From what she'd said they obviously knew about Danny. I wondered if they knew Yolande's husband. And who did they think I was? I was too old to be Yolande's love child, what else could I be? Not her mother. Her sister? From the collective curling lip and the controlled sideways glances I guessed they thought that I was some sort of out-of-place hired help. They probably thought I worked in Danny's shop on Saturdays.

Which was unfair. My grey cotton shirt was clean and even ironed for once. But looking down I could see that the toes of my black cowboy boots still turned up noticeably, despite my having polished them a week or so before. But hey, I suddenly realised I was wearing a tan leather belt. I could be a member of their Brownie pack for all they knew.

In the foot of the L of the room Sandra leaned across the table, putting last minute serving spoons on the table. Long white candles flickered in a silver candelabra in the centre of the table. The cutlery was big and shiny. I watched her efforts anxiously. I had made Yolande swear she would sit next to me. I had thought then and was sure now that I would have very little to say to these people. Or rather, as it was turning out, they would have very little to say to me. Sandra beckoned Roger over and whispered loudly that he would find a couple of extra chairs in the bedroom. She hadn't even been expecting Yolande. This was worse and worse. I wanted to call that I would be happy sitting with a tray on my lap watching TV but I realised that wouldn't fit in with the plan.

Sandra had placed me between Roger and Charles.

I ate the salad in silence while they discussed watercress versus rocket, whether you really could taste the difference between organic and non-organic food, and the possible effects of a new fertiliser being tested in Belgium.

'What does it mean when they say "Grown for the taste" about tomatoes?' I asked, but my question must have got lost in the clatter of the piling of plates.

The main course was pigeon, which suited me. I have strong feelings about pigeons. 'Did you shoot this yourself?' I asked Sandra hopefully, and suddenly the room was all silence and everyone stared at their plates. Yolande sent a little frown my way, but I'd already got the message. It was not done to discuss the way your meal had been culled. The conversation resumed, hotels in city centres versus business developments.

I couldn't even get drunk and cause a diversion because for some reason Sandra didn't leave the bottle on the table, but put it on a shelf at the side. I noticed Yolande looking at me anxiously as I leaned behind Roger to pick it up. It was half full. Sandra leapt up and took the bottle from my hands.

'No, no,' she said, brightly, 'not the red. It's time for the pudding. We're having white with the pudding.'

'Ah yes,' I said, thinking, it's all alcohol and it all goes down the same way. Roger was chortling, as he had been for most of the meal. He must have had an intravenous link to the bottle.

The pudding came, it was melon balls with ginger ice cream, and with it came a small glass of unpleasant sweet white wine, which tasted as if it should have been thrown out some years before.

Was it pity, or was it seeing Yolande blow me a kiss and my wink in reply, that made Sandra turn abruptly to me and ask, 'And what do you do, Frankie?'

Obviously afraid I might say something inappropriate, Yolande cut in, 'Frankie's a barrister.'

The effect was electric. Their faces showed shock and then cleared with relief. I was a barrister. A barrister. Oh for goodness' sake. Not a dirty hippy at all. Oh well then. Smiles bounced round the room. A barrister. I smiled back at them and noticed Roger's smile had slipped.

'Ooh, Roger, that's just what you need, a barrister,' said Barbara.

'I do not,' he said meticulously, 'I am only a witness.'

'Roger's giving evidence in the other inquiry in Birmingham,' Yolande said.

'Oh, really?' I said. 'What about?'

'His company,' said Barbara. 'Very boring.' They'd heard the story before.

'It is purely technical evidence, and Ladscore is not my company. I am but a paid employee.'

'That's not how I heard it,' Yolande said, her glass almost at her lips. She turned away from him and looked over at Sandra. 'I thought quite a few people might be grateful for some good legal advice. It's not just you who has a lot to lose.'

Barbara was looking from Yolande to Sandra in confusion.

'It is not my company. I am only a witness,' Roger repeated. His face was going white. 'The matter is *sub judice*.'

'Not really,' I said. 'The rules aren't quite the same for an inquiry.' There was a beat of silence.

Then as Sandra said, 'More wine anyone?' Barbara turned to me, 'Do you do company law?'

'No.' I hesitated. This is when the evening could turn nasty. 'My practice is family law,' I said, reluctantly. I knew what was going to happen and it did.

'I should have got you to do my divorce,' Barbara said. I smiled. 'Tell me,' she went on, 'if my ex fails to produce all the documents relating to his interests in Luxembourg what can I do?'

'Oh he's not, is he?' murmured Sandra.

Barbara nodded and looked protectively over at

Charles. 'Oh yes, completely denying the existence of the plastics business. I ask you.' She turned back to me, 'Can I ask for him to be sent to prison?'

'That's really something you should discuss with your solicitor,' I said. 'Without knowing the background I couldn't say. Money's not really my thing, actually.'

The uncertainty and suspicion crept back into their expressions. 'Oh?' 'So what do you do?'

'Public law work,' I said, 'kids being taken into care.'

'Tragic,' said Roger. Barbara's eyelids began to droop.

'I do crime as well,' I said, desperately, looking round at their faces. 'Sometimes,' I added to myself. 'That's when I get to wear the wig,' I said aloud.

Wigs, at last, something they could relate to.

Yolande murmured, 'If you'll just excuse me.'

'Oh,' Sandra said. She dabbed her lips with her damask napkin. 'You know where it is.'

'Yes,' said Yolande. She slipped out of the room. She needed at least five minutes.

'What are they made of?' Barbara asked.

'Horse hair.'

'Doesn't it get awfully hot?'

'A bit,' I said, and I told them the bad hair day story, one of the rare occasions I had been led by a QC, a man from another chambers. Our case came up on a muggy summer's day and it was so hot in the courtroom that the judges said we could take off our wigs. And my leader had not wanted to take off his wig because his toupee was not fitted as well as it should have been.

Everybody laughed. I couldn't hear Yolande. I had to keep talking. I wondered whether to tell them the off-white collarette story – they might go for the cream aspect – or the one about my leader's dog. I guessed the dog would be the best bet, people always look a little askance when you talk about unwashed linen so close to your throat. I ploughed on about my leader's time as a judge sentencing a man who had used a fox terrier as part of a blackmail threat against his ex-girlfriend. In passing sentence the judge told the defendant that he was a dog lover, which is why he regarded the case so seriously. The press got hold of the story and came and took photos of his own dog and the headlines read, 'Terrier lover judge jails terrier lover's terror lover.'

And still Yolande wasn't back. I was running out of stories and Roger looked as if he was running out of alcohol. His face was still a little strained. If Yolande didn't come soon I would have to tell them about my poor laundry habits and the difficulty of producing snowy-white tabs.

'Where is Yolande?' Roger asked. 'Do you think she's all right?' He put his serviette on the table.

'She'll be fine,' Sandra said.

'Shall I go and see?' I pushed back my chair. 'I want to use the loo, anyway.'

I knew they'd want to talk about the fact Yolande had brought me and who I was and my trousers, which would give us a few more minutes. I left the room with my fingers tucked into my belt, to draw attention to its colour, to confuse them into thinking that perhaps I was one of them.

I left the lounge and was back in the hall with the lift. I looked round desperately for the stairs. All I could see was an ocean of toffee, till I noticed a step tucked behind a door. It was a narrow staircase leading upwards to a small landing with three doors. 'Yolande,' I called in a low voice.

'Here.' She was in a cream and beige bedroom. Beige and pale blue striped curtains, beige and pale green bedspread, beige and gold carpet. How can people sleep like that? What dreams do they have?

Yolande was kneeling on the floor, groping under the bed. As I came in she stood up. 'I can't find it,' she hissed, as if it was my fault. 'You're taller than me. Look in that cupboard.' She gestured wildly.

'What exactly am I looking for?'

'You'll know it when you see it.'

I took hold of her hands and held them by her sides. 'What am I going to find, a piece of anatomy, a human hand or something?'

'Just look.'

I reached up to the cupboard and pulled it open. A shower of photographs fell out. A cream and green blanket oozed to the front.

'A blanket?' I asked.

'No, look behind that!' Yolande hissed. 'Hurry!'

I took a small stool that stood in front of the dressing table. Stepping up, I pulled out the blanket. The back of the cupboard was crammed with shoe boxes and bags and loose photographs. It was someone's memory cupboard.

'There it is!' she cried. 'The bag. The white one.'

'Are you sure?' I asked. 'This is all a bit personal.'

'I'm allowed to be personal. Get it.'

I pulled forward a white plastic bag that looked like a small cushion. A piece of Sellotape held the edges of the bag together. It rolled out of the cupboard and fell into Yolande's hands.

I was refolding the blanket, when a call came up the stairs. 'Everything all right up there?'

'Fine,' Yolande shouted, shoving the bag under the bed. I crushed the blanket back into the cupboard and shut the door.

'We're just about to have coffee.' Sandra's voice was getting louder. Yolande rearranged the valance while I jumped off the stool and slid it back in front of the dressing table. As Sandra pushed open the door, I scraped the photos off the floor and pushed them into my back pocket, and Yolande put her arms round me and kissed me hard.

'Oh. Excuse me.' Sandra giggled, whether with nervousness or irritation I couldn't tell. She backed out of the room and there was the sound of the bathroom door clicking shut.

Yolande had done this before, that was clear. And I had too, which was a spooky coincidence. I could smell her vanilla perfume. It was like kissing an exotic dessert. She lifted her head and stepped backwards, looking at me closely. She raised her thumb and wiped lipstick off my top lip. 'Nearly a nasty accident,' she whispered. 'Sorry about that.'

'Please,' I said, but she had turned away, bending down to the bed. She pulled out the plastic bag and throwing up her top, she forced the bag into the waistband of her trousers. 'Stay close to me,' she said, and pushed me towards the stairs. She followed, bending slightly so that her top billowed out in front of her.

When Sandra came down a moment later, Yolande said, 'I've got a bit of a headache. Frankie's going to take me back to the hotel. I think I'm coming down with something.'

Sandra glanced at Yolande with a curious look. Did she believe what she had seen in the bedroom? She

103

certainly didn't believe that Yolande wasn't well, but then no one was meant to believe that. I tried to look rakish but a bit sheepish, which wasn't difficult, and Yolande tried to look unwell.

Slowly, with Yolande bent over, and me beside her, looking concerned, we made our way to the door of the lift.

'Goodnight.' Sandra followed us to the hall, her arms held out to Yolande.

Yolande fluttered her fingers. 'I do feel terrible. I've heard there's something really infectious going round at the moment.' The lift door opened. Smoothly Yolande stepped inside, and blew a kiss towards Sandra. I moved in after her. 'It was a lovely evening,' Yolande said. 'Sorry we just dumped ourselves on you.' The lift door slid closed. No one had even tried to kiss me.

In the lift, pulling the bag out from her waistband, Yolande said, 'Well that was very successful, wasn't it?' She hugged the bag.

'What is it?'

'I'll tell you later.'

'What am I meant to do with these?' I asked, drawing out the photos. They showed people at something like a formal party, a group standing in a raggedy line, smiling politely, their eyes just off centre, as if they were hoping their photos weren't really going to be taken.

Yolande glanced at them. She took one and frowned at it, then gave it back to me. 'Do what you like.'

We walked in silence to the car and I drove to the hotel. 'I hope the evening wasn't too awful for you,' she said, as I pulled in, onto a single yellow line opposite the main entrance. 'Sandra's a pain sometimes, but she's all right really.'

'But she wasn't expecting either of us.'

'You said I should talk to her.'

'I didn't mean and burgle her as well.'

'It's my stuff,' Yolande said. 'And anyway, it's hardly burglary when it's family.'

I looked at her. What else was there in those bloody papers that I ought to have known?

'She's my sister.'

I couldn't think whether that made it worse or better. Mentally I checked the professional code of conduct. Theft from a family member was still theft. I put my face in my hands. 'I can't think what I was doing,' I said.

I felt Yolande's hand on my hair. 'If any of it doesn't belong to me or Danny,' she said soothingly, 'I'll give it back to her.' I glanced at her. She was looking me up and down, slowly. 'Why don't you come in with me?'

It was a cheap trick, but it worked. I smiled at her.

We walked up the red, carpeted steps into the lobby. I scarcely noticed the dark wood furniture, the enormous chandeliers and the cigarette machine, but then she said, 'Stay here,' and disappeared into a lift.

I had expected to go in the lift with her. I was ready to go in the lift, to go up to her room with her. I'd been weighing up the pros and cons since Sandra's bedroom. I'd perfected a little speech. 'If this happens I will not be able to represent Danny again, and I probably won't be able to work on his case at all. Are you sure this is what you want? What about Danny?' And she would say, 'Danny knows I find you attractive. He just wants me to be happy.' And I would say, 'If you're sure then.' And up we'd go.

But here I was, sitting in an over-stuffed, ox-blood

red, leather armchair, looking out of the window at the traffic lights where cars hooted at cabs depositing late-night, dithering tourists. Yolande tapped me on the shoulder. 'Do you want to come up?'

My stomach somersaulted. I struggled out of the chair. I felt like someone being invited to an interview.

As we went up in the lift I replayed to myself the other conversation I had prepared. I am Danny's ex-counsel, you are Danny's girlfriend, and, moreover, a married woman. Danny is something of a hard man, and who knows what your husband is? All in all, is this really a good idea? But by the time I had got to the last part of the conversation we were walking down the corridor on the third floor and she was sliding the plastic card into the slot and opening the door of her room, and it seemed churlish to bring up things that might put a damper on the evening. I made a quick deal with myself that I would let her make the running.

It was a hotel room, it had two large beds and a sofa. Someone had lit one of the bedside lamps so the light was peachy and shadowy.

'Do you want a drink?' she asked me.

'Not particularly.'

I caught a reflection of us in a mirror on the wall. We stood between the beds and the sofa. And she looked anxious. Her left hand was at her throat, toying with a button. She looked at me, her eyes narrowed with uncertainty.

I stepped forward and put my hand on the back of her neck. She quivered with something that I hoped was pleasure, and I pulled her towards me, and I was kissing her forehead, her cheeks, her lips. She was trembling.

'Are you OK with this?' I said, into her mouth.

She moved in closer and slid her arms round my neck.

'We could have a safety word,' I murmured. 'If things get out of hand, you could say "stop".'

She laughed. 'OK.'

She was soft in my arms. The creamy smell of her perfume rose from her neck.

The comb in her hair gave easily into my hand, away from her French pleat, and her hair fell forward. I stroked a blonde strand behind her ear. Then she lurched back and pulled her arms away. I looked at her, shocked, I didn't know what she meant. She lifted her hands and pulled grips from her hair. She shook her head and then she kissed me. Not like she had kissed me in Sandra's bedroom, then it had been hard and urgent, now it was soft and open.

We moved towards the bed and she began to pull at my shirt. She'd done this before too. I took her chin in my hand and tilted her head towards me. 'Is this what you want?'

'Yes,' she said and we fell onto the bed.

When I woke up it was three o'clock in the morning. I slid my feet onto the floor and reached for my clothes. Yolande lay, asleep, naked, half covered by the sheet. I was lacing my boots when she stirred and saw what I was doing.

'Wait a minute,' she said, tipping herself out of bed. She slid open the door of the wardrobe. She rifled in the bottom. 'Here.' She turned to me, holding out the plastic bag. 'Can you keep this safe?'

'What do you mean? I thought I was meant to be telling you what to do with it.'

'That's what you'd say, isn't it? Keep it safe.'

'Would I mean, put it in a cupboard when I get home safe, or take it into chambers and lock it into the safe safe? What is it?' I asked, reaching for the bag.

She put the bag behind her back. Her eyes scanned my face. 'I don't really want to tell you. It's not just about me. Do you need to know?'

She looked tired, but her face was smooth and rosy from sleep. Her hair stood out in a crown round her head.

'Is it anything illegal?' I asked.

'I don't think so,' she said. 'It just needs to be out of harm's way.'

'And you don't want me to open it?'

'No. Please take it.'

'I'll keep it for a week,' I said, although that was a decision which was ultimately taken out of my hands. I struggled to squeeze my fingers through the plastic handles. It looked as if there was another plastic bag wrapped around whatever it was, upside down.

Yolande leaned towards me and kissed me drily on the lips. 'Thank you for this evening. For everything.'

'Thank you,' I said and moved to the door. I turned. 'When am I going to see you?'

'Tomorrow? I'm busy in the day, but perhaps the evening? I'll ring you.'

I left the room and walked back down the corridor, the bag banging gently against my legs.

ELEVEN

Sunday – Mum's for Lunch

I gazed at the photos as I hugged a cup of breakfast coffee. I had found them on the bedroom floor that morning, where they had fallen in the early hours when I had thrown off my clothes. Now they were spread across the kitchen table, a memento of Yolande.

There was nothing to see. A row of uneasy people in their thirties posing for the camera, or perhaps that was just the way their clothes made them look. The three men were well-built and tall, in evening dress, with hair curling over their collars. The two women stood slightly to one side of them. Neither of them looked like Yolande, or even Sandra, but that could have been their hair – one had a long perm, the other a short basin cut. They both wore evening dresses made with Indian print cotton. The small group stood in front of a table bearing the remains of a meal, some wine bottles and two glasses that looked as if they held beer. I wondered who they were, if they were members of a deadly Midlands gang, but considering the children just visible in the background, it was more likely they were mums and dads at a works do. Or both.

Lena had rung to check that I was still alive.

'You were right to tell me not to go,' I said.

'Why? What happened?'

'I had to eat ginger ice cream.'

'What?'

I explained about the colour theme of the evening and she was not as shocked as she should have been. So I told her about the end of the evening.

'That's exactly why I told you not to go! What is it with you and straight girls?'

'Perhaps I like a challenge,' I said petulantly.

'No, that's why you're a barrister. You don't have to let that spill over into your private life.'

'I don't really go for straight women. You might almost say they go for me.'

'Frankie.' She sighed. 'So what's going to happen now?'

'Probably nothing,' I said, morosely. 'She gave me a bulging plastic bag and wished me farewell.'

'What's in it?'

'I don't know, I haven't looked.'

'How can you not look?'

I cocked my head, trying to work out why I hadn't looked. 'Because she told me not to.'

'Not good enough.'

'Because it could be something really boring like a very small duvet, or it might be something awful, like a bag of cement, that I'd have to do something about, which might at the same time incriminate Danny, and then I'd be in a quandary.'

'You'd know if it was a bag of cement,' Lena said primly.

'That's just an example.'

'If she's trying to save his bacon, why give it to you? Why not just throw it away herself?'

I considered that. I thought of Yolande's sleepy face as she gave me the bag. I'd thought she'd realised I was someone she could trust, after a battle between desire and duty. But perhaps it had been something else. 'Perhaps she didn't have time to throw it away,' I ventured.

'If you say so. But I think you should throw it away. Or bring it round here, and I'll throw it away.' I thanked her for the offer and we said goodbye.

I looked at the bag, I looked back at the pictures, trying to divine if they had anything to do with each other. Perhaps it *was* Yolande in the photo. The dresses the women wore seemed to contain some element of brown, but that could have been the photos. The colour was fading, everything had a faint pinkish tinge. I didn't know what to do with them, I didn't really want them in the house. Like finding a small feather in a book about voodoo, there was something innocent but ominous about them. But I couldn't throw them away. I pushed them into a heap at the corner of the table, under a pile of restaurant menus and pizza shop delivery leaflets. I would take them into chambers. With the plastic bag.

And why had I asked to see Yolande again? I'd almost agreed to see her today. Was I desperate? I was not. I had a schedule. I had a life. I looked at my watch. I had a lunch date with my mother.

She was living with her partner, Alan, the plastic surgeon. He had asked her to marry him but she had decided against it, saying that she wanted to see how it went living together. She kept proudly referring to her 'trial marriage' as if she was a swinger from the sixties, living the Swedish way.

* * *

111

They were renting a flat in West London while each of them maintained their original homes, my mum's in Colchester and Alan's in Brighton. It was nice to be able to drive to her place in half an hour, especially on a sunny day, which for once seemed to have made the other road users relaxed and laid back.

It was a two-bedroom flat with large, airy rooms with high ceilings. There was an enormous garden with a lawn and flowers and a patio which led off from the living room, and it was there we had our lunch. We sat on white cast-iron chairs at a white cast-iron table and ate a selection of Greek dips with pitta bread.

At the end of the meal mum scraped the plates and then carried them over to the flower beds.

'Are we having coffee with the flowers?' I said. I couldn't think of any other reason she would go this far into the garden. My mother and gardening, like me and gardening, are not concepts that go together.

'No,' she said, scraping the remains of our lunch onto a bare patch of earth, 'I'm just putting hoummous on the soil. I read an article in the paper.'

'I don't think that's the way it works, Mum.'

'But Alan loves his garden and I'm preparing this little patch for some azaleas, which are his favourites,' she said. 'I don't really know where to start, but I read the gardening section in the local paper and I thought I could combine lunch for you and gardening for Alan, the two most important people in my life.'

'That's a lovely thing to say,' I said, 'but I think you need a book. I'll get you one.'

Gardens had never really featured in our family life. Music had been the important thing. While other people's dads were sticking forks into the ground and planting potatoes my dad had been slipping 'Be Bop a Lula' onto the record player. While other people's mothers were flicking through seed catalogues my mum had been ironing her hair in preparation for seeing the Moody Blues in town. When the sun shone, in our house we just played 'Dancing in the Street' and 'Heatwave'. When it rained, we listened to 'Under the Boardwalk'. Which is why I'm stuck in the sixties.

Now we sat in the sun in silence. Mum went to get her *Guardian* to see if I could do one of the last crossword clues. 'And,' she added ominously, 'I've bought a little something for you. Although, looking at your outfit perhaps I should have bought you a subscription to *Vogue*.' I was wearing my attempt at gardening clothes for my afternoon at Iotha's. My trousers were faded royal-blue cotton with an elasticated waist (the elastic was old and tired) and the top was an old pink T-shirt that said 'I've been to Longleat.' I got it out of Lena's jumble bag. I usually wore it in bed. I have never been to Longleat.

I wasn't sure I could bear another parcel. Mum came back with the newspaper and handed me a roughly wrapped, oblong-shaped package. 'This is an early birthday present. You can take it to Birmingham,' she said, and I fantasised briefly that it was a charcoal grey silk shirt with interesting cuffs that I could wear to good effect at the inquiry. Then she said, 'I know what you and Julie are like.'

Any excitement I had been experiencing ebbed away, and when I tore off the pink and blue flowered wrapping paper the box fulfilled my worst fears. It was a Dustbuster. She saw my face and said, 'It's cream.'

'A Dustbuster?' I said. 'How could you give me a Dustbuster?'

113

'What would have been more appropriate?'

'I don't know.' I looked wildly round the room. 'A cookery book?'

'I gave you a cookery book once before, remember.'

'It only got burnt because it didn't have a recipe for chips,' I said. 'But Mum, a vacuum cleaner for my birthday. It's not very celebratory, is it? You'd have divorced Dad if he'd given you something like this.'

'I did divorce him, if you remember. Anyway, you need it and you'll thank me for it,' she said.

'How am I going to explain it to Julie? "Mum gave me this because she thinks we're both sluts"? She's doing me a favour putting me up. I don't want to piss her off.'

'Just be quiet and open it. I think it's quite pretty,' she commented, as I pulled at the intricate cardboard opening device. 'It's cream. You like cream.'

'Yes, cream telephones and cream on rhubarb crumble. I hadn't quite got round to having a favourite colour for my cleaning utensils.'

'More's the pity,' she said.

The lid gave and reluctantly I opened the box. She was right, it was neat and it was cream. But it was still a Dustbuster.

'And don't sulk.' She leaned down and picked up her folded-open *Guardian*. 'All right, you know French, what's the answer to this? French cream? Nine letters. Second letter is H.'

'You know the answer,' I said. 'You're just patronising me.'

'I'm your mother,' she said, 'it goes with the job,' and she began to hum. Together we sang about Chantilly lace and pretty faces and pony tails hanging down, doing a form of the hand jive.

'All right Mum,' I said, as we laid our hands to rest in our laps, 'thank you for the hoover.' And I leaned over and gave her a kiss.

As I was gathering my bag and the Dustbuster together, wondering whether receiving gifts of electrical goods was a sign of maturity on my part, or just old-fashioned maternalism, a thought occurred to me. 'Mum, did you ever have a long Indian print dress?'

'Oh yes, I had a maroon and cream one.'

'Did you? I don't remember that. When?'

'Well, if you don't remember it, you were probably at university. That was when?'

'I started in 1981.'

'I suppose that would be about right. I have a memory of wearing it to school, I think it was when I was working at Hayfields Primary. And that would have been 1980, 1981, yes.'

'So it wasn't a smart, evening-type dress?'

'Well, I wouldn't have worn it out for the evening. Some people did, I think,' she said, implying they were not the kind of people she would have known. 'And while we're on the subject of clothes, have you ever been to Longleat?'

'Got to go, mum,' I said. 'I've got to garden.'

I parked my car in a small turning off West Green Road in Tottenham. I rang my flat. I had no messages. So I wasn't going to see Yolande before I went back to Birmingham. I wondered if I would ever see her again. But of course, I had the plastic bag. I was bound to see her again.

I rang Iotha's door bell. I was the first person to arrive.

'Great outfit,' Iotha said.

Her own get-up was a perfect conjunction of fashion and function, long, black Lycra shorts and a close-fitting, black short-sleeved T-shirt. Her hair was knotted into plaits, which ended neatly at the level of her ear lobes. I wondered if the purpose of the afternoon was in fact to show off her style facility, but when she led me into the garden and I looked at the array of tools and potted plants it was clear that was just a vain hope.

She looked at my face and laughed. 'Let's have a drink,' she said. 'I'd hate to see you starting on your own.'

We walked back into her narrow yellow kitchen. A jug of Pimms sat on a side cupboard.

She poured each of us a glass, ice clinking and mint and strawberries tumbling in.

'Actually I did want to have a word with you. . . .' She indicated a stool tucked under a work surface. As I sat down she brought in a folding chair from the hall. '. . . in your role as the feminist conscience of chambers.' I groaned. I knew what was coming. People assume that because I call myself a feminist I have a view on all matters to do with women – which of course I do, although they don't all stand up to scrutiny. But people assume I have an evangelical approach to the world and want to change everyone. Which I know I should, but it's so much like hard work that I'm quite happy posing. But what happens is, they ask my advice. 'What would a feminist do in this situation?' and I think hard, I lose sleep, I worry, think some more and then tell them what my advice is, a little hesitantly but caringly. And then of course, guess what, the bastards don't take it. They marry the guy, or they tell their mother.

I took a large mouthful of Pimms. 'Oh yes?' I said, non-committally.

'When do office politics become sexual harassment?' she asked.

I sucked in my breath and a piece of soft fruit went straight down my throat. 'O-o-oh. Tricky question. Normally – never?' Her face indicated it was too late for that. 'What office politics are we talking about?'

'When did you last go into chambers?'

'Yesterday.'

'You have probably heard about recent chambers developments.'

'Tony's . . . elevation?'

'And things that flow from that?' She shook her glass so the ice cubes rattled.

'Forthcoming elections?'

She nodded.

'So this is not a hypothetical problem. And we're not talking about Simon?'

She shook her head. 'I don't know, it may just be my imagination.' Iotha was a sensible young woman, not known for wild flights of imagination. Unlike say, Vanya, or . . . me possibly.

'You haven't spoken to Tony about it?' Serious matters involving work colleagues were usually raised with the head of chambers but it didn't surprise me that she murmured, 'No.' Tony was a well-intentioned man, but had the discretion and sensitivity of an over-educated parrot.

The door bell rang. 'We need to talk about this properly,' I said. 'I'm up in Birmingham next week. Perhaps we could meet over the weekend some time? Is that soon enough?'

'That would be great.'

'It isn't going to be difficult this afternoon, is it?' I asked.

'Oh, no,' she said. 'Well, I bloody well hope not. The guest list was carefully constructed.'

Not that carefully, I thought, as Simon, Gavin and Jenna, all wearing loose, faded, comfortable clothes, entered the room. Simon looked even more ludicrous than I did. Iotha poured them a glass of Pimms.

'What's Pimms?' Jenna asked anxiously, lifting out a sprig of mint and looking round for somewhere to put it. She took a small sip. 'Tastes like ice-cream soda or something,' she said.

The door bell rang again and I let in five more members of chambers.

TWELVE

Sunday Evening – Yolande?

I drove back to the flat slowly. I had done three hours gardening and then had excused myself from the meal that Iotha was preparing. Wonderful odours of garlic and onions and rich sauce had begun wafting into the garden about an hour earlier, just as I was putting extra compost on a row of sad-looking flowers that I had been working with for half an hour. Two minutes later Jenna had told me they were weeds. She then inspected all the work I had done and silently removed three quarters of the neat plants I had set artistically into a new bed constructed by Simon.

Simon and I had had a brief conversation about the Danny Richards case. He had been very silent as I described my run-in with Judge Norman, which I thought he should know about. He apologised for dropping me into a difficult situation but I felt he was secretly concerned about my lack of professionalism. Which is why I didn't tell him about my coffee with Yolande in the shop, or the picnic in chambers, or the dinner with sister Sandra, or the hotel in Russell Square. I was beginning to be worried about my professionalism.

I was a crap barrister, I couldn't garden, I had a nagging sense that I wouldn't be able to help with Iotha's work problem, and as I let myself into the flat and looked round the untidy living room, I thought dejectedly that I couldn't even live properly. The flat was a mess. My life was a mess. I couldn't find myself a proper girlfriend. Yolande belonged to someone else. Two other people. Both men.

An image flashed into my mind. In the hotel, the night before, as Yolande had slid open the door of the wardrobe to pull out the carrier bag, I had glimpsed a man's suit hanging on the rail. She was unlikely to carry round one of Danny's suits as a memento. A pair of cufflinks yes, a jacket and trousers, no. It must surely have been her husband's. Where had her husband been while I was sleeping in the bed which he had presumably paid for? What if he had come in during the night? What if he *had* come in during the night? I shuddered.

I tried to think positive. One thing that was going right was my professional diary – I had a heavy case that would last for several weeks. This is the mark of success for a barrister. But it was in Birmingham. I didn't want to go to Birmingham. I didn't want to have to get my things ready for the journey, enough clothes for a week. I didn't want to stay away, I didn't want to leave London. There's something about doing a case out of town. Opponents are harder, clients are more difficult, the Robing Room more chilly. The law even seems more impenetrable in a strange town.

The answerphone was flashing. At least I had a machine that worked. And I had messages. I had two messages. The first was from Lena. 'Just reminding you that it takes at least fifteen hides to cover a sofa. Keep yourself busy, keep your mind off furniture and . . . other foolish things. Hurry back, we miss you.'

The second was a message from Yolande. She was inviting me for a drink that evening. I wondered what she was thinking. She sounded fond, affectionate. My stomach lurched with pleasure. She was suggesting a Bar at a hotel on Southampton Row near Holborn tube station.

It was quarter to seven. What I should be doing was preparing to go to Birmingham so that I would arrive with plenty of time to put the finishing touches to my preparation in the attic room at Julie's house. Going out with Yolande would be dropping myself deeper into the world of Danny Richards and his contract killing and his friends. But sleeping with someone makes you feel you've left something with them and you want to go and see that it's all right, or get it back. I made a decision. I would allow myself to go out with Yolande this evening, and in the time before I met her – she was suggesting eight thirty – I would do an hour's serious work, go out and see her, be back . . . at a reasonable time, get up at five, and, driving against the traffic, I'd be in Birmingham in a trice.

It's a good idea to give yourself time limits. Concentrates the mind. I pulled out the biggest file in my inquiry brief and flicked through the records the home had kept on each child. The rest of my clients were giving their evidence over the next few days, and I needed to ensure that they covered everything that needed to be said. The files might remind me of some salient points.

Most of the entries in the photocopied pages were in handwriting and difficult to read. There was little obvious indication of the abuse that had gone on. There were even several references to pleasant outings – coach parties to football matches, trips to pantomimes. I had already gone through with a pink highlighter marking mentions of 'punishment' and even 'requests for assistance', which is what my clients had talked about, being called out of the class to 'help' a member of staff. I stuck yellow Post-it stickers into the notes, with question marks on points that needed clarification – Did the abusers know what the others were doing? Did you ever tell any other child what was going on? Wasn't there a single adult you could tell?

As I parked the car in Red Lion Square I checked my watch – I was already five minutes late. I smiled at the thought of seeing Yolande. I wondered whether she was a punctual kind of woman.

The answer to that was clear as I walked expectantly into the bar. A quick sweep of the room showed that Yolande hadn't arrived. I like that in a woman, not being tied to time. I like it in anyone actually, given my own poor timekeeping, except clients. Because if clients are late they get into trouble with the judge, and somehow it always becomes my fault for not controlling them properly. Now I sauntered to the bar and ordered a bottle of 1997 Chablis. I know it's corny but it's Chablis. Just the idea of Chablis is romantic, let alone actually saying 'A bottle of Chablis' to the barman. Then it's the soft sound of the word in your mouth, it's like the sweetness from a grape dissolving onto your tongue. And then there's the smell, round and fruity and the taste, mystery and fulfilment all in one at the back of your throat.

I sat on a lightwood chair at a lightwood table with my back to the door so I could watch through the reflection in the mirror for Yolande's arrival. A smattering of people sat at some of the other tables, American tourists and businessmen and their female companions, and there was a low hum of conversation. The waiter brought the Chablis and two glasses and I poured a glass for myself.

'Well.' A short man behind me spoke to my reflection. He was wearing loose royal-blue running trousers and a loose orange vest, and I mean a vest, which showed the tattoos on his arms and a little chest hair. 'You're late.'

'And you're probably talking to the wrong person,' I said, thinking, with a sinking heart, but I bet you're not. You've come with a message from . . .

'Yolande sent me.' He walked round to Yolande's seat.

Twenty-two quid on a bottle of Chablis, I thought, disappointment flooding through me. And she sends her apologies through this skinny runt in orange and blue. I'd rather pour the wine down the drain than share it with someone out and about in almost his underwear.

'You'd better have a drink,' someone doing a very good imitation of my voice said.

'Don't mind if I do.'

You can't pour such pure delight down the drain, and I do hate to drink alone.

'I'm Clark,' he said, watching as I poured wine into Yolande's glass. He looked young, but his brown hair was receding, and his deep grey eyes looked tired. He could have been any age between twenty-two and thirty-five.

'And I'm . . .'

'Yeah, I know.' He picked up the glass and glugged it down like Coca-Cola. Halfway down the glass the taste must have touched his tongue and he stopped. 'Very nice. Yolande would have liked this,' he said, and winked at me.

He looked down at his chest. 'Sorry about the outfit,' he said, leaning across to another chair and picking up a track suit top which, fortunately, matched his trousers. 'I wasn't expecting to be out on the town tonight. Yolande had to go back up at the last minute.' He spoke in the soft Midlands burr that I recognised from my university days, he said 'tonoight' and 'oop'. I would have felt quite friendly towards him, except that he was Yolande's replacement. And he'd winked. And he was wearing a vest.

I didn't want to give him anything else to wink at, so I didn't ask him why Yolande had had to change her plans at the last minute and why she had chosen him to carry the message. I just poured more wine into our glasses and waited. He slid his arms into his top and zipped it up.

I picked up my glass. In repose, and perhaps through the soft glow of Chablis, he had a certain cheeky charm. The grey eyes were surrounded by surprisingly long dark lashes. When he smiled there was a dimple in his left cheek. He seemed eager to be friendly. And now his outfit was all shiny blue without the intense stringy orangeness of the vest. But he wasn't Yolande.

I wondered who he really was. 'Do you work in the shop?' I asked.

He grinned. 'Sometimes.'

'Tell me,' I said. 'Do you sell leather armchairs?'

'We don't sell much of anything,' he said. 'If you know what I mean.'

I thought, if this man is an employee of Danny's – about which I am absolutely not going to ask him – in whom Danny puts his trust, upon whom he relies, no wonder Danny has done so much time in prison. If I was a police officer, I'd cut short this conversation with Clark and I'd be straight round to the shop, looking under those comfy cushions for swag. But perhaps it wasn't Danny's shop. 'Do you know Yolande well?' I asked.

The grin slid across his face again. 'Yeah,' he said, and then his tone changed. 'I know Danny better.' He spoke almost proudly. 'Yolande says you should ring her tomorrow at the shop.' He held out his hand, a number was written in blue biro in the palm.

Why should I have to ring her? Bloody cheek. Standing me up, sending a man in ill-fitting sportswear in her place. I took a mouthful of wine, I remembered last night, and peace and serenity ran down my throat. Obediently I fished a pen out of my jacket pocket and wrote the number on the back of my own hand.

But that wasn't the real message. The reason he had come, the real task he had been set, the thing he had to say to me, just slipped out as he pushed back his chair, after I had said, 'Well, I'd better be going then,' and began to edge off my seat. He drained non-existent drops from his glass. 'Oh yeah, and also, there's some film in a left luggage compartment in Euston.' I stared at him. 'She wants you to get it developed.' He fumbled in the pocket of his shiny blue trousers and dropped a small key onto the table in front of me. 'Number 127.'

I heard him bang into a chair, as in the mirror I watched him stumble to the door. At the door he stopped, turned and picked his way back to me, groping again in the pocket of his trousers. 'It might not be 127,' he said. 'It might be 63.'

'That's logical,' I said.

'Is it?' The crease of anxiety slid from his forehead.

'No, it's hopeless.'

He drew out a handful of small pieces of paper, bus tickets, travelcards, shop receipts. He glanced at the clock on the wall. 'I'm going to miss my train. It's on one of them,' he said and squashed the small slippery heap on the table in front of me before starting his halting journey once more across the floor of the bar.

I scooped up the pieces quickly before anything disappeared and by the time I had pressed them securely into the inside pocket of my jacket, and before I had time to ask, 'If it's at Euston, why don't you pick it up on your way home?' he had gone.

It was quarter to ten and we had drunk all the Chablis. As I wandered back to the car I realised I had had nothing to eat since the Greek al fresco lunch with my mother. I suppose I had imagined a delicate, intimate dinner for two with Yolande. I was starving but I couldn't even ring someone interesting to invite them out for a late supper because I was going to go to bed in about ten minutes, because I was going to get up so early in the morning.

I turned the key in the ignition and Roy Orbison began warbling 'Only the Lonely' insistently, his voice rising and falling with the pain of his loss. This was not to be the epitaph of the evening, I told myself crisply, and fast forwarded. By the time I'd got to the Angel, the Marvelettes' stirring rendition of 'Too Many Fish in the Sea' seemed to deal with the prevailing emotions churning in my heart and my stomach. I got into the beat, and my hands were tapping on the steering wheel as I thought that it must be true that I don't need nobody

126

who don't need me. Although, I reminded myself as I cruised across the lights outside the bingo hall by Essex Road station, I don't really like fish – after an unfortunate incident in my childhood when a fish bone got stuck in my throat – and I had to admit that there were very few short, tall, blind or kind fish in the aquarium of my life and rather too many slippery eels and piranhas lurking amongst the weeds.

But I kept on humming as I ran up the steps to the house and even while I recklessly stemmed my hunger with a pile of sardines on top of a thick piece of buttered toast. Then I threw books, clothes and the handful of paper Clark had given me into a bag for Birmingham and fell exhausted into bed.

THIRTEEN

Monday Morning – Inquiry

The World Service sneaked into my room at five o'clock in the morning, telling me important things I would never hear elsewhere, but I felt that I was in the wrong place – a grey, gritty place with none of the comforts of home. It wasn't quite dark, but there was a chill in the room and I didn't want to get up. And then suddenly the clock said five thirty, and I fell out of bed with no possibility now of breakfast or even coffee.

I stood at the sink and drank a glass of water, for goodness' sake, then showered and dressed. I put on my Ede and Ravenscroft outfit. It may have been shabby, but when I took off the jacket everyone would see the fancy label. Of course you never take your jacket off in court, but maybe an inquiry would be that wee bit more casual.

As I went back into the bedroom to open the curtains I fell over a box at the foot of my bed. I looked hard at the Dustbuster. Should I take it? Oh, who was I kidding? Of course I wasn't going to take it. Perhaps if I left it in my flat, by the miracle of absence, the hoovering would be done on my return. I decided to take the chance, took the machine out of the box and plugged it in, and then I left the house and drove without stopping to Birmingham.

We were having an early-morning conference with the clients. In blazing sunshine we trooped into the side room which Mrs Gisborough had now allotted to our team. Adam was beside me. This was good. I had indicated in our email correspondence that I would like him to attend the inquiry as often as possible, but after the way Frodsham had behaved the week before I had made it very clear that he was going to have to be with me all the time. The clients needed a strong team. I had to do the advocacy and he had to glower at Frodsham. I couldn't do both. As we took our seats he said that he had had a bit of a fight to get out of the office. Which meant that the firm weren't happy that he wasn't sitting at his desk, dealing with privately paying clients, when his hourly rate at the inquiry wasn't nearly as high.

The room contained several stacks of chairs and four square metal tables piled on top of each other.

'This is a bit of a mess, isn't it?' Shelly Dean said, looking round the room. 'Gregory!' she shouted, 'you're technical, bring that table over here. Martin, you take this end.'

It was almost a full house. Most of the clients wanted to attend on the days the others were giving evidence. As we sat round the tables which had been pushed together, I noticed that the clients had started to form small friendship networks. I wondered if that reflected their time at Haslam Hall. Shelly and her husband were sitting with Leanne Scott and Janine Telford; Brian Hawkes and Martin Williams sat together, today with their wives. Slightly to one side sat Mr and Mrs Springer,

Mrs Springer still bunched up in her sheepskin coat, despite the sunshine.

We talked about the evidence of the week before. There were conflicting views about what Mr Frodsham was up to, but general agreement that all three women had held up well. I reminded the clients that they weren't obliged to give evidence, they could change their minds at any time. Giving evidence was becoming a mark of some sort of machismo and I didn't want the clients to feel humiliated in front of each other. I told them they could let me know in private if they wanted.

Martin Williams and Brian Hawkes were to be the witnesses for today. They had been two of the last to come forward to the police and had been reluctant to participate in the inquiry. Their grooming at Haslam Hall had been more subtle than some of the girls, but in the end they too had been abused. In their statements they both expressed intense guilt that they had accepted the sweets and money, so that they had somehow colluded in the abuse. Martin Williams was earnest and determined to answer all the questions that might be thrown at him. Brian Hawkes was a very short man and had been a very small boy. He had been easy pickings, abuse was the deal for protection from bullying. He sat pale and wide eyed as Shelly, Leanne and Janine leaned towards them, giving them confident and conflicting advice. 'Look him straight in the eyes.' 'Don't look at him.' 'Tell him you don't understand.' 'Tell him to sod off.'

'Can we not have the language?' Mrs Springer spoke up, her red hair bouncing in curls round her taut face.

'Oooh,' said Shelly. 'What language would that be?

Body language? From where I'm sitting you're saying some pretty scary things.'

Mrs Springer was about to reply.

'Wyatt,' I said. We had ten minutes to discuss the running of Haslam Hall.

Frodsham's reaction to the innocuous comments that Shelly had made on the first day had been excessive. Only Shelly's statement to the inquiry mentioned Wyatt, in that oblique reference to his inner-city interests. None of the others had mentioned him at all. I asked them now whether there was anything they wanted to say about Wyatt, or anyone else who hadn't been charged. They all thought about it, carefully, but one by one said that, no, Mr Wyatt had not been involved. I told them if they remembered anything they should let me know, they could make a note, or just tell me, at any time.

We moved into the inquiry room. Martin Williams walked resolutely to the witness stand and answered my questions and the questions from Catherine Delahaye in a firm and clear voice. The other lawyers posed a few questions. Then it was Frodsham's turn. Slowly he dragged himself out of his chair. 'No questions,' he said, tucked his jacket round his large waist and sat down again.

After the break Brian Hawkes stepped nervously over to the chair. His voice cracked in answer to my opening questions, and he began to shake as Catherine Delahaye put her gentle enquiries to him. By the time it was Frodsham's turn he was ashen and his voice had almost disappeared. Frodsham lifted himself two inches out of his seat. He paused. 'Nothing for this witness, thank you.'

The clients were furious. 'I weren't going to give evidence,' one woman said, 'but I will now.' 'And me,' said another.

The day was over. Four clients had given faultless evidence and Frodsham hadn't asked a question.

The others had gone, but when I climbed back up the stairs from making calls in my basement office, Shelly was tidying her papers. She was still the secretary of the Group and now her job consisted of keeping a copy of all the inquiry papers. We walked down the corridor together.

'Are you staying somewhere nice while you're up here?' Shelly asked. 'With all that's going on, you've got to look after yourself. What was Frodsham up to today, not asking any questions? You don't know where you are with him. The others are getting a bit uptight. There's been a few arguments.'

I wondered if his plan was divide and rule, getting the clients to turn on each other. I wondered if it was working.

'Do you know Frodsham?' Shelly went on. 'I don't like the way he looks at you.'

I laughed. 'Nor do I.'

Mrs Springer bustled past, enveloped in her sheepskin coat.

'Warm enough for you?' Shelly called.

Mrs Springer turned. 'Tart,' she hissed.

'What?' Shelly and I spoke together. We looked at each other.

'Is she talking to you or me?' I asked.

'Both of us, I should think,' Shelly said. 'She thinks she's something. She's only a bloody secretary. And not for much longer apparently. But you'd better keep your eye on her. Perhaps she knows something about you and Frodsham.'

'Oh yeah, me and Frodsham,' I said.

FOURTEEN

Monday Evening

'Hello?' I said, to the girl with short black hair swinging across her face who was sitting in Marnie's place on the sofa. She must be a friend, I thought.

'Oh hiya,' the girl replied in Marnie's voice.

'What have you done to your hair?' Gradually I was recognising her.

'It's a wig,' she cried triumphantly, pulling at the short bob so that her long hair tumbled down over her shoulders.

'That's very exotic,' I said. 'Is this part of your school uniform?'

'No, don't you think it's great?' She held the wig up on her fist, twisting it this way and that, admiringly. 'It's for Saturday.'

'What's happening on Saturday?'

'The demo. Are you going to come?'

'I shan't be here,' I said.

'Oh.' Her face fell.

'What demo?'

'It's the Save the World demo. You know, that inquiry.'

'The environmental one?'

'I thought that was the one you were doing. I've been

telling my friends you were in that,' she said accusingly.

'My inquiry's important too,' I said, not sure that I entirely believed that. 'But where do wigs fit into the environmental debate? Apart from the fact that yours was probably made somewhere in the Far East in a small dark room for no wages, out of some toxic material. Or is it human hair?'

'It's a disguise. Shona and me and some of the others from school are all wearing wigs in case the police take photos. Shona's got a red curly one and I chose this one.'

'And if you did a bit of back combing you could have another life as a Shangri'La.'

'This is serious,' she said. 'Or perhaps you don't care about the environment.'

'Yes, I do,' I said. 'But why do you need to disguise yourself? What are you planning on doing?'

'Nothing. You wear a wig at work, and you're not planning to *do* anything.'

'I don't wear a wig.' This felt like a replay of the dinner party. 'Except occasionally. And when I do, it's not out of choice. If it looked like yours, I might do, though.'

'Why don't you come? Mum's coming.'

'Oh my God. Perhaps I'd better not go back to London. You might need me to bail you both out.' Slip, slide, into the Family Vortex.

I walked to the kitchen. There was a piece of paper on the table in the middle room with a mobile phone number written in Marnie's round handwriting.

'What's this note?' I called hopefully.

'Someone rang. He said his name was Simon.'

I punched in the number, frustrated that it wasn't Yolande. 'Simon, where are you?' I said shortly.

'In the Robing Room. Birmingham. I was ringing to see if you'd like to go out for dinner tonight, but you sound rather distracted.'

'Sorry. No. That would be very nice.'

'Great. Chinese?'

'Must we?'

'Indulge me.'

I did some work, which I probably wouldn't have done so assiduously if I'd been staying in. I re-read the statements of the clients who hadn't given evidence, and looked again at Wyatt's thirty-seven-page opus. Talkative enough on paper, I thought. He sat so quietly beside Frodsham, I was scarcely aware he was there, Frodsham was so present, so large, and ominous. Wyatt never seemed to give instructions, he never whispered, never passed notes, unlike my clients. He sat with his fingers pressed together in the form of a church. Now I thought about it, I couldn't even bring his image to mind, just those long thin fingers. I looked back at the passages I had highlighted in his statement, his knowledge of child psychology, the children's needs, the children's hopes and dreams – he hadn't done much to protect those.

I had a shower and put on my black linen trousers and a grey shirt. As I got downstairs, I said, 'I'm going out for dinner.'

Marnie's eyes widened. 'Who with? That bloke Simon who rang? Oh you haven't gone straight, have you?' What a disappointment I was turning out to be. Not only was I appearing in the wrong inquiry, now I was becoming ordinary. Her street cred was leeching away.

'Don't worry, I haven't,' I reassured her. 'He's a man from my chambers. It's purely social.'

'Can you give me a lift to Shona's?' Shona was Marnie's best friend. She waved a video at me. 'We're going to watch the omnibus edition of Brookie.'

'I thought Shona lived just round the corner.'

'She does, but as you're going out anyway . . .'

I had arranged to meet Simon at the Golden Flame restaurant in Harborne, where he was staying with an ancient family friend. The restaurant was set back from the road, in a short row of red brick shops. I was early, so I sat in the car, watching the traffic pass. I leaned my head back against the headrest and thought about the day. Patsy Kline singing 'Crazy' filled my mind. I felt uncertain, I didn't have a grip on the case. Despite the friendly words of Shelly this afternoon, it was demoralising to think that I was a mistake, that the clients hadn't chosen me. They were unsettled by Frodsham's tactics, arguing with each other. I was going to have to get my act together, to show them it was going to be OK, to reassure them that they had made the right mistake in having me as their counsel. I was looking forward to seeing Simon, a familiar face, a shoulder to whinge on.

I strolled across the road and into the Golden Flame. The restaurant was almost empty but Simon was already at a table, gazing at one of the many Chinese paintings on the pale ochre walls. He was wearing a loud green and red Hawaiian shirt. He caught sight of me and stood up, smiling, as I approached. At least he wasn't wearing shorts.

'Frankie, how lovely to see you!' he exclaimed, kissing me on the cheek.

'Strangely, the feeling is mutual, Simon,' I told him,

overlooking the fact that we didn't kiss in our relationship.

Five minutes passed as Simon told me all the things he loved to eat in a Chinese restaurant and then we ordered them. Our selection included a pot of jasmine tea and a bottle of Gewürtztraminer. 'To take away the taste of the tea,' Simon explained.

We toasted each other with the wine as the waiter set down small plates of seaweed dusted with brown sugar.

'How's the inquiry going?' Simon asked, as we struggled with the chopsticks.

It was going to take so long. 'Let's talk about you first,' I offered. 'Say for half an hour? Then we can talk about me for the rest of the evening.'

'OK.'

'How's your trial?'

His face puckered into a small smile but he said nothing, as the waiter stood and cut away the meat from the leg bone of some crispy duck.

'This is what I deduce from your smile,' I said, brushing plum sauce over a pancake and heaping on a pile of cucumber and duck. 'The trial is effective, and Danny hasn't changed his plea. And you have met the lovely Roseanna.'

He beamed at me silently. His mouth was full. Then he swallowed. 'Yes! What a marvellous woman. She was very concerned about my foot. So was the judge, as a matter of fact.'

'I hope you played it up for all it's worth. How is it?'

'Still painful.'

'Limping?'

'A bit.'

138

'Thank God for that.'

He looked at me. 'But Roseanna's being very nice all round.'

'Is she?'

'Smart, quick, funny.'

I didn't want the whole of his thirty minutes to disappear on one topic. 'What are your jury like?' I asked.

'A lot of youth and a couple of old biddies . . .' I looked at him. '. . . women. And a guy who reads the *Telegraph*.'

'What do you reckon?'

Simon poured jasmine tea into my cup and wine into my glass. 'Hard to know. We've had the prosecution opening and one and a half police officers. I don't know how the jury are taking it. I want Danny to go in the box. It would be good for the jury to get a fuller picture. They'll like him. Without hearing him speak, the youth will just think he's an old lag. I don't think the story has enough charm to sway a tin of beans, let alone the women; and the *Telegraph* reader . . .' He shrugged dejectedly.

'Perhaps they need time to warm to him,' I said.

'Time is what I don't have. We're galloping through the evidence because Danny doesn't want me to do anything. I could win this case,' he said. 'I'm hardly cross-examining at all. This afternoon I simply asked the first officer where he was when he wrote up his notes and Danny started hissing behind me. Roseanna's doing it all. And very well I may say.' The little smile came back on to his face.

'So what are you going to do?'

'I'm seriously thinking of using that old chestnut, the one everyone says they use whenever they're in a corpseless murder case.'

I looked at him hopelessly. 'I've never done a corpseless murder.'

'OK, so, there's no body, the case against you is all circumstantial and your client has just given his evidence, saying he knows nothing about it. You say, "Your Honour, I would now like to call my next witness," and with a sweep of your arm, you indicate the door of the court and announce, "The Deceased Mr Terry Fleming," and as one, the jury swivel round to look at the door. Then in your closing speech, you say, "Members of the jury, you all turned to look, you thought it was just possible he might walk through that door, which means there is a doubt in your minds as to whether or not he's dead."'

'Sounds great, you should try it,' I said, cramming the last morsel of dripping pancake into my mouth.

'Yes, but the sting in the tail is that the jury convict.'

'Because . . . ?'

'Because the only person who doesn't look at the door is the defendant. Danny wouldn't look, if only because he's heard the story so many times before.'

'And anyway isn't there some forensic evidence in your case?' I asked.

'Oh, the blood,' he said.

'Whose blood?'

'No-one seems entirely sure. It's nothing to worry about,' he said airily.

'Where did they find it?'

'He has a shop. He sells furniture.'

So it was his shop. That was something. 'How was it found there?' I said, thinking, I know what he's going to say, that it was on a cushion which has now mysteriously but fortunately, for the defence, disappeared, and

I'm going to have to say, 'I'm sorry, but I think I know where it is.'

'It was on a piece of carpet,' he said, and I breathed again. 'In the back of the shop.'

In the back of the shop. I had been there. Sitting on the chairs, eating the Hob Nobs. Had Terry Fleming's body been dragged, badly wrapped, across the floor, on its way to a motorway pillar? Or worse, was it actually there, while he was sitting on a chair, relaxing, eating a Hob Nob, that he had come to his sticky end?

'They've cut out various sections of carpet and they've got an expert who says the trajectory of the blood is compatible with someone either having been killed in an adjacent room ("the toilet!" I thought) or someone who had blood on their clothing, received there or elsewhere, shaking it off.'

'Dr Quirk?'

'Yes, very good. But our expert says that in a shop with heavy lifting going on, you often find this type of micro-blood spot.'

Simon obviously hadn't been to the shop. It was full of soft furnishings, and my own experience, as well as Clark's description, was that not very much of anything went on there, let alone heavy lifting.

'Until we get to that point, I have very little to do,' he said morosely. 'It's all become rather boring.'

'You could go on a view to Allied Carpets,' I said. 'Compare and contrast.'

'I don't think I understand,' said Simon. We busied ourselves with rice and beef and green peppers and shrimp and noodles for a while, then he said, 'I suppose it could be Yolande's blood. She hasn't given a sample.'

'That doesn't matter does it? She doesn't seem the

141

type.' I felt myself go pink. 'To engage in violence I mean. I thought the blood letting was usually left to Danny.'

'Unfortunately that may be very close to the truth. How do you know Yolande?'

'I met her last week. After the PDH. Is that the only evidence?'

'Danny said a few clever things to the police officer that I have not been allowed to challenge. But yes, they don't have anything much at all. It's all circumstantial. But the timing's unfortunate. They say the age of the blood fits in almost exactly with Danny's release from prison. Terry Fleming was seen visiting the shop shortly before he died.'

'But if that's all there is, the prosecution are going to have trouble proving the case beyond reasonable doubt aren't they? Isn't that what Danny's doing? Keeping quiet, letting them show how little they've got? Perhaps if you cross-examined too strenuously stuff would come out that wouldn't be helpful.'

'That's what I'm worried about. Whenever a new witness goes in the box, I'm afraid what might turn up. It's like walking on eggshells. I don't like doing cases like that. I like a good strong defence, even if it is a load of rubbish. I hope you're right.' He paused. 'You haven't been talking to Yolande have you? She's not going to tell you anything I shouldn't know about?'

I took a mouthful of wine. 'Simon, I have to be honest with you. I have spoken to her, but she has told me nothing about the case that you should know, or even that you shouldn't know. She wants him to get off. She's got some theories.' I thought about the plastic bag. Should I tell him? Should I find out what was in it first?

Simon shook his head. 'Whatever Yolande may say, my instructions have to come from Danny. And he's not talking. Not about his case, anyway. You and he seem to have hit it off that day.'

'I thought he was quite interesting,' I said. 'But then I don't know any other contract killers.'

'I think he's sorry you haven't got the brief. He asked me about the inquiry. Seemed very impressed with your work there.' Simon looked at me. 'He hasn't asked you to do anything for him, has he?'

'No.' He hadn't. And I would deal with the Yolande thing as soon as I spoke to her. I willed my cheeks to remain a constant shade, whatever shade that might be.

'Just remember, easy does it. Do you want any more of these prawns?' The Danny conversation was over. I shook my head and Simon piled the last of the food into his bowl. 'So tell me all about life at the Grange, Frankie,' he said.

I gave him a brief rundown of what had been happening, the unfriendliness of the other representatives, the discovery that I wasn't the person the clients thought I was and Frodsham's strange behaviour. Simon was sympathetic and said the right things. 'The lawyers are testing you out because you're from out of town. They're probably more worried what you're thinking about them. But you are most definitely the right person for the job. Your clients couldn't have done better.'

'Thanks, Simon,' I said, comforted. I hoped he was right. It was nearly ten o'clock, time to go home. We both had work to do.

I had been in my room for fifteen minutes looking through the indictments, the charges on which the care workers had been convicted. Despite my bravado at the inquiry there were depressingly few, it was no more than a token, with a slightly longer list of TICs, the offences they had asked to be Taken Into Consideration, but which for one reason or another the police had decided not to prosecute. I heard a shout and then Marnie called, 'Frankie, it's the phone.' As I walked down the stairs she shrugged at me from the bathroom. Julie was in the kitchen making a last cup of tea. She pointed to the receiver.

Yolande said, 'I'm ringing to apologise. I really wanted to see you last night, but . . . things came up.'

Like your husband, I suppose, I wanted to say.

'Did you get it?' she asked abruptly.

'What?'

'The film.'

'No. What do you think I am? I've been at the inquiry all day.'

She tutted in disappointment. 'But you've got the key?'

'Yes, I have. And I've still got the plastic bag you gave me.' I paused, waiting for her to apologise, or explain.

She drew in a breath, with a small 'oh'. Had she forgotten the plastic bag? Was she regretting giving it to me? 'You must get the film,' she insisted. 'Soon.'

'What's the urgency? The trial has started and the sky hasn't fallen quite yet.'

'You've got my mobile number, haven't you? Give me a ring when you've got the film.' And she was gone.

Gently, suppressing my rage – but more, I realised, my disappointment – I replaced the receiver. She had rung me to check if I had been to the left luggage locker. She had apologised with something that sounded like regret for not turning up the night before, but what she was really interested in was the bloody roll of film. I wondered if she thought I was an idiot.

An idiot would be fair comment, I thought, after I stomped upstairs, and discovered that the pieces of paper which Clark had heaped on to the small wooden table in the bar, the pieces of paper on which the number of the locker was written, had disappeared. And looking carefully at my bag, I could see the holes they had disappeared through.

FIFTEEN

Tuesday

The foyer pulsated with heat as I stood with some of the clients by the coffee table, opening a small plastic pot of cream to pour into my coffee. Silently Shelly handed me a tissue as a milky way splashed across the front of my black shirt. I was worrying about the residue of tissue shreds, when Mrs Springer approached me from where she and Gregory Springer had been standing apart from the main group, over by the stairs.

'Miss Richmond,' she said, wrapping the sheepskin coat more tightly round her, 'can I see you for a moment?' Her auburn hair was caught back in a large clip and her small face was tight with tension.

'Oh God,' Shelly murmured in my ear. 'She's going to tell you about the car. She's too good for this life, her and her precious Gregory.'

We walked down the hallway. Mrs Springer looked up and down the corridor, checking that we couldn't be overheard and said, 'I want you to know that the children weren't all the same. My husband was different. My husband . . .'

'Gregory,' I said, to show I knew who she was talking about.

'. . . he knew right from wrong. He'd been brought up well. It shouldn't have happened to him. What happened to my husband was . . .'

Was she going to say 'worse'?

'Look, Mrs Springer,' I said. 'It shouldn't have happened to any of them. They were children. What they knew or didn't know doesn't come into it. It was no one's fault but the people who did it and the others who turned their backs.'

'He wasn't even in care really, it was just that his mum was ill and there was no one else who could have him. But look at those lot. You can see where they come from. We're not used to this, common talk, mixing with prostitutes.'

'We all have to make a living,' I said.

'Look at Shelly Dean, laughing like she hasn't a care in the world. That skirt. Slit up to her backside.'

'That's a fashion,' I explained. 'I know what happened was a dreadful, dreadful thing. But the children it happened to were picked on precisely because they were extra vulnerable, not because they were . . .' I searched for a word '. . . rough or something. Look, Mrs Springer, no child is ever guilty. It goes with the territory. Child equals not guilty.'

Her eyes narrowed. 'Oh yeah? So when do they stop being not guilty? One of those bastards,' she rolled her head backwards, in the direction of the foyer, 'excuse my French, let down my car tyres. . . .'

'One of the solicitors?' I asked, deliberately misunderstanding her.

If it hadn't been bad taste she would have turned and spat. 'No, one of your clients.'

I didn't think now was the right moment to remind

her that her husband was one of my clients. 'Was it a mistake?'

'If you call walking round and undoing the caps. . . .'

Shelly walked up. 'Emma, I've come to apologise about the car. It were me. I shouldn't have done it. I'm very sorry,' she said.

Nonplussed, Emma Springer turned and walked away.

'She doesn't call me a tart and get away with it,' Shelly laughed. 'Or you.'

'Ah,' I said. 'Thank you.'

Adam brought me over a fresh cup of coffee. 'Any problems?' he asked.

'Where do I start?'

Gregory Springer was giving his evidence. Perhaps it was anxiety about that which had caused his wife's outburst. His story was the same as the others. I asked his name and address and he agreed that he had made the statement the panel had before it. He clarified the dates of his stay at the home. 'Is there anything you would like to add?' I asked, as I did of each of my clients.

'Well, there was one time,' he said. I noticed his temples were shining with sweat. Unlike the other men who usually came casually dressed in T-shirts and jeans, Gregory was wearing a brown suit, with a sombre tie.

'Yes?' I said.

He raised his hand to his mouth and coughed.

Frodsham heaved himself to his feet. 'Is this in the statement?'

Gregory shook his head.

'If it's not in the statement, he shouldn't be giving evidence about it now,' Frodsham said. 'He's had years to think about this. He can't just suddenly decide to start telling a fresh story today in the witness box.'

'We don't know what the evidence is yet,' Henry Curston said. He turned to me. 'Do we?'

'No,' I said, crisply. Thinking, do I? Has he told me? Is he going to talk about Shelly and the car tyres?

'Miss Richmond, it is rather unusual to have evidence admitted in this way,' Curston went on. 'But since the rules in an inquiry are necessarily more flexible than in a courtroom, I will allow you to call the evidence, and then I will rule on its admissibility. You're not dealing with a jury here, Mr Frodsham.' Frodsham was rising again from his seat. 'If the evidence is inappropriate we will put it from our minds.'

'But it could be any wild allegation.'

'We will hear the evidence.'

Hesitantly, with a pink face, as if he hadn't meant to cause so much trouble, Gregory Springer began his story. 'It was just one time, one evening, a Sunday, when most of the carers weren't in. I was in the games room. We had a snooker table.' He was clenching and unclenching his hands. 'I got called out because the usual boy was ill.' He poured himself a glass of water and drank it noisily. 'To go into Birmingham.'

'Who called you out?' I asked.

Frodsham was on his feet again. 'This is all new. There is nothing of this in any of the papers. I demand to have this in writing at the very least, in a statement, so that I may be fully prepared for any cross-examination.' Wyatt sat impassively, his head on one side, fingertips touching, gazing at Gregory Springer.

Henry Curston sighed. 'Very well. Ms Richmond, we will break now and you can take a statement from your client. Will it be possible for you to have it typed up by two o'clock this afternoon?'

I looked at Adam. He nodded uncertainly. 'It will,' I said firmly.

We rose. The room emptied into the foyer. It wasn't yet coffee break time and the fresh flasks had not been put on the tables. Mr Frodsham and Mr Wyatt brushed past Mrs Springer, who was hovering at the doorway waiting for Gregory. I ushered Adam, and Mr and Mrs Spinger into our room and we sat at the corner of the table. The room was cool and silent. Outside were the muffled sounds of laughter and conversation. Gregory's hands were clenched in fists between his knees. He was rocking, silently. Mrs Springer sat tensely, half turned towards him, watching him.

'I think we need some coffee,' I said to Adam.

There was a light knocking and Leanne pushed the door open. The noise from the hall roared into the room. Shelly walked through with four cups of coffee on a cardboard lid. Wordlessly she put the lid down on the table and left the room.

Adam handed out the coffee. Gregory cradled his cup in his hands.

I folded open my note book. 'When you're ready,' I said quietly.

'I can't,' he said. He lifted his head and looked round the room. Beads of sweat stood out on his upper lip. He glanced quickly at his wife.

'Mrs Springer,' I said, 'could you just nip out and get me some sugar, please?'

'There's sugar there.' She pointed to two sachets on the tray.

'I like a lot,' I said, picking up a sachet and shaking

it, trying to look natural. Reluctantly, she walked to the door, turned and looked pointedly at her husband, then moved into the foyer.

'Do you want to tell me about it first, or shall we try and write something straight away?'

'I can't,' he said. 'I can't. I'm sorry.'

'Drink your coffee,' I said. 'You could probably do with a bit of caffeine.'

He put the cup to his lips. Then put it carefully back on the table. He began to cry, softly, his shoulders heaving, tears tumbling down his face. I handed him a tissue. He dabbed at his eyes and blew his nose.

'Do you want some fresh air?' I asked him.

'I want you to go out there and tell them all, tell my wife, that there's nothing to say, I'm not saying anything. I know what she says, but she can't bear the shame of it. I can't give evidence. I want to go home.'

'Are you sure?'

He blew his nose, again. He nodded. 'Yes.'

'You can tell me later, if you change your mind. You know that. Any time.'

He shuddered. 'Oh no, this is it, I've said all I'm saying. I'm not going back up there. I'm sorry.' He rubbed fiercely at his eyes with the tissue.

'It's all right,' I reassured him, as the door barged open and Mrs Springer walked irritatedly into the room, and pushed a clutch of sugar sachets onto the cardboard tray. I bent close to his face. 'At least now I shan't have to drink coffee with four sugars in.' I stood up. 'Gregory's decided he'd rather stop now,' I said. 'He won't be making a statement.'

Her expression didn't change. She stared at him.

I went out into the foyer and walked over to Frodsham and Wyatt, who were standing near the coffee table, eating biscuits.

'Mr Springer has finished his evidence,' I said. 'He won't be making a written statement and he won't be going back in the witness box.'

'Well, there's a fine thing!' Frodsham roared. 'He throws a small grenade into the proceedings, then doesn't have the nerve to carry through.'

Wyatt placed his hand on Frodsham's arm.

'I should take your client's instructions for once, Mr Frodsham,' I said. 'And shut up.'

'That were good,' said Shelly, coming up behind me, as I walked down the corridor, planning which sandwich I would buy in Marks & Spencer.

As we fell into step together I said, 'Shelly, do you know what Gregory was going to say? Could you say it?'

'I thought that were hearsay, whatever you call it. That's what DC Blane said.'

'The inquiry's a bit different.'

'But we never talked to each other about what happened, not recently and not when we were kids. I don't know, we were all too weighed down with our own secrets. You didn't know who to trust. I don't know exactly what happened to him.'

'He said something about going into Birmingham. Did you go into Birmingham?'

'Oh, no, the girls never went into Birmingham, not on our own. Sometimes for outings and stuff. But one or two of the boys did go. Getting treats and sometimes a new top or a jacket. Does it make a difference?'

'I don't know,' I said. 'It's just that Gregory was

so upset. He said there was a usual boy. Perhaps we should ask "the usual boy". Do you know who that was?'

'Not really. Like I say, some of the boys went in to Birmingham sometimes. I mean, now he's said it, I remember the expression, you know, "the usual boy". I haven't heard that for years. But I don't know who it would have been. I'll think about it.' We came to the bottom of the stairs. 'I'm just nipping off to the market, do you want anything?'

I shook my head.

'See you later, then.'

Perhaps I'd try something with roasted vegetables and a creamy cheese, I thought, as I stepped out in the opposite direction. I wondered if Gregory might tell me more tomorrow, after his initial distress had worn off. I wondered if Frodsham would make a scene in front of the panel about my client's decision not to continue his evidence. I wondered if he would tell them that I had told him to shut up.

After lunch when we were all in our seats I announced that my client had gone home.

'Is he ill?' Curston asked.

'No. In fact he wishes to excuse himself from giving further evidence. He asks me to apologise for taking up the inquiry's time.'

Henry Curston gazed at me, considering the implications. The tribunal's time had been wasted, but it was obviously a matter to be treated with delicacy. Although they had yet to be called, there was evidence in the papers, from psychotherapists and counsellors, of the depth of trauma which all my clients had suffered.

Mr Frodsham rumbled to his feet. 'My client asks me to express his complete understanding of Mr Springer's difficulty. Ms Richmond was good enough to let us know the situation before lunch.'

Creep. I wondered whose idea it was to do the smoothing over, Wyatt's or Frodsham's.

DC Robert Blane stepped into the witness box. He was a witness called by the panel which meant he belonged to no-one. His evidence covered the careful police operation, interviewing the first witnesses, making appeals for more, taking statements, organising the videotaped memorandum interviews, dealing with the distress and despair. He had guided the case through the crown court, sat with my clients during the hearings, explained the procedures, kept them informed. This was a police officer who was on our side.

He wasn't at all how I expected. He was stocky and mean looking, his hair a centimetre long. He wore a navy sweat shirt with the name of a club (a rugby club the clients told me later) across his heart. He didn't have any time for the advocate to the inquiry. He answered her questions shortly and with no smiles. I had few questions for him. He answered them curtly. The clients had wanted me to say thank you to him and I did. He nodded his head in acknowledgement.

Mr Frodsham stood up, smiling, asking him easy questions; how old he was (thirty-four), how long he'd been a police officer (fourteen years), if he was local (yes); getting friendly, getting intimate. DC Blane didn't smile. Always worked in the field of child protection? No, he'd done his time in other squads. So what did that include, traffic? DC Blane frowned. No, not traffic. Frodsham shuffled his papers as if he'd been led to believe something different. Not motorway duties? Highway patrol? No.

Traffic duty was seen as very low down the police hierarchy, even if you called it highway patrol. Frodsham wanted to discredit DC Blane. I wondered why. Frodsham drew breath to turn to another subject but DC Blane said that he had in his time investigated bank robberies, drug trafficking, and violent crime, not to mention serious public-order offences. Frodsham drew another breath, anxious to move on, but DC Blane continued.

'I work on this team because it was getting a raw deal in terms of police time and management. . . .I think I can say that it was down to me that we got any prosecutions at all.' There was a smattering of applause from my clients.

Frodsham scowled, looking at his notes. 'Making the best of a bad job, very commendable. However, being moved to this area of work was something of a demotion was it not?' He was hinting at the possibility of DC Blane having been punished for bad behaviour.

'No. I chose to come to this team. I asked to come to this team.'

'Oh so you were looking for some sort of fulfillment?' Frodsham was changing tack, trying to infer now that Blane was some sort of do-gooder. Blane remained silent. 'This was all your own work, was it? Your personal project?' Now he was implying he was suffering from an excess of ego.

'No, I had a good team, who worked long hours and put up with a lot of . . .' He looked round at the panel. 'I don't think I should use the word here. Nonsense. From your client particularly.'

Suddenly the room was still, no coughing, no surreptitious sweet wrappers crackling.

Frodsham hesitated, he didn't know whether to ignore Blane's comment or explore it. He chose to ignore it, wrapped his jacket round him and prepared to sit down, saying, 'Thank you.'

'He was obstructive and unpleasant,' said Blane. 'Actively unhelpful.'

Frodsham straightened. 'Do you know about these people?' he asked, with a sweep of his hand. I noticed I was included. 'Do you know where they come from?'

'Yes,' Blane said, 'I read some of their social services files. I had to, as part of the investigation.'

'Then you know what my client was dealing with.'

'Yes.'

'My client had a very difficult job to do.'

'The children were under his care when they were abused. I was investigating that abuse. He made my job even more difficult. He wouldn't get off his backside and help, he wouldn't return calls, he wouldn't share information.'

'That's preposterous!' Frodsham spluttered, as his client tugged on his sleeve.

'Yes, I thought so too.' Blane's expression was impassive.

I wondered if it was true.

Frodsham looked at the panel. They gazed back at him. 'My client is a very busy man. The police investigation, some eighteen years after the events complained of, came like a bolt from the blue. Everyone was in a state of shock and anxiety. The police investigation cannot have a bearing on the issues this inquiry is dealing with.' He looked round wildly. 'Therefore I will finish my cross-examination.'

'That's a matter for you, Mr Frodsham.' Henry Curston paused. 'But the panel will be considering all aspects of this case which appear pertinent. Police investigations are an important part of the story insofar as perpetrators often manage to cover their tracks because they consider, often rightly, that their victims will not be believed.'

'Quite clearly the victims here were believed,' Frodsham said with relief. 'And therefore my cross-examination is at an end.'

Curston paused. 'So be it. We will adjourn until ten thirty tomorrow.'

Julie and I spent the evening on our hands and knees painting slogans on large sheets of paper and sticking them onto card. Several said 'What's the world worth to you?'

'That's because the demo is being organised by Worldsworth,' Marnie said. She was wearing the wig again, to get used to it, and therefore could do very little painting herself. 'I'll do the music,' she said and put on a Bob Dylan CD while we painted, to keep us in the mood.

'That one's for Shona's little sister, she's three,' she said, watching me paint. It read, 'Save the world for me.' 'Shona's going to put it on her buggy.'

We painted, 'Stop toxic waste.' 'The world is everyone's back garden. Don't dump your rubbish in my garden.' And 'Clean up the Acts.'

'That's for lawyers,' Marnie said. 'They're good aren't they?'

'They are good,' I said.

At half past ten, tired and paint-spattered, I had to do some work. In the next two days, several more expert witnesses were being interposed. One was an architect, there were field workers in child abuse called by the social workers, and a couple of academics talking about paedophilia, who had been called by the advocate to the inquiry. Wearily, I looked at their statements. What could they possibly say that was new or useful?

I flicked through the reports of two earlier inquiries, one was over ten years old. The stories printed there were almost identical, the issues the same: vulnerable children exploited by a tight ring of people in a position of power. Nothing had changed. What on earth did we hope to achieve with this inquiry? Except, on current showing, more pain and anguish for the victims. Perhaps my clients should simply each be paid a sum of money for what they suffered then. If the money the inquiry was costing was divided up, the fees of the lawyers, the costs of the experts, not to mention the cost of the administration, the panel and all the paper, they'd each get quite a nice sum. Would that be a worse way of dealing with it? Or perhaps someone could just say sorry. To acknowledge the fact that the system had failed them. But that wasn't going to happen.

I made some notes, prepared some questions. And then I went down to the kitchen for a cup of tea. Julie was in the middle room, reading the paper. We sat for a while talking about inquiries. Marnie was hoping to attend the environment inquiry the following week and Julie wondered if she'd be allowed in.

Half an hour later I climbed into bed, accompanied by the rough harmonies of Sam and Dave, singing

'Soothe Me'. That's what I needed. Someone to soothe me, before everything got out of hand.

But it was too late for that.

SIXTEEN

Wednesday – Inquiry

'Nice hair,' said Shelly, as I arrived. I had streaks of paint in my fringe.

The social work experts were troubled. Twenty years ago we didn't know so much, people were not so sensitive to the issue. Training had improved now and social workers had a better idea of what to look out for. I heard Shelly comment, 'About bloody time.'

The architect was interesting, in an architectural sense. Apparently the old home was a fine example of early Victorian architecture, from the period before things got too florid. It had been decided that 'the Inquiry' would go to see the building the following week. The clients were discussing amongst themselves whether they would be able to face that.

After the afternoon tea break, when the panel had come into the inquiry room and sat down, Reginald Frodsham remained on his feet. When everyone had noticed him and silence had fallen in the room, he hitched the waist band of his trousers. 'Sir, there is a matter of some seriousness which, with regret, I must raise now.'

We all listened eagerly, the one local journalist sat forward. This sounded interesting.

'Last week, sir, you will remember that Shelly Dean gave evidence and there was cross-examination by myself, to which Ms Richmond objected.' He emphasised the Ms. 'But you, sir, felt that there was no objection to be made.' He turned and looked at me. 'At the end of the day's evidence, sir, my client, Mr Wyatt, went to speak to Mrs Dean, whom he had known as a young child, to offer her support and friendship, and he happened to overhear a conversation between Mrs Dean and Ms Richmond.' He looked at me again. My heart began to race. This story was going to be about me.

I wondered what he was going to say, because any conversation between me and my clients was privileged, confidential. He couldn't report that.

'And Ms Richmond,' he said, quickly, 'punched the air and said with a laugh, "We got them that time."'

'Ms Richmond?' Henry Curston was looking at me expectantly, his face an oil slick of disdain.

'I'm sorry?' I said. I hadn't said those precise words, and in my attempt to seem upbeat, I hadn't actually punched the air, so much as performed a sort of shadow boxing right hook. Quickly I did a mental scan of the Bar Code of Conduct – there was nothing that I could recall specifically prohibiting punching the air and being pleased about making good points.

'What do you have to say about this?'

'Nothing,' I said.

'Are you sure?'

'Quite sure. What should I say? Whatever I say to my clients, in conference, is privileged and Mr Frodsham knows that. He wouldn't want me to say anything, I'm sure.'

A sheet of paper roughly torn and folded in two was

thrust into my hand by Adam. It had my name on and I recognised the handwriting. The advocate to the inquiry was sending me a note. I unfolded the paper. There was one word written on it. 'Apologise.'

I screwed it up and put it in my pocket. 'I think in asking me what I have to say, your target is misplaced,' I said. 'Mr Frodsham says this conference took place last week? If he really had the concerns he is now claiming to have, he could have raised it with me on Monday or yesterday, this morning, at lunch, over tea – out of courtesy, as one professional to another. But not in public, in open court. That, as he well knows, is outrageous and completely unprofessional behaviour.'

The room had fallen deadly silent. No-one moved. Everyone was listening with exquisite care to what I was saying. I didn't dare to look at the journalist to see if he was writing anything down.

'I don't quite know what he's trying to do,' I said, although I knew very well. He was trying to discredit me, with the panel and with my clients. And possibly, if the story was published, with the people of Birmingham. 'Perhaps we should get on with the hearing.'

I sank into my chair, my knees trembling. 'That was great,' Adam murmured, 'till you got to the last bit. I don't think Curston will appreciate being told to get on with things.'

I knew that. I was thinking, 'They're going to sack me. The clients will think I've been unprofessional. They didn't want me anyway, they're going to sack me.'

Henry Curston QC shuffled his papers. He coughed. He was playing for time. He didn't know what to do. He knew I was right about Frodsham, but he didn't want me to know that. 'Ms Richmond, I will see you and Mr Frodsham in my room at four fifteen. Let us continue.'

Another of my women clients walked over to the witness chair. Mechanically, I took her through her name and address, then Catherine Delahaye began to ask questions.

This was just great, Frodsham wanted to discredit me, I had offended the advocate to the inquiry by not taking her advice, and I had completely pissed off the chair. My clients were bound to sack me. They wanted heads to roll as a result of this inquiry and mine was the first, and currently the only, contender. So I would go to Henry Curston's room at four fifteen and tell him it was OK, Mr Frodsham's plan had succeeded and I was off the case.

We rose at four o'clock.

'I must have a fag,' Adam said.

'I'll just go and see the clients,' I said, relieved he wouldn't be there to see this. I was shaking.

The clients were squashed round the tables in our conference room, some were standing at the back. They were all there, except for Gregory Springer. As I walked in they fell quiet and looked at me.

'Look, before anyone says anything,' I said, putting up my hands, 'I just want to say, I'm sorry. And don't feel embarrassed if you want me to go.'

'Go where?' said Shelly. 'Frankie, we're gonna get nothing from this inquiry, they're all so desperate to cover their arses. If you can scare a bit of shit out of a few people, especially that Frodsham, then we're right behind you.'

'Yeah, and if Curston has a go at you when you go

and see him, just tell us and we'll come and sort him out,' Martin Williams said from the back, and everyone laughed.

Adam peered round the door his face wreathed in cigarette smoke. 'What have I missed?' he said, and walked in. He began laughing. 'Why are we laughing?' he asked me. I shook my head.

He said, 'Oh yes, one of the administrative team gave me this for you.' He held out a piece of yellow paper.

I'd had enough messages and surprises for one day. 'Tell me what it says,' I said.

'"Ring chambers urgently,"' he read.

'Is there a time on there?' I said.

'Three o'clock.'

It was twelve minutes past four. I told the clients that I would see them in the morning and Adam and I went back out into the corridor. 'Use my mobile,' Adam said, as we walked briskly towards Curston's room. This is what a good solicitor can do for you, have a mobile phone in which the battery never fades. He even called up chambers' number from the phone's memory bank, which impressed me, and pressed the green button. However, any urgency had not transmitted itself to the clerks' room. In fact, no-one had any memory of such a message being sent. But it took me approximately eight minutes and conversations with a pupil, two clerks, and a barrister, to make that clear. I made a mental note: raise issue of personnel in the clerks' room – who is answering the phones, who is ringing out of town members of chambers and why is everyone always eating biscuits when I ring?

If I hadn't been in such a state of high tension I might have spent some time finding out where the message had come from, but I didn't have time. I arrived at Curston's room at four twenty. I could hear Curston and Frodsham laughing as I tapped on the door.

'Come in!' Curston barked, and I slid into the room. No laughter now.

The room was bare except for a large table, covered with papers, and a small book case, filled with *Family Law* books and copies of previous inquiry reports. There were three seats, one a large comfortable leather chair, occupied by Curston, and two other basic chairs with cloth-covered seats, one covered by Frodsham.

Curston indicated the empty chair. I sat down. Curston leaned back in his seat and pursed his lips. I could see he was still in a dilemma. Frodsham was obviously an old crony of his, probably instructed him, when he had to, and gave him interesting briefs. But Frodsham was a solicitor. I may have been a woman, and a pain in the arse, but I was a barrister.

'You're late,' he said, casually.

'I had to speak to my clients to see what my professional position was before I came,' I said. 'And I had an urgent message to ring chambers.'

'And what is your professional position?' Curston asked. I could almost hear Frodsham licking his lips.

'My clients are happy with my conduct of the case. They are just a little confused as to why their representative should be singled out for such . . . treatment.' They weren't confused at all, they knew exactly why, but I felt there was a need for subtlety.

'You two have got to stop bickering,' Curston said. 'It's not going to help me or anyone else to make decisions about the issues in this case to have you two sniping at each other at every opportunity.'

I took a breath to explode that it wasn't me who started it.

'Miss Richmond, you should perhaps be more aware of the sensitivities of people other than your clients.'

'They don't pay me to do that, and I don't think, professionally, I can do that if it interferes with my view of the best way to run their case.'

'They're not paying you, anyway,' Frodsham murmured.

'Reg.' Curston turned to him. 'I think it would be better all round if we tried to concentrate on the issue in hand.'

'Henry, I have duties to my client too.'

'I'm not happy with the press coverage which has been emanating from some quarters.'

'Well, I haven't spoken to a journalist about this case in the time I've been here,' I said.

'I'm not pointing the finger at anyone,' he said. 'But it does the inquiry no good at all if it looks as if members of the legal profession are arguing with each other. Now, Reg, this do you're organising for tomorrow.'

I stood up. 'I'll just leave you, then.'

'Sit down,' Curston said. I sat down.

Frodsham looked puzzled. 'The Law Society's dinner dance, you mean?'

'Are there still tickets available?'

Frodsham began to look scared. As for me, I felt my life blood ebbing away.

'I'm not sure.'

There was a sound of heavy breathing. Either Frodsham or I began to hyperventilate. No, it was both of us, concerned at what was coming. Curston wanted me and Frodsham to go to a dinner dance together. Perhaps it would have been best if my clients had sacked me. I began to think of alternative careers.

'Enough for all the legal representatives?' Curston went on. 'And possibly wives too. Or husbands.' He looked at me. 'If you want to.' I gazed at him in amazement. 'I think it would be a good PR exercise,' he continued, 'if all the parties' representatives were to attend your dinner dance.'

A dinner dance. Me? Can you imagine? 'I have nothing to wear,' I began weakly.

'Miss Richmond, I am told that there are some of the finest dress shops in the country in Birmingham.' I wondered if he knew what my requirements might be. 'I am sure that this case would pay for something appropriate. Don't look so worried, Miss Richmond, Birmingham solicitors don't bite.'

'I'm sure they don't,' I said, 'even if they want to. But you see, unfortunately, I have another appointment tomorrow evening, in London.'

'Cancel it. So, Reg, are there sufficient tickets left? Say twenty, twenty-five?'

Now that he knew he was not being required to take the floor for a paso doble with me, Frodsham's entrepreneurial spirit began to take over. 'I'm sure we can find sufficient.'

'How much does this cost?' I asked.

'Fifty-five pounds,' Frodsham said with satisfaction. 'Each.'

This is how clever judges keep control in their courtrooms. They make you buy new clothes and go out in the evening to pleasant social events. Bastards.

SEVENTEEN

Wednesday Evening

I went down to my phone booth in the basement. I balanced my papers precariously on the narrow ledge and rang Julie's house.

Marnie answered the phone. I asked her if her mother had any fancy trouser suits, because if she didn't I was going to have to buy something fast.

'Mum hasn't got anything fancy. Why?'

I told her about the social life which was being imposed on me.

Marnie drew in an excited breath. 'Oh can I go, oh can I? You honestly are the best almost aunt that I've got. And you've got really good dress sense, and . . . I love your hair.'

'There won't be any boys there,' I said.

'But there will be rich, famous people, won't there?'

'Ish.' Two cleaners were advancing towards me, lugging industrial-sized vacuum cleaners. 'It isn't really appropriate for you to come.'

'How am I going to meet important people if my own relatives won't help me out?'

'You could try doing your school work, which would mean you'd get a good job and then meet them on your own account, as equals.'

'But it's no fun if you're equal,' Marnie complained.

'Fun doesn't always come into it. Where do you get these ideas?' I said. The droning of dedicated cleaning was making it hard to hear. 'Anyway, your mum might have something to say about it.'

'She won't,' Marnie said. 'Wouldn't I be the perfect cover for you? You wouldn't have to find some boring man to accompany you, and you could go with a woman, because, and this is the best part, I'm a relative, not a lesbian.'

'I'm not sure that is the best part,' I shouted, as they unexpectedly stopped cleaning. 'But look, it won't be interesting at all. You won't enjoy it, and anyway, I've got a boring man to accompany me. Adam, my solicitor, is coming. And I'm only staying for about half an hour.'

'Oh go on, let me come, please. Please.'

The cleaners started vacuuming again, in the cubicles next to mine. The noise was unbearable.

'No.'

It was quite late, half past five, as I walked through the Cathedral Yard towards the bus stop. It had rained during the afternoon and the air was fresh in the early evening light. I'd been into Rackham's to buy something to wear but I wasn't in the mood and instead I'd drifted into the food hall and bought six figs and some very blue cheese, which I was picking at as I walked along.

Perched on a gargoyle on the wall of the cathedral, a blackbird was singing. It made me think of an old seventy-eight my mum had when I was small. She'd bought an old wind-up record player from a jumble sale, with a box of needles and a job lot of shellac discs, most of which she wouldn't let me touch because they were early Elvis Presley and Jerry Lee Lewis, but I was allowed to play 'In a Monastery Garden' as much as I wanted. Which I did. That then inevitably led on to me listening to Fontella Bass singing 'As Soon As He Touched Me' and the Edwin Hawkins Singers singing 'Oh Happy Day'. It was my spiritual period. It lasted about six months. But the music was still good.

'Hello!' It was Roseanna. She had obviously been walking towards me, smiling at me for some time.

'Sorry,' I said, brushing crumbs of Roquefort from my face. 'I was in a monastery garden.'

'Sounds interesting. Room for another one?'

'Come on in,' I said. 'Bad day?'

She grimaced.

'How's the corpseless murder going?'

'Have you got time for a drink?' she asked. 'It would be nice to talk to someone friendly.' In unison we adjusted our work bags. Roseanna's was a neat suitcase on wheels. 'There's a Bar just behind the Cathedral.'

I scrunched the cheese into its Rackham's bag and tucked it away. As we walked past the flat moss-covered grave stones, I asked, 'It's not Simon, is it? Has he been giving you a hard time?' Whatever his feelings on a personal level, in court he had no mercy. 'I could speak to him.'

'Oh, no, Simon's been lovely. He's about the only nice thing in the case.'

'Really?' I said. 'I'll tell him that.'

'Don't, he'll think he's got an advantage. You know we're running a cut throat. Well, we were.' A cut throat is where the defendants blame each other for the offence. 'Danny Richards isn't doing very much at all. What would you like to drink?'

I sat at a wooden table by an open French window while Roseanna ordered two gin and tonics. She was wearing a slick black suit with a mandarin collar and black and gold buttons. And I noticed, as I dragged my bag in under my seat and she neatly propped her case against the wall, that she was wearing black patent shoes with gold bits round the heel. When I became a barrister I made a pact – with myself, although some might think it was with the devil – that I would never wear any item of clothing that combined black and gold, in particular I would never wear black patent shoes with gold bits round the heel. But Roseanna could carry it off. Her thick black hair and bright red lipstick put the combination in a different league. I, of course, would never wear the lipstick.

'So how's it going?' I asked her as she put the drinks on the table.

'You did the pleas and directions hearing, you saw the papers, didn't you?'

'About three of them.'

'Oh yes.' She smiled at the memory. 'Well, my case should be simple. The evidence against Catcher, my client, is very thin, even weaker than the case against Danny. Catcher used to work with Terry Fleming occasionally, then about a year ago there was some trouble over a gambling debt and a few phone calls to Danny Richards round about the time Danny got out of prison. Oh, and Danny just happened to mention Catcher's name to the police when he was picked up.' I frowned at her. 'Oh yes, just a hint. The mere mention of his name. That's why Catcher was arrested in the first place. But Catcher's really just there to cover all bases.'

'How do the prosecution get away with that?'

'They shouldn't really, but as I said, the judge isn't very bright and the prosecution want this conviction rather badly. The word is that Ewan's applying for silk, so bagging a Birmingham hard man would be very useful. And your Danny fits the bill.'

'Not mine, Simon's.'

'Yes, sorry.'

'And I think Ewan is hoping that if he stirs up enough dirt, some of it will stick, even to Catcher. With any other judge I would be guaranteed to get out on a submission of no case at half-time, but with Norman I can't tell, and on top of that, Catcher's mucking around in the dock, pretending he can't bear to sit next to your client. The judge is really irritated with him.'

'So the problem isn't Simon?'

'Oh no, not at all. Simon is in quite a difficult position. I think Danny's previous convictions may go in. And that's probably my fault.'

Just as Danny had said. I added more tonic to my glass. 'You have to do your job. But we probably shouldn't talk about this.'

'Yes, you're right, sorry. I'm not trying to make you breach your client's . . .'

'Simon's.'

'Yes. . . .confidence. I suppose I'm just impressed that Simon is doing as well as he is on the material he's got.' She fished the olive out of her drink. 'He really is a lovely man, isn't he?'

'Yes, he's a good friend. I like him a lot.'

'Oh.' She put her glass to her lips, thoughtfully. 'Do you see much of him?'

'Me? I hardly ever see him.'

'Is he a social being?'

'Oh yes.' What was I saying? Simon had no social life at all. But I didn't want to make him sound pathetic – they were almost running a cut throat. 'Simon's a very nice guy,' I said enthusiastically. This could be Simon's big romantic break. And they were only two days into the trial! But starting a relationship whilst co-defending was a bit tricky. What would the clients think? Fortunately this was not my problem. 'Nice guy,' I repeated.

A smile tripped across the scarlet lips. 'Mmm. And how is your inquiry?'

I thought about the scenes of the last few days, Gregory Springer weeping, his wife's quiet fury, DC Blane's evidence, Frodsham denouncing me in front of the press, the clients in our room, laughing about him. 'Not as bad as it could be. Do you know Reginald Frodsham?'

'Oh, Reg. Don't tell me, he's giving you a hard time.'

I nodded miserably.

'That usually means you're doing a good job. He's a pain and everybody knows it. He hates all barristers. He hardly ever instructs counsel, he does almost all of his own advocacy.' So it wasn't just me. 'So it's not just you.'

That was something.

She gazed reflectively into her glass. 'I'm not sure why he's doing the inquiry at all, he's a criminal solicitor really. But I suppose he had a lot of time on his hands after he was sacked from this case.'

'Your case? By Catcher?'

'Oh, no. By your Danny Richards.'

'Danny?'

'Some people are asking the question, was he sacked or did he have to retire for professional reasons?' A common reason a solicitor withdraws from a case is because he is 'embarrassed', which usually means the client has told him something that makes the lawyer's position untenable, in a criminal case that usually means he has told the lawyer he did it.

I was still grappling with the unpleasant coincidence that connected me with Frodsham. 'Perhaps that's why he hates me,' I said. 'He heard I was part of Danny's new team.'

'It's possible, but he probably just hates you because you're against him.'

'Don't let's talk about him, it's too depressing,' I said. 'The other representatives are friendlier.' Today two of them had said hello quite cordially. 'And Adam Owen, my instructing solicitor, is a nice guy.'

'From PPR? Yes, he's sent me one or two good briefs. So it's not all bad then? Admit it, you're secretly pleased His Honour Judge Norman didn't get his wish that you should stay and represent Danny Richards.'

'Put like that, I suppose on a very fine balance, I'd rather be at the Grange and not spending the next three weeks in Court 7 with Judge Norman.'

We drained our glasses. 'You've got my card, haven't you?' she said, as we stood up and I hauled my bag up onto my shoulder and she elegantly tipped her suitcase and drew out the long handle. 'Let's go out for a proper drink one evening.'

'Some time next week? Perhaps we could all go, you, me and Simon. For a meal maybe,' I said.

Her eyes lit up. 'That would be nice.'

'Shall I ask him?' I said, with an attempt at tact.

'Yes, do. Please.' She'd gone a little pink.

'Do you like Chinese food?'

'I love it.'

They were as good as married.

I hummed 'Da Doo Ron Ron' all the way home.

Back at Julie's the atmosphere was tense and supper was a stiff affair. Marnie wasn't interested in discussing what I might wear to the dinner dance, since it was obvious from the people who were invited that it was going to be a really boring evening, and as soon as she had finished her fish and chips, she pushed back her plate, put on her denim jacket and announced that she was going round to Shona's.

'Do you want a lift?' I offered.

'No,' she said and slammed the door.

Guilt gnawed at me, like indigestion. The Family Vortex was sucking me in. Or perhaps it was indigestion.

EIGHTEEN

Thursday

I was still pessimistic about what we were doing at the inquiry. When the second academic, smiling smugly, described how impossible it is to identify men with paedophilic instincts, I wanted to shake him. 'So what can we do?' I asked.

'There are tests,' he said, 'but they are not fool proof.'

'Fool proof is what we want, isn't it?' I asked. 'To protect the weak and vulnerable.'

'Very much so.'

Without instructions from the clients, I made a suggestion. 'If you can't identify who is a paedophile, but we know from the research that it is predominantly men who abuse children, perhaps we should simply stop men working with children at all.'

A ripple of shock ran around the room. Frodsham lumbered to his feet and spread his hands in despair; I could not be allowed to continue with this line of argument, this was not serious. The advocate to the inquiry suggested this was far too wide an issue. The other lawyers expressed their disquiet. Curston looked at me.

I stood up. 'If we are serious about ways to protect children, then surely we must consider this,' I said simply.

Henry Curston didn't think twice. He made a ruling. I had asked the question, there had been an answer – a firm negative – I was to pursue that line of enquiry no further.

At the end of the morning, in our room, I asked the clients if they wanted me to judicially review Curston's decision, to appeal against his ruling, but, looking at each other, they said they didn't want to prolong the agony. They weren't sure that they wanted to stop men working with children. Shelly said she'd never thought of it like that, and in fact she'd like think about it a bit more before she decided.

She came up to me as the others were drifting out of the room. 'Would it do any good?' she asked.

'Judicial Review? It might get a bit more publicity for the inquiry. It would raise the issue, people would talk about it a bit.'

'Would we win?'

'Probably not.'

'Would that matter?'

'Might make Frodsham even more cocky than he already is.'

At three fifteen Henry Curston announced that we would resume sitting at ten thirty tomorrow morning. He gave us all a roguish grin, which meant but some of you I will see tonight.

I had two hours to buy an outfit. As we walked down the stairs I asked Adam what colour bow tie he would be wearing and whether we should go for a team look, or produce a more dramatic effect by wearing contrasting colours, or should it just be different shades? I was getting hysterical. I wasn't even planning on wearing a bow tie, and I certainly didn't want it to look as if Adam and I were a couple. The thought of the gossip was . . .

'Actually –' Adam began, mournfully.

'Adam,' I said, 'let me stop you right there. If you are about to say what I think you are about to say, that you are not coming tonight, there will have to be small but intense amounts of violence directed at pivotal points of your body.' I drew breath. He said nothing. 'Which could destroy any hope you might have of a fulfilling social life in the future.' He was silent. 'Do I make myself clear?'

'I'm sorry, Frankie,' he said. 'But I can't come. My senior partners have vetoed it.'

'How did you manage that?' I asked. 'I didn't know we could ask our senior work colleagues to make excuses for us. I would have asked Tony to write me a note.'

'I've got to go in to the office and work. Believe me, I'd rather be out on the town tonight, than stuck behind my PC.'

'Little liar.'

He looked at me blankly.

Perhaps I was using the wrong approach. I changed tack. 'I could help you with your work,' I said. 'I could come to your office, after I've bought my outfit, I could get a cab – it's not far is it? – and we could do the work together in half the time and then go on to the dance. Or better still, I could become you for the evening and do the work, and you could be me and go to the dance. You'd look great, I'm sure. If you brushed your hair over to the side.'

'I'd love to,' he said. 'All of it, any of it. But our senior partner, Mr Rutland, is going. And they wouldn't pay for me.'

'I'd pay for you!'

'I can't come. I could get Mr Rutland to dance with you.'

'Adam, not another word. It's altogether too depressing.'

I rang Gavin. 'Have I got any messages?'

Of course I hadn't. This is what happens when you leave London, people forget you. Perfect. No life in London. No one giving a second thought to me in Birmingham, not even anyone to accompany me to a delightful dinner dance, to execute a swift pas de deux across the floor.

'I see from the timetable you're not sitting on Monday,' Gavin said.

'No,' I said, guardedly.

'Could you do a quick piece of paperwork for Craling and Co?'

'How quick?'

'The solicitor said she only needs a few paragraphs, for the Legal Aid Board. Look, it'll pay you £200, no problem. And how long can it take? A couple of hours at the most.' Which shows how little he knows.

'But I've got that other advice to finish,' I said. He was silent. I looked down at my jacket. The cuffs were fraying in what I realised was an embarrassingly obvious way. 'OK, I'll do it.'

I stomped across various roads to Rackhams and bought a satisfactory outfit. And as I crossed the cathedral yard I reflected that at least it wasn't raining. The blackbird was even sitting on the gargoyle, singing. And there was no queue at the bus stop, and a number 61 was just pulling up. So, OK, it was all right. Just about.

As I got into the house, I called, 'Marnie?'

'What?' she said sulkily, appearing from the kitchen with a slice of bread and peanut butter in her hand.

'What are you doing tonight?'

'Noth . . .' Her eyes widened. 'Really? Can I? Oh Frankie!' She laughed, delightedly.

NINETEEN

Thursday Dinner – Dance

Marnie was ready at half past six, before I had even got in the shower. As I picked up my car keys at seven forty-five, and was throwing a final look at my reflection in the mirror by the front door, she decided she didn't like her hair.

'Oh Marnie,' Julie complained, but it didn't bother me what time we arrived. She came downstairs at ten past eight.

Julie and I sighed with admiration. Marnie was wearing a pale mauve silky dress with thin straps and scarcely any back. It swirled out at the hem, just below her knees. Her sandals were high and made my feet feel cold. She looked lovely. We told her.

'You look nice too,' she said to me, kindly. My suit was black and crepe. I had even bought a new pair of shoes – Hobbs, black and shiny. What they used to call loafers but clumpier, so now you couldn't so much loaf as engage in a weightlifting exercise every time you took a step.

Marnie was shrugging away Julie's hand as she tried to tidy a stray lock of hair, while I thought about the line of the jacket and whether I needed to carry any money. I asked myself again, for the millionth time, why women's jackets don't have pockets. Perhaps someone should start a campaign on *Woman's Hour*, I thought, but in the interim I gave forty pounds to Marnie to put in her small round satin bag and guard with her life. She fingered the notes lovingly and I regretted my action. In the lobby of the large Victorian building, which tonight welcomed the finest legal minds in the East and West Midlands, I pulled off my mac and helped Marnie with her short black coat. I took the ticket from the cloakroom assistant and we walked up the enormous staircase to the first floor. Marnie gazed around her at the large paintings of established lawyers. 'Why do people paint old people?' she asked. 'They're so boring.'

'That's ageism, Marnie,' I said.

She looked at me haughtily and probably would have said something cutting but we had just reached the main hall and as we stopped on the threshold were both stunned by the sight. It was a large room with a rich, polished wooden floor, the lights were blazing, a small band was playing a Beatles number and people in shiny dresses and dark suits were dancing.

'That's the kind of lampshade I want in my room,' said Marnie.

'That's a chandelier,' I said.

'Yeah, that's what I want.'

We moved into the room and, hanging closely to the wall to avoid the dancers and the tables that surrounded the dance floor, made our way to an empty spot, halfway between the band at one end and the Bar at the other. Marnie was giving me a running commentary on the dresses on the dance floor. 'I know where she got that skirt. She must have bought it last year, no one's wearing those now.' I was looking to see if there was anyone

I knew. There was no one, and I was glad that Marnie was with me. 'Look at those shoes. I was going to buy some of those but I'm glad I didn't now, that colour's dread.'

I nodded and smiled, still gazing round the room, praying that Curston would arrive soon to see that I had done my duty, and wondering how soon after that we could reasonably leave.

And then I saw Clark. What on earth was he doing here? The last time I'd seen him, in his blue and orange leisure outfit, I hadn't got the impression that he was a solicitor. Although, of course, neither were we. But I didn't think he was a barrister. Although that was possibly a conclusion born of snobbery. Perhaps, like Marnie, he had come with a relative.

The music stopped and people were drifting off the dance floor. Marnie turned to me. 'Who are you looking at?'

'The small bloke in that strange purple suit, over there.'

'Standing near that friend of yours?'

'I can't see, what friend of mine?' I said, but then he moved and I could. Clark was lounging against the wall, looking at Frodsham.

Frodsham was sitting at a table on the opposite side of the room. His size was exaggerated by the tight, formal suit he was wearing. His face was very red. Sitting at the table with him were the two male solicitors from the inquiry, also looking uneasy in their smart outfits. Frodsham was staring round the room. Occasionally he twisted his head, his neck straining against the stiff collar. Clark was about three feet from the table, standing under a large painting of another man with a red face, wearing a tight waistcoat and jacket. Clark's eyes moved round the room too, flicking from Frodsham's table, to the door, to the bandstand, and across the dance floor. And rested on mine. He eased himself off the wall, nodding in our direction, as if he had just seen some very important people. Frodsham gave no indication of being aware of his departure.

In a series of iridescent purple movements, Clark manoeuvred his way round the dance floor towards Marnie and me. I was so fascinated by his bobbing and squeezing motion, like someone weaving between tables to get to the stage to collect an Oscar, that I only half noticed a slight woman in a long turquoise sheath appear from the crowd and slide into a seat next to Frodsham. But I noticed Frodsham's demeanour slip from high tension to relaxed affability.

'Well, well, well,' said Clark.

I nodded. No one spoke. I wondered if he was wearing the orange vest under the tight pink shirt. He was jingling keys in his pocket, his eyes darting round the room. I wondered if he was looking for the same things from this side of the room as he had been from the other side.

'What are you doing here?' I asked. I thought he might say, 'I'm here with a friend,' or 'I'm a driver for Mr Big over there,' although as I discovered later, he was hardly likely to say that. Or even 'I'm thinking of doing a law degree and wanted to see exactly who I might be mixing with if I ever get that far.'

As it was, his answer seemed ominously vague. 'Oh, this and that.'

My eyes narrowed as he turned to Marnie and said, 'And this is . . . ?'

'Marnie,' she said.

'She is my fifteen-year-old niece,' I enunciated clearly. 'We are just about to go to the Bar for a drink.'

'But . . .' Marnie began. She looked at Clark helplessly.

'I'm Clark,' he said, softly, 'and I wonder if I might have the pleasure of this dance.' As he said it, I saw him through the eyes of an excited fifteen-year-old, determined to have a good time. He was the youngest-looking man we had seen since we arrived, and the suit had a curious, edgy fashion note to it. He smelled nice, something sharp and clean and not too heavy, and he was smiling at her, with those grey eyes and that little dimple. He was charming.

And Marnie was charmed. She switched on her wonderful, bright-eyed smile. 'I'd like a Coke, please,' she said and handed me one of my twenty-pound notes.

'Isn't that a friend of yours?' Clark said.

At that moment the combo of electric guitar and organ struck up an unlikely rendition of 'Nights in White Satin', while a crooner in a sparkling jacket began to whisper the words, and with surprising smoothness, Marnie and Clark moved together onto the floor.

I turned and there was Curston, standing at the entrance to the ballroom, looking anxious, as if intimidated by the lights and the perfume and the powder on the faces of the women. He hesitated and then set out in the direction of the bar.

This is another thing I hate. In post, they frighten the life out of you; then you see them away from the majesty of office (even if that majesty consists of a large municipal room with trestle tables covered with material more suited to a whist drive than the judicial process) and they are just little old men, whose hands tremble as they hold a glass. And I go all anxious and caring. Where did I get that from? Or is it a trick they learn at their public schools? In character, tough, fearless, ruthless; out of character, trembling and tragic. Either way, they've got us working-class kids taped. Or is it a woman thing? Or is it just me?

I told myself I was going over to say hello, to make a semblance of politeness and so that he knew I was there, but I knew I was really going in case he had a heart attack before he'd paid for his drink, or at least in case no one spoke to him, and he felt sad and all alone.

I tried to shadow the progress of the odd couple on the dance floor as I made my way to the bar. They were gliding easily around the room, chatting and laughing as if this was their natural habitat and dancing their natural means of progress. Clark looked relaxed and in control. I could see the dimple in his cheek flashing, and his eyes smiling down at her. I wondered how Clark had known Curston. Perhaps Curston had represented him in the past. But how would Clark know that I knew Curston?

Of course, by the time I got to Curston, it was clear that my concern for him had all been for nothing. He was standing with a group of chums. Together they all had the same aspect, sleek, well-fed, and satisfied. So now I had nothing to do there, nothing to say, and certainly not enough money to buy them all a drink. 'Hello,' I said, feeling my head tilt to one side.

'Frances!' he said. Oh God, first names, what was his? Henry? Arnold? Killer?

'Yes,' I said, with a wide smile, lifting my hands a little.

He introduced me to the men he was talking to, they were all judges or silks. We nodded at each other. 'Frances is fighting the good fight on behalf of the victims in my inquiry,' Curston said.

'Ah,' said one of the men, with a whisper of a smile.

There was a pause while I nodded like the dog in the back window of a car. 'Well,' I said, twisting my head to indicate the nirvana to which I was anxious to return. Curston nodded kindly and I was released.

'A double whisky and a Coke in a separate glass,' I breathed at the barman, and crushed the twenty-pound note into his hand.

As I was edging my way back through the crowd, the music stopped and I swivelled round to check on Clark and Marnie. They were standing waiting, looking at the band, Clark's arm resting lightly on Marnie's waist. As the mournful organ notes of 'Whiter Shade of Pale' shuddered through the room they slid easily back into each other's arms and, in time with the singer's smiling voice, skipped the light fandango across the floor.

I watched the dance floor. It was crowded now with uncomfortable-looking professionals and their partners trying seriously to enjoy themselves. Marnie and Clark floated past, and Marnie gave me a happy wave. And then a couple I thought I recognised, thin and uncomfortable, out of place, the woman with a sheen of sweat across her face. It was Mr and Mrs Springer. Mentally I checked through my papers, had I missed something? Was Mr Springer a member of the legal gang? Lena loomed into my mind, asking '*Mr* Springer? What about Mrs?' I knew very little about Mrs Springer, except that she always wore a sheepskin coat. But not tonight of course, I realised, which was why I hadn't recognised them at first. Tonight she was wearing a long-sleeved, raspberry-coloured dress. I knew she was someone's secretary, perhaps someone in the legal department. No, with her personality, she would have let me know that by now. So why were they here? Whose guests were they?

I was gazing at them so hard I scarcely noticed Frodsham, dancing past me with the woman in the turquoise sheath, moving together, smoothly in step. But as he spun her round with a professional flourish I found myself face to face with Yolande.

She nodded gravely and was twirled away.

I didn't know where to look. On the dance floor to keep an eye on Marnie, at the bar where the Springers were now waiting to be served, or over to the table where Frodsham and Yolande had rejoined their companions, Yolande flapping her hand in front of her face, laughing, commenting. As she sat down, directly across the room from where I stood, she lifted her face and I met her mocking gaze.

I didn't want to see any more of it. I'd been seen by the person who mattered. I wanted out. And I could see the flash of a camera. They were starting to take pictures. No, no. That was not going to happen. There was bound to be a notice board at the bottom of the steps where they would stick up the photo of you with your eyes closed, looking flushed and dishevelled, and you would find yourself handing over £15 to pay for it, so that nobody else saw it. I gulped my drink and took a mouthful of Marnie's Coke. As the music ended I walked onto the dance floor and said to Marnie, 'We have to go now.'

'But it's early. I haven't had a drink.'

'I have to be up in the morning.'

She turned to Clark. 'Have you got a car? Can you take me home?'

Before he could answer, I said calmly, 'We have to go. It's eleven o'clock.'

'Bye, sweetheart,' he said, his purple suit rippling with emotion. He stroked the side of her face with his finger.

'Bye,' she whispered.

As we got in the phone was ringing. Marnie quivered. She snatched up the receiver and said breathlessly, 'Hello?' Her face fell. 'It's for you.' She passed me the phone. 'I'm going to bed.'

I put my hand over the receiver. 'Did you have a nice time?' I asked her.

'Yes,' she said. 'Yes, I did. Thanks.'

It was Yolande. I waited for her to begin.

Eventually she said, 'I told you who he was.'

'No you didn't, because that I would have remembered.'

'I asked you if you knew him.'

'Yes, but you didn't say who he was.'

'Well that's him, Reg Frodsham. That's my husband.'

Terrific. Now it was me who was in the middle of a cut throat.

'So, is that how you knew this phone number?'

She laughed softly. 'I'm sorry if it was a surprise.'

'But he was Danny's ex-solicitor. Does he know about you and Danny?' My stomach lurched. 'Does he know about you and me?' An image rose up in my mind – me challenging Frodsham at the inquiry, and him slowly turning round to look at me in mock surprise and saying quietly, 'And what about my wife?' What would I do, what would I say? This was terrible. I would deny all knowledge. I wondered if I could wear Marnie's wig from now on. I would change my name. In fact, I could just become the other Francis Richmond.

'Calm down,' she said, although I hadn't said anything. 'He doesn't know anything about you. There's nothing to know, is there?'

'Oh.' I didn't know if that was worse. 'All right.'

'Emm.' She hesitated. 'The key?'

The key! And she was Reg Frodsham's wife! How dare she? I wanted to slam down the phone. 'I'll do it this weekend,' I said.

'You are very sweet,' she murmured.

'What's the number of the locker? Clark said it was 127 or 63.'

'Oh, I . . . I don't know. . . .I don't remember. Whatever he said. And . . . could you get them developed?' Her voice sank to a whisper. 'I am very, very grateful. Thank you. Thank you. I will see you soon. I'll make it up to you.'

A shiver ran down my spine.

I trudged upstairs to bed, past the bathroom where Marnie was obviously going to stay for another half an hour, and into my hot, empty room. I knew I was a fool. I was hooked on a woman who had got me caught up in something to save the man she loved. I'd been too long in the wind and too long in the rain, like the woman in the song that Millie Jackson carved out with her honey voice, and I was taking any comfort that I could. But what I really needed was some loving arms of my own to lie in. Or perhaps I just needed to get back to London.

The phone began ringing as I reached my room. I heard the bathroom door fly open and Marnie ran down the stairs.

Against my better judgment I prayed that the call would be for her. There was a pause and then her resigned voice snaked up the stairwell. 'It's for you.'

What did she want now? To whisper some more meaningless sweet nothings? Breathe in my ear to make me go anywhere? I walked down the gloomy staircase and picked up the phone. 'Yes?'

'Frankie?' It was Adam.

'My goodness, Adam, where are you?'

'I'm at the office.'

'You can go home now, I didn't mean to punish you this much.'

'Thank you, no, I. . . .' His voice was tight and thin.

'What is it?'

'Something's happened.'

'What?'

'Something terrible.'

'What, Adam, what?'

'Gregory and Mrs Springer have been in an accident.'

'Oh no. How . . . ?'

'Gregory's dead.'

I shook my head. 'What?! I just saw them, they were at this thing tonight. They were dancing.'

'It happened about half an hour ago.'

'How do you know?'

'The police rang. They found my card in Mrs Springer's bag. She's in a bad way, she hasn't regained consciousness. They've asked me to go and identify the body. Apparently they don't have any family.'

'Oh, Adam. Do you want me to come with you?'

191

'It's OK, I'm not going till the morning. I – I suppose I just wanted to tell someone who knew them.'

'What are you going to do now?'

'I'd just booked a cab to take me home when they rang. I think it's here now.'

I knew there were questions I should ask him but I couldn't think what they were. 'Ring me if you change your mind about wanting someone to come with you to identify the body,' I said.

Carefully I replaced the receiver and walked slowly up the stairs. The bathroom was empty. I tapped on Marnie's bedroom door. 'Are you OK?' I whispered.

'Mm,' she moaned, half asleep.

I put my head into Julie's room. I could see her shape under the sheet, breathing regularly. Everyone in the house was safe. I climbed up to my room.

TWENTY

Friday – Back to London

I carried my bags down into the middle room. I was driving straight back to London after today's hearing.

'I hear there was someone fantastic at the do last night,' Julie said, as I tipped Shreddies into a bowl.

I frowned.

'Someone who danced with Marnie?'

The dance seemed a very long time ago. 'Fantastic is . . . one word,' I said carefully. 'It's a bloke I met recently. He's a friend of a friend.'

'How can you eat those without sugar?' Marnie asked.

'Easy,' I said, 'watch.'

'So is he a solicitor?' Julie asked.

'I don't think so,' I said.

'Solicitors aren't any good, are they?' Marnie said, scornfully. 'Yours stood you up, didn't he? I don't think I could bear to have a relationship with someone who stood me up, or who was always late or something, who was never there when I needed him.'

'I'm not having a relationship with Adam,' I said wearily.

'Sometimes I think I should write down the traits you say you can't bear in people,' Julie said to Marnie, 'and when you're standing in church and the vicar says, "Is there any reason why these two cannot be joined in matrimony?" I could call out, "I've got a list here, I'll do it in alphabetical order: A – Always late, B – Bites his nails, C – Can't tell orange juice from Sunny Delight."'

'If you do, I shall never speak to you again,' Marnie said. 'Anyway, you're not coming to my wedding.'

'That's a relief,' Julie said.

'But Frankie can come. You'll give me away, won't you Frankie?' Marnie draped her arm round my shoulder.

'I'd feel I was not so much giving you away as throwing you to the lions,' I said.

'Why are feminists such spoil sports?' Marnie complained.

'Who took you to the dance last night?' I said.

'Huh.'

Julie looked at her watch. 'You've got five minutes, Marnie.' Marnie fled upstairs. 'Are you OK?' she asked me. 'You seem a bit distracted. You've left half your Shreddies.'

I told her about the Springers' accident.

'That's terrible. How did it happen?'

'I'm not exactly sure. I'm going to ring Adam's office now.'

It was half past eight and his weary tone made me think he'd been there for hours. 'There's a question about whether or not it was an accident.' It was something about the car, they thought it might have been tampered with. 'But that was just an initial comment,' Adam said, 'and I think they only said it to me because I'm a solicitor.' The accident had happened on Bristol Road, a clear stretch of road with good lighting. Preliminary tests indicated that neither Gregory nor Emma Springer had been over the drink-driving limit.

'Who was driving?'

'I don't know.'

'Do you know how come they were at the dance last night?'

'No idea. Although they might have been there on some corporate tickets. I know that sometimes big firms are invited as a gesture of goodwill, part of the Rotary Club sort of thing.'

'Was either of them a member of the Rotary Club?'

'Who knows?' he said, listlessly.

'When are you going to identify the body?'

'At half past nine, unless they ring and tell me that Mrs Springer is able to do it, but I doubt she will be from what they said last night. Apparently she had a lot of internal injuries.'

I wondered if she'd been wearing her sheepskin coat. If it was that which had kept her alive. How would she cope without that sad, anxious husband of hers? 'Do you want me to come with you?'

'No.'

We agreed that I would ring the advocate to the inquiry to let her know and send a card, from both of us, to Mrs Springer.

Because of my experience the year before, after Adam and I had said goodbye, I briefly checked with myself that the police couldn't in any way think that it was my fault. I didn't know the Springers were going to be there last night, I didn't know they had a car, let alone what make it was and anyway, I know so little about cars, it wouldn't be possible for me to tamper with anything. I have enough trouble tampering with my own car, although if it stops unexpectedly, as it so often does, a smart rap with a blunt instrument often works wonders. I decided I wouldn't share that information unless absolutely forced to do so.

I left the house with Marnie and Julie. 'Tell them all to wear sensible clothes and not to carry bags,' Julie said as we walked towards my car.

Advice for a demo. I had a brief flash of what it would be like, all meeting up at the start, staggering under the weight of the posters, singing together, taking up the road, feeling a bit of political power for once. Perhaps I should stay and have my own small protest about our inquiry. I couldn't think what I would put on my placard. 'For goodness' sake, just stop it.'

'And they're not to bring anything that could be mistaken for a missile. And no dangly earrings.' I hoped they would be all right. 'You've got my phone numbers, haven't you?' I said, unlocking my car door. 'Do you want me to stay?'

'No, stop worrying,' Julie said. 'This demo is going to be peaceful, this is just basic, common-sense advice. It makes people think about why they're there.'

Julie and Marnie carried on down the road to the bus stop, Marnie saying, 'Dangly earrings? Mum, what century are you in?' I started the car and drove into town.

I had deliberately arrived early. I wanted to be the first to tell the clients.

I sat by the coffee tables as the cups were brought out from the cupboards in the lobby and the flasks brought up from the kitchen area. Shelly and Leanne walked up the stairs. 'You're here early,' Leanne remarked.

'There's something I want to tell everyone.'

'About Gregory?' said Shelly. 'It were on the news this morning.'

'They showed the car. What a mess.' Leanne frowned at the memory. 'They said the police are keeping an open mind, but initial tests indicate this was not an accident.'

Gradually the clients arrived, also early, murmuring to each other as they gathered in the lobby. Today almost all of them had come. I suggested that we went into our room, and I formally announced Gregory's death and told them what little I knew about the accident. Not all of them had seen the news. They were all shocked and one or two people wept quietly.

'He had a terrible life,' Shelly said.

'Who'd want to kill Gregory?' someone said.

'You don't think it's anything to do with the inquiry, do you?'

'Will the police want to interview us?'

'I don't know what investigations the police will be pursuing,' I said. 'The main thing is to try and keep calm, not to engage in wild speculation, and certainly not to worry.'

It was half past ten. We were being called in.

Curston said all the right things about Gregory and said, as a mark of respect, we would rise at lunch time. But he felt certain that Mr Springer would have wanted the inquiry to continue.

'Not necessarily,' Shelly muttered behind me.

It was clear that no one was concentrating. The clients didn't want to give evidence and by midday we had finished the witnesses whose evidence was merely being read.

Curston announced that we would adjourn until 10.30 am on Tuesday.

As the group filed out of the room, Shelly approached me. 'Is Emma going to be all right? God, I feel terrible, what I did to them wheels. Do you think I should ring the police to tell them?'

'Adam's in touch with the police,' I said. 'Why not let him tell them, if and when the time is right. I'll make a note that you've told me, so it's clear that you're not trying to hinder the investigation. But Shelly, that happened days ago. Mrs Springer knew all about it. There's no way that could have caused the accident.' I hoped I was right.

I rang Adam. He had not come back from the mortuary and I left a message giving him all my phone numbers again, even my mother's, in case anyone wanted to talk to me. His assistant gave me all his, which, in an unusual burst of technological enthusiasm, I tapped straight into my mobile phone, in case I wanted to talk to him.

And then I headed back to London. I was going home. The car behaved well on the M1, the sound system was pretty good, and listening to 'Get Ready', flying at fifty miles an hour past a thirty-year-old Austin Allegro, I felt my life wasn't all bad. The queues began about Luton and by the time we got to the Scratchwood Services, the car began coughing and slowing down, and we had to stop for half an hour for a sandwich and a cup of tea. I thought of the two new cars that Gavin had promised I would be able to buy with the money from this case if I wanted, which of course I didn't. But as it was unlikely I would be paid until I finished the job, I was relying on my current car to carry me to and from Birmingham. I was trying to treat it with the respect and courtesy I hope to receive myself in the twilight of my days. Sometimes, however, it is just not possible, and the blunt instrument came out of the boot and soon we were back on the road.

As I drove round the North Circular, past Golders Green and Muswell Hill, I began to relax. It was the weekend and I was coming home. I drove down through Wood Green, and as Green Lanes re-asserted itself I felt that I was crossing a border. I had left Birmingham behind. Gregory's death, the mess of the inquiry, and whatever relationship I had with Yolande. It was a relief, I realised. I was back in London. The fruit and vegetables piled onto the stalls outside the Greek and Turkish supermarkets spoke to me, and Newington Green looked like my own private park. I was back on home territory.

The small clock on my dashboard said it was nearly half past four.

Walking back into my flat was like walking back into a happy memory of childhood: the coolness of the rooms, the smell of my soap, the dip in the sofa – perhaps I did need a new one. I noticed the Dustbuster had declined to do the hoovering. I felt as if I'd been away for years, I certainly felt that I'd had several years' worth of experiences in the last week. The phone rang. I threw my bag down on the sofa and papers spilled out over the cushions. OK, OK, really new bag time.

It was Gavin. 'Did it all come through?'

'Ah, the advice.' I had forgotten. I looked over at my fax machine. Pages were scattered on the floor. 'Probably,' I said.

'And you're all right for tonight?'

'I've got my chambers keys, if I need to get in. And I know the alarm code.' A set of chambers a few doors down had recently had a break in and several snazzy laptops had been taken, so security was a current concern.

'No, I mean for the chambers' meeting.'

'There's a chambers meeting tonight?' I asked. 'Perfect.'

I walked into the kitchen looking at my post, which had been waiting beside my front door. A couple of bills, a letter from an old friend in Manchester, and another postcard.

St Andrews is so far away, but the audiences are great. And the girls are coming up next week, for half-term. Thinking of you. M.

And I'm thinking of you, Margo, I reflected. But where does that leave us? In my case, eating a piece of dry toast and four green olives.

There was one message on my answerphone. Adam sounding bleak. 'DCI McLaren, the officer dealing with the case, is now ninety-five per cent certain – I quote – that it was murder and attempted murder.' I shuddered. Poor, anxious Gregory. Who had wanted him dead?

By six o'clock I had only completed the new piece of paperwork and half of one of the old ones. Now I needed authorities, so I had to go into chambers, even though I really didn't want to go to a chambers meeting. But I realised that I did rather want to go into chambers, to touch base, to feel normal.

As I was gathering my papers together, one of the photos from Sandra's flat fell off the table. It landed on a carrier bag. Photos, carrier bag. Photo. I stared for a moment at the five people grinning at the camera. Then I shoved the picture back in the pile with the others. I had no interest in them. Or the carrier bag. Perhaps I should take the bag into chambers. I could put it in the safe. We had a safe in chambers for sensitive videos, although I would never put videos of interviews with my sex abuse victims in there, because it was usually full of porn belonging to members of the crime team. Perhaps I'd leave the carrier bag where it was, happily by the sofa.

At least at eight o'clock at night there was somewhere to park in the Temple. I don't have a parking permit and during the day it's like trying to get into Fort Knox, even if you only want to stop for five minutes.

There were spaces almost outside chambers and jauntily I parked the car, but when I noticed Marcus's W-reg Mercedes, glinting in a square of sunshine, my light-hearted mood evaporated. I remembered why I didn't like going into chambers. Marcus was in chambers. That meant the meeting was still going on, because Marcus never stayed behind for a drink after the meeting, and the idea of him staying behind to do research was laughable.

But I was here now and I had to go to the library. I ran up the stairs of the building, up to the second floor.

I stood in the doorway, looking round the room. The library, which was at the back of the building, was dark at the best of times but recently half the bulbs in the fancy light fittings embedded in the ceiling had blown, so at first glance it was like walking into a cinema after the big film has started. I could make out the silhouettes of about ten people round the large table and another four or five dotted behind them on the older chairs. A single bright halogen beam shone down on Tony who was speaking. He was chairing the meeting, which was bad news. When Tony chaired, the meetings were longer, the atmosphere loopier, and the decisions woollier and potentially more disastrous.

Simon had obviously made it back in time, hurrying down from a day in Birmingham Crown Court, whereas I'd only had half a day, so it was a good job I'd come. He was staring fixedly at an agenda on his knee. Marcus, who was sitting next to him, was reading a brief. Vanya was flicking through a copy of *Archbold*, the criminal practitioner's handbook. There was an atmosphere of tired boredom. I slid along the bookcase containing the *All England Law Reports*. One of the authorities I needed was in the *All Englands*. If the meeting dragged too much, I could do some surreptitious research.

Simon raised his eyebrows in greeting and pointed a finger at the agenda. We were on AOB. Damn. If I'd been ten minutes later I might have missed it all. Marcus looked up and made a show of looking at his watch. 'Frankie,' he murmured. 'Better late than never. I think you may have missed the best part.' Doubtless he had just pushed through some dreadful item on rent increases. 'But this should be interesting.'

Tony was coughing and adjusting the hair on the very top of his head. He looked embarrassed.

'Some of you may know,' he began, 'about my recent . . . appointment to sit as the Chair of the Mental Health Appeals Tribunal.'

There was a smattering of applause, led, I noticed, by Marcus.

'You will also know that there is to be a small party to celebrate this –'

' – great achievement,' Marcus intoned.

'Thank you.' He bowed graciously. 'Another matter arises as a result of my –'

' – great achievement,' Vanya repeated.

He fluttered his hand. 'I shall no longer be able to carry out the onerous duties of head of chambers.'

There was a small sigh and a settling around the room, as if everyone was thinking, 'At last!'

'Which will leave the post empty. And I understand that, somewhat surprisingly, since it is such a heavy burden, there are two contenders for the position. I salute you both.' Tony leaned under the table and with something like a flourish brought out a large bottle of champagne. Clumsily he tore off the foil, as Vanya produced chambers' two cardboard boxes of champagne flutes. The bottle opened with a satisfying pop and Tony poured champagne into the glasses. 'So, a toast! To Simon and Marcus, may the best man win.'

So, Marcus had put himself forward. How could he do that? The natural successor to Tony was clearly Simon. He was perfect for the job. He chaired all the meetings that Tony didn't come to and was calm, concise and objective. And Marcus was an arsehole. It was as simple as that. Who on earth would vote for Marcus? Apart from Marcus?

We all raised our glasses. This was very nice champagne. Good old Tony.

Simon said, 'And to Tony, with thanks for all your great work over the years.'

'Teamwork, dear boy. Remember, it's all down to teamwork.'

We raised our glasses again. The meeting was over. People pushed back their chairs and one or two left the room to deal with their mobile phones. I asked Vanya where Iotha was.

'I assume she's at home,' she said, in a voice that indicated that she knew about the problem. 'She did say she was going to come in for this meeting. She had papers to pick up for Monday.'

'Is she OK?' I asked. I wondered if she had been my emergency caller of the other day.

'She could be better.' Vanya and Iotha shared a room, they both had mixed crime and family practices. Vanya was more senior, being six-years call. 'Why don't you ring her?'

'I will,' I said.

The library emptied and I found my authorities, then I sat down at one of the four computers on a table in a row against one wall and I finished my advices. I printed them out, signed them, and ran down to the clerks' room and put them in the DX tray. The Document Exchange would carry them to the solicitors by Tuesday morning.

It was a quarter to eleven. I had one last thing to do. Simon had asked me for my notes of the hearing I had done for Danny, some point had arisen about the witnesses. As I walked down the corridor, my paperwork now complete, I downed the contents of my champagne glass from which I had religiously taken only a few sips during the toast to Tony. I was aware of a sense of being at one with the world. I couldn't think where that came from. Then it dawned on me, completing the advices so efficiently was very satisfying. I felt pious and mature. I was becoming a proper barrister. Which made me want to go out and do something wild, something crazy, something stupid, to remind myself that I was still a risk-taker, that I was still living in the fast lane. Or I could just go home to bed.

My room was in darkness. I noticed a tiny red light flashing, like a little alarm. We really were taking security seriously. When the overhead light flooded the room the red light disappeared. I searched through my pile of notebooks, flicking quickly through four or five before I found the right pages. As I leaned down on the table to tear them out, I noticed I had a new phone, dark grey, sleek shape, very nice. I hoped they'd sorted out the wiring at the same time. I switched off the light and went back into the clerks' room, tapping out the drum beat intro of 'Let's Dance' on the first eleven volumes of Halsbury's Laws as I passed down the corridor.

I slid the pages of my notebook into Simon's pigeon-hole and turned to find Marcus standing in the middle of the room.

He seemed as surprised to see me as I was to see him and for a second neither of us spoke. He walked over to his pigeon-hole and began rooting through a pile of pale-blue fax pages.

'I see we've got new phones,' I said, conversationally.

'I can't see why the clerks can't take messages for us any more.' Marcus spoke in a complaining tone. 'What do we pay them for? Why should we have to remember retrieval numbers and pass codes?'

'I don't know what you're talking about.'

'Voice-mail,' he said. My expression remained blank. 'There's a memo in your pigeon-hole.' He turned towards the door. 'I think we're the last people here. I'll leave you to lock up.'

He left me scrabbling in my pigeon-hole. Voice-mail? *Voice-mail?* Why had no one mentioned this? I found the memo. In fact there were two. The first was dated yesterday, announcing the advent of the 21st century at 17 Kings Bench Walk (Jayne the practice manager's little joke). The new phones would start working immediately and there were instructions on how to enter words of greeting and how to retrieve messages. The second memo was also dated yesterday, four hours after the first, saying there was a glitch in the system, some people's phones weren't working and chambers would revert to the old system of taking messages till further notice. The system had collapsed before it began. It obviously hadn't been worth telling me about it.

Or had it? I looked back at the instructions on the first memo. The flashing red light was a sign of a message. I had a flashing red light, in my room. I had a message. Someone had rung me.

I ran back to my room. What if Marnie had already been arrested, practising her walk with the wig and a poster outside her house? What if Yolande was ringing to ask if she could come for the weekend . . . ? In the darkness of the room a pale line of redness blinked at me. I flicked the light switch. For a split second the room was flooded with light, and then there was a pop as the bulb exploded and the room was dark again. I switched on the desk lamp and moved the phone so that it was in the pool of light on my table. I picked up the receiver and, peering at the instructions on the memo, I tapped in the numbers to retrieve my messages.

'You have one new message,' the posh woman in the receiver informed me. 'To listen to your messages press one.'

I pressed one.

'Message received on Thursday at 3.15 pm.'

There was a pause and then a voice I recognised began to speak, in trembling, halting tones. It was Gregory Springer.

'Miss Richmond,' he began. 'I hope you don't mind me leaving this message. I did try to speak to you the other day.' He took a breath. 'I'm ringing to say that after thinking very long and hard, I have decided that I shall give evidence. Could that be arranged for next week? My wife won't be with us then. I've started to write my statement. I'm even typing it up myself which is not really allowed in this house.' He gave a thin strained laugh. 'I should finish it today or tomorrow, and then I'll pop it in the post. Please don't mention this to anyone. I haven't told anyone else. I don't want anyone to know until I give my evidence.'

I was shaking. This was the voice of a dead man. Perhaps his last message to the world. I put the phone down and then snatched it back up. I didn't know how to save messages, I didn't know how they were deleted. Perhaps by replacing the receiver I had wiped the message. I looked up to see a horrified face staring at me, my reflection in the black window.

I looked back at the instructions. I couldn't read it straight. To save messages, press what? To skip messages, what, eight? To what what what? I jumped as three insistent notes heralded the woman in the phone, urging me to please hang up and try again.

What should I do? Who should I tell? And would it wipe off the message?

I fished in the pocket of my jacket for my mobile. I rang directory inquiries and asked for the number for

Birmingham Police. I was given a generic number for all the stations. But I didn't know which station would be dealing with Gregory Springer's death and I couldn't remember the name of the officer dealing with the case.

I rang Adam.

'Hello?' He sounded confused. I looked at my watch, it was almost midnight.

'Adam, it's Frankie. I'm sorry to trouble you.' I sounded like Gregory. I told Adam about the phonecall.

'Can you save it?' he asked.

'I'm hoping that by leaving it just as it is, it is saved,' I said.

'I know that DCI McLaren went off duty about two hours ago. Gregory's message is probably important, but it doesn't sound like the most vital message in the world. I'd leave it till tomorrow.'

'That feels so unsatisfactory,' I said. 'I have this great desire to share. Have you got the number of his station? I could ring and at least leave a message.'

There was the rustling sound of a duvet being thrown back. The time I assumed it took for Adam to retrieve his briefcase or Filofax, or wherever he kept his numbers, passed and then he gave me a number for McLaren's station.

I apologised again and we said goodbye. I dialled the number. After about twenty rings someone answered and I briefly explained why I was ringing. I was told to hold. I held. I held for ten minutes and then I rang again. A different person answered the phone. I spoke and was told to wait.

'What for?' I asked.

'I'm trying to find someone to deal with this information.'

'Can't you make a note of it? If I leave my number, DCI McLaren, who I understand is the officer in charge of the case, can ring me tomorrow when he comes in.'

'Could you just hold for a minute, madam?'

Five minutes went by and I tried again. This time the phone rang and rang and no one answered. Perhaps they had a lot on.

I had a vague fear that the message would disappear with the passage of time. I pulled open the top drawer of my small filing cabinet. Perhaps I could record it. My dictaphone wasn't there. I knew where it was. It was at home.

I didn't want to leave the phone. I didn't want to leave Gregory, stammering and coughing, unused to answer machines, alone in the phone.

Which of course was stupid. Gregory was dead and there was no point in having a vigil at the side of the phone. I switched off the lamp and walked out of the room. Carefully I punched in the number of the alarm, 1407, Tony's birthday, turned both keys in their locks and left the building.

On the way home, through the dark empty streets, up Farringdon Road, across to St John Street, down Essex Road, a late-night trumpeter on the radio was playing quiet, mournful jazz. I thought about Gregory. His sad childhood, abandoned by his birth family, abused in the care system, let down by the legal system. Perhaps he and his wife had had a happy marriage. Perhaps what he loved about her was her obsession with sheepskin. I hoped so.

TWENTY-ONE

Saturday – Euston

Waking up in your own bed is such a treat. Especially when the sun is coming through the curtains and it's Saturday. I put my hands behind my head, appreciated my blue and white duvet cover, and thought about my day. A vague plan was forming in my mind. A stroll down Stoke Newington High Street, pop into the book shop to see what's new, poke round in the secondhand shops on Church Street, and maybe have a little light lunch with Lena in Fox's Wine Bar. I could even ring Iotha, maybe meet her for coffee.

And then I remembered. My life wasn't like that any more. One of my clients had just been murdered and I had been telephoned by him shortly before his death. And there was the small matter of my appointment with a left luggage locker.

Better get started, then.

I dressed reluctantly but carefully. My black jeans for strength, my Doc Martins for action, and a red cotton shirt for a bit of a lift. I rang the number for DCI McLaren. He wasn't in the office, but this time someone listened to my story, and efficiently took my name and number. 'Hang on to the message,' she said. 'He'll be back in the office this afternoon.'

I rang Lena and wailed. She was soothing but busy till tomorrow (you see, stay in London, full social life, out of London, no life). And then I rang Iotha. She wasn't in, and I left a message suggesting we go out tonight. I hadn't told Lena I was going to Euston today. I wondered if I should tell Iotha, so someone knew. But it was only Euston, a major London terminus, for goodness' sake. I followed the route of the 73 bus, turned off at Cardington Street and parked in a side road.

Euston on a Saturday. It's as busy as it is during the week, people standing stoically in front of the departures board, praying that their train will run. When I was a student I usually took the coach up to Coventry, and when I took the train it was a great event, really exciting.

Unlike today, which was not so much exciting as disquieting. I walked through the station concourse, past the glass windows of the ticket office on my left and the strange circular sweet shop on my right, and as I looked over at the newsagent's and glanced across at the flower-seller and the display boards of railway information, I wondered if I was being watched. I might have been set up. That's what Lena had said. And I had replied, 'No, Yolande wouldn't do that.' And Lena had said, 'Why isn't she collecting whatever it is herself, or that man in the vest? Why doesn't he do it?' And I had said, 'It's probably not in his job description, and perhaps he has other things to do.' Now I thought of him leaning against the wall near Frodsham's table at the dance, I thought of him gliding round the room with Marnie. Why wasn't he here? Why was I doing this?

What would Kay say? 'Don't do it!' Too negative. Like people who write to agony aunts, I considered others

211

mentors. Apparently people choose their agony aunt on the basis of the kind of reply they know they'll get. Caring, caustic, pious, ludicrous, they each have different characteristics. So Simon? 'Leave my case alone.' Too self-centred. OK, my mum. 'Is this the right thing to do, Frankie? You could be spending your time much more productively, doing some housework.' Well, there. If it was a choice between being beaten up, maybe arrested, possibly even blown up by what was in the locker, and doing housework, there was no contest.

What I needed was some money, I decided, I might have to buy myself out of trouble. I walked back past the ticket office to a cash point. I pulled my wallet out of my back pocket and took out my card. A young man with bright blue eyes and two side teeth missing appeared, smiling, by my left shoulder. 'Spare some change? Spare some credit cards?' he asked.

I laughed and gave him a pound, which I don't normally do. It seemed like a lucky token. He might keep an eye out for me, I thought. Although, watching him wander off towards a group of confused travellers, where the pickings were probably better, more chance of a big tip for a few directions, I didn't think I should rely on him.

I walked back to the left luggage area. It was very discreet, a short, narrow corridor, made up of two walls of lockers, looking out over a narrow offshoot of the main concourse, facing platforms 12–16. At the end of the corridor was a low metal counter behind which stood a bored-looking man, and behind him were rows of shelves littered with cases and rucksacks. It was all lit by fluorescent lighting, even at ten o'clock in the morning, which gave the bored-looking man a greyish, seedy tinge as he morosely hauled backpacks and cases from students and American tourists across the counter. I stood at the end of the corridor. Behind me were empty platforms and a clutch of phones. Should I just go straight up to Birmingham, was there someone I should phone? Not really.

I had money, I had the key, I had to do it.

Of course there was the small matter of what number it was. I wondered why Yolande couldn't remember the number when she seemed so desperate for the contents of the locker. You would have thought she would have written it down somewhere safe, with that slim gold pen held lightly in her left hand. If she knew the number. If she had ever known it. Perhaps she hadn't put whatever it was into the locker. Clark had said 127 or 63. I wandered up and down in front of the lockers. Neither of those numbers was there. There were thirty lockers and the numbers went from 11 to 40. Clark hadn't been sure. I wondered what the number could be. Perhaps I should consider the digits. Six and three – makes nine? One plus two plus seven? Ten. Twelve and seven? Nineteen. Why, why should it be nineteen? Why not?

I approached 19 trying to look around me without moving my head. I wasn't sure what I was looking for. My lucky token boy was sidling round a man who was probably trying to find a taxi to Kensington. Perhaps that's what I should do. Get in a cab and go somewhere flash for coffee. I was just as nervous that the bored man behind the counter would call out and challenge me for trying to break into the lockers as I was about the risk of a few Birmingham Big Men knocking me flying to get the film. But maybe the film had nothing to do with anything. Maybe it was just a few holiday snaps that Yolande thought it really was time to have developed.

The key wouldn't go in. I stood at the locker, jiggling and prodding the lock for two minutes before I decided it was the wrong key. Or, of course, the wrong locker. This was hopeless.

My lucky token boy came back, padding towards me like a panther. 'Spare a can of lager?' he asked. 'Oh, it's you. Want some help?' He was about eighteen and wore greasy-looking jeans and a shabby navy-blue fleece jacket. He exuded the smell of neglect and poverty.

'No thank you,' I said, crisply, but since he continued to stand there and I was desperate, I asked, 'Are these all the lockers there are?'

'These and the ones round the corner.' He waved his head in the direction of the counter, then reached out as if to take my hand. I stepped back. It wasn't just his filthy fingers, I simply was not ready to walk hand in hand through Euston Station with any man. But it was mainly his filthy fingers. His grin showed that he had noticed my reluctance. Perhaps he remembered the pound, or he was bored, because he growled, 'Come on,' and slithered along the wall of lockers and round the corner. There, tucked against a brick wall, awash with the smell of urine was a small dark cul-de-sac of more lockers. At least it was a discreet place for people to pee in, out of the public eye. As were he and I. We stood in front of the lockers, which were numbered 41 to 80. So, 63 it was.

'Go on then,' he said. 'I'll keep an eye out.' What did he mean, 'I'll keep an eye out'? An eye out for what? For the rest of his gang? Members of a rival gang? What did he know?

I stood motionless for a moment as I considered my options. I glanced at him from out of the corner of my eye. He was almost hopping from one foot to another, unable to keep still. He couldn't be part of any Birmingham gangland gang, not looking like that. Even Clark's bad dress sense was mitigated by soap and water. I sensed this guy couldn't allow himself to even think the word soap. I doubted he had any sink of his own to use it in.

Perhaps keeping an eye out was just the way he had to live his life. The more likely possibility was that he might mug me. And if it wasn't me, he would only wait for another sucker to come round to this row of lockers. If he was going to mug anyone it might as well be me.

But of course he didn't mug me. I stood there, once again lightly quivering the key against the key hole, and getting no joy. My lucky token boy leaned against a locker and tapped his foot, watching with interest. I tried jabbing the key in. Nothing. 'Fuck,' I said.

'You sure this is the right number?' he asked.

'No,' I said, shortly.

'Shall I have a go?'

'What do you mean?' What if he wanted to share the proceeds? What should I agree to – 70/30? 60/40? 'Even if it is the right one, there's really nothing in there worth having,' I said, doubtfully. 'In fact I don't really know what's in there at all. I'm doing this for a friend.'

'Let's have a look, shall we?' He produced a thin piece of wire from his jeans and began to poke into the key hole.

What if it was the wrong locker, and it was full of the rucksack of a desperate Warwick student, who was even now sleeping off some late-night drinking binge in the mean streets of North London, in need of cheap accommodation? How could I break into his locker and expose his meagre belongings for all the world to sneer at, and probably steal? I decided that if it was indeed a rucksack, then I would tuck a five pound note into one of the smaller pockets. Or a ten pound note.

'It's empty,' my new friend was saying, pushing back the door of the locker.

I peered in. 'No it's not.' At the back of the locker, just as Clark had said, was a small, squat black plastic tube. 'It's a roll of film,' I said, with more confidence than I felt. I reached in and grabbed it. I shook it, it was a film. 'Thank you,' I said, slipping the film and the key into my pocket. He had turned to go. I groped in my wallet. 'Here.' I gave him the ten pound note, which the Warwick student didn't need. He raised his head in acknowledgement and slunk away.

Gingerly, I moved out of the cul-de-sac, past the counter, where the attendant was arguing with a middle-aged couple about the existence of their luggage. He glanced at me as I walked casually by. I felt as if I'd been smoking behind the bicycle sheds or worse. It was worse. I had broken into a left luggage locker. 'Hey!' he called.

I turned sharply. 'Yes?' My voice cracked. My heart was racing.

'You OK?' He nodded his head towards my partner in crime, who was now doing a casual sweep of the phone boxes, feeling in the returned coin compartment. 'I keep telling the police about him. Do you want to make a complaint?'

'No, no, he . . . no.'

He frowned slightly. What else would I have been doing round there with him?

Quickly I slid round the corner and into John Menzies. Blindly, I picked up a magazine and began to flick through it, my heart still pounding in terror at what I had just done. I had broken into a left luggage locker. The smell of urine was in my nostrils. In my clothes. I needed a shower. And it was a Body Building magazine. I threw it back onto the shelf with a quiver of disgust. How can those muscles be natural?

I slunk out of the station, feeling all eyes watching me. Look at the way she walks down the street, see the way she shuffles her feet; never be any good, never ever does what she should.

Casually I turned up the collar of my shirt. Just because she doesn't do what everybody else does – I skipped across the road. I could be that person. I could be that rebel. I'd done it. I'd got the film.

TWENTY-TWO

Saturday Lunch

I unlocked my front door and heaved two plastic bags into my hallway. Somehow I had managed to buy two courgettes, a cauliflower and a packet of poppy seeds on my way home, plus, as a gesture to Marnie, a large box of Ecover washing powder. What quick, delicious lunch could I create out of that?

I lifted my head, almost sniffing the air. Someone had been in the house. Quite clearly. Everything was different. Everything was tidy. The *Guardians* were in a neat pile beside the sofa, there were no cups or glasses on the coffee table, there were no crumbs on the floor, the cushions had been plumped. Someone had been here, someone, in fact, was still here. I could hear them in the bathroom. Singing. Singing 'It's better to have and don't need, than to need and don't have.' I don't want that sentiment in my home. I marched into the bathroom.

She was leaning over the bath wearing yellow rubber gloves, which she must have brought with her because I only have one and it's pink.

'Mum,' I said.

'I'm just doing a little cleaning.'

'So I see. Where's Alan?'

'Brighton.' She scrubbed busily at the area round the plug.

'There's nothing wrong is there?'

'Not at all. When you have a trial marriage, you have to do things separately.'

'You mean Alan wouldn't want to clean my flat with you? What kind of relationship's that?'

'You haven't been using the Dustbuster, have you?' she asked. 'Have you had lunch?'

'No and no.'

'I will just say, tidy home, tidy mind. And don't forget dusting. I bought some snacky things across the road. Would that be nice?'

'That would be lovely, Mum.'

I sighed and walked back into the living room. She had done some tentative arranging of the papers on my desk, I noticed irritably, and had put some photos on top of a brief I ought to take back to chambers. I snatched up the pictures and threw myself onto the sofa. They were the ones I had lifted from Sandra's bedroom.

I looked at them again, the row of eighties party makers. Smiling stiffly, enjoying themselves, perhaps. Did I recognise them? There was something there. I looked at them closely. And then, as my eyes became accustomed to the rusty pink background, my attention focussed on a person at the side. In the background, behind the tightly cheerful line posing for the camera, turned slightly away, a young boy. He looked tall enough to be about ten, but his face, which was hardly visible, looked much younger. But his eyes were unmistakable, bright and sparkling, framed by long, dark lashes. I could even make out the dimple in his cheek. It was Clark.

Why did Sandra, girlfriend of a Birmingham gangland member, have photos – old photos – of an employee of another gangland member, currently charged with the murder of the cohort of the first gangland member? The only link I could think of was Yolande, Sandra's sister, Danny's girlfriend. How long had she known Clark?

'Shall we eat in the kitchen?' my mum called.

I got up and put plates on the table.

'Did anything major happen in Birmingham in the eighties, mum?' I asked as we chewed our way through the vegetable samosas.

'I came up to stay with you in Coventry and we went to Birmingham for the day to visit your Aunty Cath.'

It dawned on me that my family had a long, and for me, troubling relationship with the Midlands. On my dad's side there was Aunty Cath and Uncle Richard, and on my mum's there was Auntie Irene, Julie's mum, and Uncle Norman, and then I had chosen to go to Warwick University, although that was more a question of it being the only offer I had which matched my A level grades. But something, I don't know if it was the Family Vortex, or some other, geographical vortex, sucked me inexorably into something which had at its heart – Birmingham. 'Mmm. Anything really major?'

'Was that when they started talking about pulling down the Bull Ring?'

'They've been talking about that since it was built, haven't they? I mean, is there anything criminal you remember?'

'Was that when the big night-club murders were?'

'Maybe,' I said, cautiously.

'That was everywhere in the papers. Oh, a real mess. Gangsters and guns and women who were still wearing mini skirts.' She shook her head in amazement. 'All the men seemed to wear evening suits and have tightly curled hair, and there were a lot of unfunny jokes in the *Guardian* about death by curly perm,' she said. 'Didn't Uncle Richard know someone who had been there on the night?' Aunty Cath's marriage to Uncle Richard had been something rarely spoken of in our family. 'Didn't I speak to you about it? Warning you not to go into that night club? What was it called? Spats. The Spats Bar . . . Why do you ask?'

'Oh, just something someone said.'

The phone rang. It was DCI McLaren returning my call.

I repeated my story of Gregory's message. He said he thought it was interesting and was making a note, but at the moment their enquiries were focussing on local friends and relatives, and also the garage where they had recently purchased their car. Could I, he asked, make a recording of the message?

It took me an hour and a half, in between ringing Gavin in a panic and saying goodbye to Mum, to record the message over the phone onto my dictaphone. I did it twice, on two separate mini tapes for security.

And then I rifled through my inquiry papers and rang the Salthill Police Station. I asked to speak to DC Blane. I was put straight through.

I reminded him that I was counsel for the victims at the inquiry.

'And why are you playing this to me?' he asked me suspiciously, after he'd heard the tape of Gregory's hesitant stammering message.

'Because I wanted you to know. Because I thought it might mean more to you than it seems to mean to DCI

McLaren. Couldn't he have got BT to do this? To make a decent tape of this message?'

'It's probably simpler for you to do it. Have you seen this statement he's talking about?'

'No. I thought someone might be interested in finding it, in case it says something important.'

There was a rustling and Blane called something in a muffled tone. 'I've got to go,' he said. 'We've all been called out for this Ladscore demo. Hopefully by the time we get there it'll all be over. But I doubt it.'

'Is that the environment demo?'

'Yeah.'

'Is there any trouble?' My heart began to pound.

'Apparently. Why can't these demonstrators let the inquiry do its job, that's what it's there for, and then we could get on with proper police work.'

'Like our inquiry is doing its job?'

'Point taken,' he said. 'Look, I'll see if I can speak to anyone about this Gregory Springer business. There's probably someone working on it already, they just don't like to show too much enthusiasm. Thanks for ringing.'

I rang Marnie's mobile, but it wasn't switched on. I left a message reminding her of my number and urging her to call me if she needed help. Better still, to take her mum and go straight home.

When the phone rang lurid scenes filled my mind. But it was Adam. 'I identified the body. It was him.'

'And what about the idea that the car had been interfered with?'

'That's what they're working on. They think that possibly something was wrong with the brakes, and there shouldn't have been because it was a new car.'

'New cars are something I know very little about,' I

said. 'Are they sure this plan was aimed at Gregory? What colour was the car?'

'Silver I think.'

'There are so many new silver cars around, perhaps it was a mistake.'

'No, it seems that it was a professional job.'

'Well, who would have done that?'

'I'm trying not to think the obvious,' he said.

'You mean someone thought he was about to say something at the inquiry that was too damaging to be heard? What alternatives are there? What did Gregory do?'

'He worked for some big firm outside Tamworth. They both did, apparently. Which to answer your question is how they were at the dance. Some manager had two tickets but couldn't go, so they went instead.'

'Were they going to lose their jobs? Shelly made some comment about Mrs Springer.'

'No idea. Seems unlikely, certainly for Mrs Springer, she was secretary to the managing director.'

'Was it a swanky firm?'

'I don't think it's a multinational, if that's what you mean.'

'No, I just wondered whether they had air conditioning, whether that's why she always wore the sheepskin.'

TWENTY-THREE

Saturday Evening

Iotha had left a message suggesting that we meet in Fox's, which is my favourite wine bar on Stoke Newington Church Street. It was a warm evening so I told Robby, the owner, to tell her that I would be sitting outside. At the back of the bar was a small yard, whose high walls were covered in ivy and wisteria. Large pots of pink and white geraniums were placed between the wooden tables and benches, giving a sense of privacy.

I had bought a bottle of Vinho Verde. I felt the occasion did not call for deep aromatic fruitfulness, more a straightforward wry, dry kick of alcohol.

Iotha obviously thought otherwise. She arrived carrying an open bottle of Sauvignon Blanc. 'Frankie!' she scolded, as she swung her leg over the bench opposite me. 'I should be providing the alcohol, after all your work last week, and meeting me today.'

'I don't think pulling up all your decent flowers and tucking John Innes number four round most of your weeds entitles me to be provided with drink. Anyway, you supplied quite a lot last weekend. Were you pleased with the afternoon? Was Tony the last to leave?'

She nodded. 'At about half past ten. We put him in

the living room with some old videos of Kavanagh QC. I think he was asleep half the time. Every now and again you'd hear him shout, "Rubbish!" and he came out at the end saying he didn't know how the man had got silk behaving the way he did.'

'Of course. Because those are precisely the reasons why I haven't got silk. Hair too long and an accent that can't make up its mind where it comes from,' I said. 'Now then. Let's get hypothetical. What's the problem?'

'Well, you know it's not hypothetical.'

'Yes,' I said.

Iotha took a large mouthful of wine. 'Do you think I'm a person who comes on to any man I meet?' she said.

Although I knew the answer, an immediate no, I gave it fresh thought. 'From the way I have seen you behave in chambers I would not say that you come on to people. You're friendly, you're nice. You get on well with the clerks, men and women, as far as I can see.'

'Do I flirt?'

'What's flirting? If you're nice to people, if you make them feel good, is that flirting?'

'You can give out the wrong messages.'

'Aren't we starting at the wrong end here? Is this about you or about someone else?'

'Someone else.' She took a breath. 'Marcus.'

'I'll just remind you that he and I have a history.' Marcus had behaved very badly around my arrest the year before, not least by parking illegally in a disabled parking space. 'If you want someone to confront him I may not be the best person.'

'I don't know what I want at the moment. I just want to talk to someone.'

225

'OK. What's he been doing?'

'I'm not even sure about that.' There was a catch in her voice.

I pushed her glass of wine towards her and picked up my own to encourage her. She took a small sip and began.

'When I started in chambers, I was doing my pupillage, three years ago, he was really nice to me, in a completely ordinary way. Just showing me how things were done. I could always ask him questions, even if it was something stupid like how do you address a District Judge, and he would just be straightforward and tell me and that gave me real confidence.'

Already I was suspicious. This did not sound like Marcus at all.

'And when I thought I was being given too much photocopying, instead of research, compared to the male pupils, he was great and put round a note, so it didn't seem like I was making a fuss, you know, so I didn't get a name as a troublemaker. He was great. He was always saying he wanted me with him, but I thought he was being protective, not wanting me to be exploited by other members of chambers. And then, when I applied for a tenancy, he apparently spoke up for me.'

I thought back three years. I couldn't really remember, but I had no sense that Marcus had ever promoted any pupil.

'And then, for a time, I hardly ever saw him. I was always at Grays magistrates' court or Lewes Family Proceedings Court. But when I did see him somehow he always got the fact that I was his protégée into the conversation, boring but OK, then recently . . .' She shook her head and reached for her glass. She took a large mouthful of wine.

I grabbed a passing waitress and asked for anything small they had to nibble. We needed alcohol, but we needed to keep relatively clear heads. She came back with olives and warm caraway seed rolls.

Iotha ripped off a piece of bread and carefully buttered it. 'One evening I was doing some work in the library. Vanya had a heavy case on the next day, I think she'd spoken to you about it. We were for mum who was refusing parental responsibility. There was a case she'd seen in Family Law and I couldn't find it. I was standing at the photocopier, surrounded by copies of Family Law Reports and Hershman and McFarlane,' (the family practitioner's bible) 'everything was getting mixed up. The photocopier was playing up. The toner was going and it kept running out of paper.'

'What is it with photocopiers?' I tutted, and opened my mouth to say more about dreadful machines I had known. But she was rolling her wine glass between her hands in distress so I said, 'Go on.'

'It was quite late, about half past eight, you know, getting dark, and most of the bulbs, as usual, had gone in the library and so I had that reading lamp on near the photocopier. And he came in.

'So we said hello, hello, how've you been? And he asked me what I was doing and could he do anything to help. And I said, no, and, you know, joking, wasn't this a bit late for him to be out? He said he was preparing a case and he needed some authorities. But he was just standing there, so I thought, oh God, I'm the junior tenant, does he want me to find them for him? Although I thought, lazy bastard, why doesn't he get them for himself? But I asked him anyway and he said, "No, you finish what you're doing." And then he just pulled out a chair and sat there watching me.

'Of course, the photocopier kept jamming. And then needed time to "recover" and I was leaning against it, waiting, and he was making a bit of chat. Just about work, and whether my room was OK, whether I liked sharing with Vanya.

'And then the photocopier whirred back into action so I was arranging the pages, putting the lid down. And suddenly I felt his hand on my neck. Up under my hair, on my neck. It was so unexpected. I mean, I wasn't even looking nice, I hadn't been in court. I'd just come into chambers. I think I was wearing my gardening outfit as you would call it.'

'Compared to mine, yours looked quite fetching.'

'Shut up.'

'OK, sorry. But I think we know, don't we, that what you actually look like has no bearing on this kind of thing.'

'So he starts running his hand up and down my neck. And of course on one level, that's very nice. You know, someone stroking your neck. He's not a creep, he's nice, not bad looking.'

I tried to keep my face straight.

'I think for a time, right at the beginning of my pupillage, for about a month, I did actually fancy him. Oh God, does that mean it was my fault? I'd been giving out messages all the time?'

'No, for goodness' sake, no. People do fancy people. Even if you still fancied him, that doesn't give him the right to do anything he feels like doing. Unless it's OK with you.'

'So after about a second I realised what was happening and I sort of half laughed and said something like, "I've got to get volume two of the 1996 *Family Law Reports*," and ducked round him. I thought I could hang round those shelves till he went. Of course, over by the *Family Law Reports* the lights were completely off, and I thought he might come over, so I just grabbed any old book and came back. He was still standing there. He put his arm round my neck and whispered in my ear, "You know I think you're a very attractive woman and I know that you're attracted to me." And I'm like "what?" He said, "Let's pick up on this at a later date." And he stuck his tongue in my ear and then he left.'

I discovered I had eaten all the olives and we had finished the Vinho Verde. Quickly I ordered two plates of chips and some salad. We needed to make a start on Lotha's bottle of wine.

'And since then, it's as if he owns me. He hasn't asked me out, you know, it's not like he's courting me. He hasn't even bought me a drink, and there have been two or three times when he could have done, when we've been in the pub. It's the clerks' room, in front of everybody. He comes up behind me when I'm looking in my pigeon-hole and makes a loud comment that everyone can hear, like "Hello gorgeous," and then leans forward and nibbles my ear or blows into it. Sometimes he puts his arm round my waist, and once or twice he's squeezed my breast.' She was near to tears.

'He's harrassing you. And assaulting you.'

'Every time I'm in there, he seems to pop up. I daren't go into the library, and now I try not to go into the clerks' room either.'

The clerks' room, particularly for young members of

chambers, is usually a haven of security. After a horrible day in court the clerks listen with concern to your story and sometimes, if you're lucky, they make you a cup of tea. So, not only was he behaving appallingly, but he was depriving Iotha of an important line of support.

'Have you spoken to him about it?'

'Once or twice I said, "Get off" really loudly. I can't speak to him face to face, because I know I shall burst into tears. I sent him this note.'

She leant down to her bag and pulled out a folded piece of paper. It was a photocopy of a note in Iotha's handwriting, which read, 'Please don't speak to me or behave towards me in an inappropriate manner in the clerks' room or anywhere else.' It was dated two weeks before.

'And what was his response to that?'

'He left me alone for a couple of days, but gradually it's built back up. Two days ago he whispered to me, "Don't you think I deserve a little of your friendliness? You know that's what you want."'

'For goodness' sake! Right, what would you like me to do?'

She shook her head, tears in her eyes again. She poured wine into both our glasses. The chips had arrived.

'I can speak to Marcus,' I said. 'Or I could speak to Tony. Or you could use chambers' procedures to make a formal complaint against him. But we're talking about a criminal offence here. You could go to the police.'

'I don't know what I want to do. I just want it to stop.' She dipped a chip into a bowl of tomato sauce. 'Thank you for listening, I feel better for that. I'll think about what I want you to do.'

'You have my number in Birmingham. You can ring me anytime, for a chat, or if you want me to do something.'

She rubbed her eyes.

'Do you want anything else to eat?' I asked.

She shook her head.

I walked her to her car and then I walked home, thinking about her. It was a depressing situation, particularly her sense of isolation. She needed more support. I really should keep in touch. I'd put her number in my mobile. I'd have a word with Simon.

TWENTY-FOUR

Sunday Lunch

I had a lunch date with Lena. I rang her to arrange where to meet. She asked if I would go to her flat. 'It's not raining that much, is it?' I said.

'I'm ill,' she said. 'I've done something to my neck.'

I said nothing. But I was thinking a lot of gratifying things about the wages of exercise.

'There's no need to be so silent,' she said. 'It could have happened to anyone.'

'So, shall I bring round an exquisite lunch?'

'Your usual?' she said, brightly.

'I hope you're not suggesting that salami, olives and a loaf of bread is predictable.'

'I wouldn't mind a bit of predictability, I feel so rotten.'

There was a strong smell of air freshener in the communal hallway of Lena's house as silently she let me in. She rolled her eyes. At the foot of the stairs was a middle-aged woman wearing an ostentatious pair of pink Marigolds and holding a plastic bottle, which I sensed contained a powerful cleaning product. Lena was in her dressing gown and wore one of those collars round her neck. She also held a plastic bottle, hers had a large blue nozzle.

'This is my new neighbour, Sonia, from the top floor,' Lena began.

'Greetings!' Sonia hailed me cheerfully. 'Lena and I were just swapping household tips.'

'Ah,' I said, and threw a glance at Lena. She wouldn't look at me.

'Lena's been telling me about the trouble she has in her bathroom,' Sonia went on. 'I don't know what your grouting's like,' and I thought, nor do I, 'but Lena's got her work cut out for her.'

'I think I'd better take the doctor in now,' Lena said. 'She's making a special house call, and I don't want to waste her time. I'll speak to you later, Sonia, and give you back the – eh – Mister Muscle.'

'Oh, Doctor!' Sonia laughed nervously, 'And there's me talking about your grouting.'

'Not at all,' I said, with a stab at hypocratic smoothness. 'We all have grouting issues at some time or another.'

'Thank you, Doctor,' said Lena firmly. She opened her front door. 'Do come this way. Now.'

'Of course,' I said, hoping that by the force of willpower alone, the blue plastic carrier bag that contained our lunch would look as if it also carried, at least, a stethoscope. Otherwise Sonia would be ringing the BMC about untoward GPs' visits and I'd be struck off the register of doctors before I'd even decided a medical career was something I should consider.

'Grouting issues?' she asked me, when we were in the kitchen.

'You started it,' I protested. 'Doctor?'

'I had to think of something fast or she'd have been in here, disinfecting the food before we ate anything.

Anyway, we're safe now.' She put down the Mister Muscle with a small shake of her head. 'What's in the bag?'

We had a satisfying lunch – I'd added a bunch of grapes and a box of doughnuts to the menu. Lena wasn't drinking alcohol, so we made do with ginger tea and tap water, which, as a medical practitioner, I was forced to concede was good for us both. But on a personal level, I had my doubts.

We moved onto the comfy chairs, I settled myself on the sofa and Lena took the armchair. I told her about the film and then went back over my week at the inquiry, about Marnie and me at the dinner dance, and about the death of Gregory Springer.

'So do we think Shelly is a suspect?' Lena asked, plumping up a cushion and tucking it behind her neck.

'Because of what she did to the wheels? I don't think so.'

'What about Gregory? He said his wife wouldn't be with you next week?'

'You mean, she was meant to die and not him? Well, that would have been a very high-risk strategy, which, obviously, did not pay off. No, I think he was just saying she was pissed off with the inquiry and wasn't coming back. Maybe they decided between them that she shouldn't take time off work when he was at the inquiry. She's secretary to some high-up in their firm.'

'Was this a crime of passion?' she asked. 'Was either of them having an outrageous affair?'

'Not in that coat,' I said. 'Maybe it was animal liberationists feeling aggrieved about the sheepskin.'

'Let's not get carried away,' said Lena, protectively.

234

'We're rather left with the fact that he was going to give evidence. Have you seen his statement?'

'No. I just don't want that to be the reason he was killed. For a start it will freak out all my clients and secondly, who would be wanting to stop that evidence coming out?'

'Who indeed?' said Lena, who didn't know the half of it. 'What about this Frodsham? He's the one who worries me. Used to be Danny's solicitor, he's Yolande's husband and now he represents the unpleasant Mr Wyatt.' I had told her how Wyatt had dropped me in it.

'He's just a solicitor,' I said.

'Why did Danny drop him?'

'Because he wanted someone who would fight hard for him.'

'From what you say, Frodsham fights fairly hard. Perhaps he'd just discovered about Danny and Yolande and they thought it would be better if Danny had another solicitor.'

'Maybe, but I get the sense that Frodsham has known about Yolande and Danny for quite a long time.'

'Perhaps Frodsham knows what's on that roll of film, and doesn't like it. This is all very murky, darling,' Lena said, warningly. 'It's as if you're in the middle of a pincer movement, Gregory Springer and his death in your inquiry on one side, and Danny Richards and all his unsavoury pals on the other. Not good. How much longer have you got to stay in Birmingham?'

'Forever.'

'Then the first thing you must do is give up Yolande.'

'I think she's already done that.' I threw back a mouthful of ginger tea.

'That's good.'

'No, it isn't. Not necessarily. And don't look at me like that. I think she's quite sad, a small-town girl who met Frodsham, who could give her the best that money could buy, so she married him and then she met Danny; who is the real love of her life.'

'Very tragic, very femme fatale,' said Lena. 'Take my advice, get yourself some Venetian blinds and watch out. You know what femmes fatales do. They use people. They bring down everyone around them. You should leave well alone.'

'That's not proving too difficult,' I said.

Lena looked at my face and sighed. 'You and your love life. Well, given this murky world you seem to have got yourself into, I suppose you require a sidekick, don't you? And I suppose that had better be me.' I couldn't work out if she thought that would be fun or just a painful necessity.

We devised a plan which, I realised later, involved Lena sitting at home in her tranquil cream and green living room, looking out at her splendid displays of scarlet Ena Harkness roses and bushes of purple lavender, with her telephone by her side ('*right* by my side,' she assured me), while I ran through the streets of London with plastic bags and rolls of film.

It was half past three. Lena said, 'I'd better give this neck a lie down, or it might flare up again.'

'I wish something in my life would flare up,' I complained.

'No, you don't,' she said.

TWENTY-FIVE

Sunday Afternoon

I walked back into my living room and again I was struck by the overwhelming neatness my mother had created. There were colours in the room which had lain forgotten for months under their sheen of dust. Even my black sound system looked bright and sparkling. I felt benign towards my mum. I raised the lid of the record player and put on Joe Cocker singing, 'With A Little Help From My Friends'. That's how you got by. My mum had even put some roses from the garden on my desk. I went to pick up a petal which had fallen on the floor by the sofa. This part of the room looked very neat. Naked even. Empty.

The bag wasn't there. The bag that Yolande had entrusted to my care, whose contents Yolande seemed to think were in some way the answer to Danny's problem, and which I had conscientiously not looked in ever since she had told me not to, was not there. I couldn't even begin to remember the last time I had seen it. How long had I had it? A week. Most of which time I had been in Birmingham. The only other person who had been in my flat in that time was my mother. Unless I'd been burgled by someone who had broken into my flat for the sole purpose of taking the bag. I was not ready to contemplate that.

I snatched the record off the turntable and rang mum.

'Oh Frankie. Thank goodness.' Her voice sounded strange, as if she was practising being a ventriloquist.

'What, what? Mum? Are you all right? What's happened?'

'You know the Ponds Seven Day Beauty Plan?'

'Emm, no'

'You know.' Her voice was urgent but still sounded as if she was gargling. 'When you have a special occasion coming up and you want to look your best.' She was quite good at the Bs. 'The week before the event, you start using Ponds Beauty Cream, night and morning.'

'Ye-e-es?'

'Well, you don't seem to be able to get the Ponds these days, and I remembered you saying something about Vaseline.'

I didn't like the way this conversation was developing. 'Me?'

'So I spread it on, quite thickly because I haven't got much time. It's our eight month anniversary tomorrow and we're going out tonight, so I put it on about half an hour ago and now my face has gone all red and it feels like there are ants crawling up and down it.'

'Take it off,' I said sharply. 'Take it off now.' I paused. 'I didn't say anything about Vaseline to you. Except when you had that squeaky door and no Three in One.'

'Oh,' she said. Her voice was small and sad and I didn't know if it was because of the face mask or because her brilliant plan had failed, so I asked, 'How is Alan?'

238

'He's fine. Although,' she added mournfully, 'when he sees me like this goodness knows what will happen to our trial marriage.'

'Mum, he's crazy about you,' I said. 'He wouldn't care if your face was sky blue pink with spots on.'

'I think that description is rather unfortunate in the current situation,' she said. Her voice was clearer. I could hear from her tone that she was wiping off the Vaseline. She always sounded like that when she wiped her cleansing milk from her nose. I could see her reaching for another tissue.

'Mum, when you were here yesterday, you didn't see a bag did you? It was just by the side of my desk.'

'Oh that.' I could hear she was smiling.

'Yes. Where is it?'

'I brought it home.'

'Sorry?'

'I used to go out with a boy who had a jumper like that.'

'A jumper? You opened it?'

'Why, was it a surprise?'

'Mum, it's possibly evidence in a criminal trial.'

'Oh. Rather an unstylish criminal, I should say.'

'Well, if it's so unstylish, why did you take it?'

'It needed a good wash. And the memories.'

'For goodness' sake. Have you washed it? This is awful. I can't believe you did that.'

'I haven't actually. But it is filthy.'

'I'm coming to get it. Don't touch it.'

'Well, you can't come now, if that's what you were thinking, we're just going to a concert. Can I at least touch it enough to put it back in the bag?'

'All right.'

'Don't worry, it'll be quite safe here. I'll put it in the back cupboard, where it will be cool and dry.'

It was the best I could do. I replaced the receiver and stared at the wall. This was getting out of hand. It was time to go to confession. I rang Kay.

She said, 'What?' She sounded distracted, although on reflection, she always talks to me like that.

'What are you doing this evening?' I asked.

'Sorry?'

'Do you fancy going to a film? *LA Confidential* is on at the Rio.'

'Frankie, how many times must you be told? You can never be Kevin Spacey,' she said.

'I know that.'

'What's brought this on? You never ring me for social reasons.'

'I ring you about once a year. And this is it.'

We arranged to meet at the cinema at six-thirty and maybe have a drink after. The film was great. It always is. It was the drink after I was worried about.

When we came out it was still light. I had walked to the cinema, so we drove to a pub on Stoke Newington High Street in Kay's car. The pub was large and airy with wide, round wooden tables, at which sat a few hardened drinkers and a few people wearing cords and cotton shirts reading the *Observer*. I bought the drinks, we both had whisky, but I had a reason.

She knew that. As soon as I sat down she said, 'So?'

I didn't even pick up my glass. 'It's about Danny Richards.'

'What about Danny Richards, my client, who is nothing to do with you?'

I had known this would happen. I had known she

240

would get uppity. 'Look,' I said, 'I think I may have some evidence about the murder.' I should have added, 'well, my mum has', but I felt that might interrupt the flow of the conversation.

'Oh yes?'

'I've got a jumper.'

'As you know,' she said drily, 'any addition to your wardrobe is always a matter of interest to me, but I'd rather hear what you have to say about Danny.'

'No, I have a jumper that Yolande gave to me.'

'Exchanging gifts now?'

'No.' I stopped, what could I say? I didn't know what its significance was, I didn't even know what it looked like, if it really was a man's jumper as my mum had inferred or if it was more of a tank top. I didn't know what colour it was.

She cut into my thoughts. 'Are you saying it may have some DNA on it?'

I hope to God that's not what I'm saying, I thought, because the only DNA it's likely to have on it now is my mother's, with possibly a bit of Vaseline.

'What kind of DNA?'

'I don't know,' I said wildly. 'That may not be it.'

'Depending on where it's been, any DNA will be totally corrupted by now.'

I thought, you can say that again. 'Do you think so?' I said, hopefully.

'Look, save your energy, Frankie. Danny could have proved his innocence by now, if he'd wanted to. He just doesn't want to. Danny is not as other men,' she sighed. 'Not the men that we know, anyway.'

I thought of Marcus. 'That's not necessarily a bad thing.'

'I didn't say it was. In Danny's world, life isn't just about who's guilty and who's innocent.' She took a gulp of whisky. 'Sometimes it's about doing your time, to prove something else. Danny lives on another moral plane. What's considered "good" and "bad" is different. What's necessary and what's permissible are different. He has a very strict moral code. It's just different.'

'All right, I can live with that.'

'What does he say about this jumper?'

I formed various sounds in my mouth, 'mm, ww, nn, ttphw.'

'I assume that means he knows nothing,' she said. 'So butt out.'

'I love it when you talk American,' I said.

'I mean it,' she said. 'We work only on his instructions.'

'But I'm not instructed by him.'

'Come on, Frankie. You have been. That cuts you out completely. So it's just Yolande who knows you're doing this?'

'Yes,' I said, reluctantly.

'What's her game?'

'I think she loves him and misses him.'

'Yes, and I think I'm Mary Poppins – and if you start talking like Dick Van Dyke I'm leaving.'

'Oh go on.'

'No.'

'Just a little. Chim chim –'

'No.'

'All right, but what if this jumper does prove something? Shouldn't we try and see that justice is done? In this one particular case?'

'I know what you're saying. But think about this.

242

Why has Yolande given it to you? Why didn't she just straight away give it to me? Or to the police? Maybe, just maybe, and what do I know, I've only been representing him for three weeks, doing time for this murder is the price Danny has paid to protect himself or someone else from paying a far greater price for something else. You can be sure he knows what he's up to.'

'So what about this jumper?'

'Wear it,' she said.

'But it's horrible,' I said, silently adding, apparently. 'My mum wouldn't be seen dead in it.'

'Well, perhaps somebody else was, perhaps that's why your Yolande gave it to you. Why not slip it on, see how it feels?'

'That's horrible,' I said.

'I know,' she said, 'I'm sorry. Just forget it, OK?'

She was getting frosty again. By way of diversion I told her about Gregory Springer, his history, his wife in her coat, their aloofness, the phonecall on Thursday. Immediately she was captivated. What did I think? Could it really be murder? Was he the intended victim? We chewed it over for an hour or so, considering all the possibilities, and she was so matter of fact and methodical about it that the uneasy sensation I had had of being too close to it all began to fade.

It was time to go home. I hadn't mentioned the roll of film because I'd completely forgotten about it I thought, as I let myself into the flat, but she didn't really need to know about it. I hadn't even had it developed.

TWENTY SIX

Monday Morning – Clerkenwell

On my way into Clerkenwell I considered again what a stupid thing this was to do. Driving into the centre of London on a Monday morning is always madness; Clerkenwell Green is a drag to get to; I was going to have to park, and I only had three twenty-pence pieces. I was going to have to wander round gloomy, empty streets to find the building, and then reveal myself as not an artistic person.

But walking through Clerkenwell is an experience which sums up London. Straight ahead of me was the Marx Memorial Library, jostled by modern fancy restaurants and designers of expensive ethereal jewellery. Moving right past the offices of Stonewall (just relocating), on to the old Spare Rib offices, through the narrow curving streets where the film about Ruth Ellis, the last woman to be hanged in England, was made, to arrive at the Printing Workshop.

The Workshop was made up of three enormous Victorian factory warehouses, tall and forbidding. I imagined the skittering of clogs on cobbles a hundred years ago, as men and women hurried grimly to be at their places of work on time. Now though these grey, grimy behemoths were the home of young enthusiastic art workers.

A woman of about twenty-five with her head wrapped in a turquoise scarf stepped out of a pair of peeling bottle-green double doors. 'Hi,' she said, and held the door open for me. A board just inside indicated that the printers I was looking for were on the first floor. Behind the board was a small glass-walled room, with three casually dressed people chatting inside.

'First floor?' I asked.

'Just along the passage,' a young man said with a smile.

It was like an old school or an old hospital: concrete floors, the walls half bottle green tiles, half grubby cream paint. On the left of the corridor was a set of sludge green double doors leading to the stairs and the lift. The lift was the open sort, with doors of concertina metal. I heard it creaking slowly somewhere up above me. I made my way up the dark stone stairs. A notice on the first-floor landing reminded me to close the lift doors.

The corridor was lit by fluorescent lighting which beamed starkly down. Some of the doors were locked and barred, secured by heavy padlocks. Some doors were open and through one of them, the harsh, throaty voice of Eric Burdon singing a Chuck Berry classic beamed out, and I remembered that I needed an Animals CD rather badly.

I found the workshop. It was a small, untidy, cream-painted room, brightly lit by a fluorescent strip and a few spotlights. Contact sheets hung on a line, and spilled out of cardboard containers on the tables that lined the walls. Freestanding pieces of pale grey machinery stood in the middle of the room. It was empty.

I'd come to this place because of the music, not specifically Eric Burdon, but because that was the kind of place it was, cool, laid back. A photographer friend of mine had told me about them years before, that they were friendly, good and not too expensive. And if there were terrible images on this film, their first response wouldn't necessarily be to call the police.

So I was surprised when the person coming out of a back room, wiping crumbs from her mouth and smiling at me, her hand outstretched to take the film, was a girl who looked younger than Marnie. She wore a grey skirt and a pink and white striped blouse, like a school uniform. Just my luck to get the work experience person. Or perhaps it was one of those 'Take your Daughter to Work' days, which we completely agree with, to broaden girls' horizons and show them they can do anything, but which can be disconcerting. Especially when the daughter tells you the manager is just having coffee with someone in the basement and begins to enter your details in that neat, formless handwriting they have, on a spare piece of scrap paper that she picks up from the floor that looks like a shopping list. I couldn't leave this film with this child. There could be pictures of a murder on it, blood, gore, strangulation.

On the other hand, I didn't want to knock her confidence by saying that I would rather wait and see someone else, so I nudged her to take the information I thought she would need beyond my name and address, and encouraged her to tell me when the pictures, whose size, we had agreed, would be 'not that big', could be collected. She hesitated and said Friday, which I knew she was making up, but that was OK, because I was going to ring later to confirm it all.

I walked back through the corridor on the ground floor, thinking about Yolande and what I'd just done for her. From behind a peeling olive green door came the eery sound of a quite obscure version of 'Baby, Don't You Do It'. (Was it the Poets?) My message to Yolande, whispering to her not to break my heart. I sacrificed to make her happy, I tried to do my best. Then I wondered if it was a spooky message just for me, don't do it, don't leave the film, rush back and grab it out of that young woman's hands. But I didn't have time, I had to get back to the car.

There were three minutes left on the meter. I put the key in the ignition and sat, remembering the scene at Euston Station, watching my lucky token friend expertly opening the left luggage locker, swinging back the door, and my hand snaking in to the back to retrieve the film. What a business. Maybe the key Clark had given me would never have worked. Maybe Yolande or Clark had never had one and they'd given me any old key to lull me into thinking it was a legitimate exercise. Perhaps that was someone else's locker. For all I knew, I had paid money – the ten pound note – for the illicit opening of a left luggage locker in order to steal . . . a roll of film. The photos had better be good. Whatever that might mean. Oh God. Kay's words echoed round my head. This is Danny's case. We take our instructions from him. What would Danny say?

Well, it was too late to worry about it now. Images were probably emerging already in a small darkroom with a red bulb, on squares of white paper, rocking backwards and forwards in a shallow tray of developer. Whatever they might be.

I was close enough to chambers to go in. Behind Temple tube I found a meter with twenty minutes still left on it, and as a small celebration and because it was lunch time, I bought myself a cream cheese and tomato sandwich from the café.

Vanya was in the clerks' room, looking at Gavin's computer screen with him. She looked up as I walked in. 'Oh you're here! That's great. We're meant to have a Family Group meeting this evening, but everybody's back from court, so we might as well have it now. Fifteen minutes? In our room?'

She heaved her bag onto her shoulder. 'Have you heard about the band?' She looked meaningfully at Gavin and left.

'Band?' I asked.

'I've told you,' he said.

'You haven't.' Maybe my memory was going. People kept telling me they'd told me things of which I had no memory whatsoever.

'Malik and I, and a couple of others, have been playing together for about six months.' I had an uneasy prickling sensation. Something to do with heavy metal. Heads shaking violently. I was suffering hysterical amnesia, my brain was protecting me from the painful realities of life. 'Tony wants us to play at his party.'

'Ah. Has he. . . .heard you play at all?'

'Frankie, we have a range of numbers that we do. Classics, modern, sing-along. We even have guest singers.'

'OK, karaoke, great. Did you find the advices I did?'

'Nifty change of subject. Yes, I faxed them over this morning. You see . . .' He was getting that 'if only you would allow yourself, you could have a very nice paper-work practice' expression on his face.

I was too young, there was too much rock and rolling still to do. I went and made a cup of tea.

Iotha, Vanya, Deborah and Rani were already there, munching miniature chocolate bars and laughing. I felt like an outsider, because I hadn't been to a Family meeting for so long and because they'd started without me. There weren't enough chairs and I had to go to Simon's empty room and push a ridiculously large orange swivel chair back into a small space between Vanya and Deborah. They paused as I settled myself. I couldn't decide whether to apologise, ask for a chocolate or enquire what they were laughing about. Vanya pushed the box of chocolates towards me. 'We're celebrating,' she said, before I'd said anything. I took a small Galaxy Bar, unwrapped it and put it in my mouth. I let it melt on my tongue.

'I was doing a case of Vanya's today,' Deborah said.

I felt a spurt of jealousy, why hadn't it been offered to me? Then I remembered I had specifically asked Gavin to keep me out of court. But he could have asked me, I thought. I smiled. 'Where?'

'Wells Street. It was a directions appointment in a care case for Greenwich.'

I relaxed. Wells Street was just a Family Proceedings Court, the equivalent of a magistrates' court. You could be there all day on a matter that anywhere else would only take fifteen minutes. Although that was true of the County Courts in Bow and Bromley. And Romford. And Croydon. It's a waiting game we play. But Wells Street was close to Tottenham Court Road. I could have looked at leather furniture.

'Anyway my opponent was a very loud, pushy woman, from somewhere in Grays Inn. She reeked of alcohol.' We all shook our heads in sympathy. 'She was trying to say that she and Vanya had agreed the basis of the threshold criteria at the hearing before, on completely different terms from what Vanya had told me. She wanted to say that the father had agreed that all three children had been abused, Vanya had agreed abuse for one and a failure to protect the other two.'

'It was a paedophile ring,' Vanya explained. 'But the father hadn't actually abused two of them, he'd just let his mates have a go.'

'I mean, it was endorsed on Vanya's old brief. I showed her, but she wouldn't have it, so I said I was going to call Vanya. I thought that would shut her up, but she wouldn't back down. The point was that Vanya was actually in the building, her case was in Court 4 upstairs. I rang Vanya on my mobile and as luck would have it, they hadn't gone into court, so she came dashing down. Then the trouble started.'

'It got a bit loud,' Vanya said.

'A bit! You should have seen Vanya,' Deborah guffawed. 'She was fuming!'

'She was accusing me of lying,' Vanya said, indignantly.

'And then when I was showing her the endorsement, she snatched it out of my hands.'

'And so I snatched it out of hers and it was getting rather physical. Someone called security, and they were actually asking us to leave the building – the building! – when my mobile went off and I had to go back upstairs.'

'How come she reeked of alcohol at ten o'clock in the morning?' Rani inquired.

'It was probably from the night before,' Vanya said, 'but it was pretty strong.'

Deborah laughed. 'You could see the security people's heads jerking back when she spoke to them.'

'So, remember girls,' said Vanya, 'not only can we not drink at lunch time if we're in court in the afternoon, now we can't drink in the evening if we have to go to court the next day. And just as they've discovered drinking can keep Alzheimer's at bay.'

'That won't affect me,' I said. 'I'm never in court.'

'What about your inquiry?'

'Oh, yes, I forgot. Well, it's obviously too late then.'

'And for me,' Vanya said.

'And me,' the others agreed.

This is what I missed being up in Birmingham, the stories, the jokes, being able to recount awful moments, with a chocolate in your mouth and your colleagues' sympathetic laughter in your ears. I was homesick for chambers! Things were worse than I realised.

We talked about the library, the law reports we needed, the handbooks which were always out of the library just when you had to go to court, and then some recent decisions. The first was about ancillary relief – the money side of divorce – and most of us fell into a short coma of uninterestedness as Deborah tried to explain it, and the other was a case about domestic violence that we were all very excited about, which said that domestic violence was to be considered as an important issue when deciding contact cases.

'How is Birmingham?' they said at the end and I gave them the five minute upbeat version. But I had to include Gregory Springer's accident. They'd find out about it soon enough. 'Murder?' Vanya breathed.

I could see them all thinking back to the year before, wondering what kind of person I was, who carried murder and mayhem around with her in her briefcase.

Iotha and I walked downstairs together. 'How are you feeling?' I asked.

She shook her head, as if to get rid of a bad smell.

'You could try threatening our mutual friend with Vanya. Our mutual fiend. Let me know what you want me to do.'

She smiled. 'You seem to have a lot on your plate.'

'All part of the job. I'll ring you,' I said.

'Only if you have time.'

I walked into the clerks' room. 'I'm going back up to Birmingham,' I announced.

'OK,' Gavin said.

'Bye,' Jenna called.

Marcus turned round from his pigeon-hole. 'Are you in later?' he asked.

I hesitated. 'In Birmingham.'

'I'd like to ring you. It's about a case.'

I looked at my watch. 'Can't you speak to me now?'

'Not really, I haven't read all the papers yet. I don't want to waste your time.'

Marcus did almost exclusively crime. Why on earth would he want to talk to me? I wondered if he too had me mixed up with Francis Richmond. Perhaps I was Francis Richmond. This was very good news. I was no longer Frankie Richmond who slept with the wrong people. I had become a glossy, successful middle-aged man with a fabulous practice, who enjoyed discussing criminal law . . . with slimeballs. 'It would be extremely helpful,' he said smoothly.

'I'm really up to my neck at the moment, Marcus.'

He laughed and it sounded like the oil from a chip pan being poured back into the bottle.

'Well, yes, all right, if you must,' I muttered. 'The clerks have my number.'

The drive back was uneventful. I sensed that the car was starting to enjoy this new development, long journeys on the open road and the hours spent in cruise. There were no hitches, no stopping, it was a perfectly smooth ride. 'OK, we'll think about it,' I sighed, as I pulled up outside Julie's house. I was toying with the idea of having a respray and simply pretending it was a new car.

Julie had made sausage and mash. She was a good cook, when she did it, and the gravy and the onions were delicious. Even Marnie cleared her plate and sat with us at the end of the meal, joining in with our chat. The conversation was all about the demo. 'There were so many people, all talking and singing. It was fantastic. And mum nearly got arrested,' Marnie said.

'I was in the wrong place at the wrong time,' Julie sighed.

'And so I was trying to pull the policeman's arm away,' Marnie went on, 'and another one pulled my wig off. If it hadn't come off, I probably would have been arrested. Could I sue them to get it back?'

'No,' Julie and I said together.

'It was just so great.' She sighed at the memory. 'I've got loads of leaflets, shall I show you?'

I was wiping the table to avoid getting grease on the leaflets when the door bell rang. 'I'll get it,' Marnie said.

'Are you expecting visitors?' I asked Julie.

She shook her head.

Marnie came back into the kitchen, smiling shyly. 'It's Clark.'

* * *

The pub was a small, busy place, next to Selly Oak station. It was only because it was within walking distance that Julie had allowed Marnie out at all. I had been the other requirement.

Standing at the bar I could see their reflections in the mirror, Clark in a brown leather jacket, Marnie wearing a small, tight T-shirt. Marnie was standing very close to Clark. Too close. As I watched through the bottles of spirits, Clark lifted a strand of Marnie's hair and played it through his fingers. She stood stock still, a faint glow overtaking her features. Slowly she raised her eyes to his face, trust and pleasure shining out of them in equal measure. I was almost as mesmerised as she was.

Then I came to. 'A Coke, a glass of white wine and a bottle of . . . something,' I shouted at the barman as I spun on my heel and flew across the room. 'Marnie!' I said. 'Come and help me carry the drinks.' I took her arm and pulled her into the crowd.

'Frankie,' she said in disgust. 'You do pick your moments.'

'Yes, I do,' I said, leaning over the bar to see where the barman was. 'When I can.'

'Well, I wish you wouldn't.'

The barman appeared with the Coke and the wine. 'And what was it?'

'What did Clark want?' I asked Marnie.

'A Budweiser,' she said smugly. She turned to look at Clark.

I looked in the reflection of the mirror.

He was staring fiercely down at his hands, not quite muttering to himself, but looking as if he was having an internal discussion about something. His hands moved as he put forward various propositions. I hoped it wasn't anything to do with Marnie. In case the question was should he or shouldn't he make a move on her, I sent a short, two-letter answer, hoping he'd receive it through ESP.

He was actually being a very charming companion, he told stories about his flat, his fishing and his job at the furniture shop, his support for Aston Villa football club and his brothers and sisters, one of whom, Dennis, was apparently something big in the entertainment world. Marnie was completely charmed, and was obviously considering the possibility of using his contacts for a future career under the spotlights.

Marnie and I walked Clark to the bus stop and then strolled back to the house. It had just gone ten o'clock, there was still a touch of daylight, making the sky purple. It was warm and the evening felt comforting and safe. Marnie linked arms with me.

'He had this other brother right, and he saved his life. At their house one day something happened, I think it was an electric fire or something, anyway, his brother was electrocuted and I think he caught on fire, and Clark jumped on him and put the flames out. That's why he's got that scar on his arm.'

I thought back to Clark in a vest. 'I haven't seen any scars.'

'I have,' she gloated.

'When?'

'When you were getting that last round of drinks. It's just under his arm here.' She demonstrated. 'And there's another one across his chest.'

There may be an argument for making men pay for drinks. It keeps them occupied and they have to keep their scars to themselves.

'And his name's not really Clark. Well it is, it's just not his first name. It's Jimmy.'

'You should come and do my job,' I said. 'How did you get all of that out of him in such a short time?'

'My womanly wiles,' she said.

I groaned.

Simon had rung. I rang him back.

'It wasn't really important,' he said. 'Just to see how you are and chat to someone about the case. We're romping through the evidence. We'll have finished the prosecution case by next week. I've got them thinking that Catcher may be trying to set Danny up.'

'How have you done that?'

'Mainly by suggesting it to an officer.' He yawned down the phone. 'I really don't know why Catcher's even on the indictment. There's so little evidence against him. If Danny had pleaded guilty the case against Catcher would have collapsed and he'd have walked away from it all.'

'Can't that still happen?'

'No, too much evidence has been coming out. Roseanna will make a submission of no case, but I think it will have to be left to the jury. There's no love lost between Danny and Catcher. Apparently, we may even have the pleasure of Effo giving live evidence.'

'Does he really exist?' I asked.

'As far as I know. And for some reason Roseanna wants to call him to give evidence. I'm sure it's to try and drop Danny in it. We're happy to have his statement read, it just says Fleming was last seen at the Lambada. She obviously has some deeply searching questions to ask.' He paused, and then said what he'd really rung to tell me. 'Roseanna has asked me out for a meal tomorrow night, at a Chinese restaurant she says is rather good.'

'Oh Simon, I'm sorry.'

'Why? This is one of the nicest things that's happened to me for a long time. Apparently their fried noodles are second to none.'

'Yes, but I was supposed to be arranging an outing for the three of us, and I forgot.'

'Frankie, I forgive you. Because I have to say, much as I adore your company –'

'– you'd rather spend the evening with Roseanna on your own. I understand.' I was a social outcast. Nobody wanted me. Not Marnie, not Yolande, not even Simon.

'OK.' Simon yawned again. 'Tomorrow we've got an eleven o'clock start. An extra half-hour in bed. What luxury.'

'You're sleeping in tomorrow?' An idea was forming in my head. Someone who might want me. 'I don't suppose Danny will get a lie in.'

'No, unfortunately for Danny, he'll be brought from Winson Green first thing, with all the other remand prisoners.'

So Danny would have at least half an hour at court, lounging around in his cell, flicking through an old copy of the *Mirror*, getting bored, before Simon arrived. It was almost my duty to go and see him. I could be in and out in twenty minutes.

'It's all right for some,' I said casually. 'Send my regards to Roseanna.'

TWENTY-SEVEN

Tuesday – Birmingham Crown Court

Danny had definitely smartened up. He was wearing a grey suit and a purple shirt, with a deep purple tie. As he walked into the room I was aware of the scent of aftershave. Expensive aftershave, but a little overpowering. Perhaps it would calm down as the day wore on. His expression was tense and heavy, but perhaps he was worrying that he'd put on too much cologne.

His face brightened as he saw me. 'Well, well, well. Look who's here.' He grinned to himself as he pulled out a chair and sat down opposite me.

I realised that I was pleased to see him too. It could have been the power of the makeover, from army fatigues to Armani flash. It could have been his pleasure in seeing me. Or perhaps by seeing him in the flesh I could dispel some of the lurid images of myself being pummelled under his fist as he learned of the precise nature of my relationship with Yolande.

'Hello stranger,' he said. There was something reassuring about the way he had no papers with him, no creased file full of old letters, annotated statements, jotted notes, numbered insults, all of which counsel was expected to read, comment on and then use to powerful effect in court. Perhaps crime was the field to practice in. Although anyone, even someone charged with a criminal offence and anxious about the outcome of the case, is liable to keep a few documents. Danny of course was in a different league. Not my league. We smiled at each other.

'Yes. Look Danny, I really shouldn't be here, but I needed to get one or two things straight. I've got small questions and I've got big questions. Which do you want first?'

I pulled out a pack of Benson & Hedges and placed it firmly in front of me. His eyes flicked to the cellophane wrapped box and back up to my face. He grinned again. 'Let's start small.'

'I am having a roll of film developed. Do you know anything about it?'

His eyes flickered down to the Benson & Hedges. Proprietorially I put my hand on the pack.

He said, 'No, I don't know anything about that. But I hope the pictures come out well. Next question.'

I took a breath. This was going to sound even more stupid. 'What about a jumper?'

'I'm fine, but if you're feeling chilly . . .'

'Danny. Yolande has given me a jumper. It was wrapped up in a plastic bag.'

'Interesting.' Was there a shimmer of a reaction? 'What's it like?'

'My mum says it's horrible.'

'Your mum?'

'She's . . . looking after it at the moment. While I'm in Birmingham. Do you know anything about it?'

'I don't know much about horrible jumpers. These days I'm more of a suit man.' He looked down proudly at his outfit. 'Can't help you there, sweetheart.'

'She got it from Effo's flat in London.'

He raised his eyebrows. 'Oh, that jumper.' The corners of his mouth turned up in a small smile and he sat back in his chair, spreading his legs, eyeing the cigarettes. 'Yolande shouldn't be involved in all this.'

'She just doesn't want you in prison. She loves you.'

He shrugged. He was closing up. I slid the pack of cigarettes and a book of matches from the tapas bar I'd been to with Adam across the table. Slowly Danny unwound the cellophane from the box and laid it on the table. He held the pack thoughtfully, looking at it, nodding slightly, as if he was having a private conversation.

'Yolande works hard for you. She's trying to get you out of prison. She runs your furniture shop.'

'She doesn't,' he said. 'She's hardly there at all. She knows nothing. Not a thing.' He said it so definitely, compared to his usual languid responses, that I wasn't entirely convinced.

'Look, when I've talked to Yolande, or Clark for that matter, I get the impression . . .'

'Yolande can't stand the sight of blood,' he went on. 'And that's a fact.' He pushed open the lid and pulled out a cigarette.

'Are we talking about the blood on the carpet?' I said hesitantly.

'And as for Clark.' He held a lighted match at the tip of a cigarette. 'Don't,' he inhaled, 'waste your time with him. He's . . . a nice lad.' He lit the cigarette and waved the smoke away. 'But let me put it this way. He lacks elementary common sense. And he sometimes has conflicting loyalties. Which is hardly surprising.'

260

'Has Yolande known him long?'

'Yolande? As long as she's known me, I suppose. Look.' He hunched forward, his elbows on the table, his cigarette held in his cupped hands. 'The police wanted me, they've got me. If it wasn't for this, it would be something else.' He leaned back, smiling.

'Does Yolande know about the blood on the carpet?' I didn't want Yolande to know, I really didn't want her to know.

'Frankie – it is Frankie, isn't it? – you don't want to get involved any deeper. Yolande's just getting her knickers in a twist about all these jumpers and holiday snaps.'

'Who said anything about holiday snaps?'

He pulled a face. 'Good try, Sherlock.' He laughed and blew a stream of smoke up at the ceiling, tilting his chair back to watch it dissolve.

'Look Danny, we haven't got much time. I know you don't want to fight the case, and so there's no real need for me to be here at all. But what was your relationship with Fleming?'

The front legs of his chair tipped back on to the floor. 'Terry Fleming was a stupid bastard. That means he was stupid and he was a bastard. And then he had to pay for it. Ask that toe rag friend of his, currently talking to Miss Newson along there.' He indicated the corridor with his thumb. He meant Catcher. 'He knows what I mean.' He dropped his cigarette onto the floor and rubbed it out with his foot.

'Is that why you gave his name to the police?'

He raised his eyebrows at me. 'Sometimes the police need a little assistance. I like to help our boys in blue.'

There were so many supplementary questions I

wanted to ask, but there was so little time. 'And what about Effo? What's he got to do with all this?'

'That,' he said, 'is a very good question. Effo is a clever man – a bit too clever.'

'How?'

'He sees too much and he hears too much.'

'But you've worked for him haven't you?'

'When I've had to. And I've worked with some amateurs. You should never work with amateurs.'

'I thought that was dogs and children.'

He considered the comment. 'Comes to the same thing. Do you know what I wish? I wish that people like Effo didn't exist. In fact I'll go further than that, I wish he was dead.'

From a man in Danny's profession that was a blood-chilling comment.

'Danny that's a terrible thing to say.'

'He's a terrible man. Same as me. He's no better than me. Doesn't make me like him.'

'I wouldn't expect you to like him, especially as he's lined up to give evidence against you.'

'Effo? Against me? No, he won't do that. That's what Catcher wants, isn't it? He thinks if he threatens me with Effo, I'll go guilty. He's shitting himself, thinking he's going down. He's trying to be hard.' He laughed quietly. 'It won't come to that.'

'It was just something Simon said,' I murmured.

'Anyway, how've you been? I've read a bit about that inquiry of yours. Now, those are the real villains, aren't they?' He took another cigarette out of the packet and prepared to light it. 'What they do. Preying on kids.'

'You've got one on the go,' I said. With an unusual

262

show of emotion he thrust the cigarette back in the packet, breaking off the tip.

'I was sorry to see you weren't in the pictures for that do last week.' I stared at him. He grinned. 'I've got my sources. It was in the local paper. Yolande looked very nice.'

I hadn't seen the pictures. I assumed Frodsham had been standing next to Yolande, but Danny didn't seem troubled. 'Why isn't Frodsham representing you?' I asked.

He looked up at the ceiling, considering how to answer – truthfully or dismissively.

'It seemed the right time to change lawyers,' he said. 'He was better off out of this one.'

'Why?'

'I like you, Frankie.' He scratched his lip with his thumb nail, weighing me up again. 'You being friendly to Yolande.' My stomach shrivelled with guilt. 'I won't forget this.' He looked at me meaningfully.

Oh God. 'Danny, it's nothing.' Really.

'And you'll get your reward. Everything comes to those who wait.'

'No reward needed,' I said, deprecatingly.

He was smiling to himself, so I burst out, 'Danny, why don't you want to even try to get off this murder charge?'

He opened his mouth as if to say something, but he could have just been blowing smoke rings, when the door opened. We both jumped back in our seats as if we had been caught in an illicit embrace. Simon came in. I began to smile but his expression froze the curve of my lips. 'My junior?' he said to me, without even acknowledging Danny.

Danny said, 'I asked for her to come. I needed to see her.' Protecting me again.

'My junior?' Simon ignored him, and advanced into the room, throwing his wig onto the table.

In order to get in to see Danny I had had to give myself a professional position. Simon's junior was the best thing I could think of. In fact the only thing I could think of.

'But it's true,' I explained. 'In many ways. You are four years more call than me, so technically I am your junior; you ought to have a junior in this case, with all the complexities; you're taller than I am. . . .'

'Frankie, I will speak to you later,' he said. I hate that, when people I normally know as laughing and friendly start speaking with their lips so tight they can hardly get the words out.

I picked up my notebook and the makeshift brief I had thrown together, Danny's name, my name, Kay's name on a piece of white paper with red ribbon wrapped around it, which I had used as my entrance ticket. Simon moved silently to the door, his hand waiting to turn the handle. As I walked past him he hissed, 'How could you?' And then I was out in the corridor, slinking past the jailer and out into the foyer of the court.

'Bye, doll,' Danny called behind me.

I knew there was a lot more Simon had wanted to say, but not in front of the client. He would tell me later, it would be about professionalism and the Bar Council and integrity and interfering with justice and putting his own position in jeopardy. I wanted to go to sleep for a hundred years. And something told me the day could only get worse.

For a start it was twenty-five past ten and I had to be in the car park at the Grange for ten thirty. We were going to visit Haslam Hall.

TWENTY-EIGHT

Later Tuesday Morning – Inquiry/View

I flew across the road at ten twenty-nine, with a film of sweat on my forehead. My pumping heart relaxed as I saw my clients grouped round a sparkling green hired people carrier. I avoided looking in the direction of my car, which I knew had needed a wash for the last three years. No one needed to know it was mine.

'There you are!' said Shelly. 'Have you heard anything? We sent Emma a card and some flowers.'

I looked at Adam, who nodded slightly. 'Yes, so did we,' I said.

'I just rang the hospital,' he said. 'Mrs Springer has regained consciousness, but they are keeping her sedated because of the extent of her injuries.' To me he murmured, 'The police want to interview all the clients, probably tomorrow.'

'Let's tell them when we come back from the View,' I said. I didn't want them more anxious than they already were.

My clients hadn't asked for the View. Visiting Haslam Hall, where it had all happened, had been the suggestion of the teachers' representatives, and when Catherine Delahaye, in her role as advocate to the inquiry, had ventured that it might be useful, the panel had agreed immediately. I think everybody just wanted a chance to get out in the fresh air.

It was questionable whether we would see anything helpful. The place was no longer a children's home, it had been sold years before. Any forensic points we had to raise – about doors that were closed when they should have been opened; the lack of privacy in the bedrooms; what could have been heard, what could have been seen – didn't require us to visit the building. And I wasn't sure what the clients would make of it, after all these years. They had been told they didn't have to come and some had said they'd rather not. But for others it was going to be part of the process, part of the way they were dealing with it, on the route to finality.

There wasn't enough room for me and Adam in the people carrier, which is why we were going by car. I could have suggested going in mine, but I knew turning up in a dirty ten-year-old car with a slightly discoloured passenger door, would be seen as a mark of failure, and I couldn't afford that. I knew Adam's company car was bound to be something Xy, sleek and purring, that I could step out of confidently, holding a crisp blue note-book and a fountain pen, and look professional. As we walked across the car park I was proved right. Adam held out a key which unlocked the doors at thirty feet.

Adam's driving was proficient. It was his taste in driving music that made me hold on to the door handle and gasp. REM. I suppose that goes with a metallic blue car.

We arrived first. I had been navigating and had found us a clever back route which avoided some potentially choked-up villages. Adam wasn't as impressed as he could have been, but then he was worrying about various pieces of country detritus now attached to the car following the one wrong turn we had taken into a farmyard. 'If we go back the same way, we could go through the duck pond,' I said cheerfully. 'That'll get it all off.'

'If I knew you better, I might say that you could go back through the duck pond,' he said, rubbing at a grass stain near a headlight.

'If I knew you better,' I said, 'I would say that a bit of grass never hurt any car. Look at mine.'

Other cars began to arrive. Frodsham with Mr Wyatt; the advocate to the inquiry; the panel, in a rather smooth black car; the other representatives and their clients; and then my clients in the people carrier.

Shelly got out first and said, 'Bloody hell.' She stood looking round her, squinting in the sunlight. 'Bloody hell,' she repeated. The grounds were spectacular, to the right sweeping green lawn, and to the left a red brick wall, which looked as if it contained a vegetable garden, lined with beds of neatly clipped shrubs. I turned back to the lawn, to the golden fields of corn in the distance and further round to the right, where the lawn rolled down to a small lake. 'I fell in that,' Shelly said, following my gaze. She laughed. 'Someone pushed Wyatt's car in there one night.' She cast a glance at Wyatt, who was gazing at the front of the house, shielding his eyes with his hand. She frowned as if a memory was coming back. 'Didn't make him take notice of anything though.'

The others were climbing out of the people carrier, standing silently, looking around them. Fewer of the clients were here today than usually came to the inquiry. Leanne was the last out and she went and stood close to Shelly, who immediately put her arm round her. 'Y'all right?' Shelly asked.

As a group we walked towards the home. Now it was a conference centre.

We walked through the open front doorway. Shelly said, 'These weren't here then,' pushing through a set of glass doors.

'Nor was that,' someone else said, pointing to the reception desk in a corner of the large entrance hall. This whole expedition was going to be quite pointless. Everything would be different. Leanne already looked as if she was finding it hard to breathe, Janine Telford looked cautious and even Shelly was silent.

A woman in a neat tailored jacket came to meet us and Catherine Delahaye stepped forward.

We were led down a long, dark corridor, our shoes occasionally ringing on the stone floor, as one deeply coloured Persian rug replaced another. 'We never had carpets,' Shelly remarked. The place had originally been built by Victorian benefactors as a home for fallen women. It was a handsome building, the panelled walls, the thick, heavy doors, but I wondered how cold and forbidding it must have felt for the young unmarried mothers, clawed away from their families to have their shameful children, who would then be given away to the respectable childless. How must it have felt for my clients, young, troubled, unhappy, taken from their homes to be brought to this isolated spot, away from the noise and rhythms of their families and the town?

'Oh, I remember this room,' Shelly said, as we turned a corner to be confronted by a thick oak door, with a heavy metal handle. She turned to Leanne. 'Are y'all right?'

'Yeah.' A determined expression coloured Leanne's face.

'This were it,' Shelly said. 'The punishment room.'

She took Leanne's hand as Catherine Delahaye pushed open the door.

'Oh,' Shelly and Leanne said, in unison. The room was quite clearly completely different. The wood-panelled walls were lined with tables bearing computers and other pale grey plastic technological machinery. A large square table in the middle of the room was also covered with computers. Vertical blinds at the high windows were partially closed against the sunlight. In front of each screen were comfortable, modern swivel chairs, discreetly covered in a dark navy fabric.

Some of the lawyers made notes. The clients moved back to the door. But Shelly walked round the room, trailing her hand on the wall. When she reached the far end of the room, she looked over at me and raised her eyebrows. I went across to her. 'Look, just there, look,' she murmured. I looked where her hand was still lightly touching the wooden panel. I could just make out a series of faint letters, carved into a dado rail, MV, LJ, JC, R, something that could have been an F or an E Q, GS, others too indistinct to read, and numbers, 1984, 1981, 1982.

'That's me,' she said, quietly, running her finger gently over the first letters. We turned away and walked towards the door. 'We all did it,' she said, as we walked up the stairs, 'while we were waiting. I were Michelle Vernon before I was married,' she answered my silent question. 'Leanne were Jackson then.'

We walked in and out of rooms that had been enlarged, lightened, decorated. Door after door opened onto bright, airy spaces, with rows of chairs and over-head projectors and white screens. Sometimes one of the clients would say, 'Is this where the bedrooms were?' Or, 'Wasn't there a toilet here?' and someone would answer, 'No, that was the other side, wasn't it?' Sometimes one of the teachers would murmur a question. 'Is this where they did their homework?' It was a sombre group.

We were all pleased to come back out into the late-morning warmth. Shelly and Leanne shuddered, shaking themselves like dogs coming out of a pond, then they, and all the other clients, climbed back into the people carrier.

I looked in through the door. 'Thanks for coming,' I said. 'If anything you've seen this morning makes you think of something important, make a note of it and let me know.'

I waved them off, and then we had to wait as everyone else manoeuvred their cars out of the gravel parking area and back onto the long driveway down to the main road.

As we clicked ourselves into our seatbelts, Adam said, 'Did you notice, the principal was very quiet? He didn't seem to react to anything.'

'Perhaps it's just hit home what happened.'

'About time,' we said, together.

In the afternoon we heard from the training officer, who spoke about what care workers are trained to do, and the management consultant, who described how they should be properly managed. He had some criticisms of the management procedures at Haslam Hall. Frodsham asked very few questions because, he suggested to the management consultant, if someone wants to abuse children, the best management procedures in the world won't stop them. The management consultant reluctantly agreed. Then he agreed with me that good management might, however, help to control some of the worst excesses. Frodsham rose red-faced, demanding to ask more questions. Henry Curston looked at him. 'You might have known that question was coming, Mr Frodsham. In any event, isn't it almost a matter of common sense?'

Mr Wyatt, looking pained, put his hand on Frodsham's arm and whispered to him. Frodsham sat down.

I had told the clients, and Catherine Delahaye, that the police wished to interview them, and at the end of the day Henry Curston announced that tomorrow morning the police would come and talk to my clients, and, that being the case, we would adjourn the inquiry until the afternoon at two o'clock.

I walked out of the building with the clients.

As we got to the bottom of the stairs I said goodnight and turned towards the car park. A figure stepped out from the shadow of the stairwell. It was Clark. He was wearing a sleeveless navy windcheater and navy trousers with a navy bag slung over his choulder. He looked like a postman. A postman in sunglasses. His face was a mass of bruises.

'Clark! Your face. How did that happen?'

'Don't ask,' he said. The affability of the night before was gone.

'Did you want something?' I asked doubtfully. If he wanted to come home with me to see Marnie, the face would need more explanation than that.

'I've come to collect.'

'Collect what?'

'You know. Yolande said you'd got it. You know. The bag.'

I shook my head. 'I haven't got it.'

'What!?' A look of pain flashed across his face.

'Well, I have got it. It's . . . in London.'

'I've got to have it.'

'I'll get it as soon as I can, I promise.' We had reached my car. 'Well . . .' I said.

'I've got to get back to the shop,' he said, miserably.

'Do you want a lift? I can drop you off. It's not out of my way.' I had no ulterior motives.

'Yolande's not there,' he said. And still I opened the passenger door for him.

I was trying to avoid getting on to a dual carriageway, but I was confused by the one-way streets. I was coming up Price Street and not sure which way to turn when Clark said, 'Don't go down there.'

Unfortunately, my inborn sense of place told me this was the way to the shop and my left-hand indicator was on. We turned. Clark began sliding down in the seat. 'Don't worry Clark,' I said, 'no one is going to expect to see you in an L-reg Renault.'

'That's what you think,' he said.

'What are we trying to avoid?' I asked.

About two hundred yards down the road Clark said, 'This.'

We were moving past a garage. Red bunting fluttered along the perimeter of the forecourt, where five or six classic cars sat sleekly waiting to be bought. I noticed at least two Jaguars and a Bentley.

'That was Terry Fleming's garage,' Clark said.

A small shudder ran through me, but I was fascinated. I pulled into a parking bay in front of an anonymous concrete building, twenty yards further on. Clark slid down lower. 'There's no one around Clark,' I said. Clark remained hunched in his seat. I adjusted the rear-view mirror and looked back at the garage. 'I thought Terry was a small-time . . . person. Those cars are really expensive. There's one on sale for £17,000.'

'He didn't own it, he only managed it, with Dennis. Effo owns it, but he hardly ever comes over. Dennis is the man now. He's very happy.'

'Your brother Dennis? The entertainer?'

He nodded. He took off his sunglasses. His right eye was puffy and bruised. There were small cuts all over his face. 'I hate him.'

'Clark, he didn't do that, did he?'

He winced slightly as he put the sunglasses back on.

'He hasn't got anything to do with this bag has he? Why is it so important?'

'Didn't Yolande tell you?'

'No.'

'Then I can't tell you.'

'Do you want it to give to Dennis, or do you want it to give to Yolande?'

'You tell me.'

For a few moments we sat silently, as I flicked through my A-Z of Birmingham to see where we were. The afternoon was still and hot. Even the bunting now hung limp and lifeless. The maroon and navy and bottle-green cars sat shining on the forecourt. I could have sworn there was no one about.

Suddenly the passenger door was wrenched open and a face was thrust in. 'Got it then, have you?' The bulk of a man loomed over Clark, holding on to the door frame as if he would rip the car apart.

Clark cringed down in his seat.

'Fuck off!' I shouted, and turned on the ignition. The man ignored me. 'Let go of the car. Let go of the car!' I put the car in gear. The man was still breathing heavily into Clark's face and didn't move. 'I'm going now,' I shouted, and revved the engine. 'Fuck off!'

I don't know if I would have gone, but my foot slipped on the clutch and the car lurched forward. The car door flipped and the man was flung onto Clark's lap. Clark put his hand over the man's face and as I started the engine again he reared back out of the car, clutching his eyes. As I roared down the street I watched him through the wing mirror. He stumbled and almost fell into the road.

'Was that Dennis?' I asked, as we moved back into the regular flow of traffic. We were on a dual carriageway.

'Bastard,' Clark said.

'How old is he?'

'He's seven years older than me. And three years younger than Danny.'

'I was going to ask why you hate him,' I said, overtaking two cyclists. 'Are those his main professions? Managing a garage and being a hard man?'

'That and the performing. You saw him the other night.'

'At the do? Singing "A Whiter Shade of Pale?"'

'Yeah.' He looked ashamed. I didn't know if it was because Dennis was his brother or because he sang so badly. Probably both. 'That's how I got the ticket. I help him carry his equipment sometimes.'

'And he beats you up?'

He was silent.

'Clark, why didn't you pick up that roll of film at Euston Station?'

He frowned and winced. 'She wanted someone else to get it developed. She didn't trust me. She wanted you to do it.'

'Why?'

'I dunno. She didn't want it to get back to Birmingham, I suppose.'

I pulled up outside the furniture shop. 'Are you all right?' I asked. 'You don't want a drink, or something?'

'It's all right.' He shrugged.

'Why don't I come in and make you a cup of coffee?' I said. 'I know where everything is.'

'All right,' he said. He unlocked the door and we walked through the shop, past the same sofas and three-piece suites, with their crunchy smell of freshly dyed upholstery.

'How long have you known Danny?' I asked, as I filled the kettle in the small sink.

Clark had followed me and was leaning against the door. 'Since he come to live with us.'

'When was that?'

'I was about four. He's my foster brother.'

'You were in care?'

'No, well, not at first. We were living with my nan, but she was a foster mother.'

I carried the kettle back into the storeroom with the rickety chairs. Clark followed. I was noticing the pieces of carpet. I realised now they weren't offcuts, they were cut up. 'What about your mother?'

He shook his head.

I found cups in the cupboard and spooned in coffee granules. 'Did something happen to your nan then?'

'No!' He sucked in breath, his hand went to his mouth. 'She just got fed up. The police were always coming round for something or another. Then, Danny got his own place and I went in a home and Dennis stayed with Dot. That's my nan.'

'What, you had to leave your nan's and go to a children's home?' I handed him his coffee.

'It was all Dennis's fault. He was always "Jimmy's done this, Jimmy's done that". Nan reckoned she couldn't control me. Danny would have had me, you know, to live with him, instead of me going into the home, but they said he was too young or something.'

I couldn't bear to look at him, because I knew I would see Clark, the eight-year-old. Small, pale, too thin in cast-off trousers and a dirty orange vest, being led away to the children's home, the expression on his face an attempt at a cheeky grin, with a threat of tears in his eyes. Or was that me?

'But you kept in touch with him, with Danny?'

'Oh yeah. Danny's more than a brother to me. More than Dennis anyway. Danny used to come and see me, after I went away. He brought me a Villa shirt once.'

'Did Dennis not come and see you?'

'Oh yeah. He came all right.'

'What do you mean?' I began. My mobile rang.

It was Marnie. 'I'm making the supper and it will be ready in fifteen minutes, so you better be here. And your friend Simon says he wants you to ring him.'

I took a sip of coffee. It was hot and tasteless. 'I've got to go. I'll do what I can about the jumper.' We walked back through the shop together. At the door, I turned. 'Were you ever ill as a child?' I said.

'No.' He thought about it. 'Oh, one summer, I had

glandular fever. I had to stay in bed, in a dark room. It was good.'

'What children's home did you go to?'

He hesitated. 'I can't remember.'

'Was it Haslam Hall?'

'Can't remember.' He looked away.

'Why is Danny so interested in the inquiry?'

'Is he?'

'And you too.'

'I'm not.'

'How did you know Henry Curston that night at the dance?'

His eyes opened wide. He pulled the door open and manoeuvred me on to the pavement. Then he shut the door.

Marnie had made pasta and tomato sauce.

'Who's Iotha?' she asked as we carried the used plates into the kitchen.

'She's a woman in my chambers.'

'Is she a lesbian?'

'Marnie!' My cousin's shocked face snapped up from the dishwasher.

'I'm only asking. Am I not allowed to ask questions now?'

'Why are we having this conversation?' I said.

Marnie bravely fought an instinct to sulk. 'She rang just before you got in and said it was really urgent . . . What? Isn't it important if someone is a lesbian?'

'Marnie, give it a rest.' Julie was pouring soap powder into the small metal box.

'Marnie, I have no idea who she sleeps with.' My mind was racing. I hadn't spoken to her. I hadn't spoken to anyone. Damn. 'What's more important is why she wants me to ring her.'

Iotha's number was written in Marnie's neat, round handwriting on the pad by the phone. I dialled.

The sound of her answerphone clicking on was balm to my soul. I could do my duty but not have to engage. But the message gave her mobile number, which I realised was also on the pad in Marnie's writing. Damn, I would have to speak to her. I rang the number quickly. She answered after three rings. It sounded as if she was in the bath.

'Have you spoken to anyone yet?' she asked me.

'Not yet,' I said guiltily. Even though she hadn't asked me to do anything, I should have sounded out Simon at the very least. Of course, that is what I should have been doing last night, instead of planning an unwise visit to Birmingham Crown Court.

'I don't want you to.'

'Sorry, what? It's not a very good connection.'

'I don't want to go on with this. I've decided it would do my career no good. Nothing will happen to him and I will always be known as the woman who, I don't know, wanted to go to bed with Marcus but couldn't.'

'That is so unlikely,' I said, 'but I know what you mean. Let's think about this.' I was trying to ensure that my common sense wasn't outweighed by the glorious, cool sense of relief flooding through me.

'Look, if I make a complaint it will all take so long. I don't want to have to cope with any more stress.'

'Are you trying to convince me, or yourself?' I asked.

'I'm sure.'

'But how will you stop him?'

'One decision at a time.'

'If you change your mind let me know,' I said. 'Take care.'

'Well, you look miserable,' Marnie commented. The three of us stood silently in the kitchen as Julie switched on the dishwasher and water began to chug into the machine. 'So? Is she or isn't she?'

'Marnie.' Julie gave her a warning look.

'So nothing,' I said. 'It was chambers business.'

The phone rang again. Perhaps she'd changed her mind.

It was Simon. My Leader of this morning. My heart sank.

'Is this all to do with your inquiry?'

'What?'

'First I find you sneaking in to have conferences with my client and then, during the lunch break, by some complete coincidence, the co-defendant develops a black eye,' he said.

'That's nothing to do with me! Why would it be anything to do with me?'

'I assume you know that Catcher has one previous conviction for indecent assault on a child under the age of fourteen.'

'I didn't know that. I know nothing about Catcher. I only saw him that once in the courtroom. Who told you that? About the previous conviction?'

'Who do you think?'

'And who beat him up?'

'No one is saying.'

'Perhaps he beat himself up to show that the idea of a conspiracy with Danny is ludicrous.'

'Conspirators are well-known for planning a job and

then falling out about it. It doesn't stop them being conspirators. Danny obviously did it, and I want to know why.'

'I promise you, Simon, I know nothing about it. Anyway,' I became indignant, 'I wouldn't ask anyone to beat someone up because of what they've done. I might want to. Very much. But I do believe in the legal system. It may have its faults but it's better than going round engaging in vigilantism.'

'I'm glad to hear you say that Frankie, because it leads me on to my next point. Respect for our legal system.'

'I know, I'm sorry. I really shouldn't have done it.'

'Look, my main concern is you. Danny's a tricky customer. I know you have a special relationship, he likes you and your good works and your sense of humour, and you like him and his . . .'

'Women,' I added silently.

'. . . his . . . brio. But,' he enunciated slowly, 'that is no reason for you to be involved in this at all. I'm not the sort to report you to the Bar Council, but someone else might.'

I snorted.

'Just leave Danny to me.'

'Sorry. It won't happen again.'

'OK.'

'How's Roseanna?'

'Very, very nice.'

We were all right – he was going to start eulogising about Roseanna. He spoke for a few minutes about her wit and her hair and how she liked him, it was like listening to the speaking part of a Charles Aznavour song. When I felt he had forgiven me I had to let him go. 'Save something to tell me at the chambers meeting on Friday,' I said.

TWENTY-NINE

Wednesday – Police Questioning

Adam had said I didn't need to go into the Grange this morning. The only lawyers required at this stage were solicitors – barristers don't normally get involved in criminal cases until the person ends up in court. And there didn't currently appear to be a conflict between his work with the police about Mrs Springer and the interests of the other clients. In a tense, tired voice, Adam had said I should have a lie in, he would be able to cover everything.

But I went in anyway. I wanted to give the clients, and Adam, some support, to tell them that this morning's questioning was purely routine, that they had nothing to worry about. I also wanted to have a word with Shelly Dean.

The police had taken over the rooms we used as conference rooms to carry out the interviews. There would be three going on at the same time. DCI McLaren was supervising the arranging of chairs. He was a slim, pleasant-looking man, and when I gave him a copy of the tape of my conversation with Gregory, he thanked me politely. And then he thanked my clients for giving their time and assistance on this glorious morning.

The lobby was full, and to Mrs Gisborough's credit, she had provided coffee and biscuits despite the absence of the inquiry proper. All my clients were there with large numbers of their extended families. Anyone who was both connected to the group of victims and who had attended the inquiry was being questioned. And several others were there, like me, to give support. As well as have a look at the place.

Shelly, looking pale, pulling hard on a cigarette, stood in a far corner with Leanne and both their husbands. She was worrying about telling the police what she had done to the tyres.

'That wasn't what caused it,' I said. DCI McLaren had announced that it was now certain that the accident had been someone tampering with the brakes.

'Yeah, but they might think if I interfered with the tyres, I could have interfered with the brakes.'

'We're talking about a completely different type of interference,' I said. 'Adam's already mentioned what you did to them and they're not really interested.'

'They say that now.' She hugged herself, then called hello to Martin Williams and Brian Hawkes. 'Them lot went to see her last night, in hospital. We all chipped in for some flowers. We needn't have bothered. There were so many flowers, there weren't enough vases, ours'll probably be thrown out by now. Apparently they all came from this huge great bunch from her boss. I wouldn't have let them in the room. They're probably all covered with that toxic waste they make there.'

The others laughed nervously. 'Emma said it was a by-product,' Leanne said. 'When she said anything about it at all.'

'Oh my God.' Shelly jumped. Leanne's name had been called.

Leanne shook herself, ready to go. Her husband kissed her on the cheek and Shelly rubbed her arm. 'Good luck,' she said. 'You'll be all right. They won't think it's you, you never were any good at science.'

'Don't,' said Leanne. 'What about that time with those thingamies – test tubes?'

'Don't tell them about that.' Shelly laughed. 'We'll all be in trouble then. Off you go, love.'

We watched her walk towards one of the interview rooms. At the door she turned and gave a little wave in our direction.

'Frankie, can I have a word?' Shelly asked. We walked towards one of the windows, looking out over a square of brown, patchy grass.

'If you like I'll speak to the police about the tyres,' I said.

'No, it's not that,' she said. 'You know last night.'

I looked at her.

'Was that Jimmy Clark you were talking to? Has he decided to give evidence now?'

'What?'

'Jimmy Clark. You saw his initials yesterday. How did you get to him so quick? It's about bloody time.'

I shook my head.

'He wouldn't give evidence to the police, and he's not shown his face at any of the inquiry meetings. It's all right for him. He gets his heavy friends to do his dirty work for him.'

I remembered Clark's cut and puffy face. 'So he was at Haslam Hall?'

'What was it you were asking me about, that Gregory said that day?'

'The usual boy?'

'Well, I can't be sure, it was so long ago, and you know we never talked about it. But a boy would be called out, to make tea for visitors, or to go into town to talk about the home or something. I don't think Jimmy Clark was there when I first got there. He came later. He had a brother didn't he?'

'Dennis?'

'I can't remember. But I think Jimmy was the one who got called out. Would this have helped? Oh God, if I'd remembered this earlier, would it have meant Gregory wouldn't have died? He might not have felt that it was up to him to talk.' She began to tremble, and hugged herself as if to get warm.

'None of this is your fault, Shelly,' I said. 'I don't know what Clark's game is.' I remembered the cut, puffy face. Had someone assaulted him to stop him from talking at the inquiry? 'Leave it to me, I'll sort it out. Just remember, Gregory's death was nothing to do with you.'

Her name was called and I wished her good luck.

By the end of the morning the clients had all given their statements and had been told the police would be in touch if they needed further information, but that seemed unlikely. Only Shelly was worried. 'I mentioned Jimmy Clark's name,' she whispered to me as we gathered in the lobby for the afternoon session. 'I didn't know if I should, but they didn't seem interested.'

'Well, he's hardly likely to have had anything to do with Gregory's death,' I said. 'Especially since he hasn't been involved in the inquiry.'

'But what was he doing here last night?' she persisted.

I thought of the plastic bag and I thought of Clark's face. 'I'm going to be double-checking that,' I said.

In the afternoon we heard from the teachers at the home. Two of them seemed fair, expressing their despair at what had happened, now wanting to do their best for 'the children'. The third was simply dippy. She had been part time and had taught cookery. All my clients had been very fond of her. The fourth I found shifty and unpleasant. They liked him too.

It had been a long day. I really fancied a long bath with a long gin and tonic. As I stepped into Julie's house the phone was ringing.

I have to answer the phone. Some people hate the phone. Lena puts up with it, my mum's not too crazy about it, but Julie hates it. She doesn't have an answerphone, she told me that she would happily have no phone. She doesn't care who rings, what they want, why they've rung. I wondered what it would be like to be like that. For two seconds I thought about not answering it, because it wasn't my phone and it was probably one of Marnie's friends. But it was the phone.

'Hello?' I said.

'Marnie!' Julie said with irritation.

'No, it's Frankie.'

'Is Marnie there?' she said, her tone tense.

'I don't know, I've just got in. The telly's not on.' I called her name. There was no reply. 'I don't think she's here. Perhaps she's held up at school, drama club or something.'

'It's half-term. She's not at school. I've been trying to get hold of her all day. I left before she got up. Did she say anything to you about her plans for today?'

'No. The last I saw of her was last night.' After I had

got off the phone to Simon, I had gone straight to my room to do some work. Julie had been in the back room reading the newspaper and Marnie said she wanted to watch something on TV.

'I went to bed about ten and left her watching some rubbish on Channel 5,' Julie said. 'I haven't seen her since.'

'She's probably out shopping somewhere. Or with her mates. She'll be back in time for dinner.'

'You're probably right. I'll be home soon. If she's not back by then I might start worrying. At the moment I'm just angry.'

I replaced the phone. I hoped she was out shopping. If she wasn't I had a horrible feeling that I knew who she was with. And if I was right, Julie was going to kill me, with poisoned arrows of anger and disbelief and horror. And I would die. And I would never finish the inquiry and never have enough money to respray my car, let alone buy a new one. It would be my fault. All my fault.

'Don't do this to me, Marnie,' I said into the room. She had melted into his arms on the dance floor and then he had come to her house and brushed the hair back from her face, and now his face was cut and bruised so that she would want to take care of him. So she had run off with him. She had probably married him. Oh, no, she couldn't do that, she was only fifteen. But even so.

I walked up the stairs to Marnie's bedroom. It was difficult to tell anything from the look of the room. There were piles of clothes, scattered magazines, a few pages of school work that looked as if they had fallen out of a file. Her computer. Her bed with the duvet smoothed over the pillow. No clues, no signs. If she wasn't back soon, I supposed we'd have to read her diary, if she had one. Look at her recent emails.

I rang chambers for someone to speak to, and to ask for my messages. Jenna told me that no one had rung me. Then she added in a lower tone, 'Can I ask you something confidential?'

'Yes.'

'Is Iotha all right?'

'Why do you ask?'

'She hardly ever comes in to chambers. She seems a bit funny these days. Gavin spoke to her, and she said everything's OK. But I wanted to ask you.'

'Thanks, Jenna,' I said. 'I'll speak to her.'

Her voice dropped even lower, it was almost a sigh. 'Do you talk to Marcus much?'

'Did you say Marcus?'

'Mmm.'

'Not a lot,' I said.

'I'd better go,' she said abruptly.

I was grateful for that, because I couldn't discuss other members of chambers with her, especially as Iotha had said she didn't want to take it any further. But Jenna had noticed something, the clerks were talking about it, and it wasn't just salacious gossip. It meant there was still a problem.

Quickly I rang Iotha's home phone number and left a message on her answerphone.

It was almost seven o'clock and I was in the back room, reading through some files, when Julie walked through the door. 'Is she back?'

'No.'

She sat down and dialled a number. 'No reply at Shona's,' she said, looking at the notice board. She dialled another number and had a short conversation, while I anxiously moved my books about on the table.

'That was her other best friend and she hasn't seen Marnie. She said she thought Shona and her family have gone away for the holiday. What am I meant to do now?'

I pushed back my books. I was about to say, 'Perhaps we should ring the police.' But Julie was leaning over me, to snatch up a piece of paper lodged between the salt and pepper pots.

'"Gone out, don't worry, see you soon, love M",' Julie read. 'What is that supposed to mean?'

'When do you think she put it there?'

'I don't know. This morning. Last night. I didn't have breakfast today. Did you see it?'

'I don't think so. . . .Who could she have gone out with?'

'I don't know!'

'What's her boyfriend situation?' I asked hesitantly.

'Don't ask me, I'm not allowed to know. I think there is a lad, Wayne someone. But he's not a boyfriend, they're "seeing each other". Only people like you and I use the word boyfriend.' She was furious.

'Old people you mean?'

'Mmm. I suppose she could be round at Wayne's house, but it seems unlikely. He lives with his mum and dad. I'll have to get the number from her friend.' She looked again at the number on the notice board, dialled and had a brief conversation. She rang another number and spoke tersely to someone at the other end.

'No, not there. Where on earth has she gone?'

My heart was sinking. My suspicions were confirmed. She'd gone off with Clark. That had to be it. It would so appeal to her sense of the romantic. I drew a breath. 'She hasn't said anything about Clark to you, has she?'

Julie's voice came out in a strangled whisper. 'Clark who?'

'Has her passport gone?'

'Oh God, Frankie, what are you saying? Who's Clark? Not that little nerd who came round the other night?'

'Calm down,' I said, attempting to be reassuring and in control. But saying calm down to people often has the opposite effect and it did on Julie.

'What do you mean? What do you know? And who the fuck *is* Clark?'

'I'm sure she's safe, she's a big girl, you've taught her how to look after herself. Clark's nothing. It can't be Clark. I'll just make a call.'

My stomach was clenching with stress. I didn't want to make this phonecall. I had had a bad week. Simon was probably still annoyed with me, I wasn't sure about Yolande, Clark had a brother who thought nothing of beating up his sibling as well as singing like a third-rate matinée idol, and now Marnie had disappeared. I wanted to be at home, sitting in my own sagging arm-chair, watching *EastEnders*, having a takeaway, doing the *Guardian* crossword.

As I touched the receiver it started to ring.

'I've just got to tell someone,' Simon began. 'Our expert.'

'The carpet man?'

'Yes, he's having second thoughts. He thinks this Quirk man may have got it right. In fact, he may even go further and say that he now feels that the formation of the blood spots, combined with recent use of carpet cleaner, shows someone was actually killed in the shop.'

My heart flipped. 'Not necessarily by Danny.'

'Who else could it be? Yolande?'

Please, no, I thought. Let it be someone else, like Clark. Oh, really no, please don't let Clark be capable of that.

'What are you going to do?'

'I can't call our man to give evidence, that's obvious. I don't know. Kay just rang me to tell me. It's so frustrating. Not that it's going to make much difference to the way I present my case. Danny still won't let me do anything.'

'So it's back to the "Members of the jury I will now call Terry Fleming to the witness box" defence.'

'Probably.' He sighed. 'Sorry, I didn't mean to bore you. I just had to tell someone.'

'That's OK, I. . . .' Julie was hovering at my elbow.

'Have you heard anything about Iotha and Marcus?' he went on.

'Such as what?'

'That he's behaving in a bizarre fashion towards her.'

'She's told me she doesn't want to do anything about that,' I said.

'You don't think you should persuade her to mention it to Tony?'

'No. Look, I'd better go now.'

'Oh, right, of course. Are you OK, Frankie? You sound a bit . . .'

'I'm fine, fine.' I replaced the receiver. 'I have to go upstairs for the number,' I said to Julie. I rang Yolande on my mobile.

'Hello,' she said, with pleasure in her voice. Perhaps this conversation wouldn't be quite so bad.

'Marnie, my . . . niece has taken off.'

'Oh, dear. Any idea where she's gone?'

'I wondered if she might be with Clark and whether you might know how I could get in touch with him.'

'When did she go?'

'This morning. I think.'

'Have you rung the police?'

'She left a note, so it doesn't seem as if she's been taken anywhere against her will.'

'Well, I spoke to Clark this afternoon and he didn't say anything about it. And usually you can tell with Clark, what's going on in his life.'

'Can you check?'

'I'm not sure I've got his new mobile number.'

'Do you know where he hangs out?'

'There's a pub he goes to. I'll check it out for you.'

'I'll come,' I said.

She suggested we meet in the bar of a hotel on the Smallbrook Ringway.

Yolande was already there when I arrived, sitting on a low, maroon sofa. She had ordered us both a gin and tonic.

Absently I kissed her on the cheek and sat in another low, maroon sofa, at right angles to her. The place was almost empty. Two businessmen were sitting at a table across the room, and the barman and the waitress were chatting idly.

'Have a drink,' Yolande said.

'Does Clark come in here, then?' I asked, my head spinning to catch any possible arrivals. This didn't seem quite his kind of place.

'I've seen him in here once.'

'Yolande! I need to speak to him. It's very nice being here with you, but it's Clark who can sort out whether or not I'm in shit with my cousin for introducing him to Marnie.'

'Yes, they danced well together, didn't they?' she said. She tapped her cigarette in the ashtray. 'She's not with him. Believe me.'

'Did you know that all along?'

'No. I've just dropped in to one or two places and rung one or two people.'

I didn't know whether to believe her.

'Anyway, it's lovely to see you.' She leaned forward and ran her fingers across my wrist. I took a mouthful of gin. It went straight to the spot alcohol goes when you haven't eaten anything for a while. It was nice to see her too. She looked relaxed and she was smiling. She ran her nail across the back of my hand. 'I've booked a room,' she said.

I didn't quite understand what she'd said.

'Shall we go upstairs?'

I have to say, at this point, that lust took over. I can find no excuse for my actions, although her comment that Birmingham was a big place and we could drive round for hours and miss Marnie by seconds seemed, at the time, to make sense. And Yolande said we could drive round together later, when people would be out and about. And I realised as we stepped into the hotel room and she dropped her bag on the floor and wrapped her arms round my neck and began to kiss me, that I had rather missed having someone to make love to.

Two hours later, I came out of the bathroom after room service had delivered two brandies. Yolande smoothed the rumpled sheet beside her. As I slid back into bed, she lit a cigarette.

'So you found the film?' she asked me casually.

'No thanks to Clark.' I took a sip of brandy. I ran a hand down her leg.

'And . . . ?'

'The photos aren't ready yet,' I said. I had cautiously rung the darkroom the day before and they had said only that there was a backlog of work. 'I'm going to pick them up on Saturday.'

She stretched her head away and exhaled smoke. 'Thanks. So, now I can have the bag back?'

I looked at her. 'I went through all this with Clark.'

'Clark?'

'Yes, he came to meet me at the inquiry yesterday, all black and blue. Apparently Dennis did it. And almost did it again when we were in my car.'

'Oh Jesus.' Her face was ashen.

'What is it about this sweater?'

'It's a long story.' She looked up sharply. 'You mean you opened it?'

I was torn between outrage and guilt. 'No, I didn't. My mother did.'

'What! Why did you give it to your mother?' Her eyes glittered, with anger or fear I couldn't tell.

'You didn't tell me what I had to do with it. You didn't even tell me what it was. You told me not to open it.'

'So you gave it to your mother to open!' A deep maroon flush crept up her neck and across her cheeks. She took a long gulp from her glass.

'No, she just opened it. I wasn't there.'

'You still live with your mother?'

'No.'

'What did she say?'

'Nothing.'

'Nothing?'

'Just that it needed a wash, and she used to go out with someone who wore one like that.'

'And that's all? Where is it now? Has she still got the bags?'

'I don't know. I assume so, yes. I think she has.'

'OK.' She took a deep breath. 'OK. Just forget it.'

'I'll get it for you. She hasn't washed it.' We were arguing about a jumper. We were arguing about a jumper when Marnie had disappeared. 'What's the problem?'

'It's . . . obviously been missed, that's all. And . . . I'm the one who's responsible.'

She wanted to go home.

I said she didn't need to drive round Birmingham with me. We walked out of the hotel together. She wouldn't even let me walk her to her car.

I drove around for an hour or so, along empty dual carriageways, on narrow side streets, down echoing underpasses, looking for Marnie. I went to the bus stations and the train stations. It was hopeless.

When I got home it was almost midnight. Julie was in her room. An air of desolation filled the house. The heat in the attic as I prepared for bed was suffocating. I couldn't sleep, my mind was full of images I didn't want to look at. I tossed and turned.

Then Julie was knocking on my door. The room was dark, it wasn't the morning. 'It's the phone. For you.' Her voice broke with anger and despair.

I staggered down the stairs, with my eyes still shut.

'Hello!' I said.

296

'Frankie?' It was Marcus. 'It's about that case I spoke to you about.'

'What time is it?'

'A quarter to one.'

'Marcus! Could you ring back? We're waiting for a call.'

'You've done a lot of public-order cases haven't you?'

'That was years ago.' Peace demos, animal rights, poll-tax protesters. I'd represented activists when I was just starting out at the Bar, in the early 90s. I was mildly flattered that Marcus was asking me for advice, but I kept my eyes shut. 'Why not ring me in the morning?'

'I need to speak to you now.' He sounded drunk. His words were slurred, but then so were mine, but I was half asleep. Perhaps he was sleep-phoning. 'I'm representing someone who's a member of...' He said something that sounded like the name of an extreme right-wing group.

'Sorry?'

He repeated his words. I was right.

'Who on earth has sent you that?'

'A firm I do a lot of work for in South London.'

'What's the charge?'

'Conspiracy to commit affray and possibly riot, although I think we'll get that thrown out.'

'Marcus, I'm sorry, I can't help you. I don't even do crime.'

'You do it for Simon.'

'He's a friend, Marcus,' I said, 'But I really don't do crime.' I decided it was time to open my eyes. 'So I don't know anything. I don't even know what the current levels of sentencing are. But even if I did ... Look,

Marcus, I am not helping you to trash people. And you have got to get off the phone.'

'But I have to defend my client, I need assistance.'

'Well, it's not going to be from me. Marcus, I don't know why you're asking me to do this. You knew what I'd say.'

'You think you're so pure, don't you? You think you're the only one with politics.'

'If you say so. Give it a rest Marcus, and ask someone else.'

'You know you're in breach of the Code of Conduct.'

'What?'

'Failing to assist a fellow member of the Bar. You are in breach of the Code of Conduct.'

'Wow, is that a threat? Are you going to report me?'

'I could do.'

'All right Marcus, if that will make you happy, you do that.' My heart was pounding. 'Just sod off, will you?'

'A complaint to the Bar Council wouldn't be much fun for you, it might end in your suspension. Or even disbarment.'

'Join the queue, Marcus. I have more important things to worry about.'

I put the phone down, my heart still racing. What was it with these boys? Where did they get off? And if that was his idea of a good election speech, he was mistaken. He wouldn't be getting my vote.

Back up in my room I put on a tape of 'Madness' by Prince Buster to relieve the tension. Madness, madness, they call it madness. Then it occurred to me. Marcus was setting me up. He'd got wind of Iotha's complaint and he was trying to discredit me, to say that I wasn't professional, that I was driven by politics, so that I wasn't worth listening to.

For goodness' sake. I wouldn't mind, but Iotha didn't want to pursue it. But that didn't mean I couldn't make some calls.

THIRTY

Thursday Morning

There were no buses, the traffic was terrible and there was still no word from Marnie. It was quarter past ten when I arrived at the Grange. Mrs Gisborough was over-seeing the arrival of fresh coffee jugs. It dawned on me that half the clients weren't here, as if the tragedy of Gregory's death had somehow reminded them of the tragedy of their youth. They'd come on Friday to be together, to share the news, but today the sadness was too reminiscent. And perhaps they were afraid they might be next. Perhaps we should all be afraid.

It was almost ten thirty. People were starting to file back into the inquiry room as my mobile rang. The ring-ing tone was a jazz riff, which usually made me laugh, but today it didn't sound right. Not now that Marnie was missing.

It was Julie's home number. Perhaps Marnie was back. I pressed the green button to speak.

'Is she there?' Julie asked.

'Here? No.'

The line went dead.

I was thinking, 'Julie is going to come roaring into the inquiry, in front of everyone, and tear me limb from limb.' That could be embarrassing. But it's what I'd do if I had a child who was missing. Where was she? Yolande had said she wasn't with Clark, but I didn't believe her. I certainly didn't want to think she was with anyone else, anyone else who knew me. It couldn't, it just couldn't be anything to do with Gregory's death. If she was with Clark, he wouldn't hurt her, would he? A man who could dance like that couldn't be all bad. Perhaps he'd taken her to the regional heats of some ballroom dancing contest.

The morning passed in a daze of social workers, talking of their experiences. Their contact with the home had been quite marginal, but the other lawyers asked the questions I would have asked, protecting their own clients by attacking the others – Why didn't they make more inquiries? Why didn't they visit more often? Why did they place the children there?

At lunch time I slouched my way to Marks & Spencer for a tuna and cucumber sandwich and checked my mobile. I had missed no messages, so Julie obviously had no news about Marnie. Another layer of anxiety spread itself in my stomach. I threw half my sandwich away.

In the afternoon, the advocate to the inquiry rose. 'Unfortunately sir, the expert whom I had been hoping to call this afternoon has been ringing Mrs Gisborough' (we all turned to look at Mrs Gisborough, who shrank into her seat in the corner) 'to say that she is stuck on a train, somewhere outside Coventry, and the most recent information, ten minutes ago, was that there will be at least an hour's delay before a replacement locomotive will arrive to pull the train into Coventry. After that it's anyone's guess. Unfortunately there are no other witnesses to be heard today.'

Curston looked at his watch. He could scarcely keep the smile from his face. 'Then we shall adjourn until Monday.'

I went down to my office in the basement and rang chambers. There were no messages.

I walked into the street pondering the place of the individual in the ultimate scheme of things. We were getting nowhere in the inquiry. I was sure there was something I ought to be doing about Wyatt or Frodsham, not to mention Gregory. Maybe I should just leave the Bar and go and work in a furniture shop. I might get that leather armchair.

I had lost Marnie.

I didn't know if I dared go back to Julie's. I dawdled across Corporation Street and gazed, unseeing, into the windows of Rackhams. I meandered across the graveyard of the Cathedral, towards Colmore Row. The queue at the bus stop was thick across the pavement, young men chewing gum, women looking strained with three Tesco bags of shopping, and ten young women with thick gold hair, posing and chatting, all looking, from the back, exactly like Marnie.

I walked to the end of the queue, and then carried on walking. Where could she be? Where on earth could she be?

A silver grey car lurched up beside me and the passenger window slid down.

''Scuse me.' A voice from a craning head called me.

I bent towards the window, ready to give directions, a knowledgeable smile on my face, thinking perhaps a bit of common human helpfulness would make me feel better about myself and the world. I even placed my hand lightly on the window frame.

It was Clark.

'Want a lift?' he said.

'Where's Marnie?'

'Why don't you just get in the car?'

'Clark, I have things to do.'

'I got things to do too. Get in the fucking car.'

'Tell me where Marnie is.'

'How do I know? She's your niece.'

'Do you mean she's not with you?'

'What would I be doing with Marnie?' He sounded surprised and even concerned. 'Why, is she bunking off school?'

'Oh God, this is worse and worse,' I said. 'If you don't know where Marnie is, why do you want me to get in the car?'

'You'll find out,' he growled, making a stab at hooliganism.

'Clark, what's got into you?'

He glowered at me. The puffiness had gone from his face and the bruises were fading, he just looked as if he was suffering from a mild attack of jaundice. I wondered who was putting pressure on him now.

'Maybe we can do this in stages. Do you know where Marnie is?'

'No.'

'Do you know anyone who might know where Marnie is?'

'No.'

'Why do you want me to get in the car?' I peered into the back in case Dennis was hiding there. 'Where's Dennis?'

'I dunno. Look, will you please get in the car?'

'I'd love to,' I lied. 'I feel we've been through a lot together and I don't want to see you getting beaten up again.'

'I ain't going to get beaten up again.' His face creased with anxiety. 'I just . . . need . . . you.'

'Oh Clark,' I said. It's the kind of appeal I find hard to resist. 'How long for?'

'Not long.'

'But I've got to find Marnie.' I looked at his mournful, damaged face. 'Tell you what, you're a man about town, you know all the places a girl might go, and you've got a car that works. If you suggest some places we might go to look for Marnie, I'll help you out.' I got in the car. Somehow, I felt if I was with Clark I was at least in touch with the world I was afraid Marnie was in. If she was being held hostage, I could offer myself up in her place. I was desperate.

It wasn't even as if he was a good driver. And I know what bad driving can be. We squealed up to traffic lights, with my foot almost through the floor, we went down at least two one-way streets the wrong way and he entered a yellow box when his exit was not clear. Cautiously, I said, 'Clark, how long have you been driving?'

'About an hour,' he said.

'Not today,' I said. 'Altogether. Ever.'

'About an hour.'

He was such a poor hard man. 'Clark,' I said, 'get out of the car.'

He stared at me. 'You must think I'm stupid.'

'Let me drive,' I said.

'You get out the car,' he said. I could see he was grappling with the implications. If I got out of the car,

304

I might disappear. If he got out of the car, I might drive off. But he didn't like driving.

Sensibly, he took the keys out of the ignition and got out of the car. 'Move over,' he said to me through the passenger window.

I slid across to the driver's seat and Clark climbed through the passenger door. Then he didn't know what to do with the key.

'We can't go anywhere if you don't give me the key,' I said.

He handed over the key ring. It held a large plastic model car, the car key and another key. It could have been the key to a bicycle padlock, but it could have been the key to a left luggage locker.

I turned the key in the ignition, and the car melted smoothly into life. Sometimes I understand why I want to earn lots of money, it is because I want a big new opulent car.

'Where do you want to go?' I said, rearranging the mirror and the seat.

'Don't talk, drive.' He chuckled. 'You know, like that advert, "don't talk, eat."'

'Mmm,' I said, 'very amusing.' I looked at the road signs. 'I'm not going to Manchester.' We were just about to join the M6.

'We're going to Solihull,' he said.

'Solihull is miles away! And it's south,' I said.

'I know that,' he said, quickly. 'Won't take us long in this car. Nice, isn't it?'

'Very nice,' I said, as we turned easily round a sharp left-hand corner. It was an automatic. 'Whose car is this?' I had a sudden sickening thought that I might be driving a stolen car.

'Never you mind,' he said.

'Well, I do mind,' I said, 'because I'm only insured to drive cars where the owner has given his or her consent.'

'You've got that.'

'I'm sorry Clark, I don't believe this car is yours.'

He was silent. We were in a stolen car.

'So,' I said, as we waited at a junction, 'where do you think Marnie might be?'

'How do I know?'

I should have got out there and then, but Clark was my only link to the worst possible thing that could have happened to Marnie. 'Think.'

'I'll think as we're going to Solihull,' he said, with a sly grin.

'Think about pubs, think about bars, think about dance halls,' I said. There was nothing else I could do.

After about twenty minutes we approached the outskirts of Solihull. We came off the Coventry Road and down past the Rover factory. I started to slow down.

'Go left here,' he said. I turned from the dual carriageway immediately into a quiet suburban street of thirties houses, white fronts with bits of black timber.

'Where are we going?' I said. For the first time I felt anxious about my own situation. And I felt sick, not only because of what might be about to happen, but because of what these houses meant to me.

Julie had lived in a house like this in Kettering, in a long, long road full of houses just like this, with my Auntie Irene and my Uncle George. Going there seemed like going to the end of the world. Of course, their house was posher than our house – which I knew because they were buying it – but I couldn't see the advantage. There was nowhere to play and they didn't even have a shop within walking distance. As I grew older I promised myself that I would never live in a house like that.

Clark directed me into a close. Now I was feeling quite queasy. It was a warm, sunny evening and I thought I caught a whiff of an early barbecue. This was all too intimate and claustrophobic. Someone unpleasant with a soft voice and a hard fist was going to appear at some point and they weren't going to like me, I felt sure.

Clark said, 'Pull up outside that one.' The houses all looked the same, net curtains and a perfect lawn. 'Not that one, this one.' It had bunchy nets and neat mown lines on the grass. I noticed the small clumps of red, white and blue bedding plants, like those Julie and I would plant for her dad in narrow little crusts of dirt round the edge of the grass if our visit coincided with spring. It was like being back in Kettering on a cold, sharp day with her dad saying, 'Not there, there. Not a blue one, a white one,' even though they were all more or less green. And then I thought of Marnie again and I thought, if I'm scared for me, what about her? and I automatically got out of the car.

I was squeezing down the crazy paving path at the side of the garage, scratching my new Hobbs shoes on bramble undergrowth, heading towards the back of the house, before I registered that this was not the normal way one entered such a suburban house. At the very least the owners would be sorry you hadn't rung the front door bell and heard the amusing chimes, which in my Auntie Irene's case had been a long, slow rendition of 'London Bridge is Falling Down'.

I pulled at Clark's leather jacket. 'Hang on,' I said, 'Where are we going?'

'Keep your voice down,' he hissed, pulling something

like a tyre iron from the inside of his trousers. No wonder he'd had trouble driving.

'What do you mean?' I whispered. 'What are you going to do with that?' There was nothing wrong with the tyres on the car, I knew. Where was the sweet, needy Clark of half an hour ago? My stomach was turning liquid.

'Stop worrying,' he said. 'Hopefully violence won't be necessary and we can just retrieve a bit of lost property.'

'Oh, burglary. I'm sorry, I didn't understand. Of course, burglary. Lovely. Look, Clark, I noticed your use of the word "we", there. I just want to remind you that I'm a lawyer. I don't do burglary.'

'You didn't say that to Yolande, did you? At Sandra's place.' He let out a small wheeze which I assumed was a laugh. 'But that's why you're here. In case someone wants to know whether I have any lawful purpose being on the property. I can say, "Of course I have, look, I've got my lawyer with me."'

'I may not have practised crime for a long while,' I muttered, 'but unless the law has changed dramatically, I can tell you that you don't get off a charge of burglary with a defence like that. And I was invited to Sandra's flat.' In a roundabout kind of way.

I was having those flashes again, when my career glitters before my eyes, advancement, silk, judgeship, even a couple of briefs at Willesden County Court, only to fade and die. The last time I had them was when I was arrested for murder. But I hadn't done that. Today was slightly different. If there was a burglary and Clark bodged it, as I felt he was very likely to do, and I was found there in flagrante as we lawyers like to say but rarely spell, or even if it emerged at a later date that I had been there, I would have a very difficult job explaining my way out of it. For goodness' sake, I had driven us there. In what was probably a stolen car. I had even got in and out of the car of my own free will.

I turned to go. This time Clark pulled at my jacket (the long Ede and Ravenscroft one, my favourite). 'You,' he said, 'are not going anywhere.'

'But wouldn't I be more use to you as the little woman, sitting quietly in the car?'

That sounded an attractive idea to him, I could see, and as he hesitated for two seconds I made a stealthy move backwards again, preparing to slip off my jacket if necessary, but I tripped on a creeper across the path. Clark shot out his hand and stopped my fall.

'No,' he said, hooking my arm easily through his, 'no. For one thing . . .' he was working it out as he went along, '. . . .you're a lawyer, you ain't a little woman, and for another thing, the whole point is you've got to be with me, in the house, see? That's part of the plan. I thought that bit up, when I saw you in the street.'

Save us from free thinkers, I thought, conscious of the contradiction that concept posed to my own belief system, but not at this point able to explore the idea in depth.

'You're in it now, anyway,' he went on, in a chatty tone, ''cos I've got the car keys.'

'No, you haven't.' I still held them in my hand.

'Oh.' His face fell and he was thinking as fast as he could, which wasn't that fast, but he was holding my arm in a very tight hold and I was worrying about the material. 'All right,' he said, 'but look at it this way. If you do get away, I'll say you've stolen police property. But anyway you ain't going to get away.'

His plans may not have been watertight, but his grip on my arm was surprisingly vice-like. His use of the words 'police property' worried me, but I'd have to come back to that later. Right now he was dragging me, stumbling and wincing, round the side of the garage to take part in a criminal offence. My only hope of salvaging my career was that there would be a bruise round my wrist, to show that he had used force. But he obviously knew how to do it without leaving a mark, because as it turned out, there was never any sign of coercion on my arm.

When we arrived at the back of the house it was still just like my Auntie Irene's. The garden was mainly lawn except for a small patch of vegetables tucked discreetly behind a shed. The back of the house was painted white, with black pipes which stood out starkly. The white paintwork was peeling. The black paint on the back door was dull and curling off like shavings of parmesan cheese on a fancy salad. The wood underneath was dry and splitting. The window frames were in a similar condition.

'Home sweet home,' Clark said. 'This might be easier than I thought.' He brought up his tyre iron.

'You don't want to try the door handle first, do you?' I asked, thinking, would this be seen as me being an accomplice or would they realise I had been trying to mitigate the loss of the victim?

He turned the handle and the door opened, just like it would have done in my Auntie Irene's house.

'Is that you, Dennis?' a voice called from somewhere which I knew from my Auntie Irene's house would be the front room.

'Oh fuck!' He'd gone white. And so had I. Dennis? 'No, it's – eh – it's Jimmy,' he called.

He laughed uneasily, that squeezy, breathless laugh, sliding the tyre iron back down his trouser leg, as a thin woman of about seventy walked into the small black and white tiled kitchen. 'Hallo Nan! You're home early. I thought Thursday was your Bingo afternoon.'

'The caller's run off with the new barmaid again,' she said. 'He'll be back in a couple of weeks. We haven't seen you round here for a while.'

'No. I . . . eh . . . so Dennis isn't in then? That's funny, he asked me to drop round.'

Liar, I thought.

'Dennis? I'm expecting him back at any minute for his tea.' Clark's nan was wearing a pink overall and comfortable-looking check slippers. 'Don't just stand there. Make yourself useful – bring in that pot.'

I noticed a walking stick leaning in the corner. Perhaps Clark had thought he and his nan would engage in some weird fencing ritual, he with his tyre iron, she with her stick. She pushed us into the back room, taking two plates from a cupboard as she did. The table was already set for two. She laid the extra places. Clark put the tea pot onto a small ceramic stand. 'Well, we don't really . . .' he began.

'Sit down,' his nan said.

Stiffly Clark manoeuvred himself onto a chair. Carefully I took my place opposite him. Clark sat uneasily, staring at the food on the table as if it was made of plastic. I wondered why. This meal was very straightforward. It was reminiscent of all the teas I had had as a child at my grandmother's house, tablecloth, beans on toast, bread and butter and jars of jam, with marshmallows in red and white stripy silver paper to end with. And then Grandma brought in cups of tea in black and yellow contemporary china, with the sugar already stirred in. Clark seemed uncertain. Perhaps tea was a new development in his nan's regime. Or perhaps Clark had never been allowed to share in it. Perhaps only Dennis had taken tea.

Or perhaps he was worried that he was not carrying out his task.

'I'm Dot,' she said. 'And you are . . . ?'

I looked at Clark for inspiration. Was this the time to say – I am a barrister of the Supreme Court of England and Wales, or should I go for something lighter?

Our arrival had been so unconventional that I hadn't had the time, unlike, say, the Queen, to enquire who I would be meeting and where they stood in the scheme of things and thus what was the appropriate etiquette for the occasion. But I did know that Clark and I made an unlikely pair – not least because under his leather jacket he was dressed in an all-cotton outfit, a skimpy grey T-shirt and black jersey running trousers, which ended just above the ankle. And I was wearing the Ede and Ravenscroft suit, which despite its five per cent Lycra, still had an air of formality.

'I'm a j . . .' I was about to say journalist but realised this was potentially worse than being a lawyer. '. . . a judge.' Oh God, now I was impersonating a member of the judiciary. 'I judge dog shows,' I went on, trying desperately to remember the name, 'like Crusts. Crufts.' I adopted a conversational tone. 'Jack Russells are my favourites.' I flicked an imaginary dog hair from my trousers.

They were both staring at me. Then Clark said he had to go to the toilet as if he couldn't bear to hear what I would say next.

When he had gone out of the room Dot turned to gaze at me.

'So you're a judge at Crufts.' Oh God, she was going to say that she was one too, or that she exhibited. She was going to ask me questions about dogs. 'You can't be.'

I opened my mouth.

'No judge of dog shows would wear black. And Jimmy's terrified of dogs. What are you doing with him?'

'Ehh, well . . .'

'You're not his usual choice.'

'No, I wouldn't be.'

'He's a good lad,' she said, almost fondly. 'He's had a rough life, but he's too eager to please.'

I nodded mutely.

'And he's not nearly as hard as he wants you to think he is.'

'I think I'd gathered that.' Why was she telling me all this? Did she seriously think I was having a romantic liaison with Clark?

'He's probably told you his stories of his time inside.'

'Well, actually, n. . . .'

'Most of that was off the telly. The only time he was banged up was for failing to turn up at court when he'd been done for smoking dope. Oh, and a bit of kiting.' The professionals' word for dealing in dodgy cheques sounded strange on her lips. 'I don't know what trouble he's in with Dennis, but he's probably buggered something up.'

I wondered at her use of the words 'banged up' and 'dope' and 'kiting', let alone 'bugger'. They were not little old lady words. You wouldn't expect to hear them from someone who lived in a house with this wallpaper. Kiting. Only people who work with it every day use that word, like lawyers or kiters. Perhaps kiting was another of Dennis's numerous skills. Perhaps Dot was the kiter. Perhaps Clark was more afraid of Dot than Dennis. Could you really be afraid of anyone who still lived at home with their nan?

Clark came back into the room, whistling. That was ominous. What did he have to be whistling about? He seemed to be walking more easily. I wondered what he'd done with the tyre iron. There seemed to be other bulges in his trousers now, but I really didn't want to think about that.

'We better be off, Flan,' he said to me.

'Flan?' Dot and I spoke in unison.

'Whatever.' His face crumpled for an instant. I didn't know whether to share a despairing glance with Dot or try to pretend I hadn't said anything and that this was a pet name he and I used between us. I was feeling maternal towards Clark, protective, about the way he hadn't known how to eat his tea. I knew how to eat my tea. I reached for a marshmallow and began to peel off the silver paper. Of course, what I should have done was get straight up when he spoke.

'Come and finish your tea,' Dot said to him, sharply.

Clark hesitated, then swaggered over to the table in an attempt at defiance. He stood behind his chair and lifted the cup to his lips.

'Sit down,' she said again. 'There are ladies present.'

'We really should go.' My voice was muffled with marshmallow. There was probably chocolate round my mouth. I looked at my watch. 'Oh no,' I said, with genuine dismay. It was half past five. I hadn't rung chambers, I hadn't rung Julie and I hadn't found Marnie.

'I thought you wanted to see Dennis.' Dot's voice was like ice.

'Yeah, we do,' said Clark and my eyes widened. 'But look, it's late now and Flossie's got to get back.' We were getting closer, a two-syllable word that began with F. 'Tell him I'll call him, I'll call him ... tomorrow, tomorrow at eleven.'

'He won't be long and he won't want to miss you,' Dot said. 'I think he's got something for you.'

My marshmallow stuck in my throat. Whatever Dennis had to give to Clark, Clark quite clearly didn't want it. Perhaps it was something no one would want, like a thin stiletto between the ribs.

'I tell you what,' Dot said, her voice becoming more relaxed, 'why don't you send Miss Fancy Pants home in the car, and you wait here for Dennis? I'm sure Dennis will take you wherever you need to go after.'

Now then, should I take this opportunity and go? Drive away in a hot car and then ... do what? Park it outside Julie's house? It was bound to get scratched. Wait for the real owner to turn up and ... do whatever real owners do to people they think have stolen their W-reg cars? Take it to the police?

I heard myself say, 'I kind of need Clark ... Jimmy.'

'Whatever for?' Dot's expression of surprise looked genuine. It was a good question.

'He's showing me places I might find ... a room to hire for my birthday party.'

'Then we'll all go,' she said. 'I could do with a Dubonnet.'

I shot a look at Clark, but he avoided my gaze.

'Do you mind if I make a quick call?' I asked, as Dot eased off her slippers and put on a pair of very high-heeled, red patent shoes. 'I need to ring my cousin.'

'Why?' Dot took off her overall and revealed a cherry-red sweater and matching straight skirt.

'I didn't tell her we were going out hunting venues,' I said.

'Ring her later,' she said, through tightened lips as she applied cherry-red lipstick. 'I'm going to enjoy this.'

I looked at Clark and he gave me a worried shrug. I was counting on him to know where to take us. I was thinking that at least one of us, preferably me, could slip out through a toilet window and just go home.

As Dot settled herself in the front seat of the car and Clark miserably flung himself in the back, she said, 'Where are we going, Jimmy?'

I prayed he would have an answer.

'I dunno,' he said, all bravado gone.

'I know, let's go to Spats, they have rooms there,' Dot said, and chuckled to herself. What did she know? Was Marnie in a room at Spats?

Spats. Spats. And it came to me. I had my own memory of Spats.

Like old perfume, the atmosphere of the time came back to me, powerful and evocative. The memory that had been wafting in the back of my brain since my lunch with Yolande in Fleet Street, and my conversation with my mum, suddenly crystalised. A night when four of us, women I shared a house with in Leamington Spa, had gone to a Kinks concert in Birmingham. It was my idea, I said it would be a laugh. We had driven there one sunny day, all of us wearing jeans with the mildest of flares, two of us, and I refuse to say which two, with perms. The car was my old Fiat 127, like a small navy-blue matchbox on wheels. We drove into Birmingham singing 'Lazing on a Sunny Afternoon' and as we left the concert at eleven o'clock at night (four encores) we were raucously singing 'Lola, L-O-L-A, Lola', when the car stalled in the middle of town. Then the little lever between the two front seats, which was meant to start the car, lost all power, because the lead (aka elastic band) had broken, and we couldn't move. So, with me still sitting at the wheel and the others making comments about how I got all the cushy jobs, they pushed the car into a narrow alley, and, as I clambered out of the car, swearing and laughing, we found ourselves outside Spats.

Almost as one we looked up at the electric pink light above the door, which spelt out the name. Without saying anything we went as a group to ring the AA and as a group we stood on the main road to wait for the little yellow van. An hour later the repair man arrived and said he wouldn't look at the vehicle while it was down there. Silently we went back to the car and this time I steered and pushed at the same time so that we could get out into the light quicker. It wasn't until we left the city limits and were safely on the M42 that we all exploded with relief, each describing how we had been terrified of being within a hundred yards of where two hideous murders had recently occurred.

THIRTY-ONE

Thursday Evening

Driving back towards Birmingham with Dot sitting beside me I didn't know what worried me more, the prospect of being stopped for driving a hot car or not being stopped. But at least we'd be back in Birmingham.

After a few minutes Dot said in a conversational tone, 'I always liked this car. I can see why Danny wanted to borrow it. I thought the Old Bill still had it.'

'They gave it the all clear. Didn't find anything.'

'Dennis said he wanted to sell it when the police gave it back. Does he know you've got it?'

Dennis's car? I was driving the car of a man who had beaten Clark black and blue over a jumper. Clark said nothing. I felt like stopping the car and saying to him, 'You lied to me, you said the owner of this car had given permission for me to drive it. Either it's stolen police property, or it belongs to Dennis. Neither of which is likely to prove acceptable to my insurance company in the event of an accident. How can I trust you?' But I didn't. I knew the answer. Clark's lack of elementary common sense. Had Marnie mistaken that for an attractive devil-may-care attitude? Oh Marnie.

And on top of that, it sounded as if this was the car which the police thought had transported Fleming's body from somewhere in or near the furniture shop to a pillar on the M6.

Dot directed us to Fiveways, on the west side of the city. My heart lifted. There was a café at Fiveways that we'd intended to visit that night after the Kinks. It was a famous all-night place, for truckers and people called Bigwheel and Roadster, who had arranged illicit meetings with each other over their CB radios.

Maybe I could create a diversion and suggest we go into the café for old-time's sake, I could jump behind a burly man with tattoos and a beard and at the very least make a phonecall. Who would I ring? I'd have to ring Julie to see about Marnie, but right now Julie wouldn't give me the time of day and would probably tell me to rot in hell and hope they'd send me there sooner rather than later. If I rang the police what would I say? I'm driving a rather nice car with a little old lady in high heels and a young man in rather short trousers and we're making our way to a nightclub. 'That's interesting madam, and are you ringing for directions or fashion tips? If you're on the A45, madam, you won't go far wrong, and it might be worth pointing out that stilettos are bad for the calves. Happy to help, madam, and what car did you say you were driving?' Lena? She'd say 'Oh, darling,' in a doubtful way. And anyway London was over 120 miles away down the M1.

But maybe everything was OK, maybe we were just three vague pals, on a warm summer's evening, searching for a pleasant night out. And who doesn't drive around in a dodgy motor? There's always a brake light not working, or a number plate falling off.

The café wasn't where I remembered. Everything looked so different, fancy glass buildings, re-named streets. The place had probably been pulled down to make way for a Starbucks.

I carried on driving. As we drove past the Convention Centre Dot said sharply, 'Turn right just here. Here.'

I stopped abruptly, and we all shot forward a couple of inches. I turned into Bridge Street and along by the canal. And there was Spats. It wasn't how I remembered it, but I realised I'd never properly looked at it. Or perhaps it had simply changed in the past twenty years. Now it could be any pub on the corner of the street. The pink electric light had gone and the word Spats was nowhere to be seen. A pub sign that swung above the door, said 'Lambada'. The expression 'Birmingham's hottest night spot' came to me, and I wondered where I had read that. It wasn't just Clark who had been telling porkies. It had high windows like a club, certainly, but they were latticed. This seemed to be nothing more than a fairly benign local pub. I could almost smell the beer soaked into the carpet and the cigarette smoke pasted on to the walls, even with the car windows closed. And you could hear a noise, a low piano or jukebox, and laughing and coughing. We sat for a second or two, while a man in an old donkey jacket, hunched up as if it was raining, went in, and a smart-looking woman in a short skirt and sheeny legs came out.

'All right, here we are,' Dot said.

I was on a double yellow line. 'I can't park here,' I said, although why should I worry? It wasn't my car. I wasn't going to have to pay the fine. But the car might be towed away, or worse, clamped. Then how would we all get home?

'You wanted to see Dennis, didn't you?' Dot said.

'Not personally,' I murmured.

Dot twisted in her seat to face Clark. His mouth moved wordlessly, then he said, 'Dot, now I've got you on your own, we don't really need Dennis, do we? Why don't we all go somewhere else, have a drink, a bit of a laugh.'

'You can do that here,' she said. 'Make up your mind.'

'Yes, let's stop here,' I said recklessly. I was getting used to the idea of parking on a double yellow line. And I could dash in and see if Marnie was here, we would be in the full glare of the public eye. The public house anyway. I felt safe. Safer.

I could almost hear Clark's brain working. He was thinking so hard, I wanted to help him. 'Make a list of the pros and cons of staying here,' I wanted to say. Pros, I get to look for Marnie and you get to see Dennis; cons, he could beat you up. Pros, you sort out your business; cons, you could get beaten up.

He obviously read me better than I gave him credit for. Suddenly he scrabbled at the door, leaped out of the car and ran off down the road, towards the centre of town.

'That man is a martyr to his own indecision,' Dot said. She turned to me, 'Well, do you fancy a drink? Have you met Dennis? Don't be put off by Jimmy.' We got out of the car. 'It's just that Dennis has succeeded where Jimmy's failed. Come and have a drink. You'll like him.'

I didn't think that was likely. I wasn't sure why Clark had taken off like that. He hadn't said in words, come with me now, but I had a feeling that he might have said that, if he could have worked a door handle and talked at the same time.

Suddenly it all felt too much. 'I've got to ring my cousin,' I said, and walked across the road with my mobile phone in my hand. Dot stayed where she was.

From where I stood, punching in the numbers, she looked like a frail little old lady in ludicrously high-heeled shoes.

It was the elation of knowing that Marnie was back at home, had walked through the front door with a stupid grin on her face, having spent two fantastic days in London with her mate Shona, that led me to cross back to say goodbye.

'Don't go yet,' Dot said. 'How am I going to get home?'

I looked at her. Did she seriously think I was about to undertake another journey in that car, all the way to Solihull, which is to Birmingham what Waltham Forest is to London, and then find myself left with that particular stolen vehicle on my hands?

'It's my niece,' I began to explain. 'I've got to get back. Can't Dennis give you a lift?'

'If he can tear himself away from his duties. You know he runs this place?'

'I'm sure he will find the time,' I said, reassuringly, as if I had known Dennis all my life. Of course if I had known him all my life, or even for five minutes, I should have said there was very little chance of a lift or even a share in the taxi fare, and had she thought about driving lessons? I watched her walk slowly into Spats. She hadn't brought the walking stick, although she didn't seem to miss it. Perhaps she only needed it occasionally, when she fell off the heels. But her shoulders were drooping and I was tempted to run after her and say, 'Oh all right, then.' But she wasn't my responsibility, and she had Dennis.

Whereas the car had a ticket. How had that happened? I'd hardly turned my back for two seconds. Why hadn't Dot said something? I snatched the small plastic bag off the windscreen, and without thinking, got angrily into the car and turned the key in the ignition. Then I switched it off. I didn't want to go another inch in this car. It could get another twelve tickets for all I cared. I was going to have to get home under my own steam, but it was only half past six. There ought to be buses or a minicab office. I pulled the key out of the ignition, tucked it under the driver's seat, and, leaving the door unlocked, I slid out of the car.

I walked up to Broad Street. I looked up and down the street for a cab office. Nothing. There was a taxi rank, but it was empty. There was a bus stop, but there was no queue. There was no one around, scarcely any cars were passing up and down the road. Even the traffic wardens seemed to have made their final deliveries and gone home. I looked across the road towards the Convention Centre. Of course, I knew someone there.

I'd never been to Adam's office, but he'd shown me their glossy brochure so I had an idea where it might be. The Centre was clean and light and, compared to the street, full of activity. There didn't seem to be a convention or concert going on. These people were just at work. At this time of night. I had come to the twenty-first century and I didn't like it. But that was what I was relying on now. That Adam's hours were absurdly long and he would be yearning for a break. He could drive me home in one of the firm's cars and we could discuss the case, and he could describe it as a conference with counsel, for the sake of his senior partners.

And miraculously, that's what happened.

Back at Julie's, the anger had dissipated and there was an air of relief and celebration in the house.

'They went to visit the HQ of the Eco group we marched with on Saturday,' Julie said.

'It was so cool,' Marnie said. She had stayed in my flat.

'How did you get in?' I asked.

She looked at me shamefacedly. 'I made a copy of your keys. And your neighbour helped me, showed me where to put the rubbish and stuff. And your newspapers for recycling. And Worldsworth have said we can go and work there in the summer.'

'If you have somewhere to stay and your mother agrees,' Julie said. 'You may have to find a different mother before then, as I'm not sure how much of this I can take.'

'Frankie. . . .' Marnie turned to me.

'Don't look at me,' I said. 'Now listen Marnie.' After about ten minutes of constructive criticism, I said to Julie, 'Is that enough telling off?'

'I suppose so,' she said.

I pulled out the bottle of cheap champagne I had bought on the way home. 'Can we celebrate?'

'Yes, we can,' Julie conceded, 'on condition the adults get to choose the music.'

Marnie had to comply because she was still in very big trouble, although she had said she liked my living room, which is always a pleasure to hear. And then she asked if I had 'Blowin' in the Wind' but I wasn't sure it was the right mood and we compromised and played 'Corrina, Corrina', and you can't stay angry with someone who is open to that kind of debate. Then I put on 'The Wanderer', for both of us, and by the end of the evening we had pushed back the furniture and were dancing to Eddie Cochrane and Johnny Kidd and the Pirates.

I was just twirling Marnie round while Johnny complained that he'd never get over me when the phone rang. Breathlessly I leaned across the table to pick it up.

It was Yolande.

My cheeks glowed redder with pleasure. 'Marnie's back,' I said.

'That's nice,' she said. 'Having a good time?' Marnie and Julie were chorusing loudly 'found another guy-uy-uy-uy-uy.'

I walked into the middle room.

'The inquiry isn't happening tomorrow, is it?'

She had all the information. For a second I couldn't speak. 'No,' I managed. 'It's not.'

'Do you want to come for a picnic?'

THIRTY TWO

Friday – Picnic

I dressed carefully. A pair of black linen trousers, a fresh white linen shirt and then the question of shoes. Sandals were not the effect I wanted. My Doc Martens were too heavy. My black loafers were too clearly work shoes. So, it had to be my new cowboy boots. Too high? Perhaps. Too pointed? Possibly. But so delectable, so soft and tan, so comfy on my feet.

Those boots had walked out of the window display, cosied up to me on the seat in the shop and pulled the plastic right out of my wallet. They had cost an enormous amount of money, but in this case I had really got what I paid for.

Anyway, I knew I looked irresistible.

Unlike Clark, who was dressed for a session under the car, creased T-shirt and greasy jeans. Had I expected Clark? No I hadn't. But of course she would come with Clark. Who else would carry the hamper of food? Not that it was a hamper, it was two cool boxes, cracked, lime green and dirty white.

We were half a mile away from the Two Ewes, a cream-painted, half-timbered pub tucked back on a country road, off the B5000, near the river Hass. It had been rather difficult to find following Yolande's somewhat inadequate directions. But I had made the effort, dreaming of the picnic and other possible delights.

I had been thinking along the lines of small sections of warm, tender roast chicken, delicate filo parcels of spinach and cheese, hearty chunks of bagna calda with peppers and olive oil oozing out with every bite. Then possibly something sweet with tender raspberries melting into whipped cream and meringue. And wine, maybe not Chablis, maybe a simple Vinho Verde, and cold water in ceramic pitchers and white plates and linen napkins and heavy silver cutlery.

The cool boxes, it emerged, after we'd walked for half an hour and I'd scuffed my boots and had to stop to give them a discreet wipe, contained mainly cans of beer. There were also some Boots sandwiches, a mixture of Shapers (ham and salad) and three Combination packs plus some squares of carrot cake with thick white icing, wrapped in cling film.

But Yolande had brought a rug (which I had carried) and I laid it on the ground at a bend in the river, knowing that it was a faint hope that Clark would go and sit discreetly behind a thick holly bush.

I don't even like beer, but it was all there was so I gulped down a few mouthfuls, interspersed with bites of a chicken and pepper sandwich. As it turned out it was probably lucky that I drank such a small amount. I was thirsty, but I was sober.

Perhaps Yolande felt sorry for Clark, like I had till I'd had to drive him to Solihull. Apart from my own disappointment that I wasn't to spend a lazy, intimate afternoon alone with Yolande, I was slightly concerned about what his presence might mean. As far as I could make out, Clark was something of a double agent, torn between loyalty to Danny and violence from Dennis. I still wasn't sure who he would have given the sweater to, if I'd been able to produce it.

But somehow, sitting on the blanket on the sweet-smelling grass, with Yolande making soft appreciative noises, tasting the ripe tomatoes and the creamy cheese, it all seemed very far away. Clark even made us laugh, doing handstands and cartwheels dangerously close to the water. The sun beat down as we ate the last pieces of cake and swallowed the last mouthfuls of beer. I lay on my back and looked at the sky.

I woke with a start and immediately glanced at my watch – I had only been asleep for ten minutes, but I felt groggy and my throat was dry. Yolande was tidying away the sandwich wrappers that littered the blanket. I leaned up on my elbows. Clark had disappeared.

'Sorry,' she said softly, 'did I wake you up?'

I shook my head and watched her easy, languid movements, stretching her bare arms to gather the last remnants of our meal. 'Did you enjoy the picnic?' she asked.

'Very much,' I said. 'I enjoy most things I do with you.'

She leaned over me and kissed me on the mouth. 'Me too.'

'Let's go for a ride, girls!' Clark was hailing us, from the middle of the river, in a pedalo.

'Leave it out, Clark,' I said.

'What's the matter?' he called. 'Scared you'll get wet? You'll be all right, I'll do it all.' That's what he said. I remember it distinctly. 'I'll do it all. I'll go in the water. I like a paddle.'

A pedalo. I hadn't been in a pedalo since our family holidays in Clacton. I vaguely remembered laughter and splashing and wet shorts, but in what order, and who they belonged to, I wasn't certain.

'All right,' I said cautiously.

The pedalo was turquoise and orange – a colour combination I wouldn't have in my home – with two large eyes and the word Elvira painted on the mound between the two 'driving' seats. It was bigger than I remembered them, bulky and cumbersome, like a plastic tug that had lost its way.

Clark pedalled into the side and leaped onto the bank (I noticed he had taken off his trainers and socks – if he had been wearing socks). He pulled the pedalo firmly against the bank. 'Get in, get in,' he said.

'Are you sure this is a good idea?' I said.

'You go in the front,' he said to me. 'You can steer.'

I had a feeling that that was not the correct nautical term, and I wondered whether Clark knew what he was doing. Still, what is there to know about a pedalo? I stepped cautiously down into my seat and the boat rocked.

'Yolo, get in,' Clark called.

Yolo uncoiled herself luxuriantly from the rug, threw it casually over her shoulder and took a regal step onto the flat platform which was the back of the pedalo. She shook out the blanket, knelt and then sat with her back to us, stretching her long legs in front of her. And the pedalo became a yacht, a floating gin palace, a luxury cruiser, with a golden woman lounging elegantly on deck, trailing her fingers languidly in the water.

With me and Clark in front pedalling. It took us a little while to turn the pedalo round to go in the direction we wanted. Clark, who wasn't, in fact, letting me steer, was complaining about the tiller – a small piece of metal

329

sticking up between the two front seats. But when we discovered that reverse was just turning the pedals backwards, life became easier. We moved to the middle of the river and our feet moved in tandem as we forged through the water. I sensed I was doing more of the forging than he was.

But when Yolande murmured, 'Mmm, this is nice,' all concern drifted to the back of my mind and we moved smoothly and dreamily through the water. I didn't even have to worry about our stuff, since everything I had brought with me was in my pockets, and all we'd left behind was the aged cool boxes.

Yolande settled herself on the bunched-up rug, and when I glanced over my shoulder she had gone to sleep. It was peaceful and hot. No other boats, or even pedalos, passed us. There was no one to be seen, no one fishing or strolling in the fields on either side. A few trees lined the bank – a willow, some silver birch, clumps of bushes. We pedalled in silence, gradually moving slower and slower, so that our pace was lazy, less than walking. Every now and again we passed something in the water that may have been an old buggy or a refrigerator but it was hard to tell, everything was covered with swaying fronds of greenery.

Now that there was very little steering required, Clark put his hands behind his head and said, 'You take over for a bit.'

I rolled up the sleeves of my shirt, settled down in my plastic bucket seat and, with one hand on the tiller, lazily pushed the pedals round. The sky was a deep blue and the sun was burning my arms.

'You are amazing, Clark,' I said. 'Where did you find this pedalo?'

He smiled to himself, pleased. 'There was a place up the other way. It's not open, they were just there and I took one.'

Oh God, now we were out in a stolen pedalo. What would the sentence for that be? Banned from driving pedalos for three years, and three points on your nautical licence. He couldn't stop himself. If there was a minor offence to be committed, he'd commit it. I wondered if we had eaten hot sandwiches. Three points on your Weight Watchers card.

'Where did you run off to last night?' I asked.

'I had things to do, I told you.'

'I thought going to Solihull was what you had to do.' I hesitated. 'Dennis is a bit of a horror, isn't he?'

'He's my brother.' He looked away from me.

'I know you were at Haslam Hall. What was it that Dennis did, when you were in the home?'

There was a long pause while Clark stared at the bank. 'He brought them round, didn't he?'

'Who?'

'All that lot. Fleming, Catcher, the first two.' He threw a glance at me. 'The ones at Spats.'

'Fleming? Terry Fleming? Used to come to the Grange?'

'Or in town, at some crappy hotel.'

'Oh Clark,' I said.

His face still averted he went on. 'But I think it would have stopped. Dennis would have stopped it.' Was he being loyal to Dennis? This was the Family Vortex gone mad. 'It would have been alright if Effo hadn't got involved.'

'What has Effo got to do with it?'

'You know what they say, where there's brass there's

muck. Dennis was making money, he bought a new car. Effo noticed him. And that was me sorted out for the next two years.'

'What do you mean?'

'All Effo's business cronies. But Effo didn't get his hands dirty, he just poured out the scotch in the other room, talked about finance. Took the money.'

'What about Wyatt? Mr Wyatt? Did he know what was going on?'

'You're having a laugh aren't you? He jumped when Effo called, signed us out, drove us into town. Waited around, drove us home. Oh no, he didn't know anything.'

'Clark,' I began, 'why didn't you give evidence to the police?'

'I didn't need to, did I? None of them needed to. It was being sorted.' He spoke with a small show of pride. 'I'd have got it sorted out for them.'

'How?'

He looked at me incredulously. There was a small smile on his lips. 'I got friends.'

'Would you give evidence now?'

He looked down at his feet, watching the pedals turn.

'Did you know Gregory Springer?'

His feet turned the pedals.

'He was at Haslam Hall the same time as you. He's dead now.'

'That was a mistake.'

He knew! He knew all about it. My heart began to thump. 'How do you know that?'

'I've been told.'

'What do you mean? Who by? Not Dennis?'

His feet moved round and round. 'I've got to be careful.'

'Why? What?'

A voice came from behind us. 'Mmm, isn't this nice?' Yolande was yawning and stretching. 'How long have I been asleep?'

I glanced at my watch. 'About twenty minutes.' I stared at Clark.

'Look, cows,' Yolande said. 'Where are we?'

Clark shrugged. 'Haven't a clue.'

'Shall we turn back?' she suggested. It seemed like a good idea. I wanted to get Clark on his own to ask him what he knew about Gregory's death. Who had told him?

We began the arduous job of turning the pedalo while Yolande kept up a low running commentary on the loveliness of the surrounding countryside. Clark said no more.

We pedalled almost back to our starting point, slowly making our way towards the bank. Clark had taken charge of the tiller, because we were going in on his side, he said. Our feet were moving in an easy rhythm as we swished through a mass of water grasses, I could see the cool boxes, and then Clark got shot. Not a loud, smoking-gun-type shooting. It was more of a pop, like you hear at the fairground and then you expect to win a cuddly toy.

I wasn't sure what had happened. My heart was pounding and I could feel my face was drenched in sweat. I saw someone – a man – crashing through the bushes at the side of the river. I thought there was something I recognised about him, but shock had made my thought processes go into strobe mode, in and out of reality. Clark grunted and then, gradually, almost elegantly, he slid over the edge of the pedalo, and disappeared into the water. But not completely. His left foot was caught under the pedal, his ankle hooked round the stem.

'Oh, Christ! What was that?' Yolande threw herself down behind me. The pedalo rocked.

'It's OK,' I shouted.

We were drifting towards the bank. Desperately, I tried to turn my pedals, to reverse back towards the middle of the river, to give Clark space to come up, if he could come up, but his foot locked his pedals and thus mine too. 'Turn!' I shouted to the pedals. 'For fuck's sake turn!' They wouldn't move. I could see Clark bending at the waist trying to heave himself to the surface of the water.

'Is he hurt?' Yolande hissed in my ear.

'I don't know, he didn't say!' I tugged fruitlessly at Clark's foot. His own efforts to pull himself out of the water made the grip of his ankle, hooked round the base of the pedal, even more vice-like. A rusty patch of colour was spreading on the water on Clark's side of the boat.

Yolande clutched my arm. 'Who was it?'

I shook off her hand. 'I don't know who it was. Clark!' I shouted. 'For God's sake, Clark!'

Clark's head appeared above the surface of the water, in a rush of water and weeds, coughing and spluttering, and I lunged at him. 'It's fucking cold in here!' he said, leaning towards the pedalo. I clutched at his fingers and tried to bend our hands together, but he slithered from my grasp. He shouted, 'For fuck's sake!' and disappeared again beneath the surface.

Yolande had drawn her knees up under her chin and was keening softly. Clark's leg lay, scissored at the knee, over the side of the pedalo.

Suddenly, from the mass of weeds, an arm crested up out of the water and waved, in a gesture that could have been welcome or farewell. Yolande shrieked.

I threw myself across Clark's empty seat, along his contorted leg and grabbed at his arm. I caught his wet wrist, just above his watch, and heaved. The boat lurched a few inches away from the bank and Clark's head appeared above the water, knocking against the side of the boat. His eyes were closed and he was silent. He was unconscious. I leaned over futher, to catch his T-shirt with my other hand, but he was too heavy and as I grasped at the sopping cloth, the pedalo lurched over to his side, crushing him hard against the bank. His watch slid through my grip, till I was holding his palm, and then his fingers, and then I lost him altogether as his body uncurled back into the water, his foot still attached to the pedal.

The pedalo was rocking. It was knocking against something, and it wasn't the bank. It was Clark. The pedalo was rocking Clark to death, if he wasn't dead already. Yolande was right behind me, gasping for breath.

'All right! All right!' I shouted to anyone who was listening. I twisted away from the pedalo and Clark and jumped into the water. Which was not as shallow as I was expecting and I disappeared abruptly beneath the surface. Below the warm top layer, the water, as Clark had said, was icy. I nearly cried out with the cold, but my mouth sensibly stayed shut.

I knew I should have been worrying about Clark, whether he was alive or dead, how we were going to get him out of the water and then how would we get him medical help, and I was, of course, concerned about all that, but I was really worried about the water seeping rapidly into the soft supple leather of my boots. As my cheeks billowed and I pushed myself desperately to the surface, I was saying goodbye to them, to their velvety, comfortable feel and their handsome, caramel smoothness, and to all the nights I might have worn them to jive in, spinning and catching, dancing with somebody who loved me. Perhaps it was me who'd been shot, I thought with a lurch, as I surfaced, gasping and shaking my head, I was thinking in Whitney Houston.

I took hold of the boat and kicked out to pull it away from Clark. I was losing sensation in my legs from the cold. The boat pitched and Yolande toppled towards me.

'Get me off,' she said, on an inhalation of breath. 'Get me off!'

'Just keep still,' I said. 'It's a really solid boat, you're fine.'

'I need to be off!' she said. 'I can't swim. Get me off!' She started to stand up and the boat lurched and my whole body was back in the water, underwater, in a bubble bath of straw and mud, frozen in temperature and in action. I kicked my way to the top again.

'Yolande!' I gasped, 'Bloody well stay still. Don't move and you will be fine.' She sank back down, drawing herself into the middle of the pedalo.

'I hate water, I told you I hate water,' she whimpered.

'No, you didn't.' I was trying to catch my breath.

Clark's hand appeared on the other side of the pedalo and flapped weakly.

'Grab his hand!' I called to Yolande, as I tried again to pull the pedalo away from the bank. There seemed to be something holding it there. Or was there something holding Clark there? I hadn't seen anything when I jumped in the water, it had been all shock and bubbles. I didn't want to have to think about going back down.

'Yolande, do something!' I yelled. She was terrified, but, something, probably not love of Clark, possibly loyalty to Danny, maybe even simple humanity, made her uncoil her arm from her fetal position, and inch it slowly over to Clark.

'Take his wrist,' I shouted although I didn't think she'd be able to pull him in on her own.

'He's slipping,' she squeaked. 'Oh, he's bleeding.'

'Keep holding,' I shouted and then I said no more, because the thing that was holding Clark and possibly the pedalo, had got me too.

It was something large and metallic with fronds. Its tentacles were clinging to my leg and somehow pulling me under. In the grey world under the boat I could see what looked like an old Mini. Its windows were open and plants were growing in it. Long pale fronds waved gently in the current. Swirls of blood wafted softly through the water. But this was wrong. It should have been all thrashing and kicking, as Clark and I attempted to free ourselves. But Clark was obviously drifting in and out of consciousness and I – I was beside myself.

All I could see was the underside of the pedalo, the motionless mechanism that worked the pedals. Without realising it, I had drifted away under the boat and now the thing holding my leg meant I couldn't get back to the surface. I was under water with a dead car, a dying man and no oxygen.

I looked at my leg. The tentacles were actually pieces of wire wrapped round with weeds. The wires were attached to the Mini, from somewhere under the bonnet. I bent towards my leg, and pulled away several wires, but still I could not move. One wire had threaded itself through the loose linen weave of the material. It had sewn itself to my trousers. I pulled and it didn't move. I tried to gently untangle it. I pulled and jiggled. The material wouldn't even tear, it bunched up into a thick solid mass. A frightening prospect loomed. I was going to have to take off my trousers. And for that I would have to take off my boots. So in one go I would lose some good trousers and the boots. On the other hand, there was no alternative. I was bending to pull off my boots, twisting my ankle towards me, when the other end of the wire broke away from the car. I was free and I still had my boots and trousers on. I exploded to the surface.

'Call the police,' I shouted, struggling to pull my mobile out of my pocket. I threw it at Yolande, 'If you can.'

'Where are we?' she shrieked.

'I don't know.' I was gasping for breath. 'On the river. The Two Ewes. The B5000.'

'Don't leave me again,' she moaned, stretching her hand out to me. The air was fresh and dry, the sun was warm, the light was bright. I didn't want to leave her.

But Clark was still under there. I swam round to his side and dived underneath him. I tried to push him up, but there wasn't enough room between the shore and the pedalo. He was caught by wires in his T-shirt and his jeans. I took hold of the wires round his leg and ripped. They came away. The ones in his T-shirt were caught near his shoulder, mixed up with something that looked like blood and pieces of fibre. I didn't want to yank those wires for fear of hurting him. But if I didn't he would die, so I gave a sharp tug and the wires broke away from the mini. Clark started to float away from me, sinking to the bottom, but his right foot was still caught under the pedal and for a second he dangled. I could feel my lungs bursting for lack of oxygen as I swam under him again, and as my back connected with his, I pushed him to a horizontal position. In a last desperate effort, I kicked my legs, grabbed his chest and heaved. Together the two of us lurched out of the water.

'Move his leg!' I called to Yolande. She pulled at his ankle and his foot slid away from the boat. I tightened my arms round his chest and tried to squeeze hard, to eject the water from his lungs. Nothing happened. I moved my arms under his armpits, sliding my body under his. I kicked two strokes to the bank and pulled and rolled him onto the grass. He was a mass of water and blood. I heaved him upright and tried the Heimlich Manoeuvre again and this time he coughed and spat out water. I did it again and more water came out. Then we fell over together and I was giving him the kiss of life when the ambulance came.

The male paramedic bent to give oxygen to Clark and the woman helped Yolande off the pedalo. She wrapped the blanket round my shoulders.

Yolande handed back my mobile. It was dead. She had called the ambulance on her own phone, which she now lent me to ring Julie's house to ask someone to bring me a change of clothes to the hospital. I had said I would follow the ambulance in my car. We were going back to Birmingham because it was a gunshot wound.

Yolande snapped her phone shut and said she would join us at the hospital. Then she picked up the cool boxes and turned towards the sunny path we had first walked along three hours before.

After she had gone about ten yards, she turned and called, 'I want those photos.'

THIRTY-THREE

Hospital

Marnie came to the hospital with my bag, wearing sensible clothes and practising sympathetic expressions, obviously trying out the idea of working in one of the caring professions. I had told her that we'd had a small boating accident and Clark had been hurt.

Clark and I had hardly spoken to each other since we arrived at the hospital. At first he had drifted in and out of consciousness and then we were surrounded by nurses and a young doctor. They had offered to check me over, but apart from the boots, for which there was no known cure, I felt fine.

Clark was sitting on the bed in the bay where his wound had been stitched and dressed. I was sitting on a narrow hard chair. Clark's face lit up as Marnie pushed aside the curtain. 'Hello!' he said. 'It's a tonic to see you.' He was dressed in a pale green hospital gown, which stopped at his knees, and when he moved his arm to embrace Marnie the wide sleeve fell back to reveal a heavily bandaged shoulder. And, I noticed, the scars under his arm which had so entranced Marnie a few days before.

She perched on the end of the bed, smiling and nodding while I went to change my clothes and speak briefly

341

to a bored young police officer. I felt grumpy and ashamed, on my return, to see that Clark had visibly perked up, and was making little jokes about the grapes and the Lucozade that Marnie had brought.

Ten minutes later it was clear that, at the very least, she would make an excellent member of the cast of *ER*, but she was beginning to look a tiny bit fazed as Clark mentioned casually that the bullet hadn't lodged itself, it had just grazed his shoulder, tearing just a little bit of muscle. When he offered to show her the wound I suggested that perhaps Clark now needed something to read. After some caring conversation about what reading material might be light but enjoyable, Marnie went off in search of an angling magazine.

I leaned against the bed. 'Clark, I need to be clear about a few things.' I asked him why he had got shot, if we could draw any conclusions from the fact it wasn't a life-threatening injury, and if he knew why Yolande had not come back to the hospital.

Defiantly, he gazed at me. 'I haven't got a clue. That's what I told the police. They think it was kids with an air rifle. And it probably was. I've told them I won't want to press charges.'

'I can tell that you know who it was, Clark, and I expect you know why they did it, and who they intended to hit.'

He expression was sullen.

'Was it Dennis? Was it you he wanted? Or me?'

His face snapped up with a grin. 'Leave it out.'

'I'm in the inquiry, my picture's been on the news. Who's next? Henry Curston?'

'It's not you. It's not that. Look, it was a little gun, it was nothing. It was a game.'

'Tell that to my boots,' I said. 'Was it Yolande he wanted?'

'In a manner of speaking. He's always wanted Yolande. No, no.'

'Was it because of what happened at Haslam Hall?'

'Just . . . forget all of that. Forgot all of it.' He shook his head.

'Unfortunately it is etched on my memory as part of a fairly stressful afternoon. I was nearly drowned out there, not to mention my boots were ruined,' I said. 'How come I was even there?'

'Yolande said you should come with us.'

'You had planned a picnic and I was an afterthought?'

'I think Yolande felt guilty about, you know, Dennis and the bag.'

'In relation to you or me?'

'Who got the bruises?'

'So who knew about this picnic?'

'No one, Dot maybe. They were her coolers.'

'You've been back there? You're mad! Clark, just tell me what's going on.'

'Why should I?'

'Because I'm involved. Because of Danny's court case, because of the jumper, because of the photos.'

His face changed colour. 'Danny?' he breathed. My mention of the name had shocked him. 'Don't tell Danny.' He coughed and clutched hold of his bandaged shoulder. 'No, tell him not to plead guilty. Bastards. They're all bastards.'

'They had three to choose from.' Marnie appeared at the side of his bed, looking young and sweet. 'So I got you one with an article about river fishing.'

'Great.'

'There's an offer on flies,' she said. She showed him a picture. 'You can send off for them. Ooh, look at that one. Ooh.'

He laughed his wheezy laugh, holding his shoulder. 'You think those are bad,' he said. 'You should see some of the ones I've got.' What were they talking about? How did she know this about him? How did she know it at all?

'He's won competitions,' Marnie explained, as he flicked through the magazine.

They chatted and teased some more and then, surprisingly, Marnie said, 'We've got to go now.'

I raised my eyebrows.

'You should never stay too long with a patient, or you will tire them out. And mum says I've got to do some homework.' She looked at me. 'You look pretty wiped out too.'

'OK, Nurse Betty, let's go,' I said. It was fine by me. I did feel tired. I turned to Clark. The fading bruises stood out on his pale cheeks and his eyelids drooped. 'When are you coming out?'

'Dunno. Tomorrow probably.'

'Where are you going? Have you got someone to look after you?'

'I'm going back to my flat, I'll be all right.'

Marnie leaned towards him and kissed him on the forehead.

As we left the ward I looked back over my shoulder and wondered if he was safe, sitting alone there in his small bay.

I had rung chambers while Clark was being stitched. It was five o'clock. The busiest time of day in the clerks' room. Gavin had said, 'Are you sure you can't make the chambers meeting?'

'Damn.' I had completely forgotten the vote for head of chambers. And I hadn't spoken to Tony. 'Can I cast a postal vote?'

'Bit late for that isn't it?'

'Shit. Proxy?'

'We don't do that.'

'Bugger. Is Simon there?'

'He's on his way back.' I could hear his disapproval down the phone.

'Is Tony there?'

'He's on the phone and got a call waiting. And so've I.' Now he was impatient as well.

'OK. Look, the reason I can't come is that there's been an accident.'

Immediately his tone changed. 'Who? What? Are you OK?'

'Oh I'm fine, except for my boots. It's not me.'

'Want to talk about it?'

'No.'

I tried Simon's mobile but he'd switched it off. I left a message which attempted to combine something of the tragedy of my day with a request for him to speak to Tony if I couldn't get through, and a peppy expression of good luck for the evening.

I rang Gavin back. 'Is Tony still tied up?'

'Yes.'

'Can I leave a message on his voice-mail?'

'You can try. I'm not sure he'll get it.'

I left a brief message explaining what Iotha had told me.

After I had dropped Marnie back at home I drove back to London, listening to an old tape of the *Biggest Ever*

Sixties Hits, but I couldn't get into it, and when Sonny and Cher started singing 'Bang Bang', I had to turn it off and listen to the repeat of the *Woman's Hour* serial. But then *Any Questions* began so I put on the Four Tops and had done with it.

It was almost nine o'clock as I drove off the M1. I was starving and I'd started shivering. It must be delayed shock, I told myself. I needed a strong cup of tea. I wasn't even going to attempt to go into chambers. The only item on the agenda had been the election, so I would have missed it.

Miserably I let myself into the house. I didn't even have any mail.

I began unpacking my bag, pointedly ignoring the flashing light on my answerphone. It was bound to be someone from chambers with the results of the vote, but I couldn't bear to listen in case they were the wrong results. That was one of the nice things about staying with Julie. I didn't have to be a slave to the answerphone. Perhaps I should move to Birmingham. Of all the places in the world.

I threw my damp clothes in the bin in the bathroom, scrunched balls of newspaper into the toes of my boots, and turned on the taps in the shower. Ten minutes later, I came out of the shower, drying my hair, and looked again at my answerphone. I'd have to know sooner or later, I might as well listen. I pressed the button but it wasn't the results. There was a message from Julie in Birmingham. Marnie had just told her about Clark's injury and my change of clothes. She hoped I was all right.

And there was a message which sounded like someone who was very wound-up, tight-lipped, a man's voice. It said, 'You bastard.' Obviously someone who hoped I wasn't all right.

I rang Julie. 'Thank goodness,' she said, 'I thought perhaps you'd suffered post-traumatic stress on the M1.'

'I always do that on the M1,' I said. 'But I'm fine. You didn't just ring again as a joke, with a gruff voice did you?'

'No.'

I ordered a pizza and watched a video of *How to Marry a Millionaire*. It's always useful to have an alternative game plan.

THIRTY-FOUR

Saturday – Back to Clerkenwell

I should have stayed in Birmingham, I thought, lying in bed, staring at the cobweb in the corner of the ceiling. I had absolutely nothing planned for the weekend. Except shopping. I really needed to get in some tins. I looked at my watch.

But of course I had something to do, something I had been planning and talking about for days. My trip back to Clerkenwell to pick up the pictures for Yolande. Pictures of . . . who knew what? Something that would probably get me arrested. Or at the very least put the tin lid on my legal career. I didn't want to go to Clerkenwell.

I rang Simon.

The phone rang for a long time and when he answered his voice was a low groan.

'Simon, you sound like I feel, are you all right?'

'Yes,' he said thoughtfully. 'I am.'

'So?'

'You are now speaking to your new head of chambers.'

'Oh Simon, that's fantastic news.'

'What time is it?'

'Just gone ten.'

'We were up rather late . . .'

'God, Simon, I'm sorry. I'll ring back.'

'No, no. Why don't you come and have breakfast with me to celebrate. And I can tell you all my other news.' I could hear the sickening smile on his face. I knew what that meant, there was love and romance in his life. I wasn't sure I could bear it. But going out for breakfast. That could be called a social engagement.

Simon lived on a road just off Upper Street. I found myself a parking meter, and put in several pound coins which, I then realised, gave me the right to park there for almost the rest of my life, it was so cheap. Simon opened the discreet black door and I stepped into the kind of house that you spend hours looking at in magazines when you decide it's time to redecorate the bathroom. Pale wooden floors, deep, glowing rugs, muted, creamy walls and dark, polished wooden furniture, shining with a gloss only a cleaner can achieve. The place breathed with the naturalness and delicacy of 'old money'.

He led me out into the garden. A grey wooden table and chairs sat amid a mass of flowers, blue and purple clematis and ivy, on a terrace of York stone. On the table was a coffee pot and a large plate, piled with warm, golden Danish pastries. 'I'll just get the champagne,' he said.

'Oh I'm not sure,' I said. 'I've got things to do this morning.'

'I've got orange juice, how about a Bucks Fizz?'

'Damn you and your sweet talk, Simon,' I said. 'OK. Just a small one. And leave out the orange juice.'

He handed me a glass of champagne and put a chunky

painted mug of coffee in front of me. I could get used to this world.

Simon settled himself in a chair.

'So what happened?' I asked, sipping champagne. 'Mmm, fantastic. Do you know if Tony got my message?'

'Oh yes. And he went and spoke to Marcus immediately. I don't know what was said, but when the meeting began Tony announced that due to pressure of work Marcus had decided to withdraw his candidacy.'

'Well, well,' I said.

'So it wasn't a great victory. I was the only one standing.'

'Congratulations anyway. You would have walked it.' I clinked my glass against his mug. A thought struck me. 'You do realise what this means? If your Judge Norman does want to continue with his complaint against me and report me to my head of chambers, he's going to have to write to you.'

'Don't push your luck,' he said. 'We might put in a joint complaint.' Then his expression changed. 'Actually, there was something.' He paused. I felt sick. I didn't know what he was going to say – there was so much he could say. Silence hung in the space between us. A lorry accelerated along Upper Street. The glass of champagne felt sticky and warm in my hand. Carefully I put the glass on the table and folded my hands into my lap. Simon went on, 'Apparently, Marcus started burbling something about you and lack of professionalism. Said he was anxious that Tony should know that there were people whose adherence to the Code of Conduct should be reviewed before chambers got into trouble.'

Bloody Marcus and his stupid case. I opened my mouth to speak.

Simon shook his head. 'Tony said he had utmost faith in you and that you were a valued member of chambers and he would hear no more of it.'

'Did he really?' It is always nice to hear praise from unexpected quarters. Except Tony didn't know what he was talking about or what I'd been doing over the last two or three weeks.

'So,' Simon was studying my expression, 'assuming that is just an example of Marcus's pomposity . . .'

'How's the trial going?' I said, quickly, before we started talking about the wrong things.

'I'm not sure. Danny is desperate to plead guilty. I had a hell of a job yesterday convincing him he should just let the trial take its natural course. Kay's coming up on Monday to talk to him.'

'And Roseanna?'

His mouth twitched. 'Exactly. If he changes his plea, the trial ends and it's bye bye romance.'

'Love, actually.'

'What! Has she said something to you?' His eyes widened with hope.

'Sorry, no. It's the song, "Bye Bye Love". Sorry. I meant, how is her case going?'

'Ah. She's making some good points which usually bugger up anything I've managed to slip in without Danny noticing.'

'So she's good?' I asked.

Simon's eyes crinkled into a faraway smile. He was looking at her in his mind's eye, as he held a piece of pastry three inches from his mouth, and maple syrup dripped slowly onto his shirt. 'She's tough and she's a stickler for procedure.' He was imagining her in her crisp white collar and her flowing gown, I could tell. 'Even

351

the judge is afraid of her. I was thinking of asking her if she wanted to join our chambers.'

'Really,' I said, thinking, lovesickness and confectionary make such a boring combination. 'Eat your breakfast before it gets cold. How did your hot date go?' I said.

'Very well. It wasn't really a date, it was quite formal. We talked about the Bar, mainly. So that's probably that.' He looked wistful.

'But isn't it your turn to ask her out?'

He gave me a delighted, beaming smile. 'Do you think I should? Where could I ask her to go?'

'How about Tony's bash?'

'What a very good idea. Do you think she'll come to London? Should I invite her to stay here? Oh no, that would be too pushy by half.'

'I'm sure she'll have somewhere to stay, she must have friends in London. But if she needs to, she could stay at my place.'

'You're an angel.'

'Mmm,' I murmured, thinking, you probably wouldn't say that if you knew where I was going now. Perhaps Marcus had a point. 'I'd better be off,' I said. 'I have places to be.'

He walked me to my car. I still had three hours left on my meter. It seemed such a waste.

Clerkenwell was quiet. I parked easily, but more expensively than at Simon's, and walked quickly to the old, high Victorian building. Inside, most of the workshop seemed to be closed for the weekend. Somewhere in the distance someone was playing an old Beatles LP. 'It won't be long.' Probably not. I made my way up the grey concrete stairs, and along the corridor to the darkroom.

The work experience girl had gone, and it was a man of about fifty with a long grey ponytail and a navy-blue fisherman's sweater, to whom I hesitantly gave my name. Too late to think about an alias now. He went away for what seemed a very long time. I wondered if he was ringing the police.

He came back holding a greaseproof bag bulging with pictures. My heart began thumping as I offered him money. 'It's OK,' he said, 'we'll send you a bill.'

I almost asked him to make out the bill to Yolande, toying with the idea of presenting it to Frodsham on Monday morning. 'No!' I said sharply. 'I'll pay now.' I wanted it over. I didn't want to be reminded of this again.

The man with the ponytail went away again, for five minutes. Foolish. I should have let him send me the bill. He was bound to be ringing the police now. I didn't dare look in the bag. If necessary, I would claim complete lack of interest.

He returned with a scribbled invoice and I paid, £5.78 including VAT. I wondered if I could claim it back.

I walked briskly down the stairs and along to the large front doors, accompanied by George Harrison singing that his girlfriend had the devil in her heart. And we all knew how that felt.

I got back in the car, took a deep breath and slid the pictures out of the bag. My first impression was magnolia walls, beige sheets and people in a bed. Engaging in various sexual activities. On a Sunday, it looked like. A copy of the *Sunday People*, was on a bedside table. I could make out the words 'Love Rat' above a blurred picture of someone young and obviously pretty.

Not just people – Yolande, with a man. This man was neither Danny nor Frodsham. Presumably it was Terry Fleming. My heart was trembling and my breath had gone. I thought I recognised the room. The lamp. Oh God. How could she ask me to do this for her? Bastard, bastard.

OK – she was a free agent, and non-monogamy is a philosophy which is not altogether discredited. But I thought with non-monogamy, as I understood it from the old feminist days, you had to be respectful of other people's feelings, you didn't rub their noses in it. You were kind and tender and bought people presents to make up for it. That's how I'd do it anyway, if I had the chance. But this was all for Danny. I didn't count when it came down to it. I thrust the photos back into the bag.

So now what? I started the car and moved back out on to Clerkenwell Road.

I drove to my mum's flat in West London. I almost didn't care if she wasn't in, I just needed to do something, to go somewhere to work off my despair. In fact I nearly went to Wales, because I missed the motorway exit by Shepherds Bush and sailed on for a couple of miles not able to turn off. Shouting at some tourist coaches made me feel better.

I stopped outside her flat and rested my head on the steering wheel. All I had wanted was a few photos to show Terry Fleming alive and well last week. I didn't need, Danny didn't need, Yolande to be in the pictures too. I pushed the pack of photos into the glove compartment.

Mum was in, and very pleased that I had come. It was

lunch time so she made cheese and tomato sandwiches toasted in her latest electrical acquisition, a sandwich toaster. I told her she'd done them for too long, she said she'd warned me, but I burnt my mouth, and she told me not to make a fuss.

She handed me the plastic bag. 'It certainly needs a good wash.' She looked at my face. 'But, don't worry, I haven't.'

I pulled out the jumper and held it up. It was thick and chunky, something Scottish and cream with bobbles on it. It was huge. 'You went out with a boy who had a jumper like this? I thought mods were meant to be stylish.'

'Mmm. Unfortunately, in Colchester, it was always the case that a nice leather jacket or a parka would cover a multitude of fashion sins.'

I was looking through the bag, shaking it upside down. There was nothing else there.

There was a large stain on it, which looked like blood. I'm not an expert but it didn't look like it was twenty years old. I looked at the label. 'Mum, this sweater comes from Gap. Gap wasn't around here twenty years ago.'

'Oh yes, you're right. No, I would never have gone out with someone who wore a jumper like that.'

'Mum.'

This was probably quite bad news. I felt I was now in possession of incriminating evidence. Having this sweater was almost certainly an offence.

My mum and Alan were going to the six o'clock showing of a Chinese film about the fifties which had had good reviews. I drove my mum into the centre of town to meet him and then decided I'd go with them. I had nothing else to do and a good Saturday night out can start at six o'clock. I left the jumper on the front seat of the car, in case someone might want to steal something – like the jumper or the car. The photos I took with me.

After the film they asked me if I wanted to go for a meal in Chinatown, but I had things to do. I walked back to the British Museum where I found the car and its contents safe and sound. It wasn't nine o'clock. And I was going home.

My mail from the morning was piled up by the door – three catalogues, a gas bill and two postcards. I threw them on the sofa.

I rang Yolande. I wanted to say 'I've got the jumper and the photos, you bastard!' I tried the two numbers that I had. The mobile was unobtainable. The land line rang and rang. I couldn't even leave a message. I looked at the phone list that Catherine Delahaye had asked all the advocates to complete on the first day of the inquiry. Frodsham's home number resembled Yolande's in the first three digits. They must have separate lines, but I wasn't going to ring and ask him. I even tried the hotel on Russell Square. She wasn't there.

If Yolande couldn't explain the pictures, I'd have to speak to Clark. He knew about the jumper, he might know about the photos. Except I didn't have a number for him. I rang the hospital and they said he'd discharged himself shortly after we left on Friday evening. Hopeless.

I decided I would make myself a nourishing meal. I opened the kitchen cupboards, I'd forgotten to go shopping. The fridge was empty except for a shrivelled piece of fennel. The only edible thing in the house was a tin of duck liver pâté. OK, foie gras. Someone had given it to me for Christmas. And I'd had a difficult afternoon.

I lifted out a bag of flour and moved an open packet

of brown sugar. I pulled out the foie gras. And brought the sugar and a surprising bag of lentils with it. The lentils wobbled on the edge of the work surface for a second and then toppled onto the floor. All over the floor. A home-made lentil rug. I contemplated leaving them there, it looked quite postmodern. But the lentils crunched as I went to the freezer to dig out the frozen bread. Saturday night and I was confronted with serious housework. I crunched to the cupboard to find the hoover. It was behind the ironing board, the electric fan and twelve rolls of Christmas paper. Too depressing. It was time for the Dustbuster!

The Dustbuster wouldn't suck. My new, early birthday present from my mother was obviously broken. It would have to go back. I'd scarcely taken it out of the box. Perhaps this was a sign that housework has no place in the modern home. But there were lentils all over my floor. No, before I took it back, I would apply some science. I shook it, it might be a loose connection.

There was a muffled rattle. There was something in it. Someone had been using it. How horrible, someone had come into my house, while I wasn't there and, oh God, done housework. Who could have done that? It could have been Marnie, but given her parentage that seemed unlikely. It had to be my mother. I was going to have to empty it.

I prepared well. I poured myself a glass of whisky, and laid a few sheets of the *Guardian* across the kitchen floor. I prised open the cream plastic nozzle. Inside there was dust, fluff and Christmas tree spines (it was definitely my mother who had cleaned because they were underneath the settee) and, by the sound of it, a one pound coin. Some consolation. I turned my head away and shook. There was a gentle sighing of the newspaper as the contents of the Dustbuster landed softly, and the sound of something rolling away. I folded the newspaper and put it all in the bin. Then I hoovered up the lentils. Then I looked for the pound coin. It was under the kitchen table and it wasn't a pound coin.

It was about two inches long, it was shiny and hard. And unless I was very much mistaken it was a bullet.

This was what Yolande had given me to look after. A bloody bullet. A bloody sweater and a bloody bullet.

I leaned against the work surface, spreading foie gras on the toast. I took a mouthful of whisky. What a woman. I suppose you had to admire her for her complete and utter ruthlessness.

Still chewing toast, I was taking out the scrunched-up balls of newspaper from the toes of my boots when the phone rang.

It was Lena, calling me from Gino's. 'What are you eating?' she asked.

'Nothing!' I said, swallowing quickly.

'Exactly, come and have some supper.'

'And who's stood you up?'

'Never you mind, the food will do you good.'

She had to be right, and she didn't know the half of it.

In the twilight of the evening, Gino's was packed with weekend romancers, mums and dads with their Saturday-night-tidy children, groups of women having a good time, and Lena, without the neck collar, sitting at a table under the spreading leaves of a fig plant. Gino ushered me to my seat, his head bobbing with his commentary. 'Buon giorno, Signora, comment allez-vous aujourd'hui? You OK?' He pulled out a chair. His hair was a new shiny jet black, more so at the back, I noticed. 'You will share your friend's bianco?' He screwed up his face in displeasure. 'No.' He looked at me and chuckled. 'Shall I bring a bottle of vino tinto?'

I looked at the clock. It said half past nine, but it always said that. I looked at my watch, it was gone ten o'clock. There wasn't really time for two bottles, but what the hell, it was the weekend and I had just thrown away a tin of foie gras. I deserved it. 'Bring the red.'

He sighed with pleasure. 'Ah Signora, we have a saying in Italy, a woman who knows what she likes.' He waddled round to the back of the bar. Lena and I looked at each other. Lena shook her head.

I took a mouthful of Lena's wine while I waited. I was glad I was having the red. 'So who stood you up tonight?'

'Later, later,' Lena said airily, picking up the orange plastic-covered menu. 'What are you going to order?'

I knew without looking. 'Penne putanesca and a green salad. And bread.'

'That sounds nice,' she said. 'I'll have the mushroom risotto.'

We were silent as Gino placed the bottle of red wine on the table and then we gave our order. I took a large mouthful of wine.

Lena was gazing at me. 'You're not eating, you're not living at home, and you look terrible.'

'Thank you.'

'I'm sorry,' she said, 'I'm trying to give you tea and sympathy. You do look terrible. What's been happening?'

359

'All right,' I said. And I told her. About the View and the initials JC and about Marnie going missing and the trip to Spats and then about Clark's little accident in the pedalo. I repeated the part about the boots because I knew she liked those boots too.

'Oh no, that's terrible,' she said at that point, but the rest of the time she was quiet. And then I told her about the photos.

'Oh Frankie, I'm so sorry,' she said. She leaned forward and stroked my hand.

I smiled at her, fighting off the temptation to burst into tears and shout 'It's not fair!'

Gino arrived with our food and then hovered with a dish of parmesan cheese and a large pepper grinder. 'Buon appetito, Signore,' he smiled and went away.

'When does this inquiry end?' she asked, pouring more wine into my glass. 'The sooner you're back in London the better.' She toyed with her risotto. 'I asked for mushroom, what's this? It's not chicken is it?'

'Oh, don't start that again. It's a mushroom, for goodness' sake.'

'Are you sure?' Carefully she lifted something dark and glossy onto her fork and stared at it.

'All that tampering with brakes and now this shooting – I can't believe we're having this conversation – do you think there's any connection?'

'Gregory and Clark were at the children's home. From what he said, I think Clark was the usual boy and then, from what Gregory began to say, Gregory stood in for Clark if he wasn't around. Gregory was thinking of spilling the beans and he's now dead. I asked Clark to spill the beans and he got shot. So far so good.' I crammed too much pasta in my mouth.

360

Lena opened her mouth to speak. I waved her to be quiet, while I thought something through. I remembered Clark in the back of the shop. I swallowed. 'Clark said that Gregory's death was a mistake.'

'Meaning?'

'Maybe they didn't mean to kill him, just frighten him.'

'Or maybe it was the wrong car.'

'Or the wrong person. Perhaps the person they meant to kill or frighten was Mrs Springer.'

'Bit of a coincidence isn't it?'

'I know, but I'd rather think it was that. I can't bear to think that on top of everything they went through when they were kids, now they've got to think they could be killed for telling the truth.'

'There's a lot of killing going on, isn't there?' said Lena primly, surreptitiously putting something small and fleshy on the side of her plate. 'Right, I'm going to do my sidekick bit. Did you know about all of this going into Birmingham before Gregory started talking about it?'

'No. All the abuse that I knew about, that we were talking about in the inquiry, took place in the home.'

'But now you know that Clark was there as well, and we know that Terry Fleming and Catcher were in on it? And this Effo. What about Danny?'

'From what Clark said, Danny was the good guy. In his eyes.'

'Not in the eyes of the law though?'

I gave Lena a rundown of Danny's previous convictions, as well as the story of the killings he'd done and not been caught for. I remembered Clark saying, 'And the first two, the ones at Spats.'

'You know what I think,' I said. 'I think that Danny is doing over all the people who did over Clark.'

'That sounds like quite a big job.'

'And I think Danny's probably a psychopath. So it suits him. He's just not a very clever psychopath, and he keeps getting caught.'

'Who's the man with one leg?'

'I don't know,' I said, as a sickening memory trickled through my brain. The man in the bushes by the side of the river, running away, lumbering unevenly through the undergrowth. I'd thought, if I'd thought at all, that it was the rough terrain, but perhaps he was really limping. A man with a limp. A man who needed a walking stick.

'But he's not even a very effective psychopath, because in this case – sorry to go back to it – haven't you got photos that show that Terry Fleming isn't dead?'

'I assume so. If I can prove the date on the newspaper.'

'Couldn't that be rigged?'

'I wouldn't have thought so. I suppose, if necessary, I could give evidence, to say that's exactly what the room looked like the night before.'

Lena pushed my wine glass towards me. 'I think you should give those photos to the police as soon as possible, and then forget all about it. It's their job, not yours.'

'I can't give them to the police. If anyone is going to give them to the police it should be Simon.'

'Well, give them to him then. It's not your problem.'

'I've got a bullet.'

'Pardon?'

'I found it, it was in the jumper, and the jumper's got blood on it,' I gabbled.

'Police.' She looked at my face. 'All right, Simon.' She

put her face close to mine. 'OK? Agreed? This is your sidekick speaking.'

'OK,' I said.

'Good,' she breathed. She looked at her plate. 'Are you sure these are mushrooms?'

'Not really, no,' I said.

It was almost midnight when I pushed in the light in the entrance hall to the house. Inside the flat I didn't switch the lights on. I moved around in the dark in the kitchen, opening cupboards, then getting ready for bed, enjoying being back in my own place. I put on a Beach Boys tape to play myself to sleep. 'Wouldn't it be nice,' I thought, 'to have an ordinary life for a bit, where cars aren't tampered with, where people don't get shot out of your pedalo, and where tyre irons stay in the boot of the car?' And musing on why they hadn't put that into the song, since it seemed to sum up the human condition, I fell asleep.

THIRTY-FIVE

Sunday – Birmingham

I woke up singing 'Sunday, Sunday', but then I remembered the song was 'Monday, Monday'. And then I remembered everything else. I felt dreadful. Perhaps it was the last glass of Courvoisier I'd had at Gino's, or maybe the large shot of Talisker I had thrown down my throat when I got in.

I went out to buy the papers and on the way back, I looked down hopefully to the floor by my front door. No post on Sunday. But I hadn't read my mail from yesterday.

I lugged the deck chair out into the garden, made some more coffee and settled down to read how heartaches are made. The sun was hot on my head. Margo's card just said, 'Wow!' I threw the catalogues onto the floor, decided the gas bill had to be a mistake and stared at the newspaper for a few minutes, but I wasn't reading anything. I pottered around in the garden and worried a few plants. I washed up a cup.

I decided to go back to Birmingham. It was all getting so messy. Cars, guns, bad jumpers. I didn't want to think what this said about my life, that I was willing to leave London early. I knew what it said. It said, no life in London. Lena had rung at ten o'clock to ask me if I wanted to go to the Farmers' Market on Islington Green, but the thought of buying food I wouldn't be there to eat was too dismal.

I threw clean clothes and the newspapers in a bag and, just as I was leaving, went back to my desk and shuffled through the piles of paper. I found the photos from Sandra's flat and put them in the bag with Yolande's pictures.

In the car I decided to cosy up to Timi Yuro, and pushed a casette of her greatest hits into the player. Timi Yuro, what a voice. Together we were hurt, we were sorry and we urged Yolande not to make us wait. With any luck, she would pick up the phone before it was too late. She probably wouldn't tell me she loved me, but she might have some sort of explanation about the pictures. I shot up the M1.

Julie and Marnie were watching *Titanic*. I threw my bag down behind the sofa and we all watched as something happened in the ballroom. 'It's about the twentieth time,' Julie whispered as we crept into the kitchen and made a cup of tea.

'So?' Marnie shouted. It was good to be back.

Yolande was still not answering her phone. I decided to cruise past the shop. And if she wasn't there, I would look for Clark and see what he could tell me.

There were no lights on in the shop. There were two vague possibilities of where Clark might be. And I wasn't going to Solihull. Not again and certainly not on a Sunday. I'd have to go to Spats.

I got there at six thirty. The place was crowded, which seemed unusual for a pub on a Sunday in the middle of the business area. Perhaps they had come for the show. A sandwich board outside the pub announced that this evening there would be a cabaret and the Master of Ceremonies would be one Dennis De Largo. Dennis. That surname had to be his stage name. I really didn't want to see him. But I did want to see Clark. I would go in, have a quick look round and then leave. As simple as that.

I stood optimistically at the doorway and looked inside but I couldn't see beyond the first row of people. I pushed my way through the tightly packed tables. No one I knew. There was a small area near the back of the pub where a microphone and a couple of amplifiers sat, waiting for the show to begin. The ringside tables seemed to be filled with Dot lookalikes. At one table sat a group of sniggering schoolboys. I wondered if there was going to be a stripper or lap dancing. I wondered whether the place had a licence. I really didn't want to be here.

A man with green shirtsleeves stood majestically behind the bar.

'Yes, love?'

'Do you know Clark? Jimmy Clark? Have you seen him?'

Something crackled in his eyes. Suspicion, maybe concern. 'No, no I haven't. Why don't you ask Dennis? I think he's around somewhere.'

'It's OK,' I said. 'I'll catch up with Jimmy later.'

'No, he was here a minute ago. Dennis!' he called. 'Young lady looking for Jimmy.'

Damn.

A man lumbered slowly through the crowd towards me. For the first time I could get a proper look at him. He looked like Clark, a slightly older, taller Clark, who had spent several intense hours on a sunbed, changed into a green, sparkling jacket, and done some body-building to his hair. The grim expression on his face was replaced with a broad smile when he saw me. 'Well, well, well.' I wondered how much his teeth had cost him. He had a transatlantic twang. 'Nice to see you again.'

I nodded.

'Do you have something for me?'

The bloody jumper. Why couldn't people get over it? Get something modern, up-to-date, something with a hood.

'Some photos perhaps?'

For God's sake, was everybody in on this? Was I running errands for every villain in Birmingham?

I gave him my 'Are you mad?' look, while the memory of Clark's bruised, punctured face and torn, bleeding shoulder rose in my mind, and the photos throbbed to the rhythm of my pounding heart in the inside pocket of my denim jacket.

'Freddy, get the lady a drink. What would you like, how about a nice Dubonnet?' Was this the extent of Dennis's knowledge of women? Dot's favourite drink. 'Now you sit down here.' He smiled at a couple near the bar and pulled a high stool across to me.

'I'd love to,' I said, 'but I really can't stay.'

'Jimmy's bound to be in shortly. He likes a show. Perhaps he'll have something for me.' Dennis lumbered away towards the stage.

Freddy was sliding a glass of Dubonnet towards me. I nodded in thanks and raised it to my lips. Well, it was a long time since I'd had a Dubonnet. About twenty years. I'd forgotten it existed. I licked my lips, hmm. No wonder. Aromatic. Bitterish. Sweet. Undrinkable. This is what hell will be like. Men in sparkling jackets with sparkling teeth, endlessly offering you French aperitifs. This is why we should all be good.

Regretfully I pushed the glass across the bar. I had to go. I slipped out of my seat and turned away. But Freddy had moved round from behind the bar and now stood in front of me. 'Dennis doesn't want you to go,' he said. 'He wants you to watch the show.' Watching me all the time, he moved back behind the bar and topped up my glass. He pushed it back towards me.

'Lovely,' I said.

Half an hour later I had amended my definition of hell. You get the sparkling accessories and the aperitif, but you have to drink it watching a show. The lifts in Dennis's shoes were obviously giving him gyp, I thought, as he limped onto the stage, and then I remembered. I looked round and Freddy smiled at me. Dennis settled himself onto a tall stool. Accompanied by a tape of an organ, Dennis did it his way, he faced the music and danced, we flew him to the moon and he hadn't even introduced the first act. And still Clark had not arrived. I really had to go.

Freddy, his green, shirtsleeved arms folded across his enormous chest, was watching the act, but also occasionally flicking his eyes across at me. I walked towards the stage, carrying my drink, careful to stay in Freddy's line of vision, but unnoticed by Dennis. I looked interestedly at his equipment and then I came back to my seat. My glass of Dubonnet was empty. And then something happened to Dennis's ghettoblaster. The music faded and died. Dennis looked expectantly over at Freddy, who moved forward to investigate. I slid my glass across the bar and left the building.

* * *

368

I drove back towards Julie's house gnawing my lip. I had photos that would apparently help Danny. But the people who would tell me that for sure were, for one reason or another, unavailable. And Simon had said that Danny was threatening to change his plea. As soon as I safely could on Broad Street, I pulled over and stopped the car. I rang Kay. Her answer-phone, rather recklessly, told all callers that she was in Birmingham for a few days, and to leave messages for her at her office. It might just as well have said, 'Burgle me now,' but doubtless she knew what she was doing.

I rang her mobile. 'And how are you settling in to this great city of ours?' I asked. 'Where are you?'

'The Hyatt Regency.'

'Mm, fancy that. I think I've just driven past there. Do you want to go out for dinner?'

'If I must,' she said.

'Playing hard to get? I like that in a woman. Come for an Indian meal with me on Bristol Street.'

'Give me fifteen minutes.'

We ordered the food. I could have ordered it before she arrived. A dhansak and a biryani and some chicken tikka. Bread. Plain rice. We always had that.

Her hand hesitated on the bottle of Blanc de Blanc. 'Are you going to confess something terrible you've done?' She eyed me suspiciously. 'If you are, you'd better tell me now, before we drink this.'

'Nothing to confess.'

'Sure?'

I nodded. If I told her straight away it would ruin the meal, I knew.

* * *

369

'I'm not going to order another bottle,' she said, as she pushed aside her plate and poured the last of the wine into her glass. 'You're going to tell me why you were so keen to see me.'

'Did I sound keen? I didn't mean to be keen.'

'So?'

'Was that why we split up? Your suspicious nature?'

'I think that belonged to you,' she said, 'but go on.'

'All right.' I groped in my jacket, into the bag of photos. I didn't want to get the whole lot out. She didn't need to know the entire story quite yet.

She didn't actually get to know any of it that night. I put one of the pictures in front of her.

'I assume that's Yolande, but who's this?' she asked me simply.

I looked at her. 'Terry Fleming?'

'No it's not. Who took it?'

'Don't look at me like that. I didn't take it.'

'That's something, I suppose. Why are you showing it to me?'

I scraped the picture off the table. 'If that's not Terry Fleming, I don't know.' My face was hot.

'I assume you showed me that picture thinking it might be useful,' Kay said kindly. 'I don't think it is. We need to see Terry Fleming alive and well and reading a copy of yesterday's *Daily Telegraph* to impress the members of Simon's jury.' She looked over at the photo in my hand. I crammed it back into my jacket. 'Frankie, I told you to stay out of this. These photos are horrible for you. Thank you at least for showing them to me.'

The bullet weighed in my pocket like a ton of lead. If I told her where I had got it she might be compromised in representing Danny, like Frodsham had been. But she was being so kind.

'Can I talk to you about bullets?' I asked.

Her eyes narrowed in a frightening way. 'Bullets are not part of my instructions.'

'Forget it,' I said.

'You've started now.'

'All right. If a bullet comes out the other side of. . . .a person, does that indicate that the injuries are not as serious as if it had lodged itself in the body?'

'Not necessarily. Why?'

But that I wouldn't tell her.

It was ten o'clock when I got in. The TV was on in the living room. 'Marnie, can you do things on the internet?'

She sighed, quietly. 'I'm watching this.'

'When does it finish?'

She scraped her eyes from the screen and glanced at her watch. 'In about ten minutes.'

'I need your help for a case. To solve a crime.'

I was looking for a tea bag when she walked into the kitchen.

'It was only a video,' she said. 'What?'

'I need to check the headline of a newspaper.'

'Is this for Clark?' she sighed.

'Sort of. Why?' She shook her head.

We went up to her room and while she logged on, I told her the name of the paper and the headline. She found a search engine that guided her to newspaper stories for two weeks before – the day after Yolande and I had been to dinner at Sandra's, the day after we had slept together.

And there it was. The love rat story. On the front cover of the *People*.

'Thanks,' I said dully. 'Can you print that out?'

She was casual about her skill. 'Is there anything else you want me to look up?' she asked as we waited for copies.

'Not especially.'

'Do you want to see what Worldsworth dug up on Ladscore?'

'What's Ladscore?'

'It's where we went and demonstrated. I thought you'd be interested.'

'I am interested.'

'I've got loads of stuff on them, dumping waste into rivers and toxic fumes in the atmosphere. You can have it if you want.'

'Why would I want it?'

'I thought . . . Because of Clark and that photo?' She was looking at my face. 'I'm sorry, I saw it at your flat. That picture of Clark and the man from Ladscore.'

I ran upstairs and fumbled in the bottom of my bag. Back in her room Marnie was laughing triumphantly at pictures on her screen of the demonstration. 'I was standing right behind that girl. You can just see a bit of my foot.'

I gave her one of Sandra's pictures. She clicked through some pages of a website. Photos of members of the management board. She pointed at one, a smooth-faced, unsmiling man. 'That's him, isn't it?' She pointed at Sandra's photo, then read out his name from the screen. 'Roger Sumpter'.

Roger Sumpter, the man who'd chortled all the way through dinner at Sandra's, was standing in the row, with the young Clark lurking in the background.

'Do you know them all?' she asked.

I stared at the photo. One of the other men looked familiar but I couldn't put my finger on it.

'This is all a bit confidential,' I said. 'But have you got a phone number for Clark?'

I rang him. 'Clark, I need to talk to you,' I said. It sounded like he was at a party, but that could have just been his mobile.

'I'm busy,' he said. 'I don't want to talk to you.'

'I've been to Spats, looking for you,' I said.

'You've fucking what? Who did you talk to?'

'Who do you think? Dennis – who asked if I had some photos for him and who made me drink a Dubonnet.'

I heard that wheezing sound which was his laugh. 'Did you give them to him?'

'I'm not going to give Dennis photos of Yolande.'

'Not those, the other ones, from Effo's cupboard.'

'The old ones, of you?' I said slowly.

'And Wyatt, yeah.'

I looked through the bundle of photos. It was Wyatt. 'Clark,' I said, 'is this about you giving evidence?'

He was silent, then he said, 'I don't know if I can,' and the line went dead.

If Clark wasn't going to give evidence, then I was going to have to find another way.

THIRTY-SIX

Monday Morning

I had left the file containing the children's records at the Grange. I didn't have all the records, I didn't have Clark's records, just the ones of the people I was representing. I caught an early bus in to study them. They were photocopies. Someone had got bored and not bothered to see how legible the pages were. When there was a typewritten entry I fell on it eagerly, not because it said anything useful but because I could actually read it. I looked up Gregory's notes, turning to the pages with yellow Post-it stickers, reading the lines I had highlighted, searching for clues in the notes of 'punishment' and the 'requests for assistance'. There was nothing relevant there, so I went back to the beginning. 'Gregory Springer admitted June 1981.'

Twenty minutes later I found it. A note saying '23 August 1981, 6.30. Out of school to Birmingham with Mr W. Returned 10 pm.' I looked at the signature. It was very faint, and very scrawled, but it said Wyatt, I was sure of it. It wasn't much, but it was a start.

The jazz riff of my mobile warbled in my bag. It was Yolande. 'Did you get the photos?'

'Yes,' I said, 'I did.'

'I assume by that tone of voice that they've all come out.'

'Yes, it's all very clear.'

'And I want my husband's sweater back.'

'For God's sake, Yolande!' The jumper with its suspicious blood belonged to Frodsham. 'What are you up to?'

'I'm sorry,' she said, and the phone clicked on to the dialling tone.

I had scarcely anything to do this morning, very little cross-examination, which was frustrating. I didn't want to look at Frodsham and I wanted to be doing other things, like off-loading the photographs and sweater on to Yolande or perhaps more importantly, finding Clark.

At lunch time I tried ringing Clark, but there was a message saying the number was no longer in use. How do they do that? I bought a sandwich and made my way to the cathedral grounds. I wanted to find a bit of grass and sit down, but I couldn't. I needed to speak to someone. Someone who would be objective, and sphinx-like. I rang the Salthill Police Station and asked to speak to DC Blane. I was put straight through.

'This had better be quick,' he said shortly. 'And good.'

I looked at my watch. 'Can we meet in the next ten minutes?'

'This had better be extremely good,' he said. 'I'm just finishing my shift.'

'It's about Wyatt,' I said.

'Where are you? I'll meet you in five minutes.'

I walked round the cathedral twice. The sun was going behind a cloud. It looked like rain.

Blane was already there, sitting in the dim silence, in

a pew at the side. Someone was playing the organ and it echoed sadly round the church.

In an urgent whisper I told Blane about the note on Gregory Springer's record, and I showed him the old picture of Wyatt and Clark, mentioning that Clark had been at the home too.

He raised his eyebrows at the mention of Clark.

'Do you know him?' I asked.

'Oh yeah.' He looked back at the picture. 'But yes, that's Wyatt before he lost most of his hair, and Roger Sumpter.'

'How do you know him?'

'Big wheel at Ladscore. Lots of complaints about him, but nothing we could do anything with.'

Scratching through my memory of the difficult evening at Sandra's, I said, 'He was meant to be giving evidence at the inquiry, wasn't he?'

'Nasty business.'

'Was Mrs Springer his secretary?'

'I don't know,' he said. 'You should ask DCI McLaren.'

He looked back at the photo. 'Wyatt,' he said and shook his head.

I expressed my suspicions that Wyatt had been involved, possibly not abusing the children himself, but providing children to other people, possibly businessmen in and around the city.

'It's entirely possible,' he said, 'but where's your evidence? What you've got there is suspicion. There were all sorts of rumours going around at the time of the police inquiry, but we couldn't get anything to stick.'

'I know.' I'd had half a hope that he would be able

to transform it into a case that would stand up in court as it was.

'What if Clark gave evidence?'

'From what I know of Mr Clark, he wouldn't be likely to assist the police with anything.'

'Do you know Spats?' I said. 'That's where Clark's brother, Dennis, hangs out.'

'Dennis De Largo, yes, I know him.'

'I was there the other night.'

'You're brave.'

'I know. I wouldn't have gone if I'd known that Dubonnet was the drink of the house. Dennis was asking for these photos back.'

'Don't tell me. For his friend Mr Effingham.'

'Effo. Yes, probably. How come the police know all these people?'

'It's called intelligence,' he said, grimly. 'Apart from his dealings in high finance, as he sees it, we believe the way he really gets his power, such as it is, is by blackmailing all these people into doing what he wants. Of course no one will speak out. For example, Mr Sumpter there. This is a fairly inocuous photo you've got, but I bet that somewhere Effingham's got some that are a lot more explicit.'

And they're probably in a cupboard in the flat on Park Lane, I thought. 'But why?'

'Effingham owns most of the shares in Ladscore, and he doesn't want any unnecessary information being given to the inquiry. It's a race between Effo and Danny Richards really.'

There was a burst of loud music. 'I don't know what you mean.'

'I assume you know that all the men who abused

your Jimmy Clark at the home are being picked off, one by one, by Danny Richards, starting with the first two who died whenever it was in Spats. Effo was there and saw it, is what I've heard. He saw what happened. Don't look at me like that, yes we know it all, we just can't prove it.'

I wanted to say, 'I've got some proof. I've got a bullet that was in Effo's cupboard. It's here in my bag, next to some terrible photos.' But I didn't know what it was proof of. If I told Blane, would I be giving him evidence against Danny? I wanted to take legal advice.

'Spats might be operating without an entertainment licence,' I said wildly. 'And they might have under-age drinkers.' I told him about the schoolboys, giggling nervously round the table at the show.

'What night was this?' The grimness of his tone said he was thinking the same as me. The schoolboys might be there for another reason. 'I'll look into it,' he said grimly.

'Have you got anywhere with the statement Gregory Springer was going to send me?' I asked.

'I'm doing my best,' he said.

I toyed with the idea of showing him the picture of Yolande and the man, to see if he knew who it was, to see if he could work out the answer. I was desperate to show it to anyone, but he was still a police officer. And Kay would have killed me.

As if on cue my mobile rang. I could see it was Kay. I hurried out of the cathedral, gesturing goodbye to DC Blane. It was five to two. She simply said, 'Danny's going to change his plea this afternoon. I'd better have that photo, just in case.'

Oh God.

* * *

Adam was in the lobby, pouring himself a cup of tea. 'You know you've always wanted to do advocacy?' I said.

He raised his eyebrows.

'You wish to be released this afternoon?' The sneer in Curston's voice brought a hush in the room.

'Yes,' I continued more firmly than I felt. 'I had considered asking the tribunal to rise early in order that I might deal with a matter which has just arisen, but I did not wish to interfere with the smooth running of the timetable.' By the tight smile and the small shake of his head I knew that at least I had got that right.

'Mr Owen will be holding the brief in my absence, but I think, from what was said this morning and having regard to the witnesses due to be called this afternoon, it is clear that there will be no need for any cross-examination on behalf of my clients.'

I thought I heard Frodsham groan with pleasure, but there was nothing I could do.

'Well, then, since you are not asking for an adjournment, yes,' said Curston with a shrug. 'If your clients are in agreement, you may be released for the afternoon. We shall see you tomorrow then, Miss Richmond, when I understand Mr Wyatt is to give his evidence.' Adam shuffled his papers importantly, and I bowed and left the room.

THIRTY SEVEN

Monday Afternoon – Crown Court

Simon was on his feet as I crept into the back of the court. Everyone, except Simon, turned to look at me, the judge, the jury, the usher and Danny. Even the witness under cross-examination looked over at me. It was obviously a dull afternoon, evidence-wise. I almost expected Simon to turn round and ask for an adjournment so that everyone could really take in my outfit and offer advice on whether the jacket would last till the sales started.

The prosecution was still presenting its case. A police officer was in the witness box. He stood straight and confident, as if this trial was giving him great pleasure. He was talking about the inside of Danny's car and explaining why the lack of any blood or other signs of Terry Fleming was not inconsistent with the car having been used to remove the body. He'd obviously been giving evidence for some time. He kept saying to Simon, 'As I have already told the court, sir,' and turning to the judge and raising his eyebrows.

The closest I could get to Simon was two rows behind him. Apart from Simon, in his row was Roseanna and next to her, Ewan Phillips, the prosecutor, all fully robed. The row immediately in front of me was filled with solicitors' clerks bent over thick, untidy files, doodling and practising their handwriting, yawning in boredom, the work space strewn with pink and yellow flimsy sheets of paper and handwritten jottings. And Kay, taking a note of the evidence, in her fast, flowing handwriting.

I sat quietly for a moment to let everyone get over the excitement of my arrival and stop looking at me, and then I shuffled along a couple of places till I was right behind Kay, and tapped her left shoulder. She turned round and nodded haughtily, acknowledging my presence. I tilted my head towards the door. She raised her eyebrows then reluctantly mouthed at the young man next to her and he swivelled his body to one side. She moved along the row and, as Simon sat down and Roseanna rose to begin her cross-examination, the two of us moved quietly to the back of the court. As we turned to bow to the judge, his words made Kay put a hand on my arm to stop me leaving the courtroom.

'Excuse me, Miss Newson,' he said to Roseanna. 'Mr Phillips, am I right in thinking you wish to call one of your experts this afternoon?'

'Depending on when this officer finishes his evidence, today or tomorrow, Your Honour.' He sneered at Roseanna. 'My next witness is to be either Mr Effingham, or indeed my forensic expert.'

'And that is Rowland Quirk. Well, I want to say two things. First of all, I think I know the man. Why was this not raised before?'

Ewan Phillips looked nonplussed. No one said anything. Then he remembered. 'As Your Honour probably recalls, this question was raised at the Pleas and

Directions Hearing. It was established that it was a different Dr Quirk.'

The judge frowned slightly.

'A different Dr Quirk,' Ewan Phillips repeated firmly.

'Very well,' said the judge. 'Secondly, I have just received. . . .'

The court clerk stood up hurriedly and whispered to the judge. The jury sat forward with interest. In a long trial a whispered exchange between the judge and the court clerk can be the most interesting thing that happens all day.

'Yes,' said the judge, to the clerk. 'Of course. Members of the jury, I'm afraid I'm going to have to ask you to retire.'

Reluctantly the jury stood up and filed out. They knew they'd be missing something really interesting now.

'Mr Phillips, this concerns you in the first instance, since this is your witness.' He rummaged on his desk and unfolded a piece of paper. 'I have received a note of a telephone conversation, received at 2.05 this afternoon, which says that Dr Quirk is unable to attend court tomorrow. . . .' He looked up. 'Well he obviously thought he was giving evidence tomorrow.' He continued reading. '. . . as he has been taken ill. In Thessalonica apparently. His wife is at his bedside. He is not able to leave Greece due to his state of health. He will not be attending the trial at all.'

'I wonder if your Honour would give me ten minutes to take instructions,' said Ewan Phillips.

'Dr Quirk is your forensic expert, is he not?' the judge said. 'If I am not mistaken he is pivotal to your case. His absence puts this prosecution in some jeopardy does it not?'

'I will take instructions.'

'If you are going to ask me to abandon this trial as a result of your witness over-indulging on his holidays, I will be seriously considering the costs implications. I should say that I notice that I don't have a medical certificate.' Ewan Phillips may have been the judge's favourite, but if a trial had to be abandoned, someone had to pay.

Ewan Phillips said nothing.

'Very well. It is now 2.40. I will rise until 3 o'clock.'

Everyone stood up, the scattering of spectators folded their newspapers and wandered out of court, and Simon and Roseanna took off their wigs and did things to their hair. Ewan Phillips, whose wig was doubtless grafted to his head, did not touch his.

Ewan Phillips' most immediate problem was to find a member of the Crown Prosecution Service. He hurried past us towards the lifts.

Kay and I walked round the railings to stand outside Court 8.

'How did you get away?' Kay said.

I shook my head.

Simon and Roseanna came out of court. They were both grinning broadly. Simon walked over to Kay and me. 'Well, this is a turn up for the books. Frankie, what are you doing here?'

'I'm not sure now,' I said. 'I don't think you need me.'

'Is this about the famous photograph? Well, let's have a look.' I didn't want to show it to him. But I had said to Henry Curston that I was needed elsewhere, and Simon was looking at me expectantly. I flipped open my notebook and drew out one of the photos and the sheet of paper that Marnie had printed out, describing the date of the newspaper in the picture. Reluctantly, I handed him a picture of Yolande and the man doing wild sexual things in a hotel room in London.

He stared at the picture and I could see his expression change. 'When was this photo taken?' he said coldly.

'About two weeks ago. See, the printout proves it. Except I'm not sure exactly what it proves.' I could feel the temperature of the air around him go down by four or five degrees. Oh God, don't say he was having an affair with Yolande too. 'What?' I said. 'What does it show?'

'Did you take it?'

'No.'

'Thank God for that. Who did take it?'

'I don't know. Why?'

'This is a photo of Rowland Quirk. Frankie, does this have anything to do with why he isn't here today?'

I snatched it out of his hand. 'I have no idea. I was asked to get these photos developed. I had no idea why. No one else has seen them.'

'They probably didn't need to. And the other person in this photograph is. . . .'

'Yolande,' I said.

'Well, I'd better tell Danny about it. I don't think I'll show him the photo. I shall probably have to retire from this case, Frankie. There will have to be a retrial.'

'I'm so sorry,' I said. 'Would you rather I hadn't told you?'

Simon turned abruptly and went back into court. I couldn't bear to look at Kay, either she'd be furious, or she'd be feeling sorry for me. Probably just furious. But I was furious. After all I'd gone through to get the film, to take it to be developed, to pick up the pictures, to pay for them, for the sole purpose of Yolande playing some sordid blackmail scam. And I'd taken the afternoon off from the inquiry, which is almost unprofessional – goodness knew what they'd be doing to Adam while I was away – to bring the photo over as soon as possible, which, I realised now, had probably not been part of the plan. I followed Simon into court.

Danny and Catcher were being brought back in. I noticed a fading bruise around Catcher's eye.

Simon went over to them. He nodded at Danny who moved to the front of the dock. The two prison officers who flanked him registered only minor interest and remained sitting on their chairs. In a low voice Simon explained what had happened.

Danny nodded slightly towards me. 'Frankie,' he said, 'what a pleasure.'

The security guards were looking at me with mistrust, but I was wearing my black, so they weren't sure what to do. Simon turned and said in a resigned tone, 'Could you take a note of this please?'

'Yolande's a naughty girl,' Danny said. 'She shouldn't have done it. She could have got into a lot of trouble.'

'She still might.'

'Norman's too lazy to take it any further.'

Simon said 'I must have a cigarette before I tell him.'

'Can I have two seconds?' I asked.

He raised his eyebrows and went to the back of the court. 'Danny,' I said, 'I've got a bullet.'

'The one in the jumper? Well, thanks very much for telling me, doll. But it's nothing to do with me. The jumper's Frodsham's.'

'What about the bullet?'

'We'll never know, will we?'

Simon came back. 'Come on Frankie.'

'Ehh, Simon,' Danny said, 'can I have a word?'

I moved away as Danny leaned towards Simon and there was an urgent exchange of words. I could see Simon becoming more and more frustrated and his lips formed the words, 'You're a fool' as he turned to go back to his seat.

Simon went to the front of the court and asked the court clerk to put out a call for Ewan Phillips. Five minutes later everyone was in their place in court. The jury looked expectantly at Simon as he remained on his feet.

'Your Honour,' he said. 'I am instructed to ask . . .' He turned to look at Danny. Danny, his expression grim, nodded, '. . . that the charge on the indictment be put to my client again.'

There was a ripple along the front bench. The barristers knew what that meant. The judge knew too and sneered at Simon. The jurors leaned forward to learn. It meant that Danny was about to change his plea, and there was nothing anyone could do about it. The charge was put and Danny pleaded guilty to murdering Terry Fleming.

THIRTY-EIGHT

Monday – Late Afternoon

Simon and Kay were going to see Danny in the cells. The judge was reserving sentence till he had seen the reports. It would have to be life, but the judge would make a recommendation about how long he should serve. The trial against Ronald Catcher continued.

'Can I come with you?' I asked. 'As a kind of research assistant?'

Simon looked at Kay. 'No,' they said in unison.

It was raining. I went back to the Grange. I didn't know where else to go. The building was eerily quiet, but just as I reached the inquiry room the doors opened and my clients spilled out.

I went over to Adam. 'Did you miss me?'

'He did ever so well,' Shelly said.

My stomach dropped. Of course, I hadn't wanted him to do badly, but I didn't want the clients thinking that they didn't need me.

'Your face,' Shelly said. 'I'm only kidding. He didn't say a word all afternoon. Although, big boy like him, I'm sure he'd have been fine if he had.'

'The Safety Officer has just finished his evidence in chief,' Adam said, with a hint of pink in his cheeks. 'I didn't have a chance to ask a question, but I don't think we have anything to raise with him.'

Adam gave me his notes of the afternoon's evidence and then I went to collect my bag. A couple of the advocates were still in the room, chatting. 'You missed a fun afternoon,' one said. 'I think we all wished we'd come with you.'

He was so friendly, I wanted to say, 'I'm part of a blackmail heist, I need help.' I smiled and said, 'You were probably better off here,' then worried that I'd said too much.

The clients and Adam had all disappeared by the time I got to the bottom of the stairs. I pulled my mac tightly round me, and stood for a second looking out at the rain, which was now falling in dull, steady sheets. He'd just done it. Just pleaded guilty. After all that. After all Yolande's efforts. He faced years and years in prison. I shook my head.

From the gloom of a row of seats near the enquiries desk, someone started up and came towards me.

'Clark! Where've you been?'

'Same place as you.' I hadn't seen him. 'What do you reckon he'll get?'

'Well, it's going to be life. What the judge will recommend I've no idea. He might get some consideration for the fact that he didn't put forward a militant defence.'

'Danny was always going to plead guilty.'

'Why?'

'Don't ask me. Something to do with that bloody jumper. That bastard Effo's always got something.'

'But Yolande had the jumper. I had the jumper!'

'But Effo would have said he'd seen it, and then there would have been hell to pay.'

'What was it? On the sweater? Whose blood was it?'
He looked at me.

'How did Frodsham get blood on him?'

'He didn't. He wasn't wearing it.'

We both stared out of the doorway as the rain fell. 'So, what happened?'

'I don't know it all, I got this from Dennis.'

'What is it with you and Dennis?' I said. 'I thought you hated him.'

'He's my brother, ain't he?'

'OK. So what did he say?'

Clark looked round. 'Apparently, Danny had made an arrangement to see Fleming. He would have killed Catcher too, so Catcher says. Catcher and Fleming had had a falling out with Effo – something to do with not being paid for a job. He said they hadn't done it right. You don't want to know,' he said, answering the question on my face. 'So they're up for a bit of action with Danny, even though they know he's a mad bastard.

'Danny's plan was that they'd both come to the shop – Yolande and me weren't there – he'd timed it so that Fleming came first and he was going to get rid of him and then Catcher was meant to come an hour later, and he'd do him so it looked as if one had killed the other, all neat and tidy. "The police are not looking for any one else" sort of thing. Well, Catcher and Fleming came together but Catcher didn't go in, he hung around waiting. He was about to go in when Yolande turned up, and Danny says he thought it was Catcher so he called her in. He wouldn't have done that otherwise. She saw it all and she wouldn't go, and she helped Danny.

'And of course, Danny got picked up first, because he's one of the usual suspects. He likes it inside anyway.

I told Yolande there was no point taking those photos.'

'Did you take them?'

'Yeah, it was horrible. Bloody stupid thing to do, I was stuck in a wardrobe all day while he was enjoying himself. Stupid arse.' We stood in the doorway, gazing at the rain. 'Anyway he had to walk home. I nicked his travelcard. That's what I gave you. Except I gave you mine as well. I had to walk up to Euston.'

'Oh Clark.' I was sure Rowland Quirk hadn't walked anywhere. 'Why didn't you tell me?'

'You? Why? What's it to you?' Clark obviously had a clearer picture of the professional relationships than Yolande. He shook his head. 'Bastards. They're all bastards.' He was talking to himself as he had done that night in the pub with Marnie, moving his hands, thinking hard.

There was the sound of steps on the stairs. The panel members were leaving, turning towards the door to the car park. More steps, coming towards us. Clark looked over his shoulder. 'Evening, Mr Frodsham,' he murmured.

Frodsham looked at Clark and sneered. He threw a surprised glance at me, then, with a small smile on his face, he nodded, 'Clark.'

'Bastard,' Clark scowled, as Frodsham strolled out into the street, casually doing up his raincoat.

'He's a lawyer,' I said, liberally. 'He's only doing his job.'

'Yeah,' he sneered. 'And enjoying it. Where are you going now?' he asked me.

'Home,' I said.

'I'll drive you if you like,' he said gruffly.

'Clark,' I said, 'remember who you're talking to. I

know that you can't drive. And certainly not in the state you're in. Think of your reflexes.'

'Do you want to drive? I've got the car.'

'You mean Dennis's car?'

'Nah, nan, nah. It's a different one. It's legal.' He gave me a fleeting smile. 'Dennis was really pissed off about his car that night. He had a job getting it back. First Danny nicks it, then you.'

'Sorry?'

'Go on,' he said. 'Let me give you a lift home.'

We'd both had a hard day. I sighed, 'OK.'

It was the kind of car that people spend precious hours on, polishing it tenderly, fixing on stickers that say, 'My other car's a Porsche.' It was a blue Renault Five camionette, with the gear stick on the dashboard. It was so old it was almost a classic car. The tyres looked smooth and flat, as if they were the original ones.

We drove towards Selly Oak. Clark was silent. Half-way down the Bristol Road, I said, 'Did you really save Danny's life?'

'In a manner of speaking. Well, yeah, he caught on fire, didn't he? I just jumped on him and put him out.'

'Was that before or after the photo of you and Wyatt and Effo?'

'If you must know, it was about the same time.' I concentrated on the road. 'About the time, he, you know, done the first two.'

'That was a long time ago, Clark,' I said.

He made a noise in his throat, like a sob.

'Oh, Clark,' I said. I glanced at him. 'Are you all right?'

'Yeah,' he said thickly. Then he burst out, 'I love him, you know. What he's done for me.'

We were approaching the University, Clark said, 'I

need a drink.' His face was grey and there was a thin line of sweat on his upper lip.

Should I have stopped the car at that point, and said, 'Sorry Clark, that's not possible. Danny's pleaded guilty. There's nothing more for me to do. Drop me off here and I'll take a bus.' The man was in such distress. How was I to know what would happen? He hadn't even been walking strangely, like the day at Dot's with the tyre iron. He was upset, but then so was I. Nothing prepared me.

Which is why, as I turned onto Dawlish Road, I said, 'OK, let me just drop my bag off and we'll go and drown our sorrows.'

As we were pulling up outside Julie's house, Marnie turned into the street. When she caught sight of me getting out of the van she gave me a little wave and walked a little faster. 'Hello! Oh.' She had seen Clark. He wound down his window.

'We're just going for a drink,' I said to Marnie. 'Do you want to join us?' I thought she might lighten the atmosphere.

'Where are you going?' she said doubtfully. 'I've got quite a lot of homework tonight.'

'Just for a quick drink.'

She ducked down to look in the van. 'Where would I sit? It's really messy in there. I've got my school things on.'

'You could change. I'm going to.'

'No,' Clark said, urgently, although I didn't pick that up at the time.

'I'd better not. Bye Clark.'

We went inside together. 'I'm sorry,' she said. 'It's just . . . I'm more mature now. Clark and I don't really have anything in common.' She'd been to London. She'd got politics. It happens to us all.

Five minutes later, without a bag, wearing jeans and a grey shirt, I got back in the van.

'Where to?' I said. We drove back down Bristol Road.

We parked right outside again. 'Clark, it's still a double yellow line,' I said.

'That's London talk.'

'Yeah. And on Thursday, it was London action and we got a ticket.'

'I don't care,' he said.

'What about Dennis?' I said, but he had unbuckled his seat belt and got out of the van.

The seats were arranged like an ordinary pub, as if Sunday's show had never happened. The bar was in the same place. There were no schoolchildren. They were obviously still at school. The smell of stale beer and old cigarettes pervaded the room. The evening rush would begin in an hour or so and would drown out the smell with odours of perfume and aftershave.

I thought I recognised some of the women from the night before, the one in the maroon coat and the one with a large yellow daffodil pinned to her cardigan. The men looked the same too, slicked-back, brilliantined hair, red noses, thin sweaters. As I watched, one in deep discussion moved his large bulk slowly and gracefully forward, leaning across the glasses of beer on the table, to tap the ash into the ashtray.

We walked over to the bar, while I groped in my back pocket for my wallet. 'What do you want to drink?'

'Double Scotch,' Clark said.

I ordered two double Scotches. I felt Clark needed company in as many ways as possible. He had finished his drink before the barman brought my change. I ordered another double Scotch and pushed my glass towards Clark while I waited. He really was a man in need. His face was still grey, even under the peachy bar lights.

It took two mouthfuls for him to empty his glass this time. We needed to sit down. I looked around. There was an empty table in the middle of the room and I picked up my glass and shepherded Clark away from the bar.

At the seat in the window, the women were chatting, sipping from neat glasses filled with purple and maroon drinks.

Clark hadn't sat down. He shrugged and moved his neck.

'Come with me,' he said.

I looked at him with a sinking heart. 'Clark,' I said. 'It's too late. It's finished.'

'Please.' He was doing that twitching thing that my friend at Euston Station had done. The 'preparing for fight or flight or the next line of drugs' twitching. He looked dreadful. He'd lost Danny and Marnie had just dumped him. I picked up my glass and Clark led me towards the door Dennis had appeared through the night before.

We were in a chilly, white-painted lobby with three white-painted doors, one sporting the silhouette of a debonair man, one the image of a Doris Day lookalike with slender ankles and a full skirt, and the other bearing the word 'Private'.

Clark hesitated as if he might be having an identity crisis.

'I am not coming into the toilets with you,' I told him. 'If that helps.'

'Leave it out,' he said.

He pushed the door which said 'Private'.

'This is private,' I said.

'That's how they like it.' The door eased open.

Behind it was a narrow flight of stairs, covered in worn, thin grey carpeting that looked as if it had once been hairy, thin grey carpeting. The walls of the stairwell were drab green. As the door wheezed to a close behind us, we were in almost total darkness. There was a bare light bulb hanging at the top of the stairs which threw a dim gleam of light on to the top two steps. As we turned the corner and began climbing another flight of stairs I was trying to work out where we were in relation to the van. I'd completely lost my bearings. I took a mouthful of whisky.

'Are you sure you still need me?' I asked Clark, as we passed a closed door and began climbing another flight of stairs. After our traumatic day, this felt like the stairwell at Covent Garden tube. 197 steps, apparently. The deepest tube station in London. But we weren't going down into the ground, we were climbing ever upward. Perhaps it would be an oxygen issue.

'Get rid of that.' He pointed at my glass. I bristled, but threw the remains of the drink down my throat and put the glass neatly out of harm's way in a corner. We climbed on.

There were no more stairs. We walked along the bare wooden landing – the carpet had run out several flights below – and Clark turned the handle of a dirty lime-green door, that may have been Victorian but was now covered with ragged hardboard. He pushed the door open.

The light was dazzling. I blinked. There was a grimy window under the gable of the room which seemed to be some kind of office. A filing cabinet, two chairs and a messy table jostled for room. On the table stood an old Amstrad, a telephone, piles of papers and a large grimy book, which may have been an accounts book or it may have been a diary. Clark stepped into the room with difficulty, edging round the side of the table. I squeezed in after him, past the filing cabinet, easing round the door. But what, in fact, was taking up most of the room, behind the door, in a corner, was a bed.

Lying stretched out on the bed, with his hands behind his head, was a man, in smart grey trousers and a crisp blue shirt. He was sleeping. Or so it seemed.

Clark turned to face the man and grunted, 'Effo', and from somewhere – probably, I realised, his sleeve – pulled out a gun. My heart sank. My own knowledge of guns is very limited. I am only really familiar with the cowboy guns that come supplied with strips of caps. This one looked much more businesslike. It looked heavy and real. Something told me that, despite what I knew about Clark, this was not a cigarette lighter.

Effo lazily opened his eyes. Then widened them slightly, but he merely said, 'Well, Jimmy, good to see you.' His gaze flickered briefly on the gun. 'That's one of Dennis's, isn't it?'

First his car and now his gun. For goodness' sake.

'And how's that other so-called brother of yours?'

'Danny's just gone down for life for Terry Fleming's murder.'

Effo nodded. 'So I'm not needed to give evidence, then,' he said with satisfaction and made to get off the bed. There was a pause. 'I'll just finish my drink and I'll be getting off.'

'No,' Clark said.

'All right, Jimmy,' Effo sighed, sinking back onto the bed. 'What do you want? And who is this?'

Clark was silent.

'My name is Frances Richmond,' I said. 'I am a lawyer.'

He looked me up and down. 'And what does little Jimmy need you for? Parking on double yellow lines again? Naughty boy.'

I wanted to say that for some people, parking on yellow lines is quite a serious offence, with financial consequences, and I thought of the small, innocent van outside, at the mercy of any passing traffic warden. But I said nothing, and simply watched, with a degree of envy, as Effo lazily stretched over to the table, picked up a sticky-looking glass and swallowed a large mouthful of clear, tawny liquid, which gave all the signs of being Scotch. Clark and I followed its progress down his throat.

Clark looked down at the gun. It had a snub-nosed barrel and a silver-looking, chunky handle. It looked horribly realistic, like something from a movie, a movie where people in elegant evening dress and bow ties lazily shoot other people. Clark must have taken it from Dot's house. He was holding it as if he didn't know what to do with it, like a bellboy who's just been made into a bodyguard because there isn't anyone else around.

Effo settled himself more comfortably on the grey-looking pillow. An expensive-looking briefcase rested against one of the table legs. Looking at the papers on the table I guessed he had been sorting out some finances, not only for the pub, but also it seemed, for the garage. And Hombre. On the back of the door hung a jacket that matched the grey trousers. Very nice, very expensive, very Ted Lapidus. That suit hadn't come from Hombre.

'You bastard,' Clark said. The hand holding the gun was trembling. Any faint hope I had had that we were here on a mission of mercy, swinging in like the SAS to rescue a vital witness to prove even at this late stage that Danny had not killed Terry Fleming, faded and died. We – I corrected myself – he, Clark, was here to shoot someone.

But if he shot someone, what would he do with the body? Did he think the two of us would carry it downstairs? 'Effo's come over a little tired,' we'd say cheerily to the women in the window seat. 'We're just about to fold him into the back of the van to give him a run out along the canal for some fresh air.' It came to me, we weren't going to be carrying him out. Clark was planning on tipping him out of the window and straight into the canal. Presumably I was there as assistant tipper.

I was doing too much thinking and not enough talking. Someone had to take the initiative.

'Am I right in thinking that you and Mr Clark have a history?' I suggested.

'Miss Richmond, is that your name? When Mr Clark was a young man he, and indeed other members of his family, needed all the friends they could get, and I think it would be fair to say that I gave them a hand.'

'More than a fucking hand,' muttered Clark.

'Would you say,' I continued, speaking slowly, playing for time, but for what purpose I couldn't exactly say, 'that Mr Clark is justified in feeling that you did him quite a lot of damage?'

He took a mouthful of whisky. 'You might be confusing me with someone else. I am not Dennis or your Mr Wyatt,' he said. So he did know who I was. 'But then again,' he put the glass on the table, 'Mr Wyatt understood children, and what happened to Jimmy was nothing he couldn't handle, nothing he didn't need.'

This really was an unpleasant situation, an aging man in smart clothes, leaning against a grey pillow in a small room that was getting hotter and hotter, saying the terrible things that those men say, to load the guilt onto the ones they destroy.

Clark's face was white, he swayed against the table and put his hand down blindly, onto the keyboard.

'Don't do it, Jimmy,' Effo said softly, caressingly. 'There's no point.'

Clark began to shake, the keys on the keyboard jittered together, and he looked smaller, younger. He was back where he'd been, back in some room in the home, or in some sleazy hotel in Birmingham, where business guests were entertained by the young boys, alone with a man. I wanted to put my arm around him, to say it was over now, not to despair, but it wasn't.

There was silence in the room. And in the silence came the sound of steps, uneven, heavy treads, climbing up to the room.

'It's Hopalong Cassidy,' said Effo. I wondered whose side he was on.

Dennis's panstick make-up and the blue sparkling jacket looked incongruous in the grey fetid room. As did the walking stick. As I turned towards him he pushed me further into the room, till I was pressed between the table and chair. Dennis was standing six inches away from me. I could smell the rancid pomade on his hair.

'Clark and I are leaving now,' I said.

'Your brief wants you to leave,' Effo said. 'I expect she wants to see you in chambers for an important conference. Well, that's a little unfortunate.' He crossed his legs. 'Because she can go, but I'd like you to stay. We have things to talk about.'

Clark's arm jerked, the gun handle flashed in the sunlight.

'Clark,' I said, 'we're going now.'

'No,' Effo and Dennis chorused in unison, and Dennis pushed past me and grabbed the gun. There was a huge pounding explosion in the small room and a shower of thin glass from the light bulb settled on all of us. Dennis stood panting, holding the gun.

And then there was the distant sound of feet crashing up the stairs.

Effo leapt up and began to scrape the papers on the table into the briefcase. With the other hand, he pulled the jacket from the hanger on the back of the door, always the politician wanting to be well-dressed to meet his guests.

A faraway voice called, 'Nobody move, it's the police.'

Clark stood frozen by the table, like a medieval saint, the light from the window splaying round the top half of his body. Dennis pushed further into the room, wielding his stick, slashing at my legs so that I fell against Effo, who fell back onto the bed. I clutched at him, stumbling forward, and he pushed me down against the table and I slithered onto the floor. I scrabbled for the chair and began to pull myself up as Effo rose to his feet, then toppled against me so that the chair spun against Dennis's legs and he staggered back out onto the landing, and I went crashing to the ground, slithering under the table.

'Fire escape, you stupid bastard,' Effo called.

He threw himself at Clark who was still paralysed in front of the window. Then as I tried to pull myself up, Clark tripped back into the alcove, and Effo grasped his arms. Together they fell and there was a crash of breaking glass and splinters flew into the room. Then Clark reared up, elbowing Effo's arms out of the way, and threw his hands round Effo's neck. Blood was spurting from the two of them as Effo forced his greater weight over onto Clark, leaning through the window, as he scrabbled for Clark's hands at his throat. He was shaking, shaking both of them, working at Clark's hands, knocking Clark back and forth onto the broken glass.

Streams of blood ran across the floor as I dragged myself out from the table, and cautiously got to my feet. Dennis threw himself at Clark and Effo, wielding his stick like a bayonet. He stretched out his arm towards Effo, clutching Effo's shoulder as Effo and Clark rose from the window frame, and then his foot skidded on the mess of blood on the floor, and he, Effo and Clark fell towards the fire escape. There was a loud, high-pitched scream as legs and arms swirled out of the window.

THIRTY-NINE

Later Monday Evening

'And then the ambulances came and took them all away. Including both the bodies. The police didn't actually have to do anything.'

It was half past nine. Julie, Marnie and I were sitting in their dining room. Julie had laid on a comforting feast of pizza and baked potatoes, and a bottle of Montepulciano, which now contained less than half a glass.

'But how did the police come?' Marnie asked.

'They were staking the place out already. Apparently some schoolboys went in to the pub and they followed.'

'But if the police hadn't come those men wouldn't have tried to go out the window,' Marnie said, with her newly honed sense of fair play. 'If the police hadn't come, they'd probably still be alive.'

'But I might not be,' I said. 'There was a gun, remember.'

Clark had fallen through the window onto the fire escape, bleeding from his face and arms. Dennis had climbed halfway down the fire escape, but had missed his footing when his stick had slid between two rungs of the staircase and he had been flung down to the street below. And Effo had lain across the window frame, lifeless.

'Both the deaths were accidental,' I repeated. 'Dennis just fell on Effo at an angle that forced his neck onto the piece of glass that severed his jugular vein.'

I had trailed the ambulances to the hospital in Clark's Renault 5, the blood on my clothes staining the upholstery, and after Clark had been stitched up again, and the police had spoken to him again, Clark and I had had a serious talk.

'Where did the gun come from?' Marnie asked, licking mozarella off her fingers.

'It was Dennis's,' I said.

'Because I thought Clark had a gun with him when he was in the van outside.'

'Really?' I said. 'Oh, you know Clark, it was probably a banana in a bag.'

'But, anyway,' she said thoughtfully, 'Dennis was holding the gun when they found him, so his fingerprints would be on the handle.'

'Probably.'

'Perhaps I should be a forensic scientist,' Marnie said and yawned.

Julie nodded. 'Perhaps you should. But now you should go to bed.'

'Oh,' said Marnie. 'There was an urgent message from Gareth or someone. He said for you to ring him at home, Frankie. He sounded nice.'

'I don't know anyone called Gareth.'

'The number's there.'

It was Gavin's mobile. 'Thank God,' he said. I could hear someone playing cymbals in the background. He must be rehearsing. 'Look Frankie, I'm so sorry. It's your mail. Someone's been interfering with it. I've just found a load of stuff in Ellis Dangerfield's pigeon hole.' Ellis

Dangerfield was taking a year's sabbatical. 'I thought I'd better bring it with me and speak to you about it.'

'OK,' I said, thinking. Who? Marcus?

'There's a cheque for three grand.'

'Fantastic! Oh that's great, Gavin. Thanks.'

'And there's some other stuff, *Bar Mutual*, *Family Law Bar Association*, but there's something here that's marked "Strictly strictly private" and "Urgent."'

'Oh no,' I said. 'You'd better open it. But open it carefully, and remember it is strictly private.'

After a few seconds Gavin said, 'It's in another envelope that's also marked "strictly private", shall I keep going?'

'Yes.'

'There's things falling out,' he said. 'There's all sorts here. Cards, receipts, a photo.'

'Keep them safe,' I said, 'we'll come to those later.'

It was Gregory Springer's statement, dated eleven days before, the Thursday of the dinner dance. I wondered if he had posted it on his way out.

'Read it to me,' I said to Gavin.

'I'm just going into another room,' he said.

It was the story of one summer, when the usual boy had been ill, when on a regular basis Gregory had been taken into Birmingham to entertain friends of the home, engaging in sexual acts, humiliating and painful.

But no names. My disappointment was strong.

'Hang on, there's another page,' Gavin said.

'"It seems ironic,"' he read, '"that tonight we are to attend a dance at the invitation of my wife's boss now the managing director of the firm at which we work."'

'Names,' I whispered. 'Name names.'

'"A man who spent a large part of my youth terrorising me and forcing me to lose my childhood innocence. My wife is ashamed for me for what I had to experience, but she is determined that Roger Sumpter will pay for this, even if only by losing his source of income, and for that she is prepared to give evidence against him at the inquiry currently taking place in another part of Birmingham. She knows what the company has to hide, the regulations they have broken and the crude way they have silenced their critics.'"

'Go on!' I breathed.

'"But it is my burden and one that I must bear. I will speak out. I will speak out against Mr Wyatt for calling me out, for driving me to Birmingham on more than one occasion in that summer of 1981, I will speak out against Roger Sumpter, Terry Fleming, Ronald Catcher, Dennis Clark for what they did to me, as I have described above."'

I let out my breath. 'What are the receipts and cards?' I asked.

Gavin was silent, obviously digging into the envelope, then, 'There's a card here "Well done, Gregory, for step-ping into the breach, Mr W." "Thank you for your sweetness" with a puppy on it, "from Roger" and some receipts for games and things.'

'What's the date?'

'July and August, 1981.'

'Thanks Gavin. Stay on that number, I may need to call you again.' I had another call to make.

FORTY

Tuesday – Inquiry

We had a very short day the next day. I got to the Grange early, because I wanted to see everything unfold. When I arrived, the conference rooms, the lobby and the hall were empty, except for Mrs Gisborough, who was setting out the typed-up pages of evidence from the day before. The clients all turned up at ten o'clock. There was no question of a conference, they all wanted to get good seats to watch Wyatt give his evidence. Frodsham and Wyatt arrived together at ten fifteen and went immediately into their small conference room. The clients all sat patiently, except for Shelly and a couple of others who had put coats on their seats and come back out for a fag. Adam and I stood drinking coffee.

'What are you smiling about?' he asked.

'Just a little bit of rough justice,' I said.

Nothing happened until half past ten. I wondered if DC Blane had planned it that way for maximum humiliation. He could have done it the night before, after my phonecall. He could have arranged it discreetly. Contacted Frodsham. Gone to Wyatt's home. I'd given him all the phone numbers.

We were filing into the inquiry room as four police officers walked, large and navy, up the stairs.

'What have you been up to?' Leanne's husband called to Shelly. She rolled her eyes, doing a quick calculation. Car? Child? Husband? No. Past life? All dues paid. The tyres on Gregory's car? The blood drained from her face.

'It's all right,' I said.

The police officers walked into the inquiry room. Mrs Gisborough slid in behind them and threw herself at Catherine Delahaye in panic. Catherine Delahaye glided across the room, wearing a polite smile, and conferred briefly with DC Blane. Then she slipped wordlessly out of the room into the panel's chamber. We all took our seats quietly while the police officers stood near the door, their hands behind their backs.

The panel entered the room just as Wyatt and Frodsham walked in. The clients didn't know what was about to happen, so they reacted as every other day. They stood up and then sat down.

'Don't bother to take your seat, Mr Wyatt,' Curston said.

Wyatt turned as if to head for the witness chair.

'No,' Curston said, and looked across as DC Blane and another officer advanced towards Wyatt. Wyatt looked at Frodsham, who had taken his usual place behind the desk. Frodsham shook his head in amazement, and Wyatt turned towards the door to the panel's room.

The other two officers advanced. Frodsham rose to his feet. 'I wonder if this might be a convenient moment for you to rise, sir, and for me to take instructions from my . . .'

His words were lost in a round of applause from the clients, as DC Blane began intoning that he was arresting Wyatt for committing acts under the Sexual Offences Act 1956 between the years of 1979 and 1989, and reminding him that remaining silent might harm his defence.

Frodsham scooped his papers back into his barely unpacked briefcase and followed the group of officers leaving the building with Wyatt in their midst. 'If your inquiry's over,' Gavin said laconically, as I rang him from my phone booth in the basement, 'you'll be needing to remind your solicitors that you're back, and available, and I've got a nice bit of paperwork that you could get your teeth into that would just fit the bill.'

'Gavin, you sound like a secondhand car salesman.'

'Funny you should say that, my cousin's selling his Golf Convertible. I could just see you in that.'

'What colour is it?'

'Green.'

'Get back to your rehearsals, Gavin,' I said.

Curston had called all the remaining advocates into the panel's chamber and told us that he was minded to adjourn the inquiry to see what would happen with Wyatt, and then reconvene at a later date, since, if the allegations (which had been rapidly outlined to him by Miss Delahaye) were found proved, an extra dimension was added to the inquiry and witnesses already called might have to be recalled.

'You might want to cross-examine on other areas, Miss Richmond,' he said.

The thought filled me with horror. We were just getting to the end of it all. I couldn't bear the thought of starting again. He must have seen my face because he said, 'We will reconsider all matters in two weeks.'

As I walked back up from the phone the clients were hanging around the stairwell like expectant football fans. They began clapping as I reached the top.

'What?' I said. 'I thought you liked him. You never said anything.'

'Well, we just thought he was a lazy bastard, and there's no law against that, is there?' said Shelly. 'But now we know he was a lazy, conniving pimp of a bastard. Let's all go for a drink.'

Adam and I were swept away by the group – for a moment I thought they were going to raise us above their heads, which I wouldn't have liked – and out to a pub in the next street. It was almost a victory and I'd just got a cheque, so I bought a few bottles of champagne and we all felt very rakish and wild at half past eleven in the morning, celebrating.

'It's the best thing that could have happened,' Shelly said, as she poured herself some more champagne. 'Oh, these dropped out of your bag just now.'

She handed me a gas bill and a postcard I hadn't read. I'd obviously not been myself. It was a picure of Scotland, but bore a London postmark. It said, 'I've got some interesting gigs in London. Call me.' She'd sent it several days ago, so I'd probably missed her, but at least she'd written.

I rang DC Blane who told me they were currently questioning Wyatt. He was being garrulous, naming names – Dennis, Effo, Roger Sumpter.

'DCI McLaren will be writing to thank you, apparently,' DC Blane went on, 'although I wouldn't hold your breath. Mrs Springer was indeed Roger Sumpter's secretary. There was apparently some talk that she was about to air all the company's dirty laundry.'

'Did Effo know? I mean, was *that* why the brakes on the car went?'

'Unfortunately the two people most likely to know

the answer to that are now dead. Whether it was to stop Mrs Springer or Mr Springer we'll never know. It was probably just meant to scare them.'

'Thanks again for all the support you gave my clients,' I said. 'They're over the moon about Mr Wyatt.'

'Thank you,' Blane said, shortly.

'My pleasure,' I told him.

And then I rang Yolande. I tried all her numbers and no one answered. So I rang the shop. After the phone had rung for a very long time she answered. Her voice was thin and sad.

'Stupid fucking jumper,' was all she said.

'Can I come over?' I asked.

'I'm just going out,' she said.

'It'll take me two minutes to get to you. I want to say goodbye.'

The shop was closed. I banged on the door, there was no answer. I pressed the redial button on my mobile. I could hear the phone ringing inside. And then Yolande's voice – a low hello. She walked through the shop and let me in. She was wearing a large man's shirt over her jeans. I wondered who it belonged to.

We walked back into the kitchen. A saucer on the small unit held five or six cigarette butts and a smoking cigarette. 'Shall I make coffee?' I said.

'If you like.' I could feel her watching me as I went through the ritual. 'Why didn't you get the photos there before he did it?'

She was blaming me for Danny's plea of guilty! 'I did get there, as soon as I knew he was going to do it. He saw the photos before he changed his plea.'

'Then why did you show them to him? He didn't need to see them.' She began to cry.

'You didn't tell me what to do with them. I couldn't get hold of you. What . . . ? Why did he decide to plead guilty?'

'That bloody jumper.'

'What's happened to it now?' I said.

'I was wearing it.' She picked up her cigarette.

'When?'

'That night.' She inhaled deeply. 'The shop was shut. It was our half day. Clark was in Kettering, delivering a three piece, and I was meant to be going to the races with Reg. But I didn't feel well, and I wanted to see Danny – he'd only just got out of prison. I guessed he'd be at the shop, and he was. He called me in – he thought I was someone else. And there he was with Terry Fleming. Who by then was dead. Danny was in a state, there was blood everywhere. He needed to get him out of the shop. And I helped him wrap him up in some plastic off a roll of carpet.

'I was wearing the jumper. It got covered. And I found the bullet. I just picked it up. I thought the sensible thing would just be to throw it away in our bin. They collect the rubbish every night. No problem, nothing suspicious. So I took off the jumper and wrapped it up in a bag with the bullet and threw it in the bin. And that would have been all right, except that Catcher must have been hanging around outside and found it. He gave it to Effo. Sandra let something slip, so I knew where it was. It's all my fault.' She began to sob.

I put the coffee in front of her and put my arms round her. She smelt of vanilla and cigarette smoke.

She leaned against my jacket. 'Stupid bastard, he just

411

wanted to protect me,' she murmured. She shook her head, then sat up. 'OK, thanks for that. You'd better go now.'

She went into the toilet and I walked through the shop and out of the door.

I went back to Julie's, packed the car and drove back down to London. With each motorway service station that I passed my spirits lifted. By the time I had sailed past Scratchwood I was positively joyful. The inquiry was over, Wyatt would get something like his just deserts, Danny had pleaded guilty to something he'd done, Yolande – well, she'd have to work it out with Frodsham – and I was back in London. I could be an ordinary person again. And, ever mindful of my new-found status as someone who turns round her paperwork within forty-eight hours, I went straight into chambers.

It was about eight o'clock. I unlocked the front door. The Chubb lock wasn't on, and nor was the alarm. I made a mental note to speak to someone. Chambers had that empty, expectant feel as I walked into the clerks' room. Iotha was sitting in Gavin's chair, and Tony was perched uncomfortably on the edge of his desk. He looked up with a start as I walked in.

'Frankie!' he said. 'Well, that's a relief.'

I could see Iotha smiling and shaking her head.

'I just . . . Iotha has . . . There has been . . .'

'It was Marcus,' said Iotha.

'Oh no! Are you OK?'

'Perhaps I should leave you two . . .' Tony looked hopefully at Iotha. She nodded and he turned embarrassedly towards the door. He looked back at us. 'Whatever you decide to do,' he said to Iotha firmly, 'chambers will be one hundred per cent behind you. Goodnight.'

Half an hour before, unusually, Tony had walked into the library, looking for an authority to include in his first judgment. He had found Marcus pressing Iotha back against the photocopier, his hands all over her body, his mouth clamped to hers, and Iotha struggling to push him away.

'Marcus?' Tony asked in bewilderment.

'What?' Marcus looked up at him angrily. 'Want her for yourself, do you?'

'What an astonishing thing to say,' Tony said. 'For heaven's sake, Marcus. Have the decency to slink out in shame, please.'

Marcus had stood for a moment, breathing heavily.

'Iotha, shall I ring the police?' Tony asked.

Marcus had snatched up his bag and, staring straight ahead of him, pushed past Tony, out of the room. They had heard the crash of the heavy chambers door closing behind him. Tony had taken Iotha down to the clerks' room to talk and then I arrived.

'Did Tony call the police?' I asked her.

She shook her head. 'I'm still thinking about that.'

We went to Chez Gerard and had steak and red wine. And then I drove her home.

FORTY-ONE

Thursday – Tony's Do

The party was being held upstairs at an artisans' guild building in Queens Square, behind the hotel where I had first met Clark. You could tell it was a barristers' thing. There were bags up the stairs, large bags on every step of the narrow staircase. Solid barristers' bags, each one holding a story of misery, hope and destroyed rain forests. I pointed them out as I led Lena up the stairs. We climbed gingerly past. The low roar of conversation and the occasional burst of deep laughter spilled from the room above.

At one end of the room the band was setting up. Gavin was untangling wire at the base of a microphone stand. It was a good job it was a small band because the space was small. Tony was standing in the centre of a group of people who looked like judges, flushed and proud. I would go and say hello later. Kay was sitting at a table talking to Vanya and Deborah. She waved.

'Frankie!' Simon rose from a table, his face glowing pink and proud as he turned to indicate Roseanna. She was wearing a deep emerald green velvet dress, draped across one shoulder, which highlighted her porcelain complexion. She also wore an expression of unconditional love, which had to be ironic.

414

'Come and join us,' he said, pulling extra chairs across from another table. Roseanna stopped a waiter and handed us each a glass of white wine. I introduced Lena and then I leaned towards Simon and said, 'Why did he plead guilty?'

'He was worried that Yolande would still be implicated. I think he was anxious that if they investigated it further then Quirk would spill the beans about being blackmailed. He was trying to protect Yolande. Would you know anything about that?'

I took a gulp of wine. 'Not that you'd want to know about.'

'Well, it doesn't matter now,' Simon said.

'But why didn't he plead guilty straight away?'

'This is just a guess on my part, but I think he was using us. Partly he was trying to please Yolande, because she wanted him to fight it, but I think it began to dawn on him that if he pleaded right at the start, they would have let Catcher off. There wasn't enough evidence against him, and Danny would never have actually given evidence for the prosecution. But Catcher behaved so badly during the trial, raising issues in cross-examination, that there's now enough dirt against him that the matter can still go to the jury. The jury goes out next week.' He looked at Roseanna, who was discussing the material in her dress with Lena. 'Roseanna thinks he'll go down, because somehow now Danny is a hero with the jury for taking the rap. Why do they hate each other so much?'

'Long story,' I said. 'Any news about Marcus?' I looked round the room, as if he might appear at any moment.

'He's resigned from chambers,' Simon said. 'He's apparently going to set up on his own. The Management

Committee met yesterday and we decided, in consultation with Iotha, to report him to the Bar Council. She doesn't want to go to the police.'

'Well, look who's here.' Lena was shaking her head in disbelief.

There was movement over by the band stand, Gavin and Malik played a few uncertain notes on their guitars and then the unmistakable beat of 'Stand By Me' filled the room. A woman in a sparkling red dress was tapping the microphone and then she started to sing in the soft, husky voice I knew so well. And when Margo called I had to answer.

Newcastle
City Council

Newcastle Libraries and Information Service
☎ 0191 277 4100

Due for return	Due for return	Due for return

Please return this item to any of Newcastle's Libraries by the last date shown above. If not requested by another customer the loan can be renewed, you can do this by phone, post or in person.
Charges may be made for late returns.

—practically all cases of glandular fever have arisen in hospitals. The reason is not far to seek when one realizes that patients have a lowered vitality when accepted and are subject to drug therapy.

Modern Nature Cure is concerned with the application of age-old laws interpreted in the light of knowledge and experience. Nature Cure follows the cold logic of cause and effect and its success is entirely due to its working in harmony with Nature.

Since health is largely based on correct feeding, Nature Cure stresses that mankind must resolve one of its most pressing problems. We do not accept that chemicalized agriculture and factory farming is an economic necessity. Those who do accept that it is essential must also accept a lower standard of health and a moral responsibility for the degradation of land and animals.

To sum up, the naturopath, instead of using drugs to suppress disease, resorts to the principles in harmony with Nature, and these are :

Fasting. Hydrotherapy. Relaxation techniques.
Dieting. Herbal therapy.
Exercises. Manipulation (covering Osteopathy,
Chiropractic and Neuro-muscular techniques)

Chapter II

NATURAL LAWS

THE observance of natural laws does not imply a reversal to primitive type : it means the adoption of what is recognized as the fundamental laws of Nature in relation to modern standards.

Commercialism, though it may play a vital part in civilization, has rendered the world a catastrophic dis-service by its interference with Man's food. From the growth of milling and refining has come disaster. Modern technique in food processing has resulted in a depletion of the "natural" value of food. Milk is pasteurized (a poor substitute for clean, healthy cows), so that it is served—presumably clean—to the customer. Pasteurization, however, owing to the heat required in the process, destroys the vitamin C and precipitates the vital calcium phosphate mineral salt which is left in the containers and not in the milk. Balkans, Sikhs and Arabs drink sour milk and this, together with eating whole wheat, helps them to remain virile. The diet of the Sikh is a "whole" diet, in that it is grown and consumed without any artificialities such as chemical manures, refining, pasteurizing or concentrating.

Modern milling of flour demands that the germ of the wheat and the wheat-grain covering (bran) be removed from the flour, in order to save the mills and permit the flour to be kept without going sour. The germ and the bran contain the vitamins and mineral salts essential to health, but Commercialism and the inability of Britain to feed its population, decrees that we shall lose the very parts of wheat upon which we depend for health.

By the refining of sugar-cane we suffer the same losses in natural food value. Sugar found in a dilute form in fruit and honey is natural. Refined sugar, however, is a concentrated form of carbohydrate and can easily be taken in excess. Dr. Chalmers Watson says : "There is a widely prevailing opinion in the medical profession that the modern excessive use of highly refined artificial sugar is definitely detrimental to the health of the community, lowering the resistance to disease, predisposing to catarrh, dental disease and other disorders, especially in early years."

When we include tea, coffee, pickles, sauces and other artificial appetizing ingredients in the national diet, it is easy to comprehend how the natural laws of feeding are ignored. The orthodox diet of concentrated and highly refined food is one of the major items in the causation of disease.

The average family meal contains acid-forming meat, boiled-out vegetables, tea or coffee and more bread, cakes and jam. The protective foods like fruit, raw vegetables and unpasteurized milk are taken only in quantities insufficient to balance the "energising" elements in the diet and, incidentally, insufficient to provide a clean system and protection against disease.

The natural laws of feeding, therefore, are the first laws we transgress, not only as to quality, but also as to quantity. The great majority of people consume excessive meals and suffer from indigestion, lethargy, constipation and a host of other ailments as a result.

We previously referred to acute diseases as beneficial attempts by Nature to cleanse the system of impurities. In Naturopathy we encourage the inherent healing force by fasting and other methods in harmony with Nature. Orthodox civilization, however, maintains that these symptoms must be suppressed. One of the great faults of civilization is that it demands quick results and a minimum of discomfort. This has been, in part, encouraged by Commercialism, for the manufacture of patent remedies and drugs forms a lucrative business. It is an utter fallacy to assume that the treatment of symptoms by suppressive drugs will cure disease. Symptoms are certainly masked for a transient period but the ultimate result is a more highly poisoned condition and, eventually, chronic disease. The futility of patent medicines and drugs is borne out by the ever-increasing consumption of these articles.

All drugs are injurious to the system and their action is entirely one of suppression—leaving a false notion that the trouble has been cleared up. Addiction to the germ theory of disease, ready recourse to drugs and non-recognition of the healing force of Nature—plus the activities of patent-medicine manufacturers—provide the means whereby one of the basic laws of Nature is negated.

The fact is, that with intake exceeding output, the balance in the system is deranged. Elimination fails to keep pace with ingestion and an accumulation of toxins is permitted to burden the body. As a result of eating masses of starch, constipation is rife and this adds to the trouble. Lack of exercise fails to burn up the unnecessary food consumed and we are left a prey to illness. In such a state as this headaches, nerve disorders, rheumatism, high blood-pressure, indigestion, colds, catarrh and feeble circulation become common ills. When we suppress these with drugs we do our utmost to complete a vicious circle.

Ignoring the natural physiological demands of two of the eliminatory organs of the body (bowels, kidneys, lungs and skin are the organs by which normal elimination takes place) lowers our efficiency and creates the very illnesses we seek to avoid.

We have all experienced the lack of appetite that overtakes us when we are attacked by illness. Lack of appetite is a protective instinct dictated by the natural laws that govern life. It means that the efforts of the body are concerned with healing and that food is not desired, so that the main efforts may be concentrated upon ridding the system of undesirable impurities, and not engaged upon the digestion of unwanted food. In this way Nature seeks to conserve energy.

Over and over again we violate the laws of Nature without ever realizing that each transgression takes its toll of health. Such is the resilience of the human body, however, that it will withstand countless inflictions upon its functioning and still strive for health.

Chapter III

GENERAL NOTES

IN the following chapters we propose to discuss diet, fasting and hydrotherapy. The above subjects are of the most practical value to the person who wishes to gain health and to practise Naturopathy in his own immediate surroundings. Osteopathy, herbalism and other branches of Nature Cure are, of necessity, the work of the expert and can hardly be translated into practical application for home use.

The essence of Nature Cure is simplicity. Once the fundamental principles of Naturopathy have been grasped golden opportunities for health lie ahead.

It will be discovered that naturopaths differ greatly in the emphasis placed upon various therapies. No one need be confused by this differentiation. There is always a personal, psychological or economic reason for the apparent emphasis of one therapy. In all cases, however, there is the same insistence upon all the branches of Naturopathy.

One of the sharp differences between Nature Cure and allopathy is the fact that Nature Cure teaches people how to live. Nature Cure, as previously stated, is a philosophy and not a mere negative approach to disease.

Nature Cure is fundamentally simple. It is its very simplicity that deludes people. In these times we are so accustomed to scientific ideas that we overlook the fact that Nature itself is a science. The fact that it is a simple science governing the laws of life is ignored. We, who try to oust Nature, have to pay for our folly.

Once the principles of Nature Cure have been driven home, there is no need to hesitate in translating principles and theory into practical application. The reader is encouraged to test the Nature Cure theory for himself. In this he is warned to make haste slowly. If he gradually applies naturopathic methods he will find improvement in his condition. This improvement will beget confidence and appreciation of the logic of Nature Cure, thus paving the way for a complete conversion to Naturopathy and full, abounding health.

There is a general impression that Nature Cure is expensive. Nothing could be further from the truth. The simple home remedies that can be applied for next to no cost are numerous. The food-reform diet that goes with Nature Cure need not be any more costly than the orthodox diet. There is an increase in earning capacity and no expenditure on patent medicines.

But the monetary gain is nothing compared to the immense saving in health and happiness.

Apart from accidental injury, no adherent to Nature Cure need be forced into the position where an early retirement from business is necessitated on account of low health. There is every reason to assume that the adoption of naturopathic methods will add years to the physical and mental efficiency of the convert.

The really unfortunate part of the cost of Nature Cure is not in its actual cost, but in the fact that the person who takes up Nature Cure to save his health is handicapped by the nation in that he gets no redress if he has to consult a naturopath professionally. That the country has not seen fit to include Nature Cure in its National Health Scheme is, perhaps, unfortunate. While I (personally) doubt whether naturopaths wish to be included in the Government Health Scheme, that is not to say that the patient who has to subsidize the Health Scheme should not have the right either to "contract out" or to obtain equivalent benefit. There should, of course, in all fairness to the believer in Nature Cure, be some means by which he can claim financial benefit should he fall sick and not feel justified in calling in an orthodox practitioner.

At the same time, for the practitioner, it must be stated that the reasons for staying outside any Health Scheme are very concrete. These are, in the main, to keep free from the shackles that bureaucracy always tends to impose and to maintain a personal relationship that can hardly exist under any official system.

It would be a serious mistake to assume that, since the naturopath has no official connection with the State (at least at the moment), Nature Cure practitioners wish to avoid responsibility. The reverse is actually the case. No naturopath, for instance, is empowered to write out a death certificate. Any negligence on the part of a naturopath leading to the death of a patient involves severe castigation from the authorities. Serious treatment (fasting, for instance) is sometimes called negligence for want of better understanding.

Chapter IV

DIET

COMMERCIALISM AND FOOD

THE industrial Age and the growth of Commercialism may have provided manifold benefits, but, paradoxically, they have been the cause of intense misery throughout the civilized world, particularly the Western civilization. One of the major instances of the decline was the introduction of the steel rolling mill for the production of flour—white flour.

What were the immediate causes of the introduction of white flour which, at one time, was only a luxury for the upper classes? The answer lies in Industrialization, the growth of population and the decline of agriculture. To meet a growing demand wheat had to be imported and flour kept for a long time. The old milling processes did not permit flour to be maintained in a good condition over any lengthy period. This obstacle was overcome by the steel roller mill, apart from the fact that it was more economical. For efficient functioning, however, the wheat germ and the bran (the outer skin of the wheat) had to be removed—hence white flour. Unfortunately it is the germ and the bran that contain the vital parts of the wheat. These are the Vitamin B and the mineral salts. The bran, too, provides the roughage essential for peristaltic action and natural defaecation. If bread did not play such an important part in the national diet, the consequences would not be so serious. For millions of people, however, it is the "filler" food.

It is, therefore, the height of folly to take the vitamins out of flour and so deprive the masses of an essential ingredient of the natural food. The public pays for its bread minus the bran and then pays again to have the bran packeted and sold as a remedy for constipation—the constipation having been caused, to a large extent, by eating the denatured bread. Vitamins have to be manufactured and sold to make up for what is taken out of the wheat.

The only "whole" bread is the compost-grown, stone-ground wholewheat. Even the commercial brown bread is darkened and has bran added to it.

Alum, used in flour, baking powder, cheap ciders and wines, is, according to a Dutch scientist who spent years investigating the cancer problem, one of the contributory causes of this scourge.

The chemists and food merchants could not even keep their hands off the humble kipper. Artificial dyeing of kippers was at one time a menace to public health. But the rich hue imparted to kippers by chemical processes was a strong inducement to the unwary housewife.

There are very few articles of diet that the tentacles of Commercialism do not touch. Practically every time this occurs there is chemical adulteration by colouring, spicing, preserving or, in one way or another, an endeavour to stimulate the jaded appetite of the consumer by artificial flavouring.

With the vitamins and mineral salts removed from the food on the one hand, every effort of salesmanship is made to draw money out of the people's pocket for the purchase of some vitamin capsule or vitamin food. Though apparently trivial, there is, on second thoughts, solid foundation for believing that this trick of having to pay twice for food does materially contribute to the extra cost of living. Some may argue that it creates employment. But is denuding the nation's food of natural health-giving ingredients (at the same time adding harmful chemicals) productive employment?

To be fully aware of the effects of Commercialism on food readers are advised to consult such books as Franklin Bicknell's *Chemicals in Food*, Doris Grant's *Housewives Beware* and Rachel Carson's vivid and portentous *Silent Spring*.

Take a look in a grocery shop some time and note the prepared foods that are for sale. Remember that almost each one is adulterated in some way or another. There are, of course, reputable manufacturers who specialize in preparing food in either a natural state or in a condition that calls for a minimum use of preservatives.

It is unfortunate that the Food and Drug Laws of this country are inadequate. Of late years these laws have been made more sweeping but it behoves every housewife to study diligently the labels on packet food, tinned goods and any form of preserved food.

An investigation by the Infant Welfare Centre of Chicago between 1924-29 produced the following results.

20,061 infants attended the Centre during the period. Of the total number 48.5 per cent. were entirely breast-fed, 43 per cent. partially breast-fed and 8.5 per cent. entirely fed on artificial foods. The mortality figures for the entire group were as follows :

		No. of Infants	Deaths Total	Percentage of Deaths
Entirely breast-fed	...	9,749	15	0.15
Partially breast-fed	...	8,605	59	0.7
Artificially fed	... ...	1,707	144	8.4

Study of the above figures reveals the appalling danger of artificial infant foods. Contrast this with the beautiful babies we see on pictorial advertisements for baby foods. Not so much by direct encouragement as by indirect implication do commercial interests pander and foster the artificial bottle-feeding of infants. When the child puts on an abnormal amount of weight, the mother—in her ignorance—attributes special powers to artificial feeding. There is no doubt, of course, that many mothers are only too pleased to find other methods than the breast for feeding infants.

The luckless baby who is bottle-fed suffers much more from colds, stuffiness, indigestion and tonsilitis. It is also dosed with useless medicines, hence it has a bad start in life.

Sir Paul Dukes, a former British Intelligence Chief in

Russia, investigated longevity in 1938. Of 150 people over 100 years of age in Britain he visited 110. The majority of the centenarians came from lower-income groups whose diet, in the major part of their young years, has been *coarse, whole-meal bread, vegetables and dairy produce.*

Sir Paul Dukes, speaking of the centenarians he met, said : "The illnesses that overcame them in the course of their lives coincided for the most part—significantly or not I will not venture to say—with the cheapening of luxuries. Certain it is that dentistry has especially flourished since sugar and sweets became plentiful and cheap."

That beri-beri is a deficiency disease created by polished rice is already well known. What is not generally realized is that we have our own deficiency diseases—not so spectacular to be sure—but none the less having their own deadly effects. Owing to the slightly observed changes we do not attribute our deficiency diseases to the unnatural diet of the times. Yet these deficiencies, due to the tampering with food, produce a decreased resistance to disease and manifest themselves in the hundred and one common ailments to which we succumb.

The activities of Commercialism, whether with good intent or not, actually begin with the growing of food. The experiments of Sir Albert Howard, Sir Robert McCarrison, Lady Eve Balfour and others go a long way towards emphasizing the detrimental effects of artificial fertilizers and the unremitting exploitation of the soil. American authorities are already perturbed about certain features of modern agriculture. They have demonstrated too that American citrus products have a decreased Vitamin C content because the soil is exploited by artificial fertilizers and intensive cultivation.

What once were thriving granaries in North Africa, Persia, Mesopotamia, etc., are now deserts. This transformation took place because the soil was exploited, the essential humus used up and no efforts made to replace it. The humus holds the soil in place. When it became too scanty to perform this function, the winds blew away the top soil, and what we now know as erosion caused the deserts with which we are so familiar. This process, of course, is insidious. None the less, the same thing is happening in America, Australia, New Zealand, Africa and even in our own beet-growing areas.

Humus, briefly, is a "product of the decomposition of animal and vegetable residues brought about by the agency of micro-organism." It is the humus that holds the soil together and imparts a vital force to the land. A German chemist named Liebig discovered in 1840 that chemistry could, theoretically, be applied to agriculture. What the chemists have overlooked is that the soil is organic and teeming with life. Inorganic chemicals stimulate the soil, produce an abundance of crops (for a period) and produce an impression of scientific benevolence.

From *The Living Soil,* a book written by Lady Eve Balfour (Faber & Faber, London), we take the following :

> The consequence of this process of denuding the soil of its fertility is only just beginning to be realized in Western countries. McCarrison has stated : "These (certain natural foodstuffs), when properly combined in the diet, supply all the food essentials, known and unknown, discovered and undiscovered, needed for normal nutrition, provided they are produced on soil which is not impoverished, for if they be proceeds of impoverished soil, their quality will be poor and the health of those who eat them, man and his domestic animals, will suffer accordingly."
>
> Thus it will be seen that we cannot safely separate human health from the health of farm produce whether animal or vegetable. All have their origin in a fertile soil. Under field conditions a fertile soil is a live soil, and maintenance of life in such soil depends on humus.

Natural humus formation is a slow process. It is a continuity between life, decay and life as typified in a virgin forest.

Since it is imperative that humus should be applied to the soil (or maintained in it) to give it life, there must be an answer to soil fertility, soil erosion and poor-quality crops. The answer does exist, for which we are largely indebted to

Sir Albert Howard and his famous Indore Process of Composting. The making of compost heaps for the production of humus is not a difficult problem. In these heaps all residual waste from vegetables, crops, weeds, leaves, animal manure, etc., are permitted to go through a natural process of decay by bacterial action.

For a full description of composting and its advantages, the reader is referred to the works of Sir Albert Howard or to Lady Eve Balfour's book *The Living Soil*. In these and other contemporary books the reader will find a whole fund of useful information and helpful advice, all of which has a direct bearing on health.

From the Nature Cure point of view, food—the right food—is of paramount importance to health. The Nature Cure practitioner is also a dietician, and his knowledge is imparted to the thousands of patients and believers in the philosophy of Nature Cure. It is obvious, therefore, that Naturopathy is as much interested in the way food is produced (and in soil fertility) as it is in the food itself. The advantages of a correct diet are limited if the food is grown on artificial lines. Food produce must contain all the essential vitamins and mineral salts if it is to be used to advantage.

Not until one really gets down to basic facts does one discover the full deleterious impact of Commercialism upon our food resources. The ramifications of big business extend over the whole process of food cultivation and preparation. This exploitation of the soil and its produce is a vital factor in disease.

To say that Nature Cure has found an answer is an over-simplification of our whole health problem, especially where food is concerned. Nature Cure, however, points to a richer and fuller life. One of the main bugbears is the artificial processes through which our food is denuded of its natural qualities. If Commercialism could only be prevailed upon to forgo 50 per cent. of its emasculation of total food resources, then we could expect a most profound improvement in human health.

Geography and Diet

By studying the effects of food habits in other parts of the world we are led to the obvious conclusion that, to derive the utmost benefit from what we eat, the food must be essentially "whole". By that we mean that the food should be produced, prepared and consumed in relation to its natural state. This does not imply that we should consume all our food raw; though there is ample evidence to prove that raw food, particularly fruit and vegetables, should hold a high place in a commonsense diet.

Some arguments are put forward that for a food to be natural it should form an integral part of the native produce. In this event, an orange would be natural for California, but an unnatural fruit for Britain. Where favourable climatic and agricultural conditions coincide with industrial and agricultural usages, as in certain native districts, there is every reason to support this theory.

Britain, however, is a highly industrialized nation with a limited variety of food production. What is more, it has, along with other (so-called) civilized communities, suffered dire effects from the commercialization of food. While there is every indication that we could increase our native agriculture, and at the same time add to the diversity of indigenous crops, there is no sound reason why we should forgo the many advantages of imported fruits and vegetables.

Imported fruit, in particular, serves as a pleasant variety and as a most convenient source of augmenting our stock of protective foods. There should, however, be some form of inspectorate to ensure that these imported foods conform to specified standards of vitamin content. If necessary, there should be financial inducement to produce food of the highest quality from natural cultivation methods. Anything below the minimum standard should be refused an import licence.

From the foregoing it will be deduced that I do not subscribe to the "natural" food theory in so far as it restricts the diet to indigenous food products. That we should make more use of the land is obvious, but there is no valid reason for restricting our diet to what we alone are able to grow. There is, however, much to be said for a simpler diet with less variety at any one meal. Those getting on in years and those who suffer from digestive troubles will find it more suitable to have less variety at any given meal.

An example of the "native" theory which is entirely successful is displayed by the Hunzas, Sikhs, Pathans and other Himalayan tribes. These healthy specimens (they grow to six feet of healthy and cheery manhood) exist on a diet largely composed of sour curds, plenty of leafy vegetables, potatoes, wholewheat bread and little meat. These sections of India's population stand out in marked contrast to the Madrasis. The latter are very susceptible to gastric and internal ulcers, are of smaller stature and are as prone to disease as the Sikhs and Pathans are immune. The diet of the Madrasis consists of polished rice, red pepper, tamarind and dried fish. There is, of course, a difference in the climate, but the main essential difference is the wholeness of the Sikh and Pathan diet compared with the adulteration of the diet of the Madrasi. In this case, too, there is the natural cultivation that is a part of the life of the hill tribes.

Tibetans live to an incredible old age and, here again, sour milk figures in the dietary. If we include the Balkan countries, Arabs, Himalayan tribes and others we will find ample substantiation for the fact that the correct use of milk appears to be to permit it to go sour—not the civilized way of pasteurizing the milk and robbing it of its natural contents.

An astounding experiment on a mass scale has been the subject of frequent comment. This took place in March, 1917, when Denmark began to feel the effects of the blockade. Professor Mikkel Hindhede was appointed Food Adviser to the Danish Government. Denmark, at that time, had a human population of 3,500,000 and a domestic population of 5,000,000. Grains for both human and animal consumption were imported from the United States—until the blockade stopped the import of grains when America declared war.

The question facing Professor Hindhede was how the grain stocks should be distributed. He decided that four-fifths of the pigs and one-sixth of the cattle should be slaughtered, and the grain saved given to the people. The Danes were compelled to eat, coarse, wholemeal bread, vegetables, fruit, milk and butter. Only very little meat was available to the Danish public.

The Danes, therefore, were forced to live on a natural diet with the emphasis on "wholeness". The food regulations bringing about this forced existence on a natural diet lasted from March 1917 to October 1918.

Extraordinary things happened in that time. The Danish death rate, which had been 12.3 per 1,000 in 1913, dropped to 10.4 per 1,000, the lowest mortality figure that had ever been recorded in any European country. Hindhede wrote: ". . . I have emphasised the advantages of a lacto-vegetarian diet. I am not in principle a vegetarian, but I believe I have shown that a diet containing a large amount of meat and eggs is dangerous to the health." Professor Hindhede himself lays much importance on the bread consumed at the time. It consisted of 67 per cent. rye, 21 per cent. oats and 12 per cent. bran.

The impressive improvement in health, brought about in so short a time, points to a damning indictment of the commercialization of food and faulty dietetic habits.

Geography, and the diet of many races, provide numerous pointers for the selection of a sound diet. While we welcome the information from various sources of the world as proving the value of a sound, natural dietary, we should not forgo the advantages that modern dietetics have provided. The evidence from abroad, however, points to simple meals and less variety at any one meal.

Balanced Diet

The reader will already have some idea of what constitutes a balanced diet. It must be emphasized that there is no suggestion of faddism in a balanced diet. A sound dietary takes some account of the humanitarian principles involved in vegetarianism, but it is not based solely upon those principles;

its foundation lies in logic. There is no doubt that some vegetarians, in their enthusiasm, go to extremes, and have a diet that contains an excess of starch and is not conducive to health.

Diet reform, therefore, though it is not insensitive to the humanitarian element, does not base its reasoning on those lines. The real factors concerned in diet are the proper balance of food, food production, preparation and consumption in accordance with natural requirements. Proteins, starches, sugars, vitamins, mineral salts and roughage have to be considered in relation to human needs so that health can result. Apart from any broad lines that can be laid down as necessary, there is always the personal element to be taken into account. A sedentary worker obviously does not require so much starch food as the heavy, manual worker.

Two important factors influence the selection of various foods. There are the relative acid and alkaline action of the various foods. Before we delve into this problem we shall recall some factors in nutrition.

In Furneaux and Smart's *Human Physiology* (Longmans, Green & Co. Ltd., London) there is an excellent description of the need for food :

> Food is anything taken into the body for the purpose of growth, repair, the production of heat and work, or the supply of body regulators (hormones, vitamins and enzymes). This food has, however, to be first rendered suitable for absorption, *i.e.* it has to be digested. After absorption it is oxidized for the production of heat and work, or stored or used for repair and growth, as the case may be.

Food, therefore, serves the primary object of maintaining bodily functions, and is not, as some people appear to imagine, merely a way of satisfying a sensual pleasure. That food should be appetizing is not denied, for enjoyment leads to good digestion, but the main purpose of food is the continuance of life.

Food is divided into protein, carbohydrates, fat, vitamins, mineral salts and water.

Protein is found principally in meat, fish, eggs, cheese,

nuts, milk and certain vegetables. It is required for nitrogen replacement. Urea and uric acid are the forms in which nitrogen is excreted from the body as a result of wear and tear on the cells. The fact that proteins build and replace the tissues of the body, as well as supplying nitrogen, led people to overemphasize their importance in bodily welfare. Experiments on American soldiers and students of Yale University, conducted over forty years ago by Professor Russel H. Chittenden, proved the fallacy of the high-protein theory. As a result of the experiments, Professor Chittenden showed that the great majority of people overeat, and that the consumption of protein was especially excessive. The soldiers and students improved in health on a restricted diet.

Lahmann, the famous Continental Nature Cure pioneer, had stated even before Chittenden that over-consumption of protein was a vital factor in the causation of disease. The excess of uric acid was declared to be one of the causative factors in rheumatism and allied complaints. Professor Hindhede also proved that meat (one form of protein) was not only unessential, but that health could be improved on a diet with a much reduced protein content.

Though protein is necessary for health it has been vastly overrated, and an over-consumption leads to disease. Cheese, eggs, milk, nuts, fresh fish are the best sources of protein.

Fats are essential to health since they provide heat and can be stored in the subcutaneous tissues of the body. Here again, however, the consumption of fats is generally excessive. Animal fat, especially, is not easily digested, and fried starch food (fried bread, chips, etc.) is never good. Fried fat creates an insoluble coat over the starch cells and prevents digestion in the upper digestive tract. Ptyalin, a salivary secretion, has to act upon the starch and convert it into maltose. This part of the digestion is interfered with when there is a coating of fat around the starch. Incidentally, this type of fried food (like all starch) is one of the causative factors in catarrh, coronary thrombosis and colds.

Butter, olive and vegetable oil are the best types of fat.

Carbohydrates are necessary for energy. That most people

are over-conscious of carbohydrate food is one of the reasons why we fall ill. The excess of carbohydrate food (especially white-flour products and refined sugar) is a vital factor in disease. Starches and sugars are the principal containers of the above element. All carbohydrate foods (bread, rice, macaroni, potatoes, sugar, etc.) are converted into sugars during digestion. The material is stored in the tissues and liver as glycogen so that it can be quickly converted into glucose. Most starch food is acid-forming, but wholewheat bread, potatoes and other root vegetables, fruit and honey are the best sources of carbohydrate.

Vitamins and mineral salts will be discussed under their respective headings, as these merit full discussion.

For a diet to be properly balanced it must contain all the essential foods in the correct quantities. That is to say, it must contain protein, starch, sugar, fat, vitamins, minerals, water and bulk. As each individual is a law unto himself, there can be no definite statement as to how much a given person should consume, or even what proportions of carbohydrate or protein are necessary in an individual case. This is a point where studied dietetics in relation to personal health come into force.

It is generally recognized, however, in the diet reform of Naturopathy, that the orthodox consumption of proteins and carbohydrates is excessive. Nature Cure affirms also that the excessive intake of these acid-forming foods has a bearing upon disease.

Diet reform (or balanced dieting) is concerned with the correct alignment of food requirements in accordance with natural laws. Man's instinct as regards food—with the exception of when he feels sick and loses his appetite—can no longer be trusted. His perversion has been brought about largely by the use of denatured and refined food.

We previously mentioned a distinction between acid and alkaline foods. Broadly speaking, these fall under two categories. The proteins and carbohydrates are acid-forming, and the fruits and vegetables are alkaline. The alkaline foods neutralize the acid foods, and maintain harmonious balance within the system; provided, of course, that they are consumed in sufficient quantity. The alkaline foods are the cleansing elements in diet. Below is a comparative list of alkaline and acid foods.

Acid	*Alkaline*
Meat	Root and leaf vegetables
Meat extracts	Dried and fresh fruit
Bread	Buttermilk
Macaroni	Olives
Cheese	
Eggs	
Fish	
Refined sugar	
Lentils	
Peanuts	
Rice	

With the above in mind, we have now to consider the bulk in diet that is essential for efficient peristaltic action and the cleansing of the bowels. When we recall the laxative foods with a bran foundation, it seems the height of folly to take this commodity out of flour and then retail it again as packet food to relieve the very distress its absence from bread creates. This is without reference to the vitamins lost. Bulk, therefore, is best found in whole-grain cereals, vegetables and fruit.

It is quite evident that, with protein and starch being acid-forming, and the fruits and vegetables alkaline (as well as supplying the bulk and water), a sound dietary should comprise a minimum amount of protein and starch and a maximum of fruit and vegetables. It will be recalled, too, that fruits and vegetables are excellent sources of vitamins and mineral salts. This is a factor that should be borne in mind when weighing up the advantages of a balanced diet.

We have previously emphasized "wholeness" with regard to diet. Therefore, although starch should be reduced in quantity, the wholegrain cereals are advised. With "wholeness", however, we arrive at another advantage in diet—that is the use of raw food. "Wholeness" also infers grown without the use of fertilizers or chemical sprays.

Vitamin C is the most easily destroyed vitamin (hence the reason for unpasteurized or sour milk), and any cooking process has a detrimental effect upon the vitamins and mineral salts. There is every reason, therefore, to include a substantial amount of raw food in the diet. In connection with this, a large raw salad and fruit meal per day has obvious advantages.

Naturally, a certain amount of cooking is required. Heat preparation of food, however, should be cut to a minimum. Though raw feeding plays a large part in the naturopathic concept of an ideal diet, one cannot ignore popular prejudices and tastes; nor is it desirable to eliminate all cooked food, for it makes for variation and enjoyment.

Wherever possible, however, such cooking as is carried out is best done with the aid of baking, steaming, braising or conservative cooking. The latter method means cooking with the aid of a minimum amount of water.

By elimination we arrive at what balanced dieting implies. We have largely cut out protein (especially meat) and carbohydrates (especially white-flour products, refined cereals and refined sugars). What we arrive at is largely a lacto-vegetarian diet with particular emphasis on raw food.

What it virtually amounts to, therefore, is that a balanced diet comprises the following :

Wholegrain cereals in low quantities.
Fruit and vegetables in abundance.
Dairy produce in fair quantities.
Nuts and natural sugars in low quantities.

The proportion of cereals, dairy produce and nuts would be increased or decreased according to the amount of work performed. Those who do heavy work would require more of the energy-giving foods, and those doing light work and taking little exercise would have a corresponding decrease. Invalids and aged people also would consume less.

There is an emphasis on raw food (raw fruit and salads)

and on not overeating. Breakfast should be a fruit meal, lunch either a cooked or salad meal and, when lunch is a cooked meal, the evening meal should take a salad form or vice versa.

One question that inevitably arises is : if the citrus fruits are acid, and one of the basic factors in the diet is the reduction of acid foods, why advocate acid and sub-acid fruit? The answer lies in the fact that while citrus fruit (oranges, lemons, grapefruit, etc.) is acid in content its ultimate reaction is alkaline. The acid condition of the body, brought about by an excess of protein and starch and by worry or indulgence, is really a toxic condition which the alkaline elements—being eliminative—overcome.

It is true that some people, especially those with a high toxic condition, experience unpleasant reactions from eating acid and sub-acid fruit. What really happens, however, is that the acid condition of the body is stirred up with the introduction of the acid fruit. The fruit itself is not to blame. The discomfort created by eating acid and/or sub-acid fruit indicates a toxic condition of the body and demonstrates the necessity for either a highly alkaline diet or a curative fast. Once the system is really cleansed there will be no discomfort on eating acid fruit.

Vitamins

What are the vitamins? When analytical chemists were dealing with fats and oils they discovered that a certain part was "unsaponifiable". That is to say, the unsaponfiable matter would not yield to a process of boiling with alkali. From the chemists' viewpoint, this matter was an impurity. Research work by Sir W. Gowland Hopkins, from 1906 onwards, proved that the impurity was the very substance that enabled fats and oils to be fully utilized in the body.

We know that vitamins are elusive substances and that deficiencies in them definitely cause disease. We are aware also that some are destroyed by heat. So far as we are concernd it is necessary only to know that vitamins are essential and that the different classes have different purposes. It is also a known fact that the best containers of vitamins are those food-stuffs that also contain the mineral salts, *i.e.* fruit and vege-tables. We have, then, another factor in proving that the right diet is one based upon lacto-vegetarian lines, with an empha-sis on "wholeness".

All the vitamins required for bodily needs should be con-tained in a balanced diet containing plenty of fruit and vegetables, dairy produce and wholegrain cereals. It is in-teresting to record that vitamin A was formerly prepared from nettles. The herbs and wild plants that abound in the countryside are prolific sources of vitamins and mineral salts.

Since vitamins were never thought of fifty odd years ago, why should they be necessary now? At that time the normal diet was not short of vitamins. Milk was not pasteurized, bread and sugar were not refined, the consumption of de-natured foods was infinitesimal. Even beer was not put through a chemical process. Nor was the soil impoverished by artificial fertilizers, and the food was of the highest quality. And what medicines were consumed were largely of the herbalist and non-drug variety—rich in vitamins and mineral salts. There was, in effect, little need for an awareness of vita-mins.

Mineral Salts

Owing to the tremendous amount of publicity that vita-mins have received, there has been a strong tendency to over-look the part mineral salts play in health. If we break the body down into cells and then into what the cells are made of, we find the same elements that we find in food, etc.

The average body is composed of the following:

Oxygen	65%	Phosphorous	1.00%
Carbon	18%	Potassium	0.35%
Hydrogen	10%	Sulphur	0.25%
Nitrogen	3%	Sodium	0.15%
Calcium	1.5%	Chlorine	0.15%

The body contains also iron, manganese, fluorine, copper, iodine and traces of silicon and other elements.

The combination of oxygen and hydrogen accounts for

75 per cent. of body weight, of which 75 per cent. there is a 60 per cent. actual water content. Calcium is the most abundant mineral salt in the body, and its importance for growing children is emphasized. Iodine is necessary for the proper functioning of the thyroid gland. Iron is the element that enables the haemoglobin to absorb oxygen and thus permits the blood to carry out its vital task of transporting oxygen to the tissues.

The process of digestion and assimilation is considerably influenced by mineral salts. Along the tract of the small intestine lie minute, hair-like projections called "villi". Through these villi nutriment is absorbed in two ways : either directly into the bloodstream or indirectly *via* the lymphatic system. The blood carries the nutriment to the cells of all parts of the body, where it is ultimately transformed into heat and energy, or used for the repair and replacement of tissue. The passage of nutritive substances into blood capillaries and lymphatics is aided by a mechanical process termed "osmosis". Osmotic pressure is a feature of all cell life, and it is responsible for the transference of liquids and dissolved substances to and from the solutions surrounding the cells of the body and their contents. Osmotic pressure can be increased by fruit or vegetable juices which contain their full complement of mineral salts.

While on this subject of osmosis, it seems appropriate to refer to the statement of a famous German dietician, Ragnar Berg, concerning the use of common salt. Berg maintained that common salt has a paralysing effect upon the kidneys and ureters, that it disturbs the balance of osmosis and interferes with vascular endothelial activity. Salt causes an abnormally permeable state of the tissues on account of the increased osmosis induced by it.

Note that salt causes an *abnormally permeable* state of the tissues. This is not caused by the natural mineral salts, which can never be taken in such massive doses.

We have seen that the body itself is partly composed of a great many minerals and that we must obtain these from our food to maintain health. Any deficiency, such as calcium, for instance, has serious effects upon health. A recurring theme throughout this book has been that of a natural, whole diet. It has been emphasized for many reasons, not the least of which is the necessity for an adequate supply of mineral salts.

These are best obtained from fruits and vegetables and wholegrain cereals. Mineral salts are just as easily destroyed as vitamins. Any cooking process, therefore, diminishes the value of food. The importance of raw fruit and vegetables cannot be over-emphasized. A lacto-vegetarian, "whole" diet, therefore, is the soundest basis for ensuring a plentiful supply of mineral salts. A raw salad and fruit meal per day will, in itself, be sufficient guarantee against any vitamin and mineral salt deficiency and we should make more use of edible sea-weed.

Water is an important factor in the human make-up. Blood, for instance, weighs about one-eleventh of total body weight, yet it is composed of 78 per cent. water. By one means or another, roughly seven pints or more of fluid can be given off from the body in any one day.

What we eat has a lot of bearing upon the amount of fluid essential to body requirements. A balanced diet, with its emphasis upon fruit and vegetables will contain about 80 to 85 per cent. water. Less fluid is required on a sensible diet and the water from fruit and vegetables is of the purest type.

Fluoridation of the water supplies may be a possible menace to ordinary drinking water. Readers are advised to look into the question of their water supplies.

Chapter V

ELIMINATION AND FASTING

METABOLISM is the term covering all the physical and chemical processes by which life is maintained. The constructive element of metabolism—the processes by which food materials are adapted for the use of the body, repair and renewal of tissues, etc.—is known as anabolism. The destructive processes, by which energy is produced and the breaking down of tissues takes place, is termed catabolism.

Physiological income is derived from food and oxygen, and physiological expenditure is heat and work, repair of tissue, growth in the young and elimination of waste matter.

Elimination is the series of processes by which waste matter from food debris, destroyed cells, bacteria and all the catabolic processes are removed from the body.

Four organs take charge of elimination : the bowels, lungs, skin and kidneys. When these function efficiently and in harmony, providing that no undue stress is placed upon them by overeating, eating wrong foods, lack of exercise and other errors, health is maintained. Any neglect of natural laws, however, that leads to a breakdown in elimination and the retention of poisons within the system, must inevitably lead to disease.

No matter how much we may endeavour to restrict skin activity, the healing force of nature always attempts to win the day. Boils, pimples, acne and other common skin eruptions are invariably the result of an attempt by the life forces of the body to expel poisons. Where boils and acne arise one will find constipation or some other breakdown of normal elimination. The naturopath treats the case as a breakdown of normal

34

elimination, recognizes that the eruption is an outlet for toxins and treats the cause.

The way to attain skin perfection is to permit it frequent exposure to the three elements that cost nothing : sun, air and water.

As an industrialized and highly concentrated community we are unfortunately placed as regards purity of the atmosphere. Conversion to electricity can be an immense advantage, but the highly poisonous fumes that pour from the exhausts of motor vehicles will still vitiate the air. The impact of civilization upon the air we breathe is a sufficient handicap in itself without that of under-developing the lungs.

Respiration is the process by which air passes into the lungs so that the blood can absorb oxygen, and stale air (carrying off carbonic acid gas and more complex poisonous substances) is breathed out. The process is vital to life. When, however, it is limited by the air we breathe and the shallowness of the act, an accumulation of carbonic acid is retained in the system and the oxygen supply is deficient.

Postural defect (bad walking and sitting in wrong positions with the lungs and abdominal organs suffering compression effects) and shallow breathing lead to a poisoned system and a breakdown of elimination and, of course, disease. The answer to this defect is deep-breathing, better ventilation and purification of the atmosphere.

The kidneys are a pair of glands lying close to the spine in the upper part of the abdomen. Their chief function is that of separating urine from the blood. As the urine contains solids, from the waste matter of the body, a large amount of water also is excreted to keep the solids in solution. Urine is elimination of the end-products of metabolism in a liquid form.

When the other organs of elimination (bowels, skin and lungs) fail to work to capacity, the kidneys endeavour to maintain balance by increasing their activities. This condition, however, can last only for a certain period, and the ultimate efficiency of the organs is impaired.

The way in which the balance of the system is maintained can be illustrated by a natural phenomena that all have experienced. That is, in cold weather, when the skin activity is decreased, more urine is excreted. The kidneys do their best to cope with any extra tasks thrown upon them when elimination is unbalanced or when an excess of poisons is consumed (as in drug-taking, excessive starch and protein consumption or rabid tea, coffee and alcohol drinking).

Since it is the task of the kidneys to sort out and eliminate a large part of the waste products of the body, it is obvious at once that any inefficiency of the bowels, skin and lungs will demand a corresponding increase of work from the kidneys.

If the other organs of elimination take their share of the task of eliminating poisons from the body, and all excesses are avoided, especially if a natural way of living is practised, the kidneys will function automatically with no trouble.

Efficient elimination is the secret of health.

There is, throughout all Nature Cure works, an emphasis upon the fast as a curative measure which is in full accord with natural laws. At first glance it appears the height of folly to withhold food at a time of disease, or to prescribe the fast as frequently as is the practice in Naturopathy. It may even seem that the fast is applied indiscriminately, but such is not the case.

The vindication of Nature Cure and the methods employed—including fasting—is found in the enormous strides the movement has made in recent years.

Acute disease, we believe, is an expression of the *life-force* of the body. All the main efforts of the body are concentrated upon reaching a healthy state by throwing off the poisons accumulated within the system. In acute disease there is an increase of symptoms : the pulse rate rises, pain and other symptoms are increased. The digestive function is temporarily suspended, hence the loss of appetite. Even the common state of heightened emotion produces a condition of anorexia. Such a condition is purely protective; because the body, having no need for food, and with little power to act upon it, seeks to protect the suspended digestion by abstention.

It is necessary to limit the digestive functions because the energies of the body are required for the elimination of waste matter. Any energy that is used to digest food has to be diverted from the primary task of elimination. But very little energy is diverted, the consequence being that undigested food material decomposes, forms a mass of toxins poisoning the system and adds fresh fuel to the fire.

Lack of appetite, one of the first symptoms to appear in acute disease, is a protective instinct. All sorts of devices are resorted to so that the unwilling patient shall eat. Not that the patient *is* always unwilling. In minor cases of acute disease, when the appetite is lost, he is only too keen to stimulate the jaded appetite with drugs or medicines or to succumb to the blandishments of anxious but misguided relatives. Fear and tradition play a large part in this spurning of a natural instinct.

That thousands upon thousands of cases have shown the therapeutic value of the fast is sufficient evidence in itself. We have shown how fasting is reconciled with acute disease. How is it applied in the case of chronic disease? We have reiterated that most chronic disease is the result of the suppression of the simple acute diseases. The same rules, therefore, operate in such cases. Cleanse the system, with due regard to the special features of the disease, and improvement in the condition and a cure will be found.

A simple cold provides an illustration of the need for fasting. A cold, we believe, is an effort on the part of the body to supplement the normal channels of elimination by an extra outlet of poisons *via* the respiratory passages. (Skin diseases are the same, witness acne or boils.) That a cold may be occasioned by damp, infection or cold we do not deny. What we do suggest is that the toxic materials must be in the system ready for removal and that, when the right variety of conditions arises, the cold develops. It could not develop, however, within a healthy system.

Since Nature Cure claims that disease is the result of an impure system; that acute disease is an effort by the life-forces of the body to expel accumulated toxic products; that the suppression of acute disease results in chronic disease, then it follows that the fast is frequently indicated as a therapeutic measure.

The repeated use of the fast should occasion little surprise. By it disease is tackled at its very source. All the other factors in the causation of disease are studied independently, and correct measures are taken to rectify possible errors. Such errors are largely covered by the Nature Cure theory of living.

A fast achieves four main objects :

(1) It stops the intake of food which would inevitably produce toxins.
(2) It rests the digestive tract.
(3) It enables the body to concentrate its energies upon elimination.
(4) It stimulates the life-force and expels effete matter.

It is because the fast has a deep-reaching, dis-encumbering effect upon the system that it is so widely used. It is for the same reason that it is applied with due caution. Indiscriminate fasting would indeed be a menace, but such is not the case. It is, perhaps, at this point, advisable to warn those who consider that fasting is the beginning and end of Nature Cure of their misconception. Uncontrolled fasting can be dangerous. *To link it up with drugs is even more dangerous.* It must be remembered that fasting is a drastic procedure and can be carried to an extreme. When applied with ordinary common sense, however, and under some skilled supervision, it is an efficient means of healing.

Fasting may produce all kinds of disagreeable symptoms (one does not disturb a still, village pond without producing some unwelcome reactions). It must be understood that fasting so stimulates elimination, attracting toxic matter from the tissues into the blood-stream, there to be carried to the eliminating organs—that it is almost bound to cause abnormal symptoms. Fasting is almost the equivalent of opening up a dam. Some of the poisons rush out of the system and others circulate in the bloodstream, making their presence felt, until an outlet is found for them. Such a condition must naturally produce some uneasiness until a stabilization is reached.

From that it should not be imagined that a fast is uncontrollable—nothing is further from the truth. What should be appreciated is that the controlling of a fast requires a specialized technique which can only be acquired through practical experience.

There is another item in the application of the fast as a therapeutic measure requiring attention. Of the many factors in disease two are important. One of these is the reaction to disease and the other capacity for overcoming it. It is the latter factor that is important in fasting. Elimination does not follow the same rule in every case : some are slow to eliminate in the first place; in others the response is almost immediate. In all cases, however, there is an acceleration of the eliminatory processes during fasting, and the degree of elimination is conditioned by the individual response.

Fasting has become a little more complicated with the introduction of D.D.T. D.D.T. (chlorophenothane) is widely used in spraying fruit and vegetables and in ordinary households. Millions of people use aerosols containing D.D.T. and absorb this poison. It is stored up in the fatty tissues and it is only during fasting that the normal person might discover very unpleasant symptoms arising from too rapid an elimination of D.D.T. An excess of D.D.T. can cause gastro-enteritis, depression and muscular weakness.

Therefore, before fasting for the first time, it is necessary for the older person, who has probably absorbed a fair amount of D.D.T. during life, to have an eliminitive diet for a few days. The first fast should not last more than two-three days except when under expert naturopathic supervision. Fasting is physiologically correct. It is not the complete answer to disease, but it is as near perfection in the treatment of disease, whether acute or chronic, as any therapy can aspire to be.

It is obvious that the fasting methods outlined are drastic. The entire object is elimination of toxins from the body, so that the *life-force,* which is inherent in every one of us, may be given an opportunity to assert itself. The natural inclination of the body is towards health. *Only Nature Heals.* Fasting, dieting, manipulation, hydrotherapy, electrotherapy and all the other range of therapies are subject to the basic principle of *assisting* the natural powers of recovery.

The Healing Crisis

All diseases manifest themselves by certain variations from the normal which are called symptoms. Such symptoms may be an exaggeration or a lessening of normal reactions. The supernormal reaction is one that is, on the whole, favourable to recovery, while the sub-normal is unfavourable. It is the supernormal reaction that is evident in acute diseases, and the same reaction is displayed in the healing crisis. Lindlahr defines a healing crisis in the following terms : "A healing crisis is an acute reaction, resulting from the ascendancy of Nature's healing forces over disease conditions, and it is, therefore, in conformity with Nature's constructive principle."

A healing crisis is the approximation of an acute disease. We shall again emphasize the curative aspect of acute diseases, for too often are these suppressed in fear and ignorance. Such suppression invariably leads to chronic disease, and it is with this facet of medical treatment that we so deeply quarrel.

Lindlahr, in his book NATURE CURE, says :— What is commonly called "acute" disease is in reality the result of Nature's efforts to eliminate from the organism waste matter, foreign matter, and poisons, and to repair injury to living tissues. In other words, *every so-called acute disease is the result of a cleansing and healing effort of Nature*. The real disease is lowered vitality, abnormal composition of the vital fluids (blood and lymph), and the resulting accumulation of waste materials and poisons . . .

Chronic disease is a condition of the organism in which lowered vibration (lowered vitality), due to the accumulation of waste matter and poisons, with the consequent destruction of vital parts and organs, has progressed to such an extent that Nature's constructive and healing forces are no longer able to react against the disease conditions by acute corrective efforts (healing crises).

Chronic disease is a condition of the organism in which the morbid encumbrances have gained the ascendancy and prevent acute reaction (healing crises) on the part of the constructive forces of Nature.

Chronic disease is the inability of the organism to react by acute efforts or "healing crises" against constitutional disease conditions.

Acute diseases manifest themselves in conditions such as colds, fevers, diarrhoea, skin eruptions (boils, abscesses, rashes, etc.), catarrhal and other discharges. *When these acute diseases, which are Nature's attempts to increase normal elimination or to supplement the failure of normal elimination—as, for instance, acne in constipation—are treated in accordance with Nature Cure principles, then no chronic disease can arise.* We must remember, however, that the vast majority of new converts to Nature Cure spring from the ranks of disappointed medical failures, i.e. the victims of chronic disease.

The aim of Nature Cure is to help the natural forces inherent in the organism. It is quite evident, therefore, that when a position is reached, as it must be where the natural healing forces are strong enough to take the offensive—as a result of fasting or other cleansing treatment—that a healing crisis is liable to arise. We say liable, because there are exceptions to the rule. The patient, however, need suffer no alarm when, as it so appears, he suddenly relapses into a condition of acute disease. Remembering that all acute diseases are favourable reactions, and that the healing crisis would not arise if conditions were not, on the whole, conducive to recovery, we can safely go ahead and rely upon the impulse for health to gain complete control.

One extremely important point to keep in mind during a healing crisis is not to permit alarm to drive one back into the old stage of looking for a speedy suppressant drug. Medical or drug interference at such a stage can lead only to harm and the undoing of a vast amount of cleansing work.

When should a healing crisis be averted? Strictly speaking it cannot be avoided. Osteopathic inhibition of nerve impulses, it is true, can check diarrhoea. On the whole, however, it is impossible, and unnecessary, to avoid temporary flare-ups which are indicative of a healing crisis.

There are certain cases, especially with older people who have suffered for years from chronic disease, where it may be inadvisable to bring about a healing crisis, largely because of the lack of reserve powers. Graduated treatment over a longer period is permissible. Working by stages, we can minimise the cure-effects and bring about partial healing-crises, which ultimately, if all conditions necessary for recovery exist, will lead to a cure.

It is not essential to have a healing-crisis, nor does it always arise. In such cases the cure is achieved by a steady cleansing of the system. Any healing crises arising during that period are minor disturbances which are of small consequence, but the sum total of which materially assist the healing efforts as a whole.

It is the possibility of the healing crisis, and its correct interpretation, that demands either a full application of the principles of Nature Cure and/or the supervision of a skilled naturopath. The healing crisis is too often the bogey that frightens people away from Naturopathy. This can be due only to misguided fears and ignorance and can be safely set at rest by the acquisition of the true facts.

Chapter VI

HYDROTHERAPY

FOR our present knowledge of hydrotherapy we are indebted to the Continental pioneers of Nature Cure. In particular we must pay homage to Father Kneipp, the remarkable parish priest of Worishofen, in Bavaria; the German peasant Vincent Priessnitz also a great water-healer; Johann Schroth, originator of the dry diet and pack system, Bilz and others. These men all had their time in the early Victorian era.

Father Kneipp, like a great many true healers, took up his work because he had to cure himself. He came across a little book describing cold-water therapy and immediately began the more drastic of the cold water treatments and improved his methods through constant observation. As he himself said :

> The applications it enjoined were often too rough, too violent, for the human constitution. Such exaggerated treatment only serves to bring the cold-water cure into discredit, and to re-inforce the ranks of those who blindly condemn whatever they do not, or but imperfectly understand.

Though the pioneers of hydrotherapy and Nature Cure— Kneipp, Priessnitz, Schroth, Bilz, Rikli, Gossman, Just, Lahman, Bircher-Benner, etc.—were centred in Germany, Austria, Switzerland and Czechoslovakia from 1850 onwards their work was, in a certain sense, not new. The early Greeks, Romans, Egyptians and others had long appreciated the value of water as a healing medium. Most assuredly, the early water-cure methods were crude, but the elements of natural healing, even though perhaps imperfectly understood, were recognized and applied by laymen in a true spirit of healing. From Priessnitz, Schroth, Kneipp and others we progressed

43

via Lindlahr and others to our present-day standard. *Speaking of the progress of Nature Cure in general, we must emphasize the way in which laymen have dominated the scene.* True, there have been enlightened medical practitioners, but even these have encountered bitter opposition.

For an explanation of how water cures, we can do no better than have recourse to Kneipp. This is what he says :

> To dissolve; remove and strengthen : these, then, are the three principal attributes of water; and we maintain water to be capable of curing every curable disease, as its various applications, properly applied, directly attack the root of the evil and have the result—
> (a) Of dissolving the germs of diseased matter contained in the blood.
> (b) Of withdrawing the diseased matter from the system.
> (c) Of restoring the purified blood to its proper state of circulation.
> (d) Of bracing the weakened constitution, and rendering it fit for renewed exertion.

Dissolve, Remove and Strengthen are the three cardinal factors in hydrotherapy. No matter how crude the appliances used for the purpose of water treatments are, so long as these three attributes are kept in mind, the result will be the same.

The aim, therefore, of all water treatments is to dissolve and eliminate toxic matter, to stimulate the circulation and strengthen the constitution. We accomplish this in many varied ways each differing method being applied for a specific purpose, and in conformity with the patient's illness and individual powers of reaction. Not that the sole purpose of hydrotherapy is the treatment of disease—used correctly it is one of the greatest prophylactic therapies.

As a general rule, cold or cool water is applied after any treatment where hot water has been used. This is not always the case, and there are occasions when cold water alone is used, or when hot applications are advised. There are dangers in the over-enthusiastic utilization of either hot or cold-water treatments. The cold bath for instance, *should always be of short duration,* and discontinued if no warm reaction is obtained.

One of the basic laws in water treatments, as Lindlahr points out, is that of *action and reaction.* The application of any form of heat to the skin draws the blood to the surface. That is the first, immediate effect. But it is not a lasting effect, and the blood must inevitably return to the deeper blood-vessels from which it was derived. The application of cold water, on the other hand, has the first effect of *driving the blood away from the surface.* The secondary and *lasting* effect is that of warmth, since, by the law of action and reaction, the blood must circulate back to the blood-vessels and tissues from which it was expelled. In this matter an actual increase of circulation is brought about by the stimulating effect of cold water.

It is upon this basis of action and reaction that most water treatments are founded.

Tepid sprays played upon the spine are useful in neurasthenia and nervous cases, colder sprays are useful in high blood pressure, haemorrhoids, constipation and bladder troubles. The spray, in the three latter conditions, is directed towards the lumbar region. Cold showers or sprays should always be taken after hot full baths or any heat treatment. In the cold bath or cold spray we have the classic example of the action and reaction effect of hydrotherapy, for the lasting effect after the cold application should be that of warmth. With this in view we shall again emphasize that the best effects are obtained from *short-lasting* cold-water applications.

The Alternate Hot and Cold Foot Bath

For this treatment two bowls are required. One is three parts filled with water at a temperature of approximately 40 to 43 degrees Cent. and the other with water from the cold supply. Sit on a stool and place the feet first into the hot water for from three to five minutes and then into the cold water for about thirty seconds. Repeat the process three to four times, and conclude with the cold dip. This type of treatment is excellent for headaches, poor circulation, tired feet, chilblains, sleeplessness, etc. *The Hot Foot Bath* is applied in the same way as the above with the exception that there is no changing over from one bath to the other, the feet remaining in the hot water for from ten to fifteen minutes and then in the cold water for about one to two minutes. This is the most useful in the case of headaches.

Lindlahr, in his book, *NATURE CURE* says :

> Many people are under the impression that packs reduce the fever temperature so quickly because they are put on cold. But this is not so, because, unless the reaction be bad, the packs become warm after a few minutes' contact with the body.
>
> *The prompt reduction of temperature takes place because of increased heat radiation.* The coldness of the pack may lower the surface temperature slightly; but it is moist warmth forming under the pack on the surface of the body that draws the blood from the congested interior into the skin, relaxes and opens its minute blood-vessels and pores, and in that way facilitates the escape of heat from the body.
>
> In febrile conditions the pores and capillary blood-vessels of the skin are tense and contracted. Therefore the heat cannot escape, the skin is hot and dry, and the interior of the body remains overheated. When the skin relaxes and the patient begins to perspire freely, we say the fever "is broken".
>
> The moist warmth under the wet pack produces this relaxation of the skin in a perfectly natural manner . . .

The essential value of the pack lies in the way that it utilizes the natural forces of the body for healing. As previously stated, the wet sheet draws a larger amount of blood to the surface of the body, relieves internal congestion and promotes elimination. Body-warmth, it is observed, is used to create a *gentle stewing,* and it is this moist warmth that is most effective in treating disease. The moist warmth, then, acting over a period of time (varying from two to six hours), provides the means by which elimination is stimulated and decongestion takes place.

While the full-body or three-quarter pack is the most useful to apply, local packs are often advantageous and, in some ways, easier of application. It must be considered, however, that the pack draws blood to the surface, attracting more blood than is normal, and with this in mind we have to advise against the practice of applying packs to the neck and throat alone, since more blood is attracted to that area than is safe in so small a compass. It is necessary, therefore, when applying a throat pack for sore throats, tonsilitis, colds, etc., to apply a chest or abdominal pack to draw away congestion from the restricted area. Indeed, for many local conditions, especially where there is evidence of intense toxicity, it is advisable to apply either the three-quarter pack or a pack that comes well above and below the affected part. Packs for the chronic complaints—rheumatism, gout, catarrh, arthritis, asthma, etc., are best applied to the full body. There is practically no illness for which a pack is not useful. It is soothing in insomnia and neurasthenia, it is decongesting in all the acute and chronic diseases, it is an excellent aliminative measure for autotoxaemia, for sprains and bruises, it is soothing and decongesting and for even the sickest person it offers a valuable home treatment.

Apart from the rule of avoiding congestion by applying a secondary pack in local, restricted areas, the other rules are always to apply the pack in a warm room, to ensure a warm reaction from the pack (putting extra hot-water bottles into the bed if necessary) and to remove the pack when dry. *No person should be allowed to remain in a pack if a warm reaction is not obtained*. Packs are inadvisable when fasting on account of the fact that some degree of body-heat is lost during that process. On emerging from the pack it is essential to wash the skin thoroughly to remove any waste debris from the skin that has been eliminated while in the pack. For the same reason the pack sheeting must itself be thoroughly washed and aired.

The Full-Body Pack

This pack is termed thus because it covers the whole body with the exception of the head. It is more drastic than the three-quarter pack and, since nervous people feel dis-inclined to be so fully enwrapped, it is not advisable in their cases. To prepare the pack it is necessary to turn back the top bed-clothes and lay a thick blanket from the end of the pillow to the foot of the bed. The sheet (twill cotton or raw silk sheeting is the best) is dipped into cold water and well wrung out and then laid on the blanket. The patient lies on the wet sheet, which is quickly pulled over, covering from the top of the shoulders down to the feet. It is folded over the feet and legs and the arms are enclosed. The blanket is then drawn over and secured with rustless safety pins, after which the top bed-clothes are pulled over. It is advisable to have warmth with-out weight, so that a featherbed or two eiderdowns make an ideal top covering. In colder weather it is advisable to have two hot-water bottles in the bed, and the whole treatment can be converted into a sweating treatment by placing four to six hot-water bottles in the bed. In this case the pack must not last longer than two hours, though in any event, the full pack is only advised for from two to four hours. This pack is advo-cated for any decongesting purpose. It is useful for gout, arthritis, rheumatism, auto-intoxication, lumbago.

The T Pack

The name of this pack is derived from its shape. The material is usually made up from two lengths, from ten to fifteen inches wide, stitched together to form the letter T. It is made in this form so that the vertical part of the T can be drawn through the legs and the horizontal section carried around the abdomen. This pack is indicated in the treatment of haemorrhoids, constipation, indigestion, ovarian troubles, bladder and kidney diseases and practically all abdominal complaints. The outer covering, of course, has to be adapted to cover the T pack.

Local Packs

Arms, legs, chest, throat, etc., can all be treated by local packs. While it is more advisable to use the three-quarter pack wherever possible, the local packs are useful for minor ailments or injuries. Remember, however, that throat packs should never be applied singly—a chest or waist pack should always accompany it to avoid congestion in the constricted throat area.

Compresses

A cold compress supplies the answer to many household problems. Even a child can apply it. Sprains, bruises, swelling and any inflammatory condition can be treated with a cold compress. In any inflamed state there is an excess of blood within the affected area. To apply heat, bringing more blood to an already hyperaemic part, would be a mistake. The cold compress, by driving the blood away, relieves the pain and reduces the inflammation and congestion. Immediate application of a cold compress to an injured part will usually reduce the time-factor involved in healing.

Cold compresses to the back of the neck will often relieve a stubborn headache, pressure in the head, etc. Apply cold compresses to the spine and neck in feverish conditions, high blood-pressure, sunburns and minor heat-stroke effects.

Home Fomentations

In all cases where the application of heat is found to be soothing and of curative value, hot fomentations are advised on account of their simplicity. They are useful in most neuralgic conditions, toothache, indigestion, flatulence, anaemia and low blood pressure, kidney diseases, colitis, acute rheumatism, etc. The hot fomentation is prepared by placing a small towel (folded over four times) on a larger open towel. In this position the towels are laid in a large bowl so that the ends of the large towel are free of the bowl. Hot water is poured into the bowl, and the fomentation is wrung out by using the free ends of the large towel. Before applying the fomentation to the affected part rub it with olive oil to diminish any possibility of burning the skin. In cases of colitis and weak digestion it is a good plan to apply the fomentation to the abdomen immediately after a meal.

Steaming

Where it is difficult for ordinary forms of heat to penetrate as in the nose, ear and throat, steaming performs a very useful task, Haemorrhoids, for instance, can be treated by steaming. In this case it is done by sitting over a bowl of hot water and allowing the steam to penetrate the anus and dilate the blood-vessels, assisting the decongestion required for healing. Steaming of the ear, nose and throat is indicated in all painful conditions of the areas. Catarrh, colds, asthma, bronchitis and influenza can all be subjected to steam treatment. The chest and throat are steamed in affectations such as tonsilitis, mumps, sore throat and loss of voice. Steaming is very soothing and decongesting in earache, neuralgic symptoms in the face and also for styes and boils.

There is a distinct difference between direct steam heat as indicated above and the steam cabinet bath or pyretic bath which are used in institutions as a general treatment. For local treatments, as in the throat, ear, nose and chest, it is necessary to have a kettle two-thirds full of water. Bring this to the boil, and, when a steady head of steam is issuing from the spout, sit in such a manner that the steam is directed on to the part to be treated. After two to three minutes of steaming always cool down with cold water and re-apply the steam, concluding with the cold-water application. Medical steaming kettles, incidentally, can be procured from almost any chemist.

Ice

Ice packs and the use of ice in baths has largely fallen into disfavour on account of the extreme coldness. There are occasions, however, when ice is a very useful medium. Freezing treatment by the external application of ice has proved very beneficial. It must be stressed that great care should be taken in its application, and it is not advised unless the operator has some experience in the dissolving, removing and strengthening previously mentioned. Having assimilated this fact, we can appreciate the frequent insistence upon short, cold ablutions, the many alternate hot and cold baths and the advocation of cold packs and compresses.

If we were to limit our activities in hydrotherapy to what the pioneers in this work advised, we would almost certainly rule out the excessive hot or cold applications. To a large extent this is so even now, but hot applications and ice still have their uses.

The Sitz Bath

The old-fashioned sitz or hip bath provides one of the best means of combating congestion and stagnation of the circulating fluids (blood and lymph). It is one of the tragedies of our times that the advent of modern plumbing has resulted in the discarding of the hip bath. This bath is so useful that it should form a standard part of every bathroom.

Abdominal congestion is the cause of many disorders. In all cases in which a patient complains of cold extremities one can be sure that he or she suffers from abdominal congestion, and the sitz bath is ideal for the purpose of relieving this condition. Depression, headaches, many throat troubles and catarrhal conditions are a concomitant of abdominal congestion. The nervous system is adversely affected by the same physical state, and symptoms such as insomnia, irritability, nervous exhaustion, fears, worry, bad temper, etc., etc., are dispelled or decreased by the continued use of the sitz bath. In the treatment of constipation, flatulence, colitis, diarrhoea, dysentry, haemorrhoids and inflammatory conditions of the bowels, the sitz bath is supreme. These bath cans be taken cold or hot or alternatively hot and cold. Cold sitz baths of short duration are excellent for piles, constipation and sexual troubles. At the same time, the long hot sitz bath followed by a cool sponging is equally advised. For cases of heart trouble, the sitz bath can be applied when no other hot-water treatment is applicable. There is no strain upon the heart, and its function is aided by the sitz bath in lessening the pressure upon the heart and reducing abdominal congestion. Where indigestion is present, the sitz bath draws the blood to the stomach and stimulates the functioning of the digestive glands. For lumbago and sciatica, the alternate hot and cold sitz bath is an ideal treatment. Female troubles—inflammation of uterus, ovaries, leucorrhoea and any irregularity or painful periods— show a remarkable response when the sitz bath is applied. For some conditions it is applied hot and for others, cold. Bladder troubles, enlarged prostate gland and hernias should be treated with a daily cold sitz bath lasting from thirty seconds to three minutes, and also with the hot sitz bath followed by a cold sponging. The sitz bath is always advised in conjunction with fasting. The alternate hot and cold sitz bath promotes the dissolving and elimination of the effete matter accumulated in the bowels during the cleansing process of the fasting. Even if an enema or colonic irrigation is applied during the fast, the daily alternate hot and cold sitz bath or the long hot sitz bath followed by a cool sponging is advised.

As previously stated, the old-fashioned sitz bath and a foot bath is all that is necessary for the purpose. The depth of the water is varied according to the displacement arising from the size of the person being treated, but the water must reach up to the patient's waistline. The foot bath is necessary because it helps to reduce the abdominal congestion and attracts the blood from the head, lungs and liver, etc., etc.

Ebbard, co-author of THE NEW BEDROCK OF HEALTH, describes the application of the hot sitz bath in these terms :

The sitz bath is two parts filled with hot water, as hot as the patient can bear it, up to 108 to 110 degrees Fahr. The bath should last 10-14 minutes, during which time the temperature must be kept up and, should the water cool down, boiling water must be ready at hand to bring the temperature up again. By this means, all the abdominal blood-vessels and tissues become expanded, and for the moment even more blood is attracted to the abdomen. After the given time, the patient gets out of the bath and part of the body, which has been in the water, *and only this part,* is sponged with cold water for about two minutes. By this sudden cold spraying, the abdominal blood-vessels and tissues contract and the blood is forced away, at once establishing, especially by its larger quantity, an increased circulation, not only in the abdomen, but all over the body. Warm feet and the relaxing of any pressure in the body are the immediate effects of the sitz bath.

We have already stated that there are different methods of applying the sitz bath, and these are classified as follows :

(1) *The hot sitz bath,* lasting from ten to thirty minutes and terminated with a cold or cool sponging.

(2) *The alternate hot and cold sitz bath* (hot for five minutes, followed by a short cold sitz bath for thirty seconds) repeated twice or three times and *always concluded* with the cold sitz bath.

(3) *The cold sitz bath* (deeper in summer than in winter) lasting from thirty seconds to three minutes according to the case, vitality of patient and time of year. This can be a *cool* sitz bath in winter, or for people with nervous temperament or heart cases.

(4) *The blanket sitz bath,* a mild and safe sweating treatment for those with weak hearts.

The Epsom Salt Bath

This, like the previous baths, is a very simple matter and lends itself to home use. In all disease there is an accumulation of acids in the system. This is especially true of those complaints with a rheumatic character, where there exists an excess of uric acid. In such conditions the Epsom salt bath is advised because the salts neutralize the acid waste products and assist their elimination. In an ordinary bath of hot water dissolve two large handfuls of the commercial salts, and lie in the hot water for not more than ten minutes. Over this period there is a danger of enervation. Cool down after the hot bath and rest. People with weak hearts should not take an Epsom salt bath, and in no case should it be applied more than twice a week. Provided that the above instructions are observed, it will be found that the salt bath gives much relief and is efficacious in such cases as arthritis, rheumatism, sciatica, neuritis, lumbago, colds and catarrh.

The Relaxing Bath

This treatment is of longer duration than the normal. The temperature of the bath should be kept at about 30-35 degrees Cent. and one can lie in the bath for as long as forty to sixty minutes. With this temperature there is a pleasant feeling of relaxation and, if the bath is continued for the longer period, there is complete relaxation of muscular and nervous tension This treatment is particularly suited for nervous cases, for insomnia, heart trouble, general debility and depression.

The Cold Splash

All that is required for this is a few inches of cold water in the bath. In the summer this water can come straight from the running cold-water tap but in winter it is advisable to warm the water slightly. The treatment is of only very short duration and should never last for more than two minutes. The simplest method is to lie in the water and splash it all over the body, and in the winter the process should not take more than thirty seconds. As a tonic to start the day with, the cold splash is supreme. It tones up the nervous system, releases muscular tension, hardens the skin and reduces the proclivity to colds.

The Salt Rub

This is applied while lying in the warm bath. A second person sprinkles common salt into the wet hands and thoroughly rubs the patient's skin with the salt. As the salt quickly dissolves, the hands have to be constantly dipped into the salt until the skin has been quite covered with the salt rub. This treatment is indicated in all conditions where the skin activity has been lowered, when a dry scale appears on the skin and as a general tonic. It should not be applied to open sores and hypersensitive skins.

Sprays and Showers

Apart from the complete simplicity of these methods, there is their undoubted effectiveness. A cold spray played upon a varicose leg will rapidly allay inflammation and irritation.

Chapter VII

OSTEOPATHY AND NATURE CURE

Doctor Andrew Taylor Still founded osteopathy in 1874. Despite the rapid growth of the profession and the respect that osteopathy has acquired, the average person has only a vague idea of its nature.

Dr. Still based his theory on two beliefs : first, that the body is an entity, containing all that is desired to maintain health and overcome disease : secondly, that normal structure and normal functioning go hand in hand. Still found that many diseases were accompanied by faulty structure in the spine. Working on this premise, he argued that, by correcting structural imbalance, he could correct the body as a whole.

Deviations from normal structure were called "lesions" and by the adjustment of these lesions, which interfered with nerve, blood and lymph supply, a cure could be effected. Out of these beginnings osteopathy has grown into a skilled science.

Even before Still noted the relation between the spine and disease, the phenomena of spinal tenderness had been observed. Still is regarded as the pioneer of a remarkably successful system and his "Find it, fix it and leave it alone" has stood the test of time.

Since osteopathy is concerned with the correction or removal of lesions, we must first appreciate what constitutes a lesion. Dain L. Tasker, C.O., in his book *Principles of Osteopathy* (Birdey & Elson Printing Co., Los Angeles, U.S.A.) describes a lesion as follows : "Any structural change which affects the functional activity of any tissue is called a lesion." However, as Tasker himself points out, the lesion must have a detrimental influence on functional activity. Flat feet, for instance, are a structural defect, but if a person who had flat feet from birth had this structural abnormality corrected, he would find pain where no pain previously existed. There are other similar instances of structural defects to which the body has accommodated itself and where any attempt at correction would be harmful. Tasker says :

"Lesions which might have been active at a former time are sometimes non-active on account of laws of accommodation which are always active in the body. If the body has succeeded in recuperating from the effect of these lesions, it is unwise to disturb them."

A lesion is usually characterized by subluxation, thickened ligaments and contracted muscles. It is usually felt by palpation, tenderness is displayed at the area of the lesion and the functional disturbance is related to the lesioned area. By the latter, we mean that the functional disturbance must have a connection *via* the nervous system with the lesion, *i.e.* a lesion of the eleventh or twelfth dorsal vetebrae would probably be connected with the kidneys. It must be remembered that the spinal column is peculiar in that the nerves of the body radiate from it and that any structural defect may cause pressure or chemical changes which influence nerves innervating an organ or tissue some distance from the site of the spinal lesion, because the nerves of that organ or tissue arise from the area of the lesion.

Lesions are of two classes : primary and secondary. Lesions arising from injury or violence all fall into the primary class. In this case, if the lesion is not corrected at an early stage, it may further be complicated by an increase in size. Such lesions are more difficult to correct. Some indeed are never corrected, nor should they be, because of the law of accommodation which ensues. As a protective element, we often find thickening and increase of size in bone and ligaments. In any case, unless the lesion is definitely the source of functional disturbance which is detrimental to the body, it is not a true lesion. Tasker remarks :

"There can be no doubt but that the removal of a primary lesion due to violence is absolutely essential, but when we maintain that all lesions must be removed before function can right itself, we become absurd. Furthermore, if we contend that a structural lesion antedates all functional disturbances, we make of life a series of accidents, instead of a force governed by fixed laws."

Secondary lesions usually arise from the failure of the organism to adapt itself to external conditions arising in everyday life, and to functional derangements in the body.

Cold, poor diet, strain, overwork, etc., are in themselves sufficient to cause a secondary lesion. The connection between a continued draught of cold air striking on the skin and a spinal lesion may not seem apparent. Yet if we consider the average person's susceptibility to draughts on account of loss of tone in the skin and circulation, and the contraction of muscles as a response to cold, we can visualize how a lesion can be caused by cold. Lesions are osseous, muscular and legamentous. Recalling that spinal tenderness has been observed in disease and that definite spinal areas are associated with different organs *via* the nervous system, it is possible to realize the fact that overeating can be reflected in that area of the spine appertaining to the digestive tract. A stomach disorder arising from overeating would probably assert itself in a lesion between the fifth and seventh dorsal. While the correction of such a lesion would be helpful, if the same dietetic mistakes were made the lesion would recur. Of course, many lesions of a similar character occur in life and either they are corrected naturally or the law of adaptation assumes control and brings about a recovery. Few spines are normal, and adaptation after long-continued postural defects alone often creates an abnormal spine. Even osteopathically, the unity of the body is demonstrated, as Tasker shows in the following words :

"The point we desire to emphasize is that the unity of the body is exemplified by the spinal lesion phenomena. No organ or tissue can or does suffer injury without other tissues being drafted to compensate for its condition so as to maintain not only existence but the most satisfactory life of which the organism is capable. If the spinal lesion is viewed not only as a possible cause, but, also, as a quite probable effect of tissue disturbance elsewhere, we will appreciate more fully the manner in which the body strives to live up to its best."

It is commonly assumed that, in acute cases, it is of little use calling in the services of an osteopath. To help correct this erroneous belief Tasker states :

"As soon as we have an autoxaemia to deal with, our lesion picture is enlarged. This is well illustrated in the various manifestations of indigestion. In such cases, not only lesions in the areas segmentally associated, but also above and below, will be found. Some cases will complain of the whole length of the spine while the auto-intoxication is at its height. As the intensity of the auto-intoxication decreases the lesion areas become restricted to the physiologically associated spine areas. This is true in the infections as well. The backache in tonsilitis, la griffe, smallpox, etc. are well known and evidently not located in physiologically associated areas. The phenomena of spinal hypertension and hyperaestesia are very important in these cases. Nothing seems to palliate this spinal condition due to toxaemia to the same extent as manipulation. We say palliate because the toxaemia which causes the tension is not overcome by relieving the spinal tension."

Osteopathy would be of less account if it did not take cognizance of the causative factor at work. If, for instance, a case of sciatica were cured by osteopathic treatment, the same trouble would arise if dietetic indiscretions, detrimental environment, drugging, etc., which originally helped to produce the sciatica, were not guarded against. It is not sufficient merely to correct an osseous lesion. The soft tissues ranging the troubled area must all be brought back to normality and the nerve, blood, and lymph now restored. In fact, all the stresses and strains causing or arising from any lesion must be eradicated before a permanent cure can be effected. The spectacular results achieved by osteopathy in the treatment of primary lesions receiving early attention are far outweighed by the patient but solid successes gained by persistent treatment concerned with introducing normality to a disordered system. Too frequently people expect immediate results from osteopathy when, in point of fact, they have probably spent years in reaching their state of ill-health by persistent abuse of the body. Nonetheless, osteopathy does frequently achieve results in a remarkably short time where all else has failed, and it is a system of healing that should be encouraged.

Neuro-muscular technique is now increasingly adopted by both osteopaths and chiropractors. It has come to be recognized as just as essential as the osteopathic or chiropractic adjustment of bony lesions. It is, in fact, complementary.

Neuro-muscular therapy is essentially a type of specific soft tissue treatment. It was, to a large extent, developed in 1947 by the late Stanley Lief, who was not satisfied that osteopathic or chiropractic adjustments were sufficient in themselves.

After considerable research in England, America and France, Lief developed what is known as "neuro-muscular technique". The system is a noteworthy memorial to one of the most successful and gifted pioneers of Nature Cure in this country. It is almost true to say that it was Stanley Lief who placed British Nature Cure on the map.

Work of a similar nature had been going on in Germany. A book—*Connective Tissue Massage*—by Maria Ebner, M.S.C.P., published in 1962, was the result of her studies and research both here and in Germany. Connective Tissue Massage is taught in most German schools of Physiotherapy.

In England, the teaching of neuro-muscular technique is almost confined to the British College of Naturopathy and Osteopathy. There is no doubt, however, that both "neuro-muscular" technique and connective tissue massage will be increasingly incorporated in manipulative therapies.

What is the place of osteopathy in Nature Cure? It would be a brave man indeed who entered into such a controversy. The osteopath is not automatically a Nature Cure practitioner. There is no doubt that the osteopathic profession is very jealous of its code and standing, and rightly so. They do not make extravagant claims any more than the naturopath. It seems, however, that while the osteopathic teaching does emphasize the way to health, its subjects are more limited than those of the more-embracing Nature Cure system.

Osteopathy does, of course, fall into that group of drugless, natural means of achieving and maintaining health which Nature Cure must enfold. The difference between the two can be summed up by saying that osteopathy is a way to health and that Nature Cure is a way of life. In effect the two are complementary, and the value of osteopathy as a natural means of overcoming disease and maintaining health should not be overlooked.

CONCLUSION

Nature Cure should not be misinterpreted. It does not pretend to be a cure-all. It would be ridiculous to decry the brilliant surgery that saves thousands of lives or to say that all drugs are useless. What Nature Cure does maintain is that the need for surgery could be drastically reduced and that drugs should be kept for really essential cases.

The minor and chronic ailments, from which most people suffer in these days of stress and lowered food values, could be cut to a minimum when a Nature Cure way of life is followed.

Thousands of people have already proved the value of Nature Cure and each year the number increases. What is not fully appreciated, even by those deeply involved in the Nature Cure movement, is the material saving in production and financial resources that indirectly springs from adopting the naturopathic way of life.

Disease prevention is an urgent problem in the world today. It is in this field that Nature Cure excels. The naturopathic philosophy of our age is the preventative medicine of the future. This fact is slowly dawning upon the world, and recognition of Nature Cure's true worth is rapidly being demonstrated.